Copyright © 2025

All rights rese.

The characters and events portrayed in this book are fictitious. Any similarity to real persons, living or dead, is coincidental and not intended by the author.

All brand names and product names used in this book are trademarks, registered trademarks, or trade names of their respective holder. J Frances is not associated with any product or vendor in this book.

No part of this book may be reproduced, or stored in a retrieval system, or transmitted in any form or by any means, electronic, mechanical, photocopying, recording, or otherwise, without express written permission of the publisher.

No part of this publication may be used or reproduced in any manner for the purpose of training artificial intelligence technologies or systems.

Cover design by: Get Covers

CONTENT WARNING

This book is meant for mature audiences and contains content that may be triggering for some readers – including sex, profanity, drug addiction, mental health issues, infant loss, grief, domestic violence and references to suicide.

If you or someone you know is contemplating suicide then please call the helpline on 116 123 or go online to www.spuk.org.uk.

If you are the victim of domestic violence then please reach out to the National Domestic Abuse Helpline on 0808 2000 247 or go online to www.nationaldahelpline.org.uk.

If you are struggling with drug or alcohol addiction and need help then please go online to www.mind.org.uk.

SONG LIST FOR FRAGMENTED

Deer In Headlights - Sia

Leaving California – Maroon 5

Run To You – Whitney Houston

Stop Crying Your Heart Out – Oasis

First Time – Kygo and Ellie Goulding

Dakota – Stereophonics

Chasing Cars – Snow Patrol

Unstoppable - Sia

Need You Tonight - INXS

Always - Bon Jovi

Heal Me – Snow Patrol

A Thousand Years – Christina Perri

I Don't Want To Miss A Thing - Aerosmith

Angels – Robbie Williams

The Scientist – Coldplay (reprise)

Nothing's Gonna Stop Us Now – Starship

Marry You – Bruno Mars

Rainbow – Loren Allred

Lucky Man – The Verve

Nothing Else Matters - Metallica

Feels Like I'm Falling In Love – Coldplay

Never Enough – Loren Allred

A Million Dreams – Ziv Zaifman, Hugh Jackman & Michelle Williams

Over The Rainbow – Eva Cassidy

About the Author

J Frances is in her early forties and is a hopeless romantic who is addicted to books. Her love for books started as a young girl when she used to read book after book, forever visiting the library either with school or with her mum.

With a vivid imagination and a clear passion for writing, she began writing stories on her beloved typewriter until eventually finding the time in her life in her early thirties to write her first ever novel back in 2013. J Frances lives in Lancashire with her husband, two sons and pet dog, Milo.

This novel is the third and final book in the Reclamation Rock Star Series and continues directly where the second novel left off.

For My Husband

This book is dedicated to my loving and supportive husband who, without him, this series of books wouldn't have been possible.

To the husband who sat down and batted ideas around with me for the last 10 years whilst I worked on this story, the husband who solved the conundrum along with me when I was unsure about how to bring this wonderful story to its long overdue conclusion, and to the husband who donated songs to me so that they could be included in this series of books.

Forsaken Eyes, My Angel and Paragon were written by my husband and they play an important part in this series of books, bringing Reclamation's music to life.

Thank you for all that you are and for everything you do for me and our boys.

I love you endlessly.

J xx

CHAPTER 1

JONNY

I am sitting at my dining table in silence, staring at Lauren's diamond engagement ring placed in the centre of it. A note is by the side of her ring, telling me that she's gone. The house feels dark and empty once more, my mind reeling with shock, my heart broken into a million pieces.

Fragmented, that's what I am right now. Like the song I once wrote about the love I lost when Lauren left me the first time round. A song I poured my absolute heart and soul into after feeling like my life had ended the day she left me in Manchester.

Picking up the note once more, I read it again, still trying to work out why on earth she would do this to me. She loves me. This note tells me she does. So why has she done this to me again? For a third time. Why?

Jonny,

After the events of the last few days, there is something I absolutely have to do, but I have to do it alone. I am leaving my engagement ring with you so you can look after it for me, but this isn't the end for us, this isn't me leaving you all over again, this is just something I have to do for me. I hope you understand, and I hope you can find it within your heart to forgive me for this, but I promise you I will be back, because I love you. More than life itself. Please don't ever forget that. Stay strong for me – Lauren xxxx

Placing her note back on the table, I put my head in my hands and sigh heavily. I can feel the tears threatening to fall, I can feel the anger beginning to burn its way through my veins at the fact that she's gone off to do fuck knows what, all on her own. Without me. I thought we were a team, Lauren and I, and I thought that she trusted me enough to know that I would love and support her no matter what. That I would always have her back. But this? This going off on her own behind my back has shocked me to my very core.

I knew she wasn't quite herself of course, after what happened with her dad and the newspaper article. After I broke the news to her a few days ago, she just seemed to go into some sort of shock, almost in a trance, like she was going through all the motions of going about her day to day life but with absolutely no emotion attached to her at all.

The only time when I saw a flicker of emotion within her was when we were intimate, but apart from that one moment of intimacy with me, she instead pushed me away. So when she suggested she have a spa day with Stacey to take her mind off it all, I thought that was a sign she was starting to feel a bit better and I therefore jumped at the chance of her wanting to do something, anything, with her best friend. Everything was booked for this afternoon so that the two of them could be taken to the spa together and have a pamper day. What I didn't expect was for Lauren to manipulate that plan to her advantage, and manipulate it she did, down to the very last detail. A plan so clever that by the time Stacey or I realised Lauren was gone, it was far too late.

Stacey and the lads are in shock too, and after spending an age trying to calm me down, I then sent them on their way as I needed some time to think. Think about where I go from here. Because even though she has left me, albeit temporarily, as the note clearly states, this has hurt me even more than when she actually left me the last time round. The fact that she couldn't put her faith in me to tell me what was going on in her head, that she couldn't share her inner most fears and feelings with me about what she wanted to do next, hurts. It really fucking hurts.

I have to somehow put all of that anger and upset to one side for now though, because I know exactly where Lauren has gone. It doesn't take a genius to work that one out. But the thing I'm really struggling to wrap my head around, is the why. Why the fuck would she go over there all on her own? Without me? And I fear she may be putting herself in grave danger, because if I know Lauren's father, and believe me, I know him well, he won't think twice about hurting his daughter all over again.

Even after him somehow managing to convince the world he's the exact opposite of that, it won't take much for him to break out those violent fists of his when Lauren pays him a visit. Because he's a power hungry violent alcoholic who thrives on inflicting pain on his only daughter. He takes great pleasure in making himself feel strong and almighty with his fists, when in fact, he is the weakest man I have ever had the misfortune of knowing.

Picking up Lauren's engagement ring, I look down at the beautiful diamond sparkling up at me. The diamond ring that, only this morning, was sitting where it should have been, on Lauren's wedding finger. Closing my fist around her ring, the ring that was supposed to signal the start of the rest of our lives together, I come to a decision.

I only hope that my decision to fly over there to be with Lauren pays off, because if it doesn't, and her dad has moved house since we were teenagers or, god forbid, Lauren hasn't in fact gone over there to face him, then I am at a loss as to what to do or where to go.

I close my eyes, hoping and praying with all my might that I can find my girl so I can bring her home safely. I don't even want to think about the alternative. I can't think about it. Because life without Lauren is inconceivable, so I need to bring her back home to me, no matter the cost....

****

JONNY

5 days earlier....

I feel like I am broken in two. No, more than that, I am shattered, splintered apart by the fact I am about to break the heart, the very soul, of the woman I love more than life itself. This news is going to destroy her. I just know it. And she knows something is very wrong. She can see it in my eyes. Hear it in the quiet of my voice.

After I pulled her away from the bathroom where she was cleaning away and singing happily, I brought her outside into the back garden for what I called 'a talk.' And now that she is sitting down next to me, beside the swimming pool, looking at me with those beautiful ocean blue eyes of hers, she literally looks terrified. As terrified as I feel.

I swear I can barely breathe, never mind find the words to speak. How the fuck do I tell her that her dad has told the entire fucking world a lie? A complete and utter, heartbreaking lie. All about her, and all about me. But the most sickening part of all is how he's used our stillborn son in all of this.

Our Oliver never stood a chance to live after what Lauren's bastard of a dad did to her, but that very same bastard has told the world the exact opposite of what he did to Lauren. Something vile. So fucking vile, I almost feel as though I may vomit all over again like I did on my way home earlier.

"Jonny? Are you okay?" She reaches across to me and places the palm of her hand against my left cheek. I simply blink at her, trying desperately to find the words to say to her, but they won't come. They won't fucking come. *I don't think I can do this.*

When I don't respond, Lauren slowly pulls her hand away from my face and tears her gaze away from me, instead looking over at the swimming pool next to us. "Of course you're not okay, otherwise you wouldn't be home so early from the record label and you wouldn't have pulled me out here into the back garden for a talk."

Blowing out a shaky breath, Lauren then looks down at her hands and starts to toy with her engagement ring, twisting it round and round. Her nerves are really beginning to show and I know I have to do this. Right now. I can't stand to see her looking so anxious and worried about what it is I have to tell her. It's better I rip off the plaster and just get it over with. We can then start dealing with it. Together.

"Lauren...I..." Shit, how the hell do I say this to her? Running a panicky hand through my hair, I then lean forward in my chair and reach over for her hands. She gazes over at me as I take her hands in mine, and I almost crease up when I make eye contact with her, because all I want to do right now is comfort her. Hold her and soothe her and tell her that everything will ultimately be okay, even though I don't know for sure that it will be.

"Just tell me, Jonny," she says quietly, "tell me what you need to tell me and get it over with."

Steeling myself for the pain of what's about to come, I close my eyes for the briefest of moments. When I open them again, I make sure I am looking directly at Lauren, so she knows I am with her in this. All of it. Until death do us part. We may not have got to the marriage vows as yet but I am damn fucking certain of that vow. Always was. Because I would sacrifice my very life for this woman, and she needs to know that, although she most likely already does.

"Look, sweetheart, just know that what I am about to tell you is something we are going to deal with together and you are not on your own in this. Okay?"

"Jonny, please just tell me," she whispers, her eyes searching mine in desperation.

Fuck, seeing her this way, so desperate and already upset at the not knowing what it is I'm about to tell her, it nearly fucking kills me, and I swear at that moment, I nearly crumple into a heap on the ground in front of her. Why did this have to happen to us? Why? I somehow manage to compose myself just enough to find some courage from deep down somewhere.

"Okay, here goes. Lauren…your dad sold the story of our past to a tabloid newspaper. An article got printed this morning and then it went viral…all over the internet."

Her face drops immediately, almost like the happy glow inside of her is being dimmed right in front of my very eyes. Like a dozen candles being blown out on a birthday cake, Lauren's happiness is being extinguished all at once. And to think that I have to continue telling her about this vile piece of shit. I can't bear to hurt her any more than I already have done. She's as white as a ghost and is already beginning to pull away from me, her hands freeing themselves from my grip as I look on in anguish.

When she says nothing, I very reluctantly continue with what I was saying. "I've read the article, Lauren, and it's…"

"Catastrophic?" she asks me quietly. So so quietly.

I clear my throat nervously. "There's no point in sugar coating it to you, baby, but yes, it's…" I don't really want to use the word Lauren used, because even though it does feel catastrophic right now, we are going to fight our way through this. "The article is bad, yes, but it's all lies, Lauren, complete and utter lies…"

"Of course it's all lies," she whispers. Looking away from me, she then stares over into the distance, as if trying to focus all her energy on something else. Something other than the bastard who once made her life a living hell. The same bastard who is now trying to do exactly that all over again, all these years later. "Did he mention Oliver?"

Oh fuck, she's asked me the very question I've been dreading she would ask. But of course, it's not like I can hide her away from any of this. She is most likely going to read the article anyway. And no amount of me telling her not to read it will make a difference to Lauren. If she wants or feels she needs to read it then she will read it. End of.

Feeling sick and disgusted at having to say the words out loud to her, I rest my forearms on my knees and focus my angry gaze on the patio flags beneath my feet. "Yes, sadly he did," I say to her.

I want to cry right now. I want to curl myself up into a ball and scream. And I am not ashamed to admit that. Because the grief you feel when you lose a child is like no other pain you will ever feel in your entire life. It is literally unbearable, to the point where you cannot even think about that child anymore without feeling like you're being ripped apart on the inside. You will do anything and everything to numb that pain, and that's exactly what I did after it happened. I turned to the drugs to help get me through, and Lauren turned herself off from feeling anything. She never wanted to talk about what happened to Oliver. Ever. I did want to talk about it but she flatly refused, and therein began our descent into our darkest ever place. Intimacy was the only thing we had left of our relationship back then and I don't want to end up in that god awful place again. Jimmy Whittle destroyed us the first time round, but I refuse to allow him to destroy us all over again.

I almost gag whenever I think of his name, never mind actually say it. After it all happened, Lauren and I agreed to never say his name ever again, because that would have acknowledged his existence in this world. A world that had always been far too good for the likes of that evil man. But now, his name is being plastered around the globe as we speak, and people are already most likely thinking he is a wonderful middle aged man who has been very badly wronged. Wronged by an out of control, tearaway daughter and her seemingly violent boyfriend. I shudder at the thought of the lies he has told. So many lies. So many untruths. How the fuck do we come back from this?

"What did he say about our son?" she asks me, pulling me away from my own, depressing thoughts. I sigh heavily. I don't want to have to tell her this part, but I'm going to have to. *Man up, Jonny, and just tell her.* But I don't want to tell her. Because this piece of information she has just asked me about will absolutely finish her off. I know it will. "What did he say about our son, Jonny?" Lauren knows this is going to be bad, otherwise she wouldn't have pressed me for an answer.

Swiping a weary hand over my face, I look over at Lauren once more to find her still staring at something on the other side of the garden. Or maybe she's just staring at nothing. Staring into the abyss in the hope it will somehow suck us both into a blackhole and take us back to the place where we were before all of this happened today.

"He said that…" I gulp down the bile that has risen up into my throat and force it back down from where it came. "Your dad said that you and I went off the rails as teenagers. He said that when I got you pregnant, I then…" Shit, I can't say it. I can't tell her what her dad has done.

Closing her eyes, as if in pain, she says, "Please stop

protecting me, Jonny. Just tell me what that bastard said about Oliver…"

"He said I forced you into having an abortion…" I say quickly, finally ripping off the band aid and exposing the excruciating wound to the both of us.

I gag on the last word, and that's it, I can't hold it in any longer. Heaving forwards, I begin to retch like I did earlier on by the side of the road on my way home. I retch and I retch, over and over, causing my stomach a whole load of pain, but nothing comes up. I've had nothing to eat or drink since I was last sick and so my stomach has nothing to bring up other than the pain of those words. They feel like acid on my tongue, having burnt their way from my stomach, all the way up my oesophagus and into my mouth.

As I continue to retch and heave, Lauren remains next to me, sitting in her chair, motionless and silent. So very silent. When I finally manage to stop myself from all the retching and the heaving, I stand up, only briefly, so I can close the gap that was sitting between us. It may only have been a small gap but it felt like the fucking Grand Canyon to me. Because I need to be with her and hold her. Touch her and kiss her and tell her I am here with her, supporting her, loving her.

Kneeling down in front of her, I take a firm hold of both of her hands once again, and, with only my eyes, I implore her to look down at me. But Lauren doesn't look down at me. She doesn't hold my hands in return and she most certainly doesn't say anything to me. She just continues to stare into the distance, as though an invisible barrier has come down on her face and shut her off to me completely. No, this cannot happen to her again. It cannot happen to us all over again. I can't bear it. I really can't.

"Lauren, look at me," I plead with her quietly. I don't want to startle her or force her into feeling or doing anything she feels uncomfortable with. I just want her to acknowledge my presence, acknowledge the fact that I am here with her, right now, showing her how much I love her.

"This has happened because of the life you now lead, Jonny."

Lauren's words are both unexpected and hurtful, and they lash at my already wounded heart. They don't even sound like her. She suddenly appears to be void of any emotion, almost soulless and cold, like she's turned all of her feelings off. Shit, this is going to be the end of me. Because I can't watch Lauren go through this all over again. It's already tearing me apart and I don't know what to do or how to be with her. I feel absolutely helpless, and helpless is something she really doesn't need from me at the moment.

I swear this is like stepping back into the past after we lost Oliver, after she came round from her coma to discover that she no longer had our baby boy growing inside of her. I had to be the one to break that news to her, and it almost fucking killed me to do it. And now, all these years later, here I am, doing it all over again. Not quite the same as back then but in some ways, this is worse, because now, that loss we went through together has been shared for the entire fucking world to read about, if they so choose, and it has been twisted. Twisted to the point of raw, intolerable pain I know for a fact Lauren will be unable to deal with right now. If she will ever be able to deal with it at all.

I am just about treading water with all of this myself and that's due to the fact that I need to be strong for her. Being the strong one out of the two of us doesn't come easy to me but I am determined to make damn sure those therapy sessions I've had over these last few months haven't been in vain. I want to use those techniques I've learnt so I can help my girl through all of this. I will not abandon her and leave her to fall apart in front of my very eyes. If she falls, I will pick her back up and carry her back to where she needs to be. And she needs to be with me. By my side. Always.

"Baby, this is because of your dad. He's clearly seen you and me on the news or in the papers and he knew he could make some money. With him, it's always been about the money..."

"But if you hadn't been leading this rich and famous lifestyle over here in LA, if you'd have stayed in Manchester with me, none of this would have happened."

What the actual fuck? How can she even say that to me? I try to remain calm, mentally telling myself that she doesn't mean any of these things she's saying to me right now. She can't possibly mean them. She's in shock I think.

"Lauren, you don't mean that..."

"Yes I do," she spits out at me venomously.

Finally turning her gaze on me, she looks down at me angrily. Her beautiful blue eyes that are normally filled with nothing but love and adoration for me, are now cold and empty, completely emotionless. "I told you in the very beginning that I couldn't handle this lifestyle of yours, Jonny, being constantly followed around by the paparazzi and your fans as they wait around every corner wanting to get a photo or a bit of gossip about you at any given opportunity. It was only a matter of time before they dug into your past. *Our* past. And now look where it's got us! Look at where it's got us!"

I know Lauren is hurting, and I know that the anger she is currently feeling for her dad is somehow being misdirected at me, but I can't stay kneeling down on the floor while she talks to me like this. I just can't. And I won't.

Pushing myself up off the hard stone flags beneath me, I stand up and take a step backwards, putting a little distance between myself and Lauren. Because I am so angry. So fucking angry that I may end up saying something I regret.

"Look, I know you're hurting right now, Lauren, but so am I. And don't forget that you wanted this life out here with me, so don't pretend otherwise. I know you were unsure about it all in the beginning but you then told me you wanted me to go back to the band. Just a few months ago, you told me no when I offered to give up my music career, which I would have done by the way. I offered to give it all up for you. For us. I would have given up the life here in LA, the band, the fame, and the money. But you said no. So don't now turn around and throw all of that in my face just because that evil, murderous bastard of a father of yours has finally decided to crawl out from which ever rock he went and crawled under all those years ago! Don't you dare blame me for something he's done!"

"I can't talk about this right now," Lauren says to me in response, like everything I've just said to her hasn't even registered. She stands up from her chair and turns away from me, dashing up the stone steps that lead up to the back of the house, as fast as her legs will carry her.

And I know I should leave her to digest everything I've just told her about her dad and the article, I know deep down I should allow her to walk away from me so that both she and I can calm down, but for some stupid, unknown reason, I go after her into the house.

She's in the hallway by the time I catch up to her but she continues to walk off. "Lauren, don't walk away from me!" I shout over to her, desperate for something I say to sink in with her. "Don't make me feel like I'm the one in the wrong here! *He* was the one in the wrong, Lauren, not me. He was always the one in the wrong, and he still is now! Do not defend a murderer like him!"

I didn't mean for those last few words to slip out, but as usual, my big fucking mouth ran away with me, and now I can't take them back, even if I wanted to.

Whirling around to face me, she storms over to me in a fit of rage. "Did you just say that I defended my dad? After everything you know about the abhorrent things he said and did to me all those years ago, and you seriously think I would defend *him*?!"

"Look, I didn't mean..."

Lauren shoves angrily at my chest, causing me to stumble backwards slightly. "Then why did you say it?!" she screams up at me, her eyes sorrowful. Shit, she looks broken. So fucking broken. I am a prize idiot for saying what I said to her just now. In fact, I am more than that. I am a bastard. A hurtful, unfeeling bastard who is so fucking weak for not being able to get a lid on that ridiculously short temper of mine.

"I'm sorry," I say, "I didn't mean it how it came out."

I automatically reach out for her, to comfort her. All I want to do is pull her into my arms and absorb her pain. I want to soak up every single drop of sorrow from her eyes so she can finally be free from all of this, free from the pain her father inflicted on her for so long, the pain he is still inflicting on her now, but she pushes me away.

"Fuck you, Jonny!" she yells, and then she sprints away upstairs. I hear the slamming of a door a few seconds later. I decide to leave her be this time, something I really should have done a few minutes ago.

Well, I handled that badly. Really fucking badly. So badly that I decide to go back outside and smoke my way through half a packet of cigarettes. The cigarettes do little to calm my ever spiralling mood and I find myself hating the fact I am suddenly out here alone. I really want to ring my friends and ask them to come over, but I don't.

I have to prioritise Lauren and her feelings. I've literally just dropped a bombshell on her and she needs time to take it all in. How much time she will ultimately need is anybody's guess, but I bet she's reading that article right now, drowning in the very pain I had finally convinced myself I could protect her from.

I have literally just sparked up another cigarette when my mobile starts ringing. I lift it up from the table and see Stacey's name flashing up at me from the screen. I swipe to answer the call. "Hey, Stacey."

"Oh my god, Jonny, I've just read the article online after Ben came home and told me what happened. I've tried ringing Lauren but she isn't picking up. Is she with you right now? Can I talk to her?"

Stacey's concern for Lauren is heartwarming and something I obviously expected, but she can go from zero to a hundred miles an hour within seconds and therefore I have to put a stop to her million and one questions before she gets carried away with herself.

"Stace, just take a moment to breathe and I will answer your questions," I say to her calmly.

"Oh, I'm sorry, Jonny, I'm just worried sick about her. I can't believe that that bastard has gone and done this to her. After all these years of nothing and now this!"

"He's seen an opportunity to make money out of his daughter and he's taken it, just like he always did. He's a mother fucking bastard and he's going to get what's coming to him…"

"Jonny…"

"Look, you can try to talk me down all you like, but he isn't going to get away with this. He got away with a fuck load of shit long ago and this has to stop. I won't allow him to hurt Lauren anymore...I won't."

I quickly finish off my cigarette and then stub the end into my ashtray. I can feel the anger beginning to bubble its way to the surface all over again, the tears welling up in my eyes as I fight with all my might to push them away. To push it all away. If only it was that easy. Life would be so much simpler if it was.

Stacey sighs at me down the phone. "I wasn't going to talk you down, Jonny, I was...shit, if I could kill the bastard with my own bare hands then I would. I really would." She goes silent for a moment, as if thinking about her next words carefully. "We all need to really think about how you two go from here, but right now, as I'm sure you already are doing, we need to look after Lauren...how is she, Jonny? How is she really?"

Sitting back in my chair, l look up at the clear blue sky above my head, the warm LA sunshine beaming down on me in the early May afternoon. Hard to believe that on a day as sunny and bright as this one is, the darkness of our past is still surrounding us, blanketing us in a painful fog that neither of us can fight our way through. Not just yet anyway. That fight is yet to come.

Pinching the bridge of my nose, I close my eyes, effectively shutting out the wonderful LA weather, so I can focus on my conversation with Stacey. "She's..." I'm struggling to get my words out again. Those damn emotions of mine are playing holy havoc with me today. "She's not good, Stace. She...we... fuck, I'm sorry..."

"Hey, it's okay. I'm sorry, I know this is really upsetting for you both."

I shake my head even though Stacey can't see me. "No, it's fine. Don't apologise. It's just...we argued earlier because... she...well, Lauren blamed me for the life I now have over here in LA. Instead of blaming her dad, she turned on me, and… well, in my usual defensive manner I said a few things I shouldn't have, that I truly didn't mean, and she stormed off…"

"Oh, Jonny," Stacey whispers, sounding mortified.

I can't help the small sob that somehow manages to creep its way past my lips. "I know," I say to her, my inner strength finally beginning to weaken, "she's in shock I think."

"Yeah, I bet." She lets out a heavy sigh down the phone. "Listen, do you want me to come round? Maybe try and talk to her? Just me. Not Ben, or anybody else."

I swipe at my eyes with the back of my hand and then sniff loudly, feeling so fucking grateful right now for Lauren's best friend. But as grateful as I am to her, I don't think that now is the right time to allow her to see Lauren. I think I should at least give her the rest of the day and the night ahead to wrap her head around the events of today. I decide to suggest tomorrow to Stacey instead.

"I'm so grateful to you, Stace, I really am, but I think we should give her a bit of space to allow her to digest everything that's happened today. Maybe you could swing by tomorrow instead? Maybe bring Ben and I can chat with him well away from you and Lauren. I can let you know in the morning how she is and we can take it from there. Is that okay?"

"Yeah, of course. I think you're probably right. I don't want to overwhelm her, I remember what she was like last year when…well, after you two split up. She was a mess, but I kept hounding her and hounding her. It didn't do her any good at all but I thought I was helping her. Maybe staying away for a little bit longer will help this time. I hope so anyway."

"She loves you, Stace, and she knows you'll always have her back. And I know it too."

"Thanks, Jonny. Take care of yourself and Lauren tonight, and hopefully I'll see you both tomorrow."

"You will. Bye, Stace."

I end the call and throw my mobile back on to the table in front of me. I ponder over whether or not I should go upstairs to check on Lauren. I decide against it for the time being and instead take myself off to my music studio. It's about the only thing in the world that will provide me with some solace right now. Here's hoping.

CHAPTER 2

LAUREN

I am lying on our bed upstairs, clutching my mobile phone against my chest after reading the devastating article online that my dad sold to the tabloids. An article about his own version of my past. My past with Jonny. I want to scream and cry and rip apart this very bedroom I'm currently in, but I don't. I can't.

For some reason, I feel paralysed, numb and lifeless, devoid of all emotion. I don't even feel like my normal panicky self. In the past, I would have gone into a full blown panic attack right about now after hearing something, anything, even remotely related to my dad, but for some reason, I just feel numb. Numb and in complete shock about the events that have occurred today.

Reading those poisonous words my dad had printed about me and the son we lost has tipped me over the edge I think. To the point where I don't think I can face the world ever again. Because that world out there now knows everything about me and Jonny, or at least, they think they do. In truth, they know absolutely nothing about our lives from back then and have instead been given an extremely warped version of both me and Jonny.

And that's the part that has absolutely broken my heart. How he has painted us to be the bad ones in all of this, when in fact, we were the victims. The victims of his endless bouts of threats and violence. But the most innocent victim in all of this isn't Jonny or even me. It's the one who never got to take his first breath or say his first words, the little boy who never got to take his first steps or enjoy his first day at school. *My little boy.*

As I remember the baby boy I never got to know, I begin to feel a rage building inside of me, the likes of which I don't think I've experienced ever before. All I felt after it originally happened to me was devastation. Total devastation at the depth of loss my own flesh and blood had inflicted upon me. My dad cruelly snatching my unborn son away from me by beating me to a pulp.

My dad had turned up at my flat asking for money. After months of hearing nothing from him, he just turned up out of the blue one night when Jonny had gone out to play at a gig at one of the local pubs. I should never have opened the door to him that night, but regretfully, I did. And it was so stupid of me to tell him I was pregnant. So bloody stupid. But he became violent with me when I told him no to giving him more money, and because he got violent, I thought that if he knew I was pregnant, then he would back off, but he didn't. In fact, the knowledge of my pregnancy just seemed to tip him over the edge. He literally went insane. It was as though a switch went off in his head, adding fuel to my father's already burning rage.

I shudder at the last memory I had of him kicking me in the stomach, me writhing around the floor of the stairwell outside my flat in absolute agony before he went on to kick me down the stairs. It all went black after that. I remember when I woke from my coma, days later, to find Jonny sitting by my hospital bed.

I remember it so vividly, how he held my hand tightly as he broke the devastating news to me that our son hadn't made it. That the doctors had made the decision to perform an emergency caesarean section on me in an attempt to save his life, but sadly, it was too late for that. Oliver had already passed away by the time they got in there and at only twenty one weeks gestation, his chances of survival would have been slim anyway.

I am surprised to feel an errant tear slipping down my right cheek, the painful memories finally cutting their way through my seemingly emotionless state. Dropping my mobile phone on to the bed, I swipe that single tear away in anger. I will not cry about it. Not today. I have cried so many tears for my little boy over the years since I lost him, but tears are not what I need at the moment.

Right now, I need to hold on to the anger I feel towards my dad. The burning rage I want to finally use against him. Because I never sought to get justice for my little boy. I just walked away from it all without ever pressing charges against the murderous bastard. And all because I was terrified of him. Truly terrified of what he might have done to me and Jonny.

Because in the aftermath of it all, Jonny lost his head one day and finally let my father have it. He rained down on my dad hard and left him badly beaten. My dad eventually went on to make a full recovery and no harm was done, but he wielded that threat over Jonny, telling me he would press charges for assault and battery against him if I so much as went near the police station to report him for what he'd *apparently* done to me.

Hard to believe that my dad actually had the nerve to deny what he'd done, but he did deny it. He denied it until he was blue in the face, proving to me yet again that he was nothing more than the cold, heartless liar he'd always been. And so, as much as it pained me to do it at the time, I stayed silent. Like the weak and pathetic victim he had moulded me into.

Jonny and his parents tried desperately to talk me round. They'd found some witnesses who had arrived on the scene just as my father was kicking me down the stairs. Those witnesses had even been willing to testify against my father, but without my statement, nothing could be done. And that's when I closed myself off to everyone and everything. I shut down my emotions and told Jonny I didn't want to talk about my father ever again. I also refused to talk about the incident, wanting to silently move on and remember Oliver in my own way. In my head, I could pretend he hadn't been snatched away from me, and so that's what I did. Until now.

I can't keep up the pretence anymore, not now every man and his dog outside these four walls have been given a snippet of what went on all those years ago. A very skewed snippet but a snippet nonetheless. And I will make it my mission to set the record straight. I don't know how I get to that point as yet but I know what I need to do in the meantime. A plan is already forming in my mind of the very thing I should have done when all of this originally happened. It's not going to be an easy feat but I have to do it. Both for myself and for Oliver. I owe it to my little boy to finally face up to my fear and deal with the consequences of what happened that night. Only then will I truly be able to move on.

****

I must drift off to sleep because I wake a short while later to the feel of the mattress dipping as Jonny climbs on to the bed to lie next to me. I feel his right arm wrap its way around my body from behind as he buries his face into my neck. He doesn't say anything to me, instead allowing the silence and the feel of him just lying here next to me being comfort enough.

I was awful to him earlier. Absolutely awful. Blaming him and his life out here in LA instead of laying the blame on the true guilty party in all of this. But I was in shock, and so angry. I didn't even know how to process it all at first. I still don't, not really, but now I've had a bit of time to myself to digest the information and to think up a plan, I feel a little calmer than I did earlier on.

The trouble is that this plan I've got swirling around in my mind cannot include Jonny. Because I can't put him through any of that shit all over again. I need to protect him from our painful past and protect him I will. He always deserved so much better than me. Always. Maybe his dad was right, maybe I just wasn't good enough for his son after all. Because I only ever brought trouble to his son's door, and looking back on our time together, I know that to be true. Without me, Jonny would have lived a much simpler, happier life, and he would have still achieved worldwide fame with the band, one way or another. He just would have done it without me bringing a whole world of pain to his doorstep.

Yes, Jonny Mathers is definitely better off without me in his life, but I will never convince him otherwise. He simply refuses to accept it, putting me on some sort of pedestal like I'm this amazingly strong, independent woman who somehow put her life back together after her dad almost destroyed it. But I am not that person, and I never was. I am weak and naïve and I easily give in. I gave in to my dad whenever he physically attacked me and I never fought back. Not once. I gave in to Jonny's dad when he threatened me with his words, not his fists, and again, I never fought back. Not really. I may have mouthed off at Pete but in the end, I always gave him exactly what he wanted. This is why I know it's time to step up to the mark and become the person I always wanted to be. A person who fights back, who stands up for what she believes in and defends not only herself, but the people she loves.

"Thank you for loving me, Jonny," I whisper to him, suddenly feeling upset.

I promised myself I wouldn't get upset, that I would instead hold on to my anger from earlier so I could power on through with my plan. But now that he's here, lying next to me on the bed with his arm wrapped tightly around me, holding me against him, how can I possibly stay angry at him? After all, Jonny has done nothing wrong in all of this, other than love me, body and soul, for over fifteen years of his life. We may not have been together for all of those fifteen years, but he still loved me in between, in all those years we were apart, and I loved him, more than I've ever loved anyone. Which is what makes this whole sorry business so much harder. But I can't put him through any more of this heartbreak and pain, I just can't.

"Hey," says Jonny, trying to get me to turn and look at him. When I don't, he continues regardless. "What do you mean? Thanking me for loving you? Baby, are you okay? Stupid question I know but what's going around in that head of yours?"

Unwrapping his arms from around my body, I then roll out of his embrace and sit myself up on the side of the bed. Looking down at the floor, I sigh heavily. "I don't deserve you, Jonny, I never did..."

"Oh no, you're not doing that with me, Lauren. That's bullshit. You do deserve me, and a whole lot more. In fact, you deserve so much better than me. I failed to protect you from that bastard the first time round and now, all these years later, I've gone and failed you all over again."

I shake my head at him. "Protecting me from him wasn't your responsibility, Jonny, and it never was. It still isn't. I am the one who failed to defend myself against his violence. I am a weak person. I was weak with my dad, and I was weak with your dad. I am weak."

"Weak?!" he shouts over at me, sounding exasperated. "Lauren, you were a young girl when your dad started with his violent ways. You were only fifteen years old when I met you and he'd been doing it long before I came into your life! Just what were you supposed to do as a young girl who had nobody else in the world other than *him* to supposedly look after you and protect you? Instead of giving in and becoming a tearaway or a child in the system, you fought back by getting out of that house every day and getting yourself little jobs. You fought back by carrying on in spite of everything he ever did to you. You got back up and went to school. You got back up and made a life for yourself. You got back up and then went on to meet me! Jesus Christ, Lauren, if that isn't strength then I really don't know what is!"

I stand up from the bed, tears now streaming down my cheeks, angry at myself and at Jonny for reducing me to this pathetic blubbering mess all over again. Angry at myself for being the weak young girl I always. "You see?!" I shout over at him. "You see me right now? This is weakness, Jonny! Not strength! So quit putting me up on this ridiculous pedestal you've always put me on and accept the fact that I am weak and I'm just not good enough for you!"

He slides his way across the bed so he can reach over to me but I wrench my arm away from him. "Don't!" I snap. "Please don't touch me."

He looks like I've just burned him with my words. And I hate I'm the one who can do that to him. Hurt him so easily. I hate the pained look on his face he's wearing right now, which is why I walk away from him again. I can't look at him and so I need to put some distance between us. I storm out of the bedroom and head downstairs, desperate for some peace and quiet on my own.

I'm happy to find the door to his music studio is unlocked. I walk into the only room in the house that can perhaps quieten my mind amidst all of this chaos. Thankfully, the mattress that Jonny had originally brought downstairs when we were sleeping in this room is still in here, over in the corner. There are sheets and a duvet still on top and so I pull back the duvet and lie down on the mattress.

I'm still wearing my tank top and jeans and I have no clue what time it is, but right now, I just need to rest my mind, and my body. I don't care if I'm not wearing my pyjamas and I don't care if the sun is still shining outside, I am exhausted. Well and truly exhausted. I hope and pray for sleep to find me fast, and for Jonny to leave me alone just long enough to allow that to happen.

****

I don't know what time of night it is but I know that it must be late when I eventually wake up later on, because I turn over on the mattress to find Jonny lying fast asleep next to me. The lamp over on his desk is on I notice, basking the room in a warm, comforting glow, allowing me to really appreciate the man lying next to me.

Jonny is topless, wearing only his light grey pyjama pants, which tells me he's actually turned in for the night. And I'm so glad he decided to come down to his music studio to sleep in here with me, because, for the second time tonight, I feel absolutely terrible about how I spoke to him earlier. The things I said. The guilt is really beginning to pluck at my heartstrings as I watch him breathe in and out, his chest rising and falling softly. Oh so softly. He looks as peaceful as can be, as though there is nothing at all wrong in our world, almost like everything is normal. I only wish it was.

I inch that little bit closer to him, so I can snuggle up against him quietly, admiring him for the beautiful, kind hearted soul he is. I drink him in as much as I possibly can in this moment, from his dark locks of hair and the dark lashes of his eyes, to the walking work of art that are his arms and his chest, his many tattoos almost like a mural of his life so far.

Propping my head up on my right hand, I glance down at the large tattoo that completely adorns the left side of his upper body. My favourite tattoo of them all. Even above the tattoo of my name on his inner right forearm. And all because of the meaning behind it.

I feel the urge to reach out and touch him, to place my hand over his heart, his huge, beautiful heart that beats with so much love for me, and only me. I give in to that urge and rest my hand on the tattoo of the winged angel he had inked on to his skin after I left him in Manchester. The winged angel ascending into heaven with a baby in her arms. *Our* baby.

I bite back a fresh wave of tears as I remember Jonny telling me the sentiment behind getting this particular tattoo. He said it was the first tattoo he got done after I left him, and whilst he has never been particularly religious, he said he wanted to get it done as a way of remembering Oliver…and me. The angel with the baby in her arms is supposed to be me.

A teardrop falls on to his chest, unbidden, uninvited, as I think back to how Jonny must have felt back then. After I left him. Because not only did he lose a son, he lost me too, all over the course of six months. And now I am about to hurt him all over again. Because I still need to go through with my plan. I just hope that when my plan comes to fruition, Jonny remembers how much I love him, and I hope he can forgive me for what I am about to do, and still take me as his wife at the end of all of it. Because I will marry Jonny. We will unite as husband and wife one day in the not too distant future, but for now, I need to start planning for what is to come next.

But not before I give in to the magnetic pull of the man lying next to me. The love of my life who is now opening his eyes and blinking up at me in wonder. He's probably surprised to see me staring down at him, my hand splayed out across his chest, over his heart.

Jonny says nothing, instead reaching up with his hand to touch my face, my hair. And I let him reach out for me this time. I let him touch me. Oh, I let him. I allow my emotions to take over as I lean in to his touch, and what starts off as me kissing the palm of his hand, soon turns into more. So much more.

Slowly sitting myself up on the mattress, I reach down for the hem of my tank top and pull it up and over my head. Jonny watches me intently as I then remove my bra and my jeans, swiftly followed by my knickers.

The silence becomes the backdrop to a highly emotional union between two people who have been more than scarred by their painful past. But I don't want to think about any of that right now. I just want to be in this moment with him, and only him.

I slowly climb on top of him, my legs either side of his, and I cup his face gently in my hands. I look deeply into his beautiful brown eyes, those openly honest and loving eyes of his I adore getting lost in. They are like deep pools of molten brown, swirling around in such a way, that whenever I gaze into them during our most intimate moments, I feel like I am being swallowed up by them, drowning myself in the depths of their invisible hold over me.

I kiss him gently on the lips, once, twice, three times. When I pull back, our eyes lock together for another long moment, Jonny's hands clasping at my face as he silently checks in with me to make sure I'm okay. Right now, in this moment, I am more than okay, and I am right where I need to be.

Without breaking eye contact, I pull down Jonny's pyjama pants, just enough to free his erection, and more than enough to make my intention well and truly clear. That I want him. I want him so very badly.

Taking a firm hold of his cock, I place the tip at my entrance, before slowly sliding him inside me. I let out a soft cry of pleasure as I take the full length of him, the deliciously familiar ache burning like a wildfire between my thighs already. An ache only he can relieve.

Leaning over, I dip my tongue into his mouth and lose myself in Jonny completely, kissing him with a desperation I can't even begin to explain. I ride him slowly, drawing out each deliberate thrust for as long as I possibly can. Because I want to savour every single second of this moment, taking a mental picture in my mind of Jonny coming undone beneath me.

Pulling back slightly, I watch him closely as he gazes up at me from his pillow, his dark eyes a heady concoction of both love and pure need. My riot of blonde curls sweep across Jonny's face as his fingers knot their way into the long, silky strands, and he tugs on them hard, dragging my mouth back down to his in a kiss full of so much fire and passion, I can barely form a rational thought. Hell, I don't want to form a rational thought right now. Not while we live in this moment, only for each other. Jonny's mouth greedily devours my own, his hands now moving down my body, moulding the curves of my bottom before finding their rightful place on my hips.

Wrenching my lips away from his, I then pull myself up into a kneeling position so I can up the tempo between us, Jonny hauling himself up right along with me so we are face to face, chest to chest.

It is so intimate this way, gazing into each other's eyes, his hands on my hips, mine threaded around the back of his neck. I start to rise and fall in his lap, increasing the pace of our thrusts, Jonny's fingernails almost digging into the skin of my hips as he starts to really lose his mind with pleasure. Over me. Only ever for me. And me for him. In fact, screw that, I'm not losing my mind with pleasure over Jonny right now, I am actually being driven insane. Absolutely insane over this man and what he does to me. How he makes me feel. Oh my god, I just want him. I'm having him right now and yet I still want more of him. *What the hell is wrong with me?*

In a bid to hide my reeling emotions from Jonny, I break eye contact with him and instead tug at his hair, pulling his mouth down to my breasts, and he groans loudly. I almost come apart in his arms as I feel his tongue slide its way across my left nipple, the sensation driving me wild with need.

I find myself rocking against him in desperation as he flits between my breasts, kissing, licking and sucking on them for dear life. All the while, he is panting, groaning and cursing with every thrust, and I take great delight in the fact that Jonny is now at my complete and utter mercy, as I control every thrust, every ounce of pleasure, so I can blow his mind.

Jonny tears his mouth away from my breasts so he can place his forehead against mine, his hand now pressed firmly at the back of my head, keeping me in place, forcing me to look into his eyes once more as we reach our climax together. His mouth drops open, his hot breath against my lips as he pants like a mad man. I watch as Jonny's beautiful face screws up in pleasure, his hand pushing my head even harder against his as the fingers of his other hand make their way down to my clit. It only takes one sweep with those magical fingers of his and I crack wide open.

"Oh my god...Jonny..."

I feel as though I am being ripped apart at the seams as my orgasm tears through me like a raging fire, but I don't close my eyes, and I don't turn away from him. Not for a second. And neither does he. We stare deeply into each other's eyes as our mouths smash together in a joint groan of release. It is sweaty and intense, our bodies still hungry and greedy for more, the pair of us so desperate to erase the last few hours from our minds in the only way we know how.

We lie together in the peaceful haven of Jonny's music studio afterwards, and I allow myself to fall into a restful sleep in the arms of the man I love. For now, I want to forget about the fight that is yet to come, because once it comes, there will be no turning back from it, whether I want to or not. I have to fight to the bitter end this time round, and fight to the bitter end I will....

CHAPTER 3

JONNY

Back to the present....

It's 8.00 am when Stacey, Ben, Will and Zack arrive at my house the following morning, all trying to get an early start with me so we can get a plan together. I barely slept a wink all night just worrying myself sick about Lauren.

When I wasn't trying to get some sleep, I was on my mobile constantly, trying to call her, so many times I've now lost count. I've also sent text message after text message, but to no avail. This is the part about it all that makes me so angry with her. The fact that she's gone off all on her own and not even sent a text to tell me she's okay. I fear this article with her dad has really pushed her over the edge, to the point where she's just cut and run, and maybe even put herself in real danger. Which is why I need to get over there to find her as quickly as possible.

Not long after my friends arrive, Lara turns up at my door, armed and ready with piles of paperwork in her briefcase, ready to get me booked on to the next flight over to Manchester as well as go through some really important details about what I intend to do next.

And that's where my dad comes into the equation. Last night, after the initial shock of everything had started to wear off, I actually plucked up the courage to ring him and ask for his help, because of all the people in the world who can bring down the likes of a violent man like Jimmy Whittle, then he can.

Lara, Ben, Will and Zack settle themselves around the dining table while Stacey puts on a pot of coffee for us all over in the kitchen. As Lara sets about pulling out her laptop and paperwork from her briefcase, I hear the doorbell ring, signalling my dad's arrival. After we spoke last night, I gave him the new code for the gate and decided to put everything that's happened between us to one side, for now at least. I am far from forgiving him for what he did, but right at this very moment in time, I need him. More than I've ever needed him, I think.

I can't pretend I don't feel that familiar anger with him when I open the door to see him standing on the other side of it. Wearing a casual cream coloured suit and a dark blue polo shirt beneath, my dad still looks as healthy and as well as he always has done. I have to hand it to him, he is always immaculately presented and really takes care of himself and his appearance, and at fifty six years old, I do admire him for that, for always putting in the effort and looking after himself.

Apart from the sprinkling of grey in his hair and a few lines around his eyes, my dad looks far younger than his years, although I would never actually tell him that. My dad's head is big enough, or at least, it used to be. Not so much these days, not after everything that's happened over these last few months. I think my dad and his overly inflated ego have well and truly *deflated*, that air of self-importance he used to walk around with no longer being an issue. Thank god, because it used to bug the absolute shit out of me.

"Hi, Jonny," my dad says, nodding his head at me. He looks a little unsure about how to greet me and he doesn't smile I notice. I can understand that of course, this is hardly the reunion he had hoped for with me but then, this isn't exactly a reunion. This is a means to an end for me and he needs to know that.

"Hey," I say back to him. "Thanks for coming." I step back from the door and gesture for him to come inside. As he walks past me, I can't help but remind him of why he is here. "Before we proceed, I need you to know that you're here because I need your help, Dad, nothing more. I think you owe me that much at least."

My dad stops in his tracks. Turning towards me, he looks me straight in the eyes as he says, "No reminder needed, Jonny. I'm here to help. Nothing more."

I can't be sure but I think I detected a hint of bitterness in his tone just now, which almost betrays the look of guilt I still see swimming around in his eyes. Whether or not he intended to sound bitter, I'm not entirely sure, but I decide to let it go. I've far more important things on my mind right now other than raking over this long drawn out feud with my dad.

I close the front door and my dad follows me through the hallway and into the kitchen where Stacey is busy pouring out cups of coffee for everyone. An awkward silence descends on the room as soon as my dad enters, Stacey immediately pausing what she's doing so she can glare over at my dad.

Over at the dining table, Lara already looks uncomfortable at being in the same room as my dad again, after everything that transpired between them, whilst Ben, Will and Zack just look downright angry. And they have every right to be angry with my dad, as have I, but anger is not what I need from them today. I need a team of people to pull together for Lauren, and so I make it known.

"Before anybody says anything at all to my dad, then don't. I asked my dad to come here this morning so he can help me with bringing down the bastard that is Lauren's father.

It's why we're all here. To get Lauren back home safely where she belongs and to make damn fucking certain Jimmy Whittle can't harm her ever again, either physically or verbally. We're all here for the exact same reason and so we all pull together today, whether we want to be in the same room with each other or not. Agreed?"

I hear a few murmurs of agreement from one or two of them but that isn't enough for me. "I said, are we all agreed?"

I finally get a resounding yes from them all. Well, all except Ben. Ben looks less than impressed with the entire situation, but he'll just have to suck it up and deal with it, and the quieter the better for me because I am not in the mood for him and his big mouth this morning. Mind you, I'm not in the mood for much of anything at the moment, and I won't be until I have Lauren safely back in my arms once more.

Stacey quietly finishes off making the coffee in the kitchen before bringing everything over to where we are sitting around the dining table. She sets down a jug of milk, teaspoons and a bowl of sugar in the centre of the table before placing a mug of coffee down in front of each of us, one by one, leaving my dad's cup until last.

Slamming his cup down in front of him, she casts a glare in his direction before taking her own mug of coffee with her. Sitting down next to Ben, she continues to pin her frosty gaze on my dad as she blows over her coffee. Ben then wraps an arm around her shoulders and pulls her against him, looking over at my dad with a scowl of his own. And that's when my dad snaps.

"Look, if you two have something to say to me, then just say it," says my dad, looking less than enthused with the pair of them.

Stacey looks affronted at my dad's sudden outburst whereas

Ben just snaps right back at him. "Oh, I have plenty to say to you, mother fucker," Ben snarls. And that's when I lose it.

"Hey! You wanna watch your mouth or what?!" I shout over at him. He's sitting on the opposite side of the table to me but I will pull him over the fucking table if he carries on. As I said before, I am not in the mood for this shit and I won't put up with it.

Ben just sneers in response, looking over at my dad as if he's a piece of shit on the bottom of his shoe. "You defending him after what he did? I'd say what I just called him is polite compared to what you've been saying about him since you found out the truth about the shit he did…"

Scraping my chair back in anger, I stand up and slam my hands down on to the table. Leaning towards him, I offer him out. "You wanna go right now, Ben? Because I swear to god I will put you through this fucking table if you carry on speaking to my dad like that!"

Ben shoves his own chair backwards and stands up when I say that to him. He then walks around the table towards me, goading me in a way that really gets my back up. And he knows it gets my back up which is exactly why he's doing it. "Come on then, Jonny! Do it!" he shouts, beckoning with his hands for me to go towards him. Oh and I take the fucking bait.

I push myself away from the table and storm my way over to him. I square up to him, right before I shove him in the chest. "Come the fuck on then, Ben! Let's get this over with!"

Ben shoves me back just as hard, and that's when I really lose it. I get the first punch in, my fist landing smack bang on Ben's left cheek, and that's it, we're off. Ben throws a punch in my direction but I manage to dodge out of the way. That royally pisses him off and so he lunges at me again, the pair of us grappling with each other like wrestlers in a wrestling ring.

The next thing we know, we're in the midst of a full on fight that neither of us are willing to back down from, least of all me. I am so fucking angry with him. For ruining my plan this morning, for trampling all over it with his big fucking mouth and getting in the way of me finding Lauren.

Before we know what's happening, Will, Zack, and even my dad, are pulling us apart, Stacey screaming at the pair of us to stop. Neither of us let up that easily though; I'm trying with all my might to free my arms from the grip of Will and my dad whilst Zack is pulling Ben back by the arms as best as he can on his own. Zack is pretty well built though and stands firm against him, and so Ben eventually gives in, scowling over at me in his usual, childish way.

"Just stop this madness!" screeches Stacey, looking between the pair of us. And that just riles me up even more.

"Madness?" I snap at her, "you and Ben were the ones who started all of this! I specifically told you all to leave the past behind us, just for this morning, so we could all pull together to help me find Lauren, but instead, *he...*" I manage to break my arms free from the grip of both Will and my dad so I can point over at Ben, "...and his big fucking mouth just couldn't stay quiet as I requested, and you, Stacey, you were eyeballing my dad from the word go, and don't pretend that you weren't..."

"Hey! You speak to Stacey like that again and you'll have me to deal with!" shouts Ben, stalking towards me all over again, ready for round two. I'm about to meet him in the middle to do just that, but I get hauled back again by Will and my dad, Zack yanking Ben backwards at the same time.

"Oh for goodness sake!" Lara's high pitched voice suddenly cuts through all the anger in the room like a knife.

We all slowly turn our heads toward her, as if we'd forgotten she was even in the room with us. In all honesty, I had forgotten she was here, too angry with Ben to think about anything else in that moment.

Lara is standing by the table, looking between us all, absolutely disgusted with the lot of us I think. "Fighting between ourselves isn't going to bring Lauren back to Jonny any sooner," she says firmly, "which is why Jonny asked you all to just be civil with his dad. If I can do it then I'm damn sure you all can." She glares at us all individually, before taking her seat at the table once more.

A moment of silence descends on the room as the gravity of the situation hits us all. I feel Will and my dad loosen their grip around me, and Zack does the same with Ben.

After a beat, I decide to just swallow down my pride and apologise. "Look, I'm sorry for flying off the handle like that, I'm just..." I swallow down the lump of emotion that seems to form in my throat whenever I think about Lauren at the moment.

"Yeah, we know," says Will, placing a reassuring hand on my shoulder. I nod my head at him and then I glance over at Ben.

"I'm sorry," I say to him, "okay?"

I can tell his pride is hurt, more so than his face, although from the looks of things I've given him one hell of a shiner on his left cheek, as well as a slight cut above his right eye. I look down at my knuckles and see that they're a little bloodied and sore from where I hit him, but they'll heal. And Ben's face will heal too. But his pride? Not so much.

Ben nods a simple thanks in my direction and then goes back to sit down in his chair, Stacey fussing over his bruised cheek and the cut above his eye. He bats her hands away, not wanting any sympathy from her whatsoever. Normally, Ben would be lapping up the attention from Stacey round about now, but when it comes to fisticuffs, Ben likes to come across as the strong macho man he professes to be.

In all honesty, he's not as tough as he thinks he is, and I've more than proven that point to him a good few times in our past, the pair of us having come to blows on many occasions before today. Not that I like fighting with one of my best friends, or anyone for that matter. I am not a violent man and I never have been, but if somebody brings the fight to my door then I will react, and unfortunately, Ben and I have a knack of being able to wind each other up so easily.

Thankfully, we have two other much calmer friends by our side to diffuse these situations as and when they arise, and those friends have done exactly that this morning. With a little help from the others in the room of course. Which reminds me....

Walking over to Stacey, I place a hand on her shoulder and say, "I'm sorry for what I said to you, Stace, I was just angry."

Thankfully, Stacey is a lot more forgiving than Ben is. She smiles up at me and says, "No need to apologise, Jonny, but thank you all the same. I'm sorry too."

I smile back and give her a nod of thanks before taking my place at the table once more. Turning to Lara, I throw a grateful smile in her direction. "And thank you, Lara, for reminding us all about why we are here this morning."

"No problem," she says, nodding. Turning to the paperwork she's now spread out across the table, she says, "Okay, so, I think I am able to build a case against the newspaper for printing the article, and I've been in talks with your lawyers about this and they are on it as we speak."

I nod my head, grateful for her work on all of this. "That's good to know, but this isn't just about the newspaper who printed the article. How likely is it we can sue Lauren's dad for defamation of character? Because that is what he's done here, both to me and to Lauren."

Lara looks around at the paperwork in front of her. "I know that's originally what you wanted to do, Jonny, but taking her dad to court over defamation of character is probably something the lawyers will advise against…"

"Advise against?" I ask, feeling annoyed.

"Simply because he has nothing to lose, as in, no property, no assets, no money…"

"Except for the money he made from the god damn article!" I snap, quickly losing my temper. "And anyway, this isn't about the fucking money! I don't want to sue him for any money! I want to make an example out of him and show the world exactly what that man is!"

I can feel myself getting all riled up again and my dad puts a hand on my shoulder in a show of reassurance. "Hey, you will get your day with him, Jonny, and you will get justice for Lauren." Justice for Lauren? Like he gives a shit!

"Justice for Lauren? Well, nice to know you care about the woman I love after all."

I can't help it. Tensions are running high in here this morning and even though I leaped to his defence before, I am now turning on him myself, angry at the fact he has the nerve to sit next to me, pretending he cares about the woman he ripped away from me…twice!

I feel my dad's hand fall away from my shoulder as he shrinks back into his chair. "I suppose I deserved that," he says with a sigh, "just as I deserve to be scowled at by everyone sitting at this table right now, but I'm here this morning because you are my son, and…I want to make amends for all the wrongs I've done over the years. Not only to you and Lauren, but…to others as well."

My dad glances over at Lara when he says that, but she looks away from him, not wanting to make eye contact. My dad continues. "I don't expect for you to forgive me for what I did, Jonny, but at least allow me the chance to prove myself to you, to help you with this, in any way I can."

That was quite the apology, and whilst my dad appears genuinely sorry for his past misdemeanours, I can't allow my emotions to cloud my judgement when it comes to him. I need to focus on the job in hand and make it crystal clear what I want from him in all of this.

"You can help me by bringing down that violent bastard, Jimmy Whittle," I say to him. "So there won't even be a need to sue him for anything…"

"As in…"

"As in, you deploy every source you have at your disposal and you dig up every slither of information you can find on him. I want to know everything about his life. The life he led before Lauren was born, the life he led when Lauren was born, the life he's been fucking living over the last decade when Lauren moved down to London. I want you to leave no stone unturned, because I am going after that bastard, all guns blazing, and he will regret the day he ever laid a finger on his daughter."

With a determined nod, my dad says, "I will throw everything I've got at this, Jonny, I promise you I will. No stone unturned."

"Good," I say, nodding my head in return.

Turning back to Lara and the rest of my friends sitting around the table, I look at each one of them individually, taking the time to appreciate every single one of them. Even

Ben, who is looking a little more at ease now than he did just moments ago.

"As for the rest of us, we pull together now so I can get to Lauren as soon as possible. Lara, I need you to book me on the next flight over to Manchester, whenever that is. I don't care when it is, I just want it booking straight away. Will, Ben and Zack, can you try and manage our socials while I'm not here and keep an eye on things as they progress and liaise with Lara as and when needed, because there's going to be a continuing media fallout as a result of all of this. Stace, can you just keep trying Lauren for me, at any opportunity, and maybe fire off a few texts to her that might just persuade her to get in touch before I get over there."

I sound like I'm firing off commands to them all, like they're an army unit about to go out on manoeuvres, but they all nod their heads in agreement, smiling at me in a show of support about how I want to forge ahead with things. And speaking of forging ahead.

"Lara, in light of all of this, I obviously want to respond to this news article in due course, given the media frenzy surrounding it all, but I need time to think about what I want to say and in all honesty, I really want Lauren by my side when I do that, so for now, I want to hold off on responding to anything. That sound okay?"

Lara grimaces. "I understand why you want to hold off with any sort of press release but can you deal with the constant press intrusion before then? It's four rows deep with the paparazzi outside your front gates this morning."

"I can second that, Jonny," says my dad, "I almost had to knock them over to get them to move so I could drive up to your gates this morning." Stacey and the lads all nod their heads in agreement. Talk about suddenly feeling ganged up on.

Running an impatient hand through my hair, I let out a heavy sigh. "I couldn't give a fuck about how many vultures are waiting out there. I'm more than used to them by now, and believe me, they are the least of my worries at the moment. They can fucking wait for a statement. All I'm bothered about right now is how I get from here to Manchester without being seen by them. I need to go under the radar when I go over there and I honestly don't know how to do that."

I can feel the nerves about this whole sorry situation beginning to get to me, my fingers trembling as my craving for nicotine gets the better of me. Reaching into the pocket of my jeans, I pull out my packet of fags and proceed to light one up. I don't normally smoke in the house but I'm not in the mood for obeying any rules right now, especially my own, and so I puff on that fag of mine as if my life depends on it.

"You want one?" I say to Ben, offering the fag packet to him across the table. Unfolding his arms, Ben looks over at me and gives me a grateful nod, before leaning over to pluck one out for himself. "Anyone else? Zack?" Zack also takes a fag and before we know it, the three of us are sitting around the table in a cloud of smoke. Normally, my dad would protest about something like this, but he keeps quiet, remembering his place.

"I would normally apologise to the rest of you around this table who don't smoke but I'm afraid that needs must today."

I pull deeply on the cigarette, taking the time to allow the nicotine to work its magic. Nicotine barely hits the spot with me these days, my past drug addiction making my dependency on the cigarettes feel so much stronger than it used to be, but I'd rather smoke my way through a load more cigarettes than fall back into the destructive life of being a drug addict again. If anything, this situation with Lauren and her dad has made me even more determined to never re-visit that dark place from my drug fuelled past ever again.

"Listen, Jonny, it won't be easy going under the radar," says Lara, "but if we handle this discreetly and trick the paparazzi into thinking you've perhaps gone somewhere else when in fact you haven't, then that might buy you a couple of days to find Lauren and get her back home to LA before they latch on to your whereabouts. Plus, Lauren somehow managed to slip under their noses, as well as ours, and considering she's also well known to the paparazzi, I'd say we should just about be able to manage it. And if we don't, then…we'll deal with it, if and when it happens."

Blowing out the smoke from between my lips, I lean my forearms on to the table and give Lara a determined nod. "Okay then. So the plan is born."

And so it starts, right now, the beginning of the end for that son of a bitch….

CHAPTER 4

LAUREN

It's been over twenty four hours since I left LA, since I left behind the love of my life, and I am still lying on the bed in my dingy hotel room, just outside the city of Manchester. I've been lying here for the last two hours, just looking up at the ceiling, wondering what the hell I am doing with my life. I was supposed to be going to see my dad tonight, to face him, to finally stand up to him like I've been planning to do ever since the article got released.

He is about a fifteen minute taxi ride away from here. That's all. Just a short distance away from where I am staying in this budget hotel. It isn't the nicest hotel I've ever stayed in but that's the point. I'm so paranoid about anybody recognising me from the newspapers that I've really gone all out on the whole incognito thing.

I gave a fake name at the reception desk downstairs when I arrived this afternoon and I've been wearing a cap and sunglasses so I can walk outside during the day without being noticed. It's highly unlikely I will be recognised around here but I can't risk being seen, and so I have fought to stay well and truly under the radar.

Even though it has felt like an age since I last saw Jonny, this is only my first night here in Manchester. The flight I boarded back in LA took over twelve hours to get me to where I wanted to be, and with the eight hour time difference between LA and Manchester, I only landed on UK soil this afternoon.

And then there was the whole getting through airport security where I had to expose my face of course. I was absolutely terrified somebody at the airport was going to recognise me, but, if they did, they certainly didn't let on that they knew who I was. Thank god. I grabbed my luggage as quickly as I could after that and set about finding myself a hotel that had some free rooms at short notice and somewhere located near to where my dad lives. In one of the roughest parts of Manchester.

I can't quite believe I am back here after all these years. Sadly, most of the memories I associate with this city are painful ones. So painful that I don't want to dwell on them anymore. I'd rather remember the happy memories I made when I was here, when I met Jonny. *Jonny.* God, I miss him. I miss him more with each passing second, and I hate myself for doing what I've done, but I hope he'll find it within himself to forgive me and understand my reasoning for doing this without him.

Tearing my gaze away from the ceiling, I roll on to my side and pick up my mobile phone from the bedside table, suddenly intent on torturing myself that little bit more by scrolling through photos and videos of me and Jonny.

I gasp as about a million missed calls from Jonny flash up on my screen, as well as another million missed calls from Stacey. I scroll through text after text from the pair of them, my eyes filling with tears as the guilt really starts to cut through my skin and seep into my heart.

I want to text them, I really want to text them both, just to reassure them that I am okay, but if I text them, they will then ring me, and if they ring me after I have communicated with them then I will crumble and I will pick up that phone. And I can't do that. Not until I have done what I set out to do. But not tonight. I can't go and face my dad tonight. My fear has won yet again and I instead decide to wallow in self-pity, by flicking through my phone and looking at the photographs and videos of me and Jonny from the last few months.

I smile as I see Jonny coming into focus on a video I got of him when he came running towards me on the beach when we were in the Maldives. He was dripping wet from his swim, covered in sand, and he came barrelling towards me in a deliberate manoeuvre to get me all mucked up right along with him, something he did a few times to me while we were over there. I can hear my squeals of laughter on the video as he plucks the phone from my hands before cutting the video short. It was one of very many magical moments we had together on that wonderful island.

That holiday turned out to be the beginning of the healing process for Jonny, as well as the beginning of a new chapter for us. His romantic proposal on the sandy beach at some unearthly hour of the morning, the love we made in our villa after his proposal, the candlelit dinner he arranged for me the following evening so we could officially celebrate our engagement. And now I am without him. All over again. *Just for now.*

I keep telling myself that. I haven't left Jonny again. This is a temporary thing I needed to do, but now I'm here, all on my own, I'm beginning to wonder if I've gone about this all wrong. *No, Lauren, you need to do this, for you.* The voice in my head wins again. I do need to do this for me, and Jonny will understand that. At least, I hope he will.

Tomorrow night. I will psyche myself up for the next twenty four hours and I will visit my dad tomorrow night. No more excuses. I need to do this.

****

I am standing outside the scruffy looking council house I once lived in with my dad. It looks much the same as it always did, dirty and downtrodden, like the man living inside it. The front garden is an absolute tip, as it always was. Empty bottles of alcohol lie scattered across the path that leads up to the front door, some broken, some not, the front hedgerow is massively overgrown and is taking over most of the pavement and the grass is so tall, I don't think it's seen a mower in years. Even the light on the front wall just to the left of the front door has been smashed in. Despite the fact it's dark, I can still see this house for what it truly is.

Council houses or not, a lot of people on this estate I once lived on with my dad look after their homes, and they take pride in the fact they have a roof over their heads, as I always did. I tried so hard to make this place a home, to prove to myself l could be better than him. I really thought I could create a loving environment in spite of everything I had to endure at the hands of my violent father. Oh, how wrong I was.

Feeling sick to the pit of my stomach with nerves, I look away from the house of horrors standing in front of me and instead turn my gaze upwards, towards the sky. It looks dark and foreboding tonight, the clouds are thick and heavy and the drizzle is really beginning to put a dampener on my already low mood. I know the UK is famous for its changeable weather but with it being May, I expected some half decent weather at least. Not tonight though. Perhaps the weather is building me up for seeing my dad. Preparing me for the storm I am about to face.

Turning my attention back to what was once my childhood home, I take an unsteady step forward. My heart is thudding like mad in my chest and my breathing is beginning to accelerate. I can feel the onset of fear and panic already beginning to wrap its way around me like a vine, but I need to breathe through it and force myself to do this. Why am I so afraid of him? I have moved on and made a life for myself.

I am a thirty year old woman who doesn't have to take those beatings anymore. I can do this. I *have* to do this.

"So this is why you ran off to Manchester without me, is it?"

I whip my head round in shock, almost stumbling backwards when I see Jonny standing across the street from me. I watch as he slowly steps out from the shadows, from behind a car I assume is a hire car he's driven here in.

Wearing a black cap, his black leather jacket and black jeans, he looks as incognito as I do. I feel partly relieved he is here, because I've missed him more than words could ever say, but at the same time, I am so taken aback by his sudden appearance that I feel in shock. Holy shit, this is not what I was expecting at all. This isn't how all of this was supposed to go and I am already beginning to struggle to process this turn of events.

"But...how did you find me? How..." I am speechless. I can't find any more words to say to him and so I fall silent.

As he walks toward me, from across the narrow street that is sitting between us, I try to gauge the look on Jonny's face, but it's difficult to read his expression right now. Apart from the dim glow of a streetlight a few feet away, we're pretty much in darkness out here.

"I fly thousands of miles over an entire ocean to try and get to you without knowing exactly where you are, I wait for you tonight for hours on end on this estate in a hire car, hoping against hope you would turn up here at some point, *praying* that I hadn't missed you perhaps visiting your dad before tonight, and the first thing you say to me after doing your whole disappearing act is 'how did I find you?' Really, Lauren? That's all you have to say to me?"

Turns out I don't need to read Jonny's facial expression after all, as he makes his feelings about me coming over to Manchester without him abundantly clear. "No, of course not,

I'm just in shock that you're here. You're…really here?"

My question sounds as pathetic as I feel, but I just can't find the right words to say to him. What can I possibly say right now that will make him feel any better about me coming over here on my own? Nothing at all. Which is why I fall silent for the second time in as many minutes.

Jonny seemingly ignores my ridiculous question and instead nods toward my dad's house behind me. "So, if you had gone in there tonight, before I arrived, what were you planning on saying to him?"

Jonny's question catches me completely off guard, and I find myself scrambling around in my mind to find the answer. *The truth, Lauren, just tell him the truth about why you came here.* The truth. Of course. Nothing quite like speaking the truth in a situation as delicate as this one is.

Blowing out a shaky breath, I look down at the floor as I finally pluck up the courage to tell him what's been going around my head these last few days. "I wanted to face my dad head on. I wanted to finally speak up for myself after spending years of suffering in silence, to show him that I am now strong and that he hasn't in fact destroyed my life like he thought he had. I wanted him to see what I have become since I left Manchester, that I am no longer the weak girl he once knew."

"And you thought you had to do all of that alone? Without me?" Jonny asks, sounding hurt.

"This isn't about you, Jonny," I say to him, trying to ignore the hurt in his voice, "this is about what my dad did to *me*. How he made *me* feel. I wanted to face him on my own so that I could prove to him, and to myself, that I'm no longer scared of him. I wanted him to openly admit what he did to me…and to Oliver, because I want…I *need* closure, Jonny. I thought you of all people would understand that."

"You don't think I understand your need for closure?" he asks in exasperation.

"Jonny…"

"Jesus, Lauren, you really know how to stick the knife in, that's for sure." He sighs and then turns away from me, running an angry hand down his face.

"I'm not trying to hurt you, Jonny, I just need to do this by myself. You need to let me do this…"

Throwing his hands up in the air in anger, Jonny then whirls back round to face me once more. "And you need to stop running away from me, Lauren! Because when the going gets tough and you can't handle the situation, you just cut and run. Every single time…"

"That is so not true," I say, immediately going on the defensive, "that isn't what this is!"

"It isn't?"

"No!" I shout at him.

Jonny raises his eyebrows in surprise. "Oh, okay, so you leaving your engagement ring behind together with a goodbye note, wasn't you running away? Well, that's good to know…"

"I told you I loved you in that note, I said I'd be back…"

"Yeah you did! When it fucking suits!" Jonny exclaims.

I draw back from him in shock at hearing that remark. "What the hell is that supposed to mean?"

Jonny sighs impatiently. "It means exactly as it sounds, Lauren, because I am done with the whole walking on egg shells around you in all of this. I love you, more than anyone or anything, so fucking much that I would die for you. And despite everything, despite you leaving me twice before, despite you breaking my heart not once, but twice, I still took you back, because I love you. *That much*. And yet somehow, that love still wasn't enough for *you* to put your trust in *me*. You didn't trust me to get you over here safely. You still decided, for whatever reason, to handle something as difficult as this, all on your own, which brings me to my next question...where does that leave me?"

"Jonny, I'm sorry...but why...how can you throw me leaving you in my face like that? You know why I left you twice before. You know it was because of your dad..."

"Whether it was because of my dad or not, you should have shared it with me at the time. All of it. I understand why you left me the first time and I can accept that now. I was stuck in rehab and you were out here, all on your own...but last year, when my dad visited you in London and warned you off, you should have just told me. Everything. But you just cut me off and ran a fucking mile. And you're still running now, and I feel like you'll always be running away from me. I just don't know why..."

I shake my head at him, tears now swimming around in my eyes as I realise the consequences of my actions. "Jonny... please..."

"I will watch you go inside that house to talk to your dad tonight. I will stand guard outside so I know you are safe, and I would have done that for you anyway, had you bothered to ask me. I would have respected your decision to go in there and face him on your own, and I'm absolutely heartbroken that you think I would have done anything other than respect that decision."

"Jonny...I'm sorry..."

"Sorry isn't really doing it for me right now, Lauren, but I'll wait here for you because I would never walk away and leave you on your own. Never. Just remember that."

I raise my eyebrows in surprise. "And you expect me to go in there and face my dad now? After everything you've just said to me?"

Appearing unaffected by my remark, Jonny says, "It's why you came here, isn't it?"

Feeling a little defeated with the entire situation, I think about turning away from facing my dad at all. I'm hardly in the right mindset for it now, not after everything Jonny's just thrown at me. But then, that would be running away all over again. Something I do all too often apparently. I feel a little bitter and twisted about those hurtful comments Jonny has just hurled at me, but is he really that far off the mark? Looking back over our time together, I fear probably not.

I really want to make things right with Jonny, but I also need to face my dad and combat my fears. Maybe only then I will truly stop running. Once I have the closure I so desperately need. Straightening my stance, I give him a determined nod. "You're right," I say to him, "that is why I came here."

Gesturing towards my dad's house, Jonny then says, "So go ahead, get your closure. I'll be waiting right here for you when you come back out."

I give him a grateful smile. "Thank you."

He doesn't smile in return, instead simply nodding his head in acknowledgement. "If at any point he tries anything at all, you shout for me. Okay?"

"Okay," I say, feeling relieved. Relieved that he's here with me after all. Looking out for me, making me feel safe. He always made me feel so safe. Why the hell did I think I could do this without him? What on earth was I thinking? I wasn't thinking, not properly anyway. In my usual anxious like state,

I came up with a plan that isolated him all over again. I have so much making up to do where Jonny's concerned, I know that, but for now, I have to turn around and finally face him. Face my dad.

Swallowing down a bout of nerves, I turn towards his house and start walking down the path, approaching the front door. *It's now or never, Lauren, you can do this.*

When I reach the door, I reluctantly raise my hand in the air. Balling my hand into a fist, I take the deepest breath in I think I've ever taken, and I punch through my fear by knocking on his door. And then I wait....

CHAPTER 5

LAUREN

It feels like the longest moment of my life, waiting for my dad to come to the door. I very nearly turn away and run off towards where Jonny is waiting for me on the pavement, my panic rising within me to the point where that familiar fight or flight is beginning to kick in, but then my dad suddenly opens the door.

For the first time in over eleven years, I set eyes on the man who was supposed to be my father. He looks much the same to me as he always did, large round belly bulging out from his white stain ridden vest, light grey joggers with holes in that look like they haven't been washed for months. His bright red cheeks match the colour of his bloodshot eyes and the little wisps of greying hair he has left around the side of his head and neck look greasy and unkempt.

With his usual bottle of vodka in one hand, my dad places his other hand on the door jamb, swaying slightly as his bloodshot eyes zone in on me. His daughter. Even though I'm standing a little bit further back from where he is in the doorway, the stench of stale sweat mixed with alcohol hits my nostrils immediately, almost making me gag.

Now that I'm here, seeing him in the flesh all over again, smelling the foul odour of the man who took my entire childhood away from me, I can't believe I ever lived in this house with him for so long. I must have grown accustomed to the smell when I lived here but now that I am being thrust back into it, by my own choice this time, I suddenly feel proud of myself. Proud that I survived the years of abuse I endured at his hands. I am not the weak young girl I thought I was after all. Jonny was right all along. I am strong. Strong for getting out of this shithole and for making a life for myself.

Before tonight, I had doubted myself for so long, punished myself in fact for thinking that I had been the weak girl my dad had always told me I was. Well, this is certainly an eye opener for me, and a complete revelation. I came here tonight for closure but what I've got already, within the first few seconds of seeing my dad, is inner peace. I am finally making peace with myself for coming out of this hellhole alive and for never giving up, and that in itself is glorious.

It takes a good few seconds for my dad to realise it's me standing in front of him. His own flesh and blood. In his inebriated state, I'm actually surprised he managed to drag his lazy drunken ass up off the sofa to get to the front door, never mind open it and hold a conversation with someone.

"Well, well, well, if it ain't my loving daughter come… come…back to see her…old man after…these years."

My dad is already slurring his words but as usual, he brings that vodka bottle back up to his mouth and takes another gulp of the alcohol anyway, before belching his satisfaction afterwards. Eurgh, this man is so vile that I look at him and wonder how the hell I came from him.

"So…to what do I owe this…this…honour," he says, taking another swig of the vodka.

Jeez, why did I come here? I should have known that he'd be off his face on alcohol. He always was. I'm surprised that the alcohol hasn't poisoned him to death before now, which is a shame, because my father deserves nothing less than a death as painful as that one would be. So I've heard anyway.

I honestly wouldn't wish a painful death on my worst enemy, but this man standing in front of me is not my enemy. He is my dad. The most evil man I have ever had the misfortune of knowing.

"You coming in?" he asks, frowning over at me. Pointing drunkenly down his hallway behind him, he says, "Because I've got some...some...food..." He hiccups right before he lets out another loud burp and then steadies himself against the door jamb once more. When I don't answer him, he blinks at me and then says, "I asked you a fucking question."

Oh, here we go, he's becoming angry with me already and that took the grand total of two minutes. Me staying silent would of course make my dad think I'm being deliberately ignorant, which in turn would get his back up, as it always did in the past. In truth however, I only haven't answered him because in all honesty, I'm dithering. Dithering over whether I actually want to walk back into this house I suffered in for so many years. But this isn't about what I want right now, this is about what I need to do. It's why I flew over here in the first place. To face him and to tell him a few home truths before I walk away with my head held high and that closure I so desperately need.

Yes, I need to go inside and not stay standing out here on the other side of the front door like I'm afraid of him. Because I'm not afraid of him, not anymore. That ship has long sailed and he's about to find out just how far it's gone.

Finally mustering up the courage to open my mouth, I answer him, being sure to keep my voice calm but firm, without even the slightest hint of emotion. Emotions are being left at the front door tonight. "Yes I will come in," I finally say to him, "but not for long. This isn't a social call. Far from it."

I'm giving him a warning now so he doesn't fly off the handle at me later. It was always the same with him. If you pretend to go along with the things he wants or apparently needs and then backtrack out of fear or sheer panic, that's when he strikes, like a python, sinking its teeth in and injecting its venom into your veins until you have nothing else left in you other than the worst type of pain imaginable.

My new found confidence and openly audacious words hit the mark with him straight away and he stares at me coldly, his bloodshot eyes giving me the usual look of disapproval they always gave me if I so much as spoke back to him. I admittedly didn't speak back to him very often, for fear of making things so much worse than they already were, but when I did, my god when I did, did he make me regret it.

"You better watch your tongue, Lauren…and remember your place."

Normally, that type of threat from my dad would have had me running a mile but seeing how drunk he is tonight and knowing that Jonny is hiding behind the front hedgerow, only a few feet away from me, makes that threat of his seem so empty. Even so, I am still wary of my dad and what he is capable of.

He was always at his angriest when he was drunk, which was often, but sometimes, he would get so off his face that he'd end up passing out on the sofa in a drunken stupor. Those were the moments when I found myself feeling thankful for his terrible drinking habit, but sadly, those moments were extremely rare.

Most of the time, my dad just seemed to strike that oh so perfect balance that sat him exactly between being slightly drunk and being completely off his face. And that balance of his was what I called 'control.' That power hungry control he held and wielded over me for so very long. Well, not anymore. Tonight, I say my peace and then I leave. I close the door on this bastard and this stinking rotten house of his for good. But not until I've walked into this house and faced my past. And facing my past starts right now.

Taking a calming breath in, I mentally talk myself into stepping over the threshold and into his house. When I step into his hallway, I notice the corner of my dad's mouth turning upwards, almost like he's smiling to himself over something. That something most likely being me doing exactly as he says. Nothing gave him greater pleasure in life than that, once upon a time. Well, he can think that for now if he wants, but that smile of his will soon be wiped off his face when I've finished with him.

My dad turns away from me and stumbles his way through the hallway as I close the front door behind me. Closing the front door almost sets me off in a panic, the gravity of the situation suddenly hitting me in the face. I am sealing myself in here with my dad, a man so violent that he almost killed me. And I was originally going to do that on my own tonight. Until Jonny turned up unexpectedly. Like a knight in shining armour turning up on his steed to save his damsel in distress.

Well, I'd hardly call our love story one of knights and steeds and I'm certainly no damsel, but Jonny is, when all said and done, my white knight. He'd probably call himself a dark knight, but to me, Jonny is the brightest person in my life to have ever existed. He is the day to my night and he is the light to my dark. My unending love that never ever faltered. I shouldn't have excluded him from any of this. Jonny is right where he needs to be right now. Outside that front door, waiting for me, keeping guard, protecting me. Just like he always did the first time round, like he always will. Yes, with Jonny by my side, I can achieve anything. Absolutely anything. Including standing up to the man I once thought I would never be able to stand up to.

Ignoring the shit heap and the musty walls of my dad's

hallway, I find that inner strength within me that Jonny helped me to find, and I walk through to the kitchen at the back of the house. I find my dad sitting at his kitchen table, picking his way through the last bits of what look like a Chinese takeaway.

The kitchen is small but the size of it never mattered. This room could have been so lovely had it been looked after, but it looks much the same as the rest of the house, dirty, run-down, battered and broken, just like the man sitting in the middle of it.

Piling a forkful of what look like dried up noodles into his mouth, my dad speaks to me as he chews up his food. "So, what brings you back to Manchester then?"

His question is so nonchalant, as if he doesn't already know why I'm here, but then, my dad was always so pig ignorant and narcissistic. A lack of empathy or understanding about anything or anyone in his life was always his major problem, hence the violence. He really doesn't have an ounce of love or kindness within him and seeing him now at his kitchen table, still drinking himself into oblivion and munching away on his takeaway like everything is normal, is living proof to me of the monster he really is.

I take a moment to think of the words I want to say to this man. I don't want to start shouting the odds at him for fear of riling him up, but I also want to get everything off my chest and purge myself of the years of violence he inflicted upon me. I decide to speak up about the one thing that hurt me the most out of all those years of violence. The moment when my dad snatched everything away from me. My little boy. My son. My Oliver.

Walking slowly over to where my dad is sitting at the kitchen table, I look down at him through angry eyes, swallow down my nerves, and finally find my voice. "He was called Oliver," I say to my dad, who is still munching away on his fucking takeaway, like everything is normal. Well, everything might still be normal in his world but it isn't normal in mine, and it hasn't been normal for a very long time. Because of *him*.

When my dad says nothing in response, I repeat my words back to him through gritted teeth. "I said, he was called Oliver."

Finishing off his food, my dad then takes a swig of his vodka before wiping his mouth on his arm. Resting back in his chair, he folds his arms. He eventually bothers to look up into my face, his reddened eyes now bleary with so much alcohol, I'll be surprised if he even remembers anything about my visit tomorrow. Well, come tomorrow morning, I don't give a shit if he remembers me visiting or not, all that matters is that I get to remember this moment. The moment where I stood up to him after all these years.

"I have no idea who the fuck you're talking...ab...about..." He somehow manages to slur his way through a few words in response before his eyelids begin to close. Oh no, this bastard is not going to sleep on me. No bloody way is he getting away with this after all I've gone through to be here.

Slamming my palms down on to the kitchen table, that gets my dad's attention, jolting him awake out of his drunken daze. "Fuck that for?" Jeez, he can barely string a sentence together, and that's pissing me off. Really pissing me off.

"Oliver was my son!" I suddenly scream at him. "Oliver was mine and Jonny's son! The son you took away from me when you almost beat me to death that night when you came wanting money! Do you remember that night, Dad?!" When he doesn't answer me, I ball up my fists this time and slam them hard into the kitchen table once more.

My dad reacts badly to me thumping my fists into the table. Swooping his arm across the table, he knocks his empty plate and the half full bottle of vodka on to the kitchen floor tiles below. They smash to pieces at his feet and his face reddens with fury. Standing up from the table, he sways from side to side as he points to the floor.

"What a fucking waste!" he shouts, so angry at the fact he's spilt his precious vodka, his lifeline that gets him through every day. Oh, such a hard life he has, my dad. Such a hard life.

"Oh, boohoo!" I shout over at him. "Boo-fucking-hoo!"

Shit, I'm beginning to really lose my temper now and I know that will only serve to add fuel to my dad's already burning rage but I can't help it. He is such an unfeeling bastard, a piece of shit that deserves nothing at all in life. In fact, he deserves less than nothing. He doesn't deserve to even have a life. Why wasn't my son allowed to live? While this bastard got to continue living and breathing, why was my son allowed to die? Why? Why? Why?

My dad manages to somehow lean on to the kitchen table for some sort of support. "You fucking what…what you say?"

"I asked you a question!" I scream at him. I am literally seething with fury. Shaking from head to toe and absolutely seething. He has to answer my question. He *needs* to answer me. I need to hear him say it out loud to me before I leave here tonight.

Flailing his arms around the place, my dad then stumbles backwards slightly but somehow manages to keep himself upright…just. "You fucking whore," he slurs, "you were a whore then with that…boyfriend of yours…although…" He hiccups. "…he's certainly come up in the world…ain't he…eh? My girl did good in the end I s'pose…"

God, I can't stand this vile man who is just about managing to stay standing as he slurs his way through yet more bullshit. "Managed to get me some money…at last…" Another hiccup and he falls into his chair again. "Won't get me that far though…not outta here anyway…" Sniffing loudly, he then says, "So as you're…here and all, why don't you ask that rich boyfriend of yours…for more money…for your old man…" He then has the audacity to smile over at me. Like everything I just said to him about the son he took away from me hasn't even registered.

Trying to breathe through my anger, I lean on the table and narrow my eyes on the bastard. Time to let him have it. All of it. Even if he doesn't take it all in or even remembers any of it tomorrow, I want him to sit there in that kitchen chair while I tell him exactly what I think of him.

"You beat up my mum and made her feel like she had no other option but to slit her own wrists and kill herself. You then started taking your anger out on me, beating me with your fists as often as you saw fit, and because that's all I knew, I don't even remember how old I was when it started!"

My dad blinks at me drunkenly, but I don't even give him the chance to say anything back to me, instead continuing right where I left off. "You beat me so badly that I could have gone off the rails or even ended up in care, in the system, but I didn't, I kept on going! I went to school, I got little jobs, and I earned my own money. I went on to meet Jonny and I fell in love. I then got pregnant, and despite being young at the time, I loved that baby with all my heart and soul. And so did Jonny. But *you*… you took our baby away from us the night you nearly killed me! So admit that you did it! Admit that you are a murderous bastard who took everything away from his own flesh and blood!"

"Oh fuck off you insolent little bitch!" He makes a grab for me over the kitchen table but I quickly back away from him. He then tries to stand up again but ends up falling backwards on to the kitchen floor, missing his chair by a mere few inches.

His lazy fat arse hits the tiles as he goes down with one hell of a bump and he groans in pain. I highly doubt he's sober enough to feel any sort of pain, although I wish he was. I wish him a world of pain, and a whole lot more to boot.

"You see what you made me do you fucking bitch?!" he screams up at me from the floor. "Do you see now why you made me do those things to you?!"

I walk around the table to watch him squirm on the floor. When he sees me approaching, he starts to crawl his way across the floor towards me so I back up a bit, putting a bit of distance between us. But he's far too drunk to even drag himself across the floor tiles, never mind get up and attack me. Not that I'd allow him anywhere near me. Not now. If he even attempted to hit me again, I would make damn sure I fought back. And I'd fight back hard. So hard, he wouldn't know what had hit him.

"You are worthless, Dad," I say, as I watch him trying to get his sorry ass up off the kitchen floor. "A worthless piece of shit and a complete waste of oxygen." I use his own words against him as I watch him become increasingly angry, his face almost purple with rage. "And you won't get another penny out of me or Jonny. You are done, Dad. Completely and utterly done!"

He groans in frustration, his soulless eyes burning up into mine from where he's lying on the floor. "I'm glad I took your baby's life away from you…getting pregnant so young…you whore…you were nothin' but a whore…and you needed to be taught a lesson…and him…that scumbag of a boyfriend that…that…beat me…"

Pain slices through my heart when I hear him not only admit out loud what he did to me, but the fact he was glad he did it, that he intended to do it, to take away the life of an innocent baby, *his* grandchild. What a sick and twisted man he really is.

I somehow manage to rein in my tears as I allow his venomous words to burn their way through my skin, right through to my very heart. Well, I have more than got my answer from this bastard tonight, and I did that for my boy, for the son I lost. And even though justice will never be served for what my dad did to Oliver, I feel like I'm getting my own justice right now by watching the man I used to fear roll around the floor in a drunken state. The man who used to control my entire life. Whether I had a good day or a bad day all depended on this man writhing around in front of me. Jimmy Whittle. The man about the town who begged, borrowed and stole from anybody he could, the man who, at one time, people on this estate feared.

While he's never been particularly tall, standing only at five foot ten, my dad's overly large frame, portly belly and reputation with his fists always made him appear threatening. And he used that threat to his advantage to get him what he wanted. Always. But not anymore. Not with me anyway.

Seeing my dad now, reduced to this, nothing but a drunken wreck who can barely string a sentence together or even get up and walk, has made me realise that I really have come full circle. I went through hell for so many years while living at home with him but I survived. I survived to tell the tale and I am stronger as a result. Strong enough to walk away from this monster once and for all and never look back.

Crouching down to the floor, I set my hardened gaze on him, the hatred I feel for this man literally flowing its way through my veins as I say the words, "Goodbye, Dad. For the last time."

"You bitch!"

He makes a grab for my ankle but I'm too quick for him. Standing up, I take a step backwards and give him one last look of revulsion before I turn on my heel and walk away from him.

Forever. Never again will I see this man and that in itself feels so freeing. I feel elated, as though I've had a huge weight lifted off my shoulders. A weight that has been dragging me down for far too long. But no more.

I walk through my dad's hallway and stop as I reach the front door. I chance one more glance around the grimy hallway, my dad still shouting and balling at me from the kitchen at the back of the house. "Goodbye childhood," I mutter to the house, "and good riddance."

I turn the door handle and wrench the door open. I find Jonny standing on the other side of the front door waiting for me, his face etched with concern. "Lauren, are you okay? I heard him shout…I was going to come in but you didn't shout for me and so I thought I'd let you be, like you wanted…"

"I'm fine, Jonny." I smile up at the man I love and step willingly into his embrace. He folds me into his arms and I instantly relax. This is my safe place right here, my warmth, my love, my life. And I'll never run away from that life with Jonny ever again.

We close the front door behind us and we walk away from the man I once called my father. We close the door on both him and our painful past, and it feels liberating. We still have many things to face following the fallout of all this but just for now, I want this quiet time with Jonny in order to heal.

I know I have a lot of making up to do where Jonny's concerned but we will find our way together, somehow or other, because we have to. Our love has certainly been put to the test over the course of our time together but I will make this right with him, because I love him, and our love will endure, I'll make damn sure of that.

CHAPTER 6

LAUREN

The atmosphere in the car as we drive away from the council estate I once lived on with my father is quiet and sombre, and I know it isn't entirely to do with what just transpired between me and my dad. Jonny is bristling with tension and I know for a fact that it's because of me. After what I did. I've broken that trust with him all over again and in doing that, I've hurt him. I didn't intend to hurt him by what he now sees as me running away from him again, but somehow or other, I have. And I hate that I have.

Initially, he appeared to want to hold me and comfort me when I walked out of my dad's house, most likely because he was worried about me. Worried about the fact I was holed up in that god awful place again with my violent father. But now that his worry is wearing off, I can see how tensed up he is, and I honestly don't know how to broach the subject with him.

Maybe I should just leave him be, until he feels ready to talk to me about it all. The last thing I want to do, especially with Jonny, is start apologising my ass off all over again, as I try to explain why I did what I did, because that won't work on him. Not this time. I've more than burned my bridges in that respect and I hate that I've done that to him, over and over, when, in my head, all I thought I was doing was protecting him. Protecting the man who I always thought deserved so much better than me. But I need to stop thinking like that, I need to stop tearing strips off myself because of where I came from. I am nothing like my father and I never belonged in that shitty, dead end life with him. I belonged with Jonny from the moment we met and I've always belonged with him, even when I wasn't with him.

Hating the silence, I decide to go for small talk, in the hope Jonny will at least start talking to me about something. Anything. "So, are we going to pick up my stuff from my hotel or…where are you staying?"

I realised as soon as I started asking that question that I have no idea where Jonny is staying, or where he's even driving to in this hire car of his. I say hire car, it's still a top notch Range Rover we're driving around in, as seems to be the norm with us these days. Jonny clearly has a taste for a particular type of car. Mind you, these fancy cars I keep being driven around in are also beginning to grow on me, and I never used to care about cars at all. I still can't believe Jonny owns and drives around in a brand spanking new Porsche, but then, so much has changed since he took the music world by storm. One might say too much. Especially when it comes to having a twisted version of your past being splashed about for the entire world to read.

I can feel the elation and relief from moments ago already beginning to evaporate. Knowing that we still have to face one hell of a shitstorm when we get back home to LA is suddenly hitting me. Facing my dad was one thing but facing the rest of the world after everything my dad said in that newspaper article, that is something else entirely, and I don't think I'm ready for that. I highly doubt Jonny is either.

"For now I'm just…driving," Jonny says absently.

He doesn't look at me, instead keeping his gaze pinned on the road in front of us as he steers the car through the many back streets and roads that lead us out of this part of Manchester. A part of Manchester I thought I'd never see again. Not that I can see much of it in the dark. And not that I'd want to. This part of my life is something I'd rather forget about and the sooner we are out of here and away from my dad, the better.

"Okay," I reply, not entirely sure what to say to him next. Clearing my throat, I then decide to just go with what I was originally asking him, in a bid to keep things casual. "So, where are you staying then?"

Jonny sighs heavily and then removes the black cap from his head, instead tossing it on to the back seat behind us. He then runs his left hand through his hair in agitation.

"I can't do this with you, Lauren. Not right now. I can't do fucking casual with you after everything that's happened between us this week. And then tonight, with your dad…" He breaks off for a second or two, as if gathering his thoughts. "What did you say to him in there? What…what took place between you two…did he…did he try and hurt you?"

I frown over at him. "No, he didn't try and hurt me. I told you before. He…he was too drunk. Jonny, I promised you I would have shouted for you if he had tried to attack me…"

"Yeah well you've promised a lot to me over these last few months, and you've broken most of those promises, so forgive me for being so fucking cynical."

I would normally hit him right back with an apology or an explanation, but I know that will only serve to anger him even more, and so I don't. I say nothing. I sit back and remain silent, allowing Jonny the time to think and stew or bubble and boil over, if that's what he needs to do. Although I'd prefer for him to not be driving if an argument is on the horizon. I'd rather we went back to my hotel, or wherever Jonny is staying, and talk about all of this properly, or even sleep on it. Maybe sleep is what we both need. Sleep off the events of the last few days and wake up tomorrow with clearer heads.

"So what did he say?" Jonny presses me for an answer.

"What did that mother fucking violent bastard say to you? Did you get the closure you wanted?"

I sigh. "Jonny..."

"I want to know what he said to you, Lauren," he snaps. "I *need* to know. Okay? This is part of *my* fucking closure now and I need it just as much as you, so what did that evil, conniving waste of a life say to you?"

Shit, I hadn't even thought about Jonny needing some closure in all of this. I just selfishly thought about myself and how I needed to close the door on that part of my life I'd absolutely hated. I never even gave a thought to Jonny and how he would want closure. Closure for the son we both lost. Not just me. Jonny too. We both lost Oliver. My god, I really am nothing but a selfish, thoughtless bitch at times.

"He..." Taking a shaky breath in, I try to compose myself for what I'm about to say to him, because he won't like hearing what I have to say, hearing what my dad admitted to. It's going to hurt him to hear it as much as it hurt me. But he wants to hear it. He *needs* to hear it, just like I needed to. "He said he was glad that he'd done it...glad that he'd taken the life of our...our son...he said I was a whore and that you were the scumbag that got me pregnant...words to that effect anyway."

"Jesus...I'm..." Jonny shakes his head in anger, almost choking on his words. "I can't believe any human being could...shit..." Swiping an angry hand over his face, Jonny tries his best to concentrate on his driving, but I can see he's getting upset.

"Jonny, why don't you pull over somewhere..."

"He's only lucky I wasn't in that god damn house with you and him, because if I had been there, he wouldn't have lived to drink his way through another fucking day...piece of shit..."

Jonny blows out a huge breath from between his lips as he struggles to calm the raging storm within him that rears its ugly head wherever my dad's concerned. And the storm that rages within Jonny is one of the reasons why I didn't want him to come with me to Manchester. I was trying to protect him. Protect him from my past life and what that life I once lived out here did to him.

"And where would that have got us, Jonny? Huh? You finish my dad off once and for all and then what? You go to prison for the rest of your days?"

"He deserves nothing less than death after what he did to you and Oliver!" he shouts over at me. "In fact, death is too fucking good for the likes of that man!"

"And this is exactly why I didn't want you to come to Manchester with me. I was trying to protect you, like I've always protected you..."

"Wait, you...you thought I would have gone storming in there tonight to finish the fucker off, don't you? You really thought so low of me that you truly believed I would have actually gone in there and done that? That's the real reason why you didn't want me to come to Manchester with you, isn't it? Because you thought that's what I was going to do when I've actually just done the exact opposite of that! As much as I hate the man for what he did to you and Oliver, I stood outside his god damn house tonight and I watched you go in, all on your own, as difficult as it was. And I did it because you asked me to. I may talk like I want to kill him down dead but they're just words, Lauren! Angry fucking words because of how much hatred I feel towards him!"

Oh my god, he's got this all wrong. So wrong. "Of course I don't think you would have actually finished him off! Not at all! I meant I was just protecting you from my shitty past life!"

"Protecting me from *your* past life?!" He laughs humourlessly. "Jesus, this *was* my past life, Lauren. With you. Once upon a time."

"Yeah it was!" I shout over at him. "Because I dragged you into that life with me! And look where it got you? Look where you ended up? Because of me! Everything that happened in your life back then…the violence with my dad, losing our son, the drugs, you going berserk at my dad after what he did, that only happened because of *me*!"

Without warning, Jonny suddenly swerves over to the side of the main road we are currently travelling on, bringing the car to an abrupt stop. Thankfully, with it being so late, there are hardly any other cars around, which is a good job really, considering how quickly he stopped just now.

Killing the engine, Jonny turns to me and fixes me with a determined stare. "And I'd do it all again in a heartbeat if it meant having you in my life!" he shouts. "Fuck, I'd do it all over again five times, ten times, if it meant still having you at the end of all of it!"

I shake my head at him, tears now swimming around in my eyes at hearing his declaration of undying love for me. His words, so beautiful and heartfelt, so passionate, seep into my skin, my heart, my very soul. But he doesn't get it. He doesn't understand what his love does to me sometimes. It wrecks me. Completely wrecks me.

"But I didn't want any of that for you again," I say to him through my blur of tears, "I want only good things for you, Jonny. I always did. But please know that anything I ever did, whether it was walking away or staying silent, keeping you at arm's-length while I came over here to face my dad, it was all for you. I only ever wanted to protect *you*."

With a defeated sigh, Jonny briefly closes his eyes before

looking away from me. He fixes his gaze on the windscreen, looking out at the dark road in front of us.

"It feels like ever since we got back together, you've struggled to accept my love, like you feel you don't deserve it, and yet, we had four years together before all that terrible stuff happened with your dad. Four entire years before it all went completely wrong, and in all those four years, you accepted my love without question. God, we were so…"

Jonny's voice fades away as he tries to rein in his emotions. I watch as he struggles to compose himself, my own tears now falling freely from my eyes as I think back to all those wonderful years I spent with him before our world came crashing down around us. Four years of nothing but being madly in love. Of course we had our arguments, our disagreements, like every other couple, and we were young of course, probably too young at the time, but we didn't care. We were in love and that was that, and nothing and nobody could come between us. Or so we thought.

"Jonny, I…" God, now I'm having difficulty getting my words out. Words that really need to be said to the man I love sitting across from me. "I think you're right." His head whips round to look over at me and he frowns. "I do feel like I don't deserve your love and…only the other day I told you that I felt as though I never deserved you, that you were too good for me…"

"And as I recall, I told you that what you said was bullshit," he snaps, looking angry again, "complete and utter bullshit."

"Whether you think it's bullshit or not, it's what's been ingrained into me, Jonny! It's how I've been made to feel all these years. Ever since my dad completely tore our lives apart, I've felt it. Felt like I didn't deserve you or any happiness that may have come my way, and…any happiness that does come my way now just makes me feel afraid."

"Afraid?" Jonny asks me, his eyes desperately searching mine for answers. "You're afraid of being happy?"

"Yes! I'm afraid of being happy only to have it all ripped away from me again!" I shout. "Terrified of either my dad or your dad or somebody else breezing their way into our life and shitting all over it again. Like now, with this god damn newspaper article, this twisted story that's been plastered around the world for every man and his dog to read about, it's just another example of people wanting to tear our happiness away…"

"No," says Jonny, shaking his head determinedly, "the ones who read that article aren't the people who want to rip our happiness away, Lauren. Your dad was the one who did that. Not them. The people out there will ultimately get to know the truth about everything that happened, but for now, let's focus on the fact that tonight, you went in there and you stood up to that bastard who made your childhood a living hell, and you did that on your own without anyone else standing next to you, and for that, you should be proud, because I know I am. I can't pretend that I'm still not a little upset and angry over how you went about facing your dad tonight, at how you ran off to do this all on your own, but…I am proud of the woman you are, proud of the girl you once were, and proud of the fact that I am the one who gets to love that woman for the rest of my life…if she'll still have me…"

"If I'll still have *you*?" I manage to blurt out through my tears. "Jeez, are you for real right now, Jonny Mathers?"

We reach for each other at exactly the same moment, Jonny dragging me into his arms and cocooning me in his warmth, his love. He holds the back of my head as he slowly pulls my mouth against his, his lips moving over mine so softly, and with such tenderness, that it makes me want to weep. Weep in his arms as I finally allow the man I love to kiss away the last painful parts of our past, for good this time.

It really is time to move on with our lives, and I think visiting my dad and being back here in Manchester has finally allowed us to do that. Together. It's me and Jonny against the world once more. Just me and him. Always.

CHAPTER 7

JONNY

"You're not seriously expecting me to climb over that fence with you...are you?"

Lauren looks over at me, and even in the darkness of the night, I can tell that she thinks I've lost the plot and gone completely mad. Maybe the events of the night have sent me mad. Or maybe, just maybe, I want to do a little bit of reminiscing with the girl I love while we are still here in Manchester together. Even if it is nearly midnight.

"Oh come on, it isn't like we haven't climbed this fence before."

She raises her eyebrows up at me and says, "Jonny, we were fifteen years old when we started coming to this park. That was fifteen years ago. This fence has grown a whole lot taller since we were last here."

"And so have we," I reply with a grin.

I get the usual Lauren eye roll for that smart ass remark. "Oh, very funny. Seriously, Jonny, we are not climbing over this fence and breaking into Heaton Park in the pitch black at nearly midnight."

Leaning back against the metal railings of the fence Lauren is referring to, I fold my arms across my chest and shake my head at the unadventurous person she has become. "It never stopped us when we were teenagers. Why should it stop us now?"

"For the reasons I just gave you, plus...it's pouring down, we're going to get absolutely soaked if we start wandering around a bloody park at gone midnight!"

"Lauren, it isn't pouring down, it's drizzling..."

"Drizzling still means us getting wet, Jonny, plus, what if we get caught?"

I roll my eyes at her. "Yeah, I can see a police car just pulling up on the road over there where I parked the hire car...seriously, Lauren, where's my wild girl gone from all those years ago?"

"Erm, she's still here..."

"Oh yeah? Then prove it."

I love to challenge Lauren. Challenging her is pretty much a surefire way into getting her to agree to something she's seemingly oh so reluctant to do. Of course it works both ways too, Lauren challenging me on many an occasion before now.

Walking over to where I'm standing with my back to the railings, Lauren gives me one of her disapproving looks, but she doesn't fool me. Not one bit. I can make out the hint of a smile playing on her lips as she considers my challenge.

Looking up at the fence behind me, she says, "You were always such a bad influence on me, Jonny Mathers. And you still are."

Pushing myself away from the railings, I close the gap between us and gaze down into the eyes of the woman I love, the girl I did all of my firsts with. And I want to relive some of those firsts with her right now. Take her back to where it all began for us here on this park. I have so many happy memories of our time here as teenagers and I want to leave Manchester with those in my mind, as opposed to all the painful ones.

"As I recall," I say, holding my hand out to her, "you were always the bad influence on me."

She flashes me that cheeky smile I love so damn much and, as predicted, she takes a hold of my hand and accepts the challenge I laid down to her a moment ago. *That's my girl.*

"Go on then," she says with a sigh, "but if we get arrested and go to prison, I'll be making you *my* bitch, not the other way around. Agreed?"

I burst out laughing when she says that to me. Got to love Lauren and her wicked sense of humour, and I'm so happy to see that her smart mouth and killer humour is slowly returning. Mine too. This is why I really wanted to bring her here after the events of earlier. I just want to spend a bit of quiet time with her in a special place that at one time, meant a lot to us.

Heaton Park was our go to place where we got up to all sorts of things. The sorts of things teenagers probably shouldn't be doing but end up doing anyway. Well, some of them do. We certainly did. And ultimately, this park became a safe haven for the both of us, once I found out about her dad's abusive ways. That was much further down the line in our relationship but nevertheless, this place provided a security blanket to us at a time when we really needed it the most, and it continued to be our go to place until we parted ways.

"Oh, I'll happily be your bitch, sweetheart, any day of the week. You just say the word and I am there for all of that."

She chuckles. "Why doesn't that surprise me with you?" Nodding towards the fence, she then says, "Come on then, let's get on with it and hope to god we don't break any bones in the process."

I grin and then give her hand a quick squeeze. "Okay, let's do this."

****

After climbing our way over the fairly high fence with relative ease, Lauren and I take a nostalgic tour of the park we once loved. With the help of the torches on our phones and the various street lamps dotted around the park, it takes us about half an hour to find the very thing I came on this park to find. The tree. The great big Eucalyptus tree to be exact, the one that is apparently the biggest of its species and one of Heaton Park's most notable features. Well, it certainly was to us anyway.

It's only a pity we're re-visiting this park in the dark as the photos we could have taken during the day would have been an amazing thing to be able to do after all these years. Sadly, my lifestyle these days and recent events have put a dampener on all of that but, night time or not, the important thing is that Lauren and I are here, and we've found our tree. Our special place. A place where we partook in, shall we say, a few of our firsts together. A fair few, if my memory serves me correctly.

We walk over to the huge beauty that is the Eucalyptus tree, our shoes sloshing their way through the muddy grass as we take in the beautiful sight before us. We may be missing out on a whole lot of scenery by visiting this park at night, but this tree is so big and so imposing, so beautiful, that you can't not see it for what it truly is. History. A beautiful part of history that has seen so much over the past however many years it's been growing here. So many events, so many people, us included. If this tree could talk, it would have a whole lot to say about us two, believe me.

"I can't believe we're here," says Lauren, looking up at the tree in awe. "After all these years, you and me, we're finally back here...back where it pretty much all began for us."

Standing beside her, I wrap my arm around her shoulders and gaze up at the tree right along with her. "Back where all the making out really began you mean?"

She lets out a little chuckle. "God, the stuff we used to get up to." Biting down on her bottom lip, she looks up at me and smiles. She's got that naughty glint back in her eyes already and after the god awful week we've had, I am so fucking happy to see it. "You know, for a boy who supposedly had no experience when he met me, you certainly seemed to know what you were doing."

Yep, that fifteen year old teenager I once was really did know what he was doing and for some reason, with Lauren, he always did. I'd honestly never experienced anything sexual with any other girl ever before until Lauren. Not properly anyway. Sure, I'd snogged plenty of girls before Lauren came along and I'll admit to feeling a few pairs of tits on the girls that had wanted me to, but, anything more than that just hadn't happened. Until her. The one who hooked me in from the moment I laid eyes on her.

It was like a bomb went off that day at my school bus stop. We just seemed to have this instant connection that sparked to life as soon as our eyes met from across the road. Sounds all soppy and romantic and some might say we were way too young for anything as serious as falling in love but, we did. We truly did. And that connection has remained for over fifteen years.

Even when we were apart it was still there. Because Lauren was still a part of me in all those years I was without her. She had been burned into my very skin, scorched on to my heart and soul, branding herself on me in ways I never thought possible. My beautiful, blonde ray of sunshine I simply couldn't live without. I somehow managed to live without her for ten whole years but thinking about living without her again now, even for a second, is something I don't want to even contemplate, and thankfully, I don't have to. Not anymore. And certainly not after tonight. Tonight has given us many things, pain, heartache, doubt, so much doubt, but now, it's time to embrace what we still have. And what we still have is each other.

Grabbing a hold of her hand, I smile down at the love of my life before giving her a quick kiss on the lips. When I pull back, I say, "And for a girl who apparently had no experience, you also seemed to know exactly what you were doing when you met me."

She grins. "I know we've both said this before but…two peas in a pod, Jonny. That's what we are."

Turning my body toward hers, I reach for her hips. Snaking my arms around her waist, I pull her hard against me. "I couldn't agree with you more, sweetheart." I press another kiss to her lips before resting my forehead against hers. "So, you wanna come and lay down with me under this tree of ours? I know it's dark and it's late and yes it's a little wet and cold but I thought that we could, maybe…create a bit of nostalgia? You know, as we're here and all."

Threading her hands around the back of my neck, she breaks out into a smile. A great big smile that makes my insides turn to mush. "It might be dark and late, it might also be cold and wet out here on this park of ours in the middle of Manchester, but, I don't care about any of that. I just want you, Jonny. And I want all the nostalgia and the memories right along with you. Because I love you. Always have. Always will."

I don't wait another second before making a grab for her hand, pulling her along with me so we can both take a seat under our tree. It's a little bit muddy and a whole lot of wet under here but we don't care. And that's one of the very many things I absolutely love about Lauren. How she was always so wild and carefree, so full of life and incredibly passionate about even the most insignificant of things. Things that probably wouldn't have mattered to others but mattered a hell of a lot to her.

Money and material possessions were never high on Lauren's agenda and I think her upbringing, as shitty as it was, made her appreciate the smaller things in life even more. I really did appreciate the smaller things in life right along with her, way back when, I just seemed to lose sight of some of those things once my music career took off. My reunion with Lauren however is really beginning to make me remember what life was like before all the fame and the money came along, and boy am I loving remembering it now. Beneath this tree. With her. My one and only.

Linking my fingers through Lauren's, I rest my head against the tree trunk behind me and I take a moment to look at her. I mean, *really* look at her.

"You okay there, rock star?" she asks, flashing that dazzling smile of hers over at me.

My eyes rove over her beautiful face, her ocean blue eyes sparkling over at me in the darkness. "Oh, I am now," I whisper. And I really am. Now I've got her back safely by my side again.

"Yeah, me too." She plants a soft kiss on my lips, and I smile.

"Do you remember the very first thing I did to you under this tree?" I ask her, hoping she remembers. When she pretends to give the matter some serious thought, as if she's forgotten, I give her a prod in the ribs for that. "You better be fucking joking with me right now," I say, pretending to be offended.

"Well…I may need you to jog my memory for me, Jonny," she murmurs, her right hand now reaching for the zipper on my jeans. "But while you jog my memory, how about I jog yours?

By reminding you of the very first thing *I* did to *you* under this tree."

Fuck me, could she get any more fucking perfect than she already is? I swear this woman was made for me. When Lauren said we were two peas in a pod earlier, she wasn't fucking kidding.

"Sweet Jesus," I curse, Lauren slowly freeing my erection from the tight confines of my jeans. It may be cold and wet under this tree tonight but man are things really beginning to heat up between us, Lauren already pumping my cock in her fist, reminding me exactly of what she first did to me under this tree all those years ago. Not that I needed reminding. I remember absolutely everything from back then. All the naughty firsts we got up to together are literally burned into my core memory, and they will never be forgotten. Ever.

And I know for a fact Lauren won't have forgotten the very first thing I did to her under this tree either. But, as she wanted a reminder and all, who am I to say no to that? My hand makes its way into her jeans a moment later. Pulling the flimsy material of her g-string to one side, I then sink my fingers inside her, groaning at how wet she is already. So hot and so wet. For me. Only ever for me. It feels like we're the naughty teenagers we once were all over again. Making out and getting up to things we shouldn't be doing out here in the open. But that's the thrill of it all. With Lauren, it was always that way, and I know for certain it always will be.

Once we've finished "reminiscing," we tidy each other up and just lie back against the tree again, our arms wrapped around each other, both enjoying the darkness and the silence of the park surrounding us.

"Thank you for convincing me to climb over the fence with you tonight, Jonny. It's been lovely being back here again. Not necessarily in Manchester, but here…on this park…with you.

The park that meant so much to us once upon a time."

I kiss her forehead and then rest my head on top of hers. "Yeah, I just...after what happened earlier, with your dad, I just needed to focus on something happy, something that would make us forget, and then this place popped into my mind and that was it, I had to bring us here."

Grasping on to my leather jacket, she snuggles into me, even closer than she was before. "You always manage to make me forget all of the bad, Jonny, and you always did."

I gently brush my knuckles back and forth across the skin of her right cheek, my lips in her hair. "And I always will," I whisper. "I promise."

"I know you will."

"And now can you promise me something in return?"

She looks up at me curiously. "Of course."

Resting the tips of my fingers against her cheek, I say, "Promise me that we're always open and honest with each other about everything from now on, and that we start anew, right now, meaning that we leave all the shitty parts of our past behind us here in Manchester and we just take away the happy memories when we return home to LA."

"I promise," she whispers, without hesitation. "And I also promise to never run away from you ever again. I'm so sorry I did that to you, for putting you through that after everything you've been through..."

"Sssh, baby, it doesn't matter now, because it's in the past. Am I right?"

She smiles up at me. "Right."

I kiss her softly on the lips and then rest her head back against my shoulder. After a beat, I say, "You know, I think it's time for a bit of music."

"Music?" asks Lauren, chuckling. "What if we disturb the neighbours?"

I grin. "I think if there were any neighbours to disturb then that would have happened about five minutes ago, when we were in the throes of passion under this tree."

She covers her mouth with her hand to stifle a laugh. "Shit, it's just like being a naughty teenager all over again."

"Well, that was kind of the point," I say, smiling at her suggestively. She smiles at me right back.

Pulling out my phone from the pocket of my jeans, I bring up Spotify and start scrolling through my playlists. "I think I have the perfect song for us right now," I say, "a song by one of your favourite bands."

"You're my favourite band," she murmurs, pulling my mouth on to hers for another quick kiss.

I smile against her lips, relishing the fact that this beautiful woman of mine really cannot get enough of me or my music. However, on this occasion, my music is being kept to one side, at least for now anyway. Looking down at my phone, I click play on a song that was actually released a year after Lauren and I split up, a song that reminded me so much of her and how I felt about her, it was almost like I'd written it myself.

I've written more than enough songs about Lauren over the years, about the love we had, the unbearable yearning I felt every single day in the weeks and months that followed after she left me in Manchester. But this song by Snow Patrol, a favourite band of ours from our early days, was almost like it had captured the very essence of what it felt like for me when I first met Lauren.

The guitar strings and the lyrics of Chasing Cars begin to

filter into the silence around us. Lauren's eyes meet with mine and I see them light up as the lyrics and the music wrap their way around the both of us. "Oh, I love this song," she whispers. "I remember when it came out. I was down in London by then of course, but…it instantly made me think of you." I smile. "And then, not long after that, you took the music world by storm right along with them."

I run my hands through her blonde curls as I look over at her with so much love, so much emotion, I feel like I can't breathe. "Do you know why the lead singer gave it the name, Chasing Cars?"

"No." She shakes her head at me.

"It was to do with a girl he was infatuated with apparently. Ever heard of the phrase, like a dog chasing a car? Well, he was the dog chasing the car and the car was the girl he couldn't stop thinking about."

Her eyebrows shoot up in surprise. "Really?"

"Really," I say, loving how enraptured she is by the meaning behind songs. She was always as enthusiastic as I was when it came to music and song writing, especially when it came to what I was writing. "When the song came out, I actually felt jealous that they'd written it and I hadn't."

"You felt jealous of somebody else's song?" She laughs. "You? Jonny Mathers? Seriously?"

I narrow my eyes on her in jest. "Seriously. But only because I felt like I should have been the one to have written it. This song just seems to speak to me on so many levels, about how infatuated I was with you, how much I wanted you, even though I already had you…back then, and now. I mean, let's face it, I'm still a dog chasing you around like you're a fucking car."

We both burst into laughter when I say that, but it's true. So true that it's actually ridiculous. I'm a thirty year old man still chasing after the woman lying next to me under this tree. And all because she drives me absolutely crazy. Wild and crazy with love and passion and everything else that comes with being so madly in love with a woman like Lauren.

"So…how about we stop with all the chasing around then, for now, and let's just…lay here together, under this tree, *our* tree, and forget the world. Just for tonight."

I smile at her little reference to some of the song lyrics there. I could perhaps make a song writer out of my girl after all. She says not, but I'm not so sure. I really think that Lauren could achieve anything. Absolutely anything. And with me by her side, back where I belong, I will make damn fucking sure she gets to achieve any dreams she sets her mind to. Lauren's dreams from when we were teenagers were my dreams too. And they always will be.

CHAPTER 8

LAUREN

I look out of the window as our plane takes off from the runway at Manchester airport, the early afternoon sun finally making an appearance, cutting through the thick clouds at long last. I think this is the first time I've seen the sun since I arrived in Manchester.

When it hasn't been raining, the clouds have still been thick and heavy, the weather so grey and overcast. I certainly haven't missed the UK weather while I've been living over in LA. Even London was a lot sunnier and warmer than up here in the north west. Typical that the sun decides to now make an appearance as we're leaving but, maybe there is something in that. A sign perhaps that the clouds hanging over me when I arrived are now parting, clearing their way in the hope I can finally find some sunshine in my life and reach for that long awaited happiness with Jonny after all this time.

I watch as Manchester falls away beneath us, the bustling city that brought me so much pain and heartache in my childhood, but a city that also brought Jonny into my life. Without this place, I would never have met him, and for that, I am truly thankful.

As the cityscape and surrounding boroughs of Manchester grow ever smaller, I rest my head back in my seat and breathe a sigh of relief. Relief I finally faced my fears and visited my dad, stood up to him for everything he ever robbed from me, and relief from the glare of the paparazzi who finally discovered us as we were leaving our accommodation for the airport this morning.

I checked out of my hotel two days ago so I could stay with Jonny in the first floor apartment he had rented out for his stay over here. We thought it was the best idea at the time as it was small and unassuming and hidden away in the suburbs of Manchester somewhere. Or so we thought.

How the hell they discovered where we were staying, I honestly don't know, but the vultures that they are were well and truly circling when we left that little apartment of ours. And with Jonny coming over here all by himself, we had no bodyguards with us either, meaning we literally had to push the waiting crowd of reporters out of the way just to get to the hire car.

Jonny was absolutely livid, swearing under his breath at the lot of them as he quickly tossed our bags into the boot of the Range Rover before safely bungling me into the front seat, speeding away as fast as the car would carry us. He managed to reel in his anger as best he could, not wanting to add fuel to the fire of our life in the tabloids that is burning hotter by the day.

Our names have been more than dragged through the mud thanks to my shitty father and with each day that passes, that mud begins to stick more and more. Our silence since this story broke hasn't helped the shitstorm that is currently brewing but Jonny and I have needed the privacy in order to be able to deal with the fallout of that newspaper article.

How we deal with it going forward is yet to be decided but I've been mulling it over in my mind for the last day or so and I think I know what I want to do. Whether Jonny agrees with my idea is anybody's guess, but I think he will. He may just need a bit of persuading to get him to jump on board right along with me.

"You okay?" Jonny slips his hand into mine, knotting our fingers tightly together. I look over at him and give him a small smile.

"I am now we're on the plane," I reply, and he grimaces.

"Yeah, this morning was..."

"Shit," I say, finishing his sentence for him.

He nods. "Yeah, it was shit, but we got through it and now we're on our way home..." He brings my hand up to his mouth and presses a kiss to my knuckles.

"To face more shit," I say, before turning my face back towards the window. Manchester is long gone already and all I can see below us now are green fields, as far as the eye can see. Very soon, as the plane climbs even higher, I won't be able to see anything other than clouds and blue sky, and with my mood being so low, that suits me down to the ground.

"Hey, we'll get through it," Jonny says, giving my hand a gentle squeeze.

With a heavy sigh, I look over at him once more. I honestly feel defeated this afternoon. So fucking defeated. And it's all thanks to those reporters and their god damn cameras. "I just hate what they've been printing about us. Some of the stuff they've been saying about me, about you..."

"Is all complete and utter bullshit and very soon, that lot will regret the day they ever fucking printed all those lies because I am taking every single one of those tabloids to the fucking cleaners for what they've been saying about us. For defamation of our characters without knowing any of the facts..."

The arrival of an air hostess offering us some food and drinks briefly halts our conversation. I decline the offer of food but welcome the offer of a glass of champagne. Travelling first class with my rock star certainly has its perks and as I still feel so churned up and anxious about the episode with the paparazzi earlier, I think an alcoholic beverage or two might be just what I need to take the edge off. Drinking champagne is kind of ironic, considering we have absolutely nothing to celebrate at the moment, but I decide to raise a toast to the fact I stood up to my violent father after all these years.

Jonny joins in with that personal little toast right along with me, the pair of us relishing the bubbles as well as the peace and quiet of our very own private suite on the plane. Something that is very much needed right now, after everything that happened this morning. But this sort of luxurious lifestyle comes at a high price, and I only wonder just how much more of a price Jonny and I will have to pay when it comes to living out our life in the tabloids for the rest of our days.

I'd like to think that one day the media will become bored of us, but I can't see it happening, not for a good while anyway. Before all this shit happened with my dad, I used to tell Jonny that myself, that the world will eventually become bored of us and hopefully move on to somebody else far more interesting. Talk about eating my words. Because those vultures out there won't be getting bored of us any time soon, that's for bloody sure.

Once the air hostess has sorted us out with our drinks, she leaves us alone once more, sliding the partition door closed behind her. Content that we're alone again, Jonny sets down his glass of champagne on the little table in front of us and continues with what he was saying.

"Look, sweetheart, I know everything appears shit right now, but I promise you those tabloids will get their day. Lara, along with my lawyers, has been working on this tirelessly since the story broke and my dad is also working in the background to bring down your dad, because believe me when I say that he will get his day too, in the not too distant future."

My face screws up in confusion, because I'm sure I haven't just heard him quite right. Jonny has enlisted the help of his dad? After everything that happened? "Did I just hear you correctly?" I ask, my brow creased up with concern, "that you went to your dad for help?"

Jonny gives me a reluctant nod. "Yes, you heard me right, but don't worry, he knows his place. Asking my dad for help is simply a means to an end, and I've told him that…"

"And you think he can be trusted to help you with something like this? You know, the dad who ripped me away from you? Twice! The same dad who threatened to do the exact same thing to us that *my* dad has just done? Selling our fucking history to the entire world!"

Jonny frowns. "Hey, calm down…"

"Calm down?" I snap, raising my eyebrows at him in surprise. "Are you serious?"

Jonny runs an impatient hand through his hair and then sighs. "Look, my dad is the very person who can dig up all the shit on your dad that I want him to dig up. He's the chief manipulator who I need right now, and he wants to help us, he wants to make amends…"

"Oh, he wants to help us and make amends now, does he?" Reaching for my glass of champagne, I take a large gulp before slamming it back down on to the table in front of us. But one gulp of the bubbles just isn't enough to calm the anger and upset now stirring up inside of me after hearing that. I need more champagne and I need it right now. "Can you ask the air hostess to bring the rest of the champagne bottle please?"

Jonny looks on at me in disbelief. "Oh come on, Lauren, don't you think you're overreacting just ever so slightly?"

Taking a moment to gather my anger, I take a few calming breaths in and out before downing the rest of my champagne.

As I set the empty glass back down, I turn to look at Jonny and say, "Look, nobody would love to see you reunite with your dad more than me, and I truly mean that. I hate that you're at odds with each other and I hate this whole shitty mess that somehow still seems to centre around me, but, after everything he ripped away from us, twice over, you really think I'm overreacting right now?"

I have to get that point across to him. I need him to know that I would love nothing more than to see them happily reunite as father and son. But the huge cloud of doubt that hovers over me whenever I so much as think about Jonny's dad will not blow away so easily. If it will ever fully blow away at all.

Jonny's eyes turn sorrowful and he instantly reaches for both of my hands. Taking them firmly in his, he looks me straight in the eyes and says, "I'm sorry, I shouldn't have said that to you. You're not overreacting, not after everything my dad did, but… this isn't some sweet reunion between me and him, it's about him finally helping us. If he sees it as him making some sort of amends with us then I'll let him think that. If it's his way of repenting for the sins of his past then I'll let him do it. If he's of use to me then I'll allow him to do it, but once he's been of use, he can then walk away, like I want him to…"

"But, do you?" I ask him, suddenly feeling guilty for my angry outburst. "Do you really want him to walk away and never see him again? Never have your dad in your life ever again?"

I can tell Jonny is torn. Torn between wanting to hate his father for the terrible things he's done to us in the past, and done to others along the way, and torn over the fact he still loves him. Loves his father in spite of everything cruel he ever did. And I hate to see him looking so tormented over something I now have absolutely no control over.

Once upon a time I had that control and I used it, however wrong that may have been. In my defence, I only did it so I could protect Jonny from the massacre I knew would ensue once he learned of what his father had done. Now that the truth is out in the open, as it should be, that control is now firmly in the hands of Jonny. Only he can decide whether or not he wants to rebuild some bridges with his dad.

If he did want to rebuild those bridges, then I would rebuild them right along with him. I would shove all my anger, anxiety and hurt to one side and I would focus on supporting Jonny through it, but I won't ever forget, and I certainly wouldn't be able to trust Pete Mathers ever again. Not fully. I would always be watching him from afar, as would Jonny. But, maybe that's the new type of relationship they could work on, a distanced association between father and son they could perhaps build on over time.

Releasing my hands from his grip, Jonny sits back in his seat and lets out a heavy sigh. Pinching the bridge of his nose, he says, "The truth is, I don't know. I hate him for what he did to you, to me, to us, but…he's still my dad and I…well, I still love him…I guess. I just don't think I'll ever be able to forgive him for what he did. And if I can't forgive him then…where does that leave my relationship with him?"

Jonny looks over at me once more, his eyes searching mine, as if looking for the answer to his dilemma. Reaching across, I place the palm of my hand against his right cheek. Rubbing my thumb back and forth across the skin just under his eye, I say, "I don't have the answer for you, Jonny. I only wish I did." He gives me a sad smile.

"But know this," I continue, "that whatever you do ultimately decide to do where your dad's concerned, then, I will support you, no matter what. I know I jumped down your throat just now about you going to him for help but...if you wanted to rebuild those bridges with your dad then, I would rebuild them right along with you. We would both go into it with our eyes wide open and we would stand together, side by side. Always."

"You and me against the world again?" he asks, his eyes lighting up with renewed hope. So much hope for our future. A future full of endless possibilities for the both of us.

I smile over at him longingly. "How could it ever be anything else?"

"Come here," he says, pulling me against him.

His lips meet with mine in a soft, tender kiss that somehow manages to make everything shitty about this morning completely melt away. He tastes of champagne and aftershave and he smells delightful, that familiar masculine scent of his mixed with the smell of the leather from his jacket sending me absolutely wild for him.

"How many hours have we got on the plane?" I ask him between kisses. So many kisses.

Jonny smiles against my mouth as the tips of his fingers begin to trail their way down my neck, all the way along to my collarbone, the barely there touch making me shiver with delight.

"Plenty," he whispers, his voice full of dark promise, "and even if there wasn't, it still wouldn't stop me from doing what I'm about to do to you on a plane for the very first time." *Oh my.*

I bite down on my bottom lip, trying my best to quell the sudden rush of hormones that have arrived courtesy of my rock star and his dirty mouth. Oh, how I love that dirty mouth of his. Mmm, looks like I might be joining the mile high club with him after all....

CHAPTER 9

JONNY

Due to the time difference, it's early evening by the time Lauren and I arrive back home in LA. And thank god we are home, after the ordeal we faced at LAX. We thought it was bad this morning in Manchester when we were mobbed as we left our apartment, but that was nothing to what we've just experienced over here.

We were met with dozens upon dozens of reporters with their intrusive cameras as we walked through the airport after our plane landed. Thankfully, Tony and Andy were there to meet us, quickly ferrying us away from the world's media, along with our luggage. A lot of pushing and shoving took place and a few choice words were said to the reporters from our bodyguards, but once we were in the Range Rover, we were out of there.

Arriving home wasn't a whole lot different either, even more paparazzi camping outside our front gates as we drove through the waiting crowds. Lauren was as anxious as I was, the pair of us gripping each other's hands as tightly as possible as we heard the shouting coming from outside the car. Questions being fired at us about her dad, her past as a so called tearaway teenager and most recently as a lap dancer who lived down in London. We tried to block out the hurtful questions and comments, but even through the car windows, we heard them all.

It's funny how the media can just turn on you without so

much as hearing your side of the story. Clearly, we've so far stayed quiet and haven't responded to the newspaper article as yet, but those bastards out there, at the very least, should give us a fighting chance. A chance to explain our side of the story without making such wicked and hurtful assumptions.

A couple of months ago, when I released my press statement to the world about my suicide attempt, the outpouring of sympathy and well wishes was astounding, not only from my fans but from the paparazzi too. Now, those very same reporters have done a complete about turn and are now painting me out to be something I am not. A violent man. A man who, as a teenager, apparently beat up his girlfriend's dad before making her have an abortion after getting her pregnant.

Honestly, I feel sick at what I am being forced to read and listen to at the moment. Physically sick. Because this time, the media have gone way too far, and they are going to know just how far they have gone very soon. This situation has already spiralled way out of our control and it needs to be reined in, and fast.

"I can't begin to tell you how wonderful it is to have you back home again," says Stacey. She wraps a comforting arm around Lauren's shoulders, cuddling her gently.

We are sitting outside in the back garden with Stacey and the lads who turned up at our front door not long after we arrived home. Stacey simply couldn't wait another minute to see her best friend and to say she's relieved to see her would be an understatement.

Lauren smiles. "Yeah, me too. It's certainly been a tough week but I'm so glad to be back home again, where I belong."

"You just promise me and the rest of us sitting here that you won't go running off like that ever again. You gave us such a fright..."

"I know," says Lauren, looking suddenly guilty, "and I'm sorry." Looking around at all of us, she then says, "I'm sorry to each and every one of you for doing what I did. I...had my reasons but, I now know that I shouldn't have gone off on my own, and I'm sorry. Thank you all for being there for me, and for Jonny, we couldn't have got through it without all of you. And I really mean that."

"Come here," says Stacey, pulling Lauren in for a proper hug this time.

"We're just glad to have you back home again, Lauren," says Will, smiling over at her, "we all are."

"Too true," says Ben, "and now that you are back home, how about we break open a few bottles of beer and order in some food? Take your mind off all the shit that's going on outside these four walls. Just for an hour or two."

"You know, I think that's one of the smartest things you've ever said, Benny boy," I quip, as I reach for my packet of cigarettes from the table. I offer him one and he begrudgingly accepts.

"Oh, here we go, Mr Comedian returning with a vengeance I see," he retorts, pressing the fag between his lips.

"Well, I've had a shit week so I need some light relief. It may as well be you." I grin as I lean across the table towards Zack. "You want a fag?"

"Is the pope Catholic?" Zack smirks, plucking a fag from the half empty packet.

I spark up my cigarette and then pass the lighter round so that Ben and Zack can do the same.

"Well, I have to say, I'm glad to see the usual banter has returned between you two," says Stacey. "Making up with each other is the best part after all." She chuckles at her own joke and Ben scowls at her from across the table.

Lauren looks confused. "Make up?" Turning to Stacey, she says, "What do you mean?"

"She means nothing," Ben says, looking annoyed.

"Oh, but she does," I say, unable to keep the amusement from my voice.

Lauren sighs impatiently. "Okay, will someone tell me what's going on? What private joke am I missing out on here?"

Taking a puff of my cigarette, I ignore the daggers I am currently receiving from Ben and instead turn to Lauren. "No private joke, sweetheart, Ben's just pissed that I whooped his ass the other day, that's all."

"You two fought?" asks Lauren, suddenly looking concerned.

"Well, a fight is when two people partake in an exchange of fisticuffs. There was no exchange really."

"Oh fuck you, Jonny," snaps Ben. Looking over at Lauren, he says, "There was an exchange, an angry fucking exchange actually, and there'll be another one if this conceited asshole sitting next to me carries on winding me up like he is doing." Turning his angry gaze on Stacey, he then says, "And thanks for that, darlin'. I love how you take the piss out of me the minute these two return home."

I roll my eyes at him. "Oh come on, Ben, we were only winding you up…"

"Yeah, exactly. Winding me the fuck up as soon as the opportunity presents itself." He puffs on his cigarette angrily. "And to think I was actually looking forward to seeing you two today. Well, Lauren anyway." He grins over at Lauren and flashes her a cheeky wink.

She gives him a genuine smile in return. "Well, it's lovely to have been missed and, even though you two fought, for whatever reason..." Her eyes seem to land on me when she says that. "...I'm glad you've now made up and are back to your usual comical selves."

Balling up my fist, I give Ben a gentle bump on his shoulder. "It's good to be back home again...even with you..." I grin and he just shakes his head at me.

"Asshole," he mutters, before taking another drag of his cigarette.

"Sooo, am I forgiven?" asks Stacey, giving him the usual mushy eyes routine from across the table.

Resting his right leg over his left knee, Ben sits back in his chair and pretends to consider Stacey's request. "I'll think about it," he says, with an air of arrogance about him.

And just like that, I feel right at home again, with my fiancée and my friends, listening to their usual banter and chatter, almost like everything is normal. Well, for now, I will pretend everything is normal. Just for tonight. The shitstorm brewing outside can wait for a little bit longer.

****

After spending a lovely couple of hours with our friends, eating a takeaway and drinking a few beers, Stacey and the lads finally leave later on so Lauren and I can get an early night. We head upstairs, deciding to leave the unpacking of our bags until the morning. I head for a shower while Lauren gets herself ready for bed.

When I come out of the en-suite after my shower, dressed in my usual t-shirt and pyjama bottoms, ready to turn in for the night, I find Lauren sitting at the dressing table in our bedroom. She's staring at a small wooden box in front of her, running her hands back and forth over the smooth surface. She's got dressed into her pyjamas I notice but she suddenly looks...melancholy. I walk over to where she is sitting.

"Hey. Are you okay?" I ask her, feeling concerned with her sudden change of mood.

She lets out a shaky sigh. "While you were in the shower, I decided to...look for Oliver's ashes."

Fuck, I was not expecting her to say that. Glancing down at the wooden box sitting on the dressing table she is still caressing so softly, so gently, I take a deep breath in and fall to my knees beside her. Placing one hand on her arm, I then rest my other hand next to Lauren's, on top of the box containing Oliver's ashes. The tips of her fingers slowly reach out to touch mine and she looks over at me, her eyes all watery and sad. So fucking sad. God, I hate seeing her like this.

"When you were in hospital and I first flew over here with Stacey to try to get in to the hospital to see you, I...I had to bring them with me. Bring *him* with me. Wherever I've been in the world, since the day we lost him, he's always been with me, no matter what."

I take a hard swallow before resting my head on Lauren's shoulder. Turning my gaze back to the box containing the ashes of our son, I try to think of the right words to say to make all of this better. But none will come. And so I stay silent, my fingers still linked with Lauren's on top of his box.

"After everything that's happened this week...with my dad, being back in Manchester, I came up here tonight and I just wanted to see him. Because even though he's always been with me, since the day he left us, I still kept him hidden away at the back of my wardrobe. Out of sight. Out of my mind's eye. But... that was wrong of me..."

Lifting my head up from her shoulder, I look over at her and say, "It wasn't wrong of you, Lauren. It was a way of coping with your grief…"

"And what about your grief?" she asks me, her guilt ridden eyes now fixated on mine. "What about yours? Back then, after it happened, I just completely ignored your grief and look what it did to you."

Tears begin to slip down Lauren's cheeks and I bring my hands up to her face so I can gently swipe them away. "We agreed that we would leave all of that behind us in Manchester. Do you remember the other night? Under the tree on Heaton Park? The promises we made?"

She nods her head gently. "Of course I do."

Pressing my forehead against hers, I say, "So, we stick by those promises. We forget all about the bad stuff from back then and we focus on the here and now. And the here and now is us two grieving for our son in private as we look on at his ashes. What we decide to do with his ashes is something we've yet to make a decision on, but in all honesty, now that I've seen them again, after all these years without laying my eyes on them, I don't think I want him going at the back of a wardrobe ever again."

Lauren shakes her head at me. "Me neither," she whispers.

Looking over at the wooden box once more, Lauren sighs. "You remember last year when we'd not long been back together and we went to stay in Yorkshire with Ben and Stacey?"

"Of course I remember, it was an amazing couple of days away."

"And do you remember what I said to you on the beach that day?" Lauren turns her sorrowful gaze back on me. "When I said that I might want to spread Oliver's ashes down in

Newquay because of the fact we made Oliver there?"

I nod. I remember absolutely everything about that conversation. It was the first time we had spoken about Oliver in over ten years. "I remember everything about that conversation, Lauren. Why wouldn't I?"

Her eyes fill with fresh tears. "Well, thinking about it now…I don't think I can bear to spread his ashes down there, knowing that we're living over here in LA. In fact, I don't want to spread his ashes at all. Not yet. Maybe even never…"

Lauren then bursts into tears, proper tears this time, full on sobs, and all I can do is pull her against me and hold on to her tightly. So fucking tightly. "We never have to let him go, sweetheart," I say to her, my own voice beginning to crack with emotion.

I run my hands through her hair as she sobs uncontrollably into my neck, and I just allow her to cry, for as long as she needs to. My tears soon join hers, and there we remain, in the privacy of our bedroom, finally dealing with our grief.

It's taken us eleven years to get to this point, but here we are, finally talking and opening up, soothing each other and grieving together, as we should have done when it all originally happened. But grief is different for everybody and no one person will ever experience the same journey. This journey is ours, and as painful and as heartbreaking as it is, I feel like we're finally beginning to move on from that horrific time in our lives. Lauren facing her father and us visiting Manchester has started the whole process for us I think. And it needed to happen.

When Lauren's sobs eventually begin to ebb away, she pulls away from me and looks over at Oliver's box once again. "Where should we put him?" she asks, "until we move house I mean?"

Pressing a kiss against Lauren's left temple, I say, "I know exactly where we can put him."

"You do?" She looks over at me in surprise.

I nod. "Yeah...yeah I do." And I really do. Until we move house, I can't think of anywhere else more appropriate for our son's ashes to rest than downstairs, in my beloved music studio.

"Come on," I say to her, "let's carry him together."

"Where to?"

Brushing my knuckles across her right cheek, I give her a warm smile. "To my music studio. He can sit on top of my desk in there by the window and spend some time with me while I write my music...if you agree..."

Her eyes take on that sorrowful look all over again. Placing her palm against my left cheek, she whispers, "Oh, Jonny, that's...that's..."

"I know." Not wanting her to break down and cry all over again, I silence her with a soft kiss.

After we place Oliver's ashes in their rightful place in my music studio, a very emotional Lauren and I then take ourselves up to bed, but before we switch off the bedside lamps, there is one last thing I want to do before we go to sleep.

Reaching into the drawer of my bedside cabinet, I pull out the small box containing Lauren's engagement ring. Rolling over on to my side to face her, I place the box on to the bed and rest my index finger on top. "I know we've had an emotional night. In fact, we've had an emotional week, but this box right here is our future. Our happy future."

Lauren smiles over at me lovingly and then reaches for the box excitedly. I put my hand out to stop her and she cocks an eyebrow up at me. "But before you open this box and before I slip your engagement ring back on to your wedding finger, you must make me one more promise."

A look of uncertainty crosses her beautiful features. "Okay."

Linking my fingers with hers, I say, "Promise me that once this engagement ring goes back on your finger, you will never take it off ever again. Apart from the day you marry me and you need to take it off to put the wedding ring on, but other than that, this engagement ring stays on this time. Forever."

The penny instantly drops, Lauren's eyes suddenly swimming with guilt. "Oh, Jonny, of course I promise. I swear on my life."

She places her hand over her heart and then reaches across the bed to place a reassuring kiss to my lips. "I swear," she whispers, "forever and always."

"Forever and always," I repeat back to her.

Reaching for the box, I remove the lid and pluck out the beautiful diamond ring that sparkles up at the pair of us. Taking Lauren's left hand in mine, I slowly slip the engagement ring on to her wedding finger, back in its rightful place, where it belongs.

"To new beginnings," I whisper. Gazing over at the woman I love with all my heart, Lauren smiles her happiest smile.

"To new beginnings, Jonny."

CHAPTER 10

LAUREN

It's almost lunchtime before I wake up and drag my overly tired ass out of bed the next day. Jonny is still lying fast asleep next to me I notice. And it's no real wonder. The pair of us are absolutely exhausted, and not just with the jet lag. It's been a horrid week, full of nothing but stress and high flying emotions and needless to say, it has drained us both dry.

I sit on the edge of the bed and smile down lovingly at my sleeping fiancé. He just looks so comfortable and at peace with the world that I simply don't want to wake him up. And so I don't. I leave him be, instead deciding to stay in my pyjamas and set about making us both some breakfast, but not before admiring my engagement ring first. I look down at the sparkling diamond ring in wonder, Jonny having finally placed it back on my finger last night before we went to sleep.

For the first time in over a week, I feel a flicker of excitement beginning to light up within me again, our happy future within touching distance once more. I can't wait to start planning our wedding. In fact, scrap that, I just can't wait to marry the man lying next to me. Lord knows, it's taken us so bloody long to get us to this point, but now that we're finally here, I don't think I want to wait much longer to make this man my husband. *My husband.* I love the sound of that.

Turning to look at Jonny once more, I start to reflect, thinking back over everything we have ever been through together, the years both with him and without him, and the years that are yet to come. *This time it's for keeps*, I think to myself. Neither my dad, his dad, or anybody else for that matter, is going to rip us apart ever again. Not even those god damn reporters.

Like a water balloon popping all over my new found excitement, my happy thoughts are soon dampened as my mind turns to the tornado of paparazzi currently wreaking havoc and shitting all over our lives. The idea that has been swirling around in my mind for the past couple of days begins to resurface, reminding me of the need to respond to those greedy vultures outside these four walls who are constantly circling. And they will continue to circle until we give them a statement.

Well, a press statement isn't the route I want to take. Not this time. I need to talk to Jonny about my idea but I can talk to him about it when the moment is right, most likely over breakfast. I say breakfast, it'll be more like a brunch looking at the time. It's almost noon and my stomach is telling me as much. Yes, I will cook us both a delicious brunch, and then I'll run my idea by Jonny. Fingers crossed he'll be in agreement with what I want to do. Here's hoping.

****

It isn't long before the waft of bacon and sausages emanating from the kitchen entices my rock star from his bed, and I smile as I feel his tattooed arms winding their way around me from behind.

"Mmm, smells good," he says, nuzzling his nose into my neck. Looking down at the various pans of food I've got simmering away on the hob, he then says, "Food smells good too." I laugh.

"Good morning, rock star, or should I say, good afternoon." I turn my face up to give him a quick kiss.

"I thought about telling you off for not waking me up, but

now I've seen what you're up to in the kitchen, I'll let it slide."

Leaving the mushrooms and the chopped tomatoes to simmer away for a moment, I turn around in Jonny's arms and grin up at him. "Oh, so you'll let it slide, will you?"

He smiles against my mouth. "Only this time. Next time, I'm afraid I may have to punish you for leaving me to sleep while you're wide awake."

"Oh yeah?" I tease, loving the sound of that.

Sliding his hands down to my bum cheeks, he gives them a quick squeeze through my pyjama shorts. "Hell yeah."

Sinking my teeth into my bottom lip, I say, "Well, I might leave you to sleep every single time then, because I kind of like the sound of being punished by you."

"Oh, you do?" He raises his eyebrows in mock surprise.

Placing my hands around the back of his neck, I giggle. "In the words of Jonny Mathers, fuck yeah I do."

He grins at me suggestively, right before he plants one hell of a smacker on my lips. And I can't help it, I kiss him right back. Hard and deep, enjoying the long overdue playfulness that is finally returning between us. The banter, the flirting, the back and forth I love so damn much.

And just as things are beginning to really heat up between us, the pans of food on the hob behind me begin to let me know that they are also well and truly heated up. Beyond heated up actually. In fact, both the tomatoes and the mushrooms are beginning to burn to the bottom of both pans. Damn it. Bloody Jonny and his never ending wicked ways of distracting me from the job in hand.

"Oh shit," I curse, gently shoving Jonny away as I turn back to the hob to deal with the mess. Jonny chuckles behind me.

"This is your fault," I grumble, although I'm smiling. That kiss was well worth me burning a few items of food.

His arms encircle their way around my waist from behind once more. I can feel him smile against my cheek as he says, "Oops."

I chuckle. "I'll give you oops in a minute."

"I'd rather you gave me something else..."

I try to bat his wandering hands away with my wooden spoon. "Save that for later, rock star. Now, we eat. Because this brunch of mine is beginning to burn..."

"I'm beginning to burn," he murmurs, nibbling at my neck as he presses his erection into my lower back. "For you."

Jeez, what is he doing to me? *What he always does to me, that's what.* Bloody well distracts me and makes me want him so badly that every rational thought or action goes right out of my head. But I'm honestly starving. And I also really want to talk to Jonny about my idea on how we handle the car wreckage that is currently our life being played out in the world's media.

Elbowing him away, I try to ignore the look of rejection on his face. "You can burn for a bit longer," I say to him. Pointing to the pans on the hob I have now turned off, I then say, "These can't."

"So this is what it feels like to be rejected," he sighs in jest, "never happened to me before."

I prod him in the chest with the end of my wooden spoon for that remark. "It'll be happening a whole lot more if you carry on talking like that, you conceited idiot. Now grab some plates and some cutlery and make yourself useful."

Narrowing his eyes on me, he says, "You are one bossy female sometimes, you know that?"

I shrug. "Yeah but you love it."

Breaking out into a slow smile, he says, "Yeah, I suppose I do." Sauntering back over to me, he takes my face in his hands and kisses me once more, before finally doing as I ask of him.

He lays the table and then helps me to plate up the food and before long, we are indulging in a slightly overcooked, but delicious all the same, full English breakfast come brunch. "Baby, this shit is good," says Jonny, piling some scrambled egg into his mouth.

I smile. "You see? You're glad I forced you to eat now, aren't you?"

He smirks. "If you're asking me whether I would prefer to be eating this or be inside you right now then I'm sorry, sweetheart, but being inside you wins. Every. Single. Time."

His eyes rake over me as he piles another forkful of food into his mouth and I deliberately avoid his searing gaze. I want to clear my mind of all things dirty, just for this once, so I can get things off my chest and out into the open.

"Okay, when you've quite finished with all the smutty talk, there's actually something I really want to discuss with you today. Something important."

"Oh?" Immediately looking concerned, Jonny places his fork back down on to his plate. "Are you okay?"

I am quick to reassure. "Of course I'm okay." Reaching across the table, I take a hold of his hand. Giving it a gentle squeeze, I say, "But what isn't okay is the constant media circus taking place outside these four walls, and that's what I want to talk to you about. About how we deal with the media now that we're home."

Jonny's brow pulls into a deep frown. "I told you. They will get their day. You don't need to worry about any of that…"

"Stop telling me I don't need to worry, Jonny," I say, snatching my hand away from his. He raises his eyebrows at my sudden annoyance and I sigh. "Sorry. I didn't mean to snap. It's just… I have an idea. An idea about how to deal with those vultures out there, and I want you to hear me out and really consider it, without dismissing me within the first few seconds of me suggesting it."

With a heavy sigh, he says, "You know, I love how much faith you have in me. You think I won't sit here and listen to what you have to say? You think I won't hear you out?"

"Of course I have faith in you. I just know how over protective you are of me, and sometimes, because of that overwhelming need to protect me, you fly off the handle or immediately go on the defensive…"

"I don't go on the defensive," he snaps.

Gesturing over towards him, I say, "I think I've just proven my point."

Sitting back in his chair, Jonny folds his arms across his chest and glares over at me like a petulant teenager. "Oh, thanks for that," he mutters. I roll my eyes at him. "Fine," he sighs, relenting, "I go on the defensive and I'm over protective of you but I have my reasons, and you know those reasons."

"I know I do," I say, suddenly feeling a little guilty. "But I really want you to listen to what I have to say…"

"I'm listening," he interjects, becoming ever more impatient.

Taking a quick sip of my coffee so I can glean some Dutch courage from somewhere, I then rest back in my chair and lock eyes with Jonny once more. "I want to do an interview. A live television interview..."

"What the fuck?"

I shoot Jonny a warning look and he quickly simmers back down, remembering his promise to stay quiet and listen to what I have to say.

"I want to do a live interview so I can tell the world, in my own words, *our* own words, what actually happened to us back in Manchester. I want to tell the truth so that the lies and the twisted story my dad sold to that tabloid can finally be put to rest. I also want to talk about the violence I endured at the hands of my dad, so that I can help others out there. Just like you did, when you released your press statement telling the world about your suicide attempt. You told the truth to the world that day, Jonny, and now I want to do the same. For me. For you. For Oliver. But most of all, for all the other poor children, men and women out there who are currently suffering a similar fate to me.

"I want to speak out so that others may find that inner strength within themselves to find help, to be able to get out of a violent home or relationship. I want them to see how far I've come, so that they too can find their way out of the darkness and back into the light. There were so many times in my life, before you came along, when I very nearly gave up. So many times. But then I found happiness. With you. My bright light in the darkness. And others can find their bright light too, they just might need a bit of help along the way to find it. And I want to be that help. I can be that help. I just need to know you're with me in this. Are you with me?"

I hesitate, trying to gauge his reaction to my idea. After that long drawn out explanation, I've kind of stunned him into silence I think. Straightening himself up in his chair, Jonny then places his forearms on to the table and blows out a huge breath from between his lips. "Wow," he says, finally breaking the silence, "just...wow."

Running what looks to be a shaky hand through his hair, Jonny then looks over at me proudly. Eyes shining with adoration, he says, "You fucking astound me, Lauren Whittle."

Feeling a little taken aback by this unexpected reaction to my idea, I start to stutter some sort of a response. "I...well..."

"You are the bravest woman I have ever fucking met," he says in awe, "and when you sit in front of those cameras and do your interview, that world out there will fall in love with you, just as I did, all those years ago." Holding his hand out to me from across the table, he says, "Come here."

I don't take his proffered hand. Standing up from my chair, I instead rush over to where he is sitting and he pulls me straight on to his lap. He wraps his loving arms around me and I nuzzle my face into the soft skin of his neck, taking delight in his masculine scent and his warmth. "I am so proud of you," he says, "so fucking proud."

Resting my head on his shoulder, I smile up at him as he gazes down at me fondly. Gently pushing the curls back from my face, he says, "I support you every step of the way with this, but, if you will allow me, I want to do the interview with you. I want to sit beside you, holding your hand, supporting you, looking on at you proudly as you inspire others. Because you will. I have no doubt about that."

Running the tips of my fingers back and forth over his jawline, I say, "Of course I want you sitting beside me when I do the interview. I never want you to leave my side ever again. I was wrong to run off to Manchester to face my dad all on my own...and you were right what you said even though I didn't want to hear it at the time. I have been running. For far too long. But no more. It's time to stand together and put on a united front for that lot out there, and boy had they better watch out."

"Too fucking right they better watch out," he murmurs, "because the age of Lauren is coming, and they better be ready for that. I know I am."

I let out a little giggle of happiness and Jonny chuckles. "Oh, I do love you, Lauren Whittle. I know you've heard me say it to you a million times before but I can't seem to be able to tell you anywhere near enough."

Trailing my fingers into the back of his hair, I say, "You could never tell me enough, Jonny Mathers, because I will never ever tire of hearing you say those three words to me. And just so you know, even though you already do, I love you too. With all my heart and soul."

Brushing his knuckles tenderly against my cheek, he says, "So tomorrow, we begin to set things in motion with the interview, but for today, just for the rest of today, I want this. I want you. Just you, and nobody else."

"Just us two," I whisper.

Jonny smiles. "Just us two."

CHAPTER 11

JONNY

I am sitting next to Lauren, holding her hand tightly, gazing down at her with pride as she sits in front of the television presenter and tells her, along with the rest of the world who are currently watching us live on air, the truth about what happened all those years ago back in Manchester.

Lauren never ever thought she was strong, having always been made to believe she was weak, thanks to both her own father, and mine, but she absolutely is. She's the strongest person I have ever met. Sitting in front of a television presenter who she only met with this afternoon is one thing, but sitting in front of an entire television studio full of people, with cameras at every angle, telling the entire world her heartbreaking story live on air, is something else entirely.

Sophie, the lady news anchor from LA News who is interviewing Lauren, is conducting the interview as impeccably as my PA, Lara, assured me she would, giving Lauren the time and space to really open up and being both empathetic and quiet when needed. Something I insisted upon when it came to choosing the correct news network for doing something as important as this. Because when Lauren first suggested this interview idea to me a few days ago, I admittedly wasn't keen. I was in awe of her idea and I wanted to support her of course, but for me, Lauren putting herself out there by talking about something that was a really painful and difficult time in her life, was deeply concerning for me.

Mainly because I've seen what triggers her, the anxiety and the panic attacks suddenly overwhelming her when her thoughts and feelings from that part of her life completely take over. She's managed to overcome a lot of those fears and anxieties since her most recent trip over to Manchester to finally face her dad, but they're still there. And they'll probably always remain, like an internal part of her make up, part of who she is and what shaped her to become the beautifully brave woman she is today.

Lauren looks ravishing in her all black trouser suit with white silk blouse and black lace high heels to match. Her blonde curls have been pulled up into a high ponytail and her makeup left more natural, with just a touch of blusher on her cheeks and a light coating of pink gloss on her lips. Not that Lauren needs makeup of course. Her natural beauty simply shines through. And it's certainly shining through today, for the entire world to see.

The way she is speaking right now, growing ever more confident as she tells Sophie about the reasons why she wanted to do this live interview today, about her passion for wanting to help others like her, it honestly makes me want to weep at her feet. With pride. So much fucking pride that I could burst.

In fact, after this interview is done with, I am going to show my girl exactly how proud I am of her. But for now, for this moment, the floor is well and truly Lauren's, and I continue to sit in silence, with my hand in hers, nodding every now and again and offering a supportive smile when I need to.

No matter what happens after today, we can walk out of this television studio with our heads held high again. And whether the fans or the paparazzi believe what Lauren has told them today doesn't really matter. All that matters is we have now told the truth. *Our* painful truth. Meaning we can finally move on with our lives. That next chapter of ours is now well within our reach, and fuck am I going to grab on to it, I'm going to grab on to it with all I've got and I'm never going to let it go.

****

After the interview is done with, I surprise Lauren by whisking her off for a meal with our friends. I thought it was about time we stepped out into the world again, having only spent time with our friends behind closed doors of late, either at our house or at theirs. The quaint Italian restaurant where I made the reservations for all six of us is the perfect place to celebrate Lauren's bravery.

Needless to say she is well and truly bowled over when we arrive to find Stacey, Ben, Will and Zack waiting for us at the back of the restaurant. Sitting around a large rectangular table, all four of them leap to their feet and start clapping and whistling at us as we walk towards them. Lauren's jaw drops to the floor in shock and then she turns to eye me suspiciously. "You sneaky man, you."

I grin like a Cheshire cat and she beams up at me, reaching in for a quick kiss before officially greeting our friends. "Oh, stop with the whole standing on ceremony for me." She laughs, waving away their applause.

"Erm, we will stand on ceremony for you all night long after what you just did, girl!" shouts Stacey, edging herself around the table, past Ben, so she can head straight for Lauren.

Stacey pulls Lauren into a massive hug and Ben just can't help but pass comment. "Hey, you two wanna get up on to this table and celebrate properly?"

I give him the usual Jonny scowl. "Knock it off, Ben."

"Oh come on. Like you wouldn't want to see *that*." Ben grins from ear to ear, knowing full well he's already winding me up.

"See what?" asks Stacey, pulling away from Lauren.

Sitting back down, Ben rests back in his chair and smiles. "See you two get up on to this table and give us a night to remember, just like old times." Ben winks at both Lauren and Stacey and I roll my eyes heavenwards, trying to keep my cool. Tonight is about celebrating Lauren's victory and I am determined not to lose my temper but with Ben, anything is possible.

"In your dreams...*Benjamin*," Lauren jokes, and her and Stacey laugh.

"Joke away but, you two don't know how true that statement actually is." Ben flashes another wink in their direction and that's it, I'm done.

"Right, Ben, when you've quite finished," I warn.

"But I haven't..."

"You have now," says Stacey, swiping him around the back of the head as she squeezes past him to sit herself back down between both him and Will.

"Erm...ouch," he protests, rubbing at his head.

Shaking my head at him, I then pull out a chair for Lauren and she sits down between both me and Zack. I sit opposite Ben, a deliberate move so I can keep him in check. Something tells me he's had one too many drinks already and the more he drinks, the louder he becomes.

"You lot start drinking before we arrived then?" I throw another scowl over at Ben and he sniggers.

"Fuck me, you're wound tight tonight. We went for a couple of drinks at a bar before we came here to meet you two. That okay...Dad?"

"Oh, very fuckin' funny," I say, narrowing my eyes on him.

"Wow, it's like being back at school all over again," quips Lauren, giving both Ben and I 'the look.'

"He started it," I mutter.

Holding her hands up in exasperation, Lauren says, "You see? *Just* like being back at school."

Will, Zack and Stacey burst out laughing and being the grumpy asshole I am, I instead turn away and shrug out of my leather jacket, hanging it on the back of my chair. It's becoming increasingly hot in here and for some reason, I'm suddenly feeling agitated. Really agitated. In fact, I need a drink myself.

"Any actual waiters or waitresses around in this place?" I ask, glancing over towards the bar area opposite our table where several staff seem to be milling around doing nothing much else other than standing about. "They going to actually do their fucking jobs and come over or what?"

"Hey." Feeling Lauren's warm hand on my arm pulls my angry gaze away from the bar area for a moment. Leaning in close, she whispers, "Are you okay?"

I nod. "Yeah, I'm just…Ben wound me up, that's all…"

"Well…how about I unwind you then?"

Mmm, now we're talking. As soon as Lauren's lips meet with mine, I'm gone, my irritation with Ben and the waiting on staff instantly melting away. And now I'm suddenly wishing we weren't in this god damn restaurant. Because I want her. I want her so fucking badly, and I have done all day long. No real change there but today is different. Today, that pride for Lauren I was talking about earlier is literally waiting to burst out of me. So much so that I can't even begin to put into words how watching her today has made me feel.

When I said I wanted to fall to the floor and weep at her feet during the interview, I actually meant it. Maybe that's why I'm wound so tight tonight. Maybe Ben's right after all. Not that I would ever admit that to him of course. Wouldn't want to blow any more air into that already inflated ego of his.

Wolf whistles and suggestive comments from our friends sadly put a dampen on the fire that is now burning hot inside of me. Burning hot for the woman sitting next to me. The woman who is now looking up at me through hungry eyes as she slowly pulls her lips away from mine. Leaning up, she places her mouth against my ear and whispers, "Until later, rock star."

Fuck, she really is a naughty little tease sometimes and I swear it takes every ounce of restraint within me not to just yank her away from this table and march her off to the toilets somewhere so I can pin her against the sinks and have my wicked way with her. *Classy, Jonny, very classy.* But classy doesn't really come into the equation when it comes to having my way with Lauren. And certainly not after today. Today has been pretty overwhelming for me, watching her go through something as tough as that while I just sat back and stayed quiet. But that was what she wanted and it was what I wanted for her too.

It wasn't easy though, staying silent as I listened to her talk about all the dark and painful moments from her past with her dad, especially when it came to her talking about that one painful moment in particular, the most painful moment of them all. The moment when he ended the life of our unborn son. *Our Oliver.*

My overwhelming need to constantly protect her was desperately fighting to get out at that point and because it wasn't allowed out, I had to shove it down. All the way down. Out of sight and out of my mind. Until now. Now, that tremendous urge to just comfort her and protect her is literally trying to rip its way through my skin to get to her. *Not now, Jonny. Not now.*

Pulling my mind back from the dark parts of our past, I somehow manage to simmer down my reeling emotions by remembering why I brought Lauren here tonight. Forcing a smile to my face, I press another quick kiss to her lips.

"I'll hold you to that, sweetheart," I whisper into her ear, and she giggles.

"Okay, okay, enough with the mushy shit," says Ben, "we ordering some drinks or what?"

Turning my gaze back on Ben, I say, "Sure. The ladies can have whatever they want, me, Will and Zack will have a beer and you can have lemonade. Sound good?" Everybody laughs.

"Hilarious, Jonny, as always," he retorts, flipping me the middle finger. "Lemonade is for pussies, and I ain't no pussy."

"Glad we got that all cleared up then," I say, flipping him the middle finger right back.

"Please tell me now if this sort of school boy shit is going to continue for the entire night," says Lauren, sighing. She folds her arms and then looks over at Stacey sitting opposite her. They both roll their eyes at the pair of us.

Finally joining the conversation, Zack leans in and nods toward me and Ben. "Apologies, ladies, but this is pretty much the norm for these two on a night out."

Will grimaces. "Yep, standard night out I would say."

Lauren and Stacey both groan their annoyance. Turning to me, Stacey then says, "If I remember correctly, you two lovebirds seemed to get on like a house on fire when we went to Yorkshire last year."

"Lovebirds?" Ben screws up his face in disgust.

"Oh, you mean when we went to the pub for the meal and Jonny and I ended up doing karaoke?" Lauren says to Stacey. Stacey nods.

"Yes, that night. It was a wonderful night…and they got on so well…"

Stacey and Lauren both turn their gazes on us, staring down both me and Ben like a pair of school teachers disciplining their pupils. Ben and I exchange amused glances. "Yeah well, we were just easing you in gently back then," I joke, "now that we have, this is how we really are together. Isn't that right, Ben?"

"Too true," he agrees, and we both grin.

Time to make light of it all now, and it works, everyone around our table laughing once more, because as much as he winds me up, Ben is one of my best mates and I'd never be without him. Sure, we come to blows sometimes, as we did only recently, and he also has a really annoying knack of being able to anger me so easily with all of his smart ass quips and wind ups but then, he gets it back from me tenfold. It's how we roll.

Sadly for Ben, how we roll with each other usually all depends on what mood I'm in, which can then send our playful banter and wind ups either way. Tonight is a prime example of that, me overreacting to a comment of his that normally wouldn't bother me. I have my reeling emotions from Lauren's interview to thank for that, but, I've somehow managed to get a handle on them now and it's time to enjoy an evening with our friends and have some much needed food and a few drinks.

"Right, let's get this celebration started, shall we?"

CHAPTER 12

JONNY

The night turns out to be such a good laugh. The food is delicious, the drinks are flowing, and the banter back and forth around the table is just the tonic I needed to get my mind back to its happy place. Looking at Lauren now, chatting away and laughing with our friends, you wouldn't even think that just a few hours ago, she'd gone live on air to talk about her painful past. She has literally shared her life with the entire world and yet she seems completely unphased by it all, unlike me.

Maybe it was her way of healing or purging herself of everything she had deliberately locked away inside of herself for so long. Too long. Either way, it's clear to me that Lauren's interview has been a resounding success. For her. I couldn't give a shit about whether or not it was a success outside of our little bubble, although it would give Lauren a real boost if it was. Especially as she set out to do the live interview in order to help and inspire others like her who haven't as yet found that help.

As the night eventually comes to a close, we bid our friends goodnight and we head home, Tony and Andy picking us up in the Range Rover. As soon as Lauren and I are in the back of the car, we are all over each other, kissing heavily, making out, touching, panting. It's been a very emotional day for the both of us and those emotions are running seriously high tonight. In the back of the fucking car. But I won't take her here. Privacy screen or not, what I want to do to Lauren tonight goes way beyond the confines of this Range Rover.

As soon as Tony and Andy drop us home, Lauren and I are stumbling through the front door together, pulling at each other's clothes in desperation. Kicking the front door closed, I then back Lauren up into it, pressing my denim clad erection against her as I cage her in with my arms. She grinds her hips against me in desperation and it sends me wild. Wild with need for the woman standing before me. This beautiful brave woman who I simply cannot get enough of. I kiss her madly, deeply, and she kisses me right back, her lips almost bruising mine with their onslaught.

I groan against her mouth and that just spurs her on for more. Making a grab for my leather jacket, she quickly pushes it over my shoulders and on to the floor. My t-shirt soon follows and then it's my turn. I remove her suit jacket with ease but pause momentarily when I reach for her white blouse. My eyes drop to her breasts which rise and fall beneath the silky material and I trail my index finger back and forth across the buttons as I contemplate my next move.

"This blouse new?" I whisper, Lauren still panting madly beneath me.

"Yes," she whispers, her voice coming out all breathy and desperate.

My eyes blaze down into hers as I hook my fingers into the gap between the buttons. "Then I'll buy you a replacement," I growl. The buttons scatter across the hallway floor tiles as I literally tear the blouse away from her body. Lauren gasps loudly in shock but then suddenly makes a grab for my face, kissing me hard and deep, her tongue slashing against mine as her hips grind against me once more.

"Fuck me," she begs, sounding impatient, "fuck me right now."

Jesus, hearing her beg for it is driving me insane. Fucking insane. Reaching for the zipper on my jeans, she yanks it down and only manages to get my jeans and boxer shorts partway down my legs before I'm spinning her around and slamming her against the front door.

Pinning her hands against the door, I place my mouth against her ear and whisper, "Lose the bra, the pants and the thong but *they* stay on." I point to the black lace high heels on her feet that have been distracting me all day long.

She does exactly as I ask of her, quickly removing her bra, pants and thong. I then take a moment to really admire the sexy temptress standing in front of me. Bent over and ripe for the taking, her hands are splayed against the front door, her long blonde curls still tied up in that ponytail from earlier. My eyes drop to the black lace high heels on her feet and I drag my teeth back and forth over my bottom lip as I start to feel the last shred of control completely slip away.

Standing behind her, I place my hands on her hips, and she whimpers as she rocks back against me. Her bare ass rubs against my erection, her thighs grazing against the denim of my jeans. Fuck, I won't last long. Not tonight. Leaning over, I press a soft, tender kiss to her shoulder.

"I can't be gentle with you tonight," I whisper. "Because I want...I *need* you. So badly. So fucking badly."

She turns her face towards me and our eyes meet once more. "I don't want gentle either," she whispers, her eyes blazing with heat. "So take me, Jonny. However you want me. I'm yours. Always."

At hearing her declaration, my mouth smashes into hers head on in a kiss so hot, so wet, that it re-ignites the fire within me that has been silently raging for Lauren all day long. She moans loudly into my mouth and that's it, I am done for. Well and truly done for. Wrenching my mouth away from hers, I position myself behind her. I pause only briefly before I plunge myself inside her. We both groan loudly but I don't hold back. I can't hold back.

Lauren feels the full brunt of me as the agonising wait to be inside her finally comes to an end, pleasure engulfing me completely. My thrusts are hard and rough, Lauren bracing herself against the front door as she meets me thrust for thrust, rotating her hips in a way that simply blows my fucking mind. The lap dancer within her is still there, teasing me, pleasuring me, moving lithely like only Lauren can. Except this time, she moves only for me. She dances only for me. And that knowledge alone threatens to rip me apart at the seams.

And if she's ripping me apart with her lap dancer magic then it's only fair I rip her apart right back. With my musically talented fingers. Leaning over her bare back, I close one of my hands over hers against the door as the other one makes its way down to my favourite place. Between her legs. Fuck, she's wet. Dripping wet. My fingers slip and slide over her clit, my cock still punishing her relentlessly from behind.

"Ah...fuck," she moans, bucking wildly against my fingers, and I surge into her, desperate to feel her tighten around me.

"That's it, baby," I breathe, "let go and come with me."

She turns her face just enough so she can kiss me, her mouth practically devouring mine as she kisses me hungrily, almost like she's been starved for so long. Too long. I feel the animal unleash within me as I take us both to the brink, my cock throbbing with the desperate need for release.

"Jesus...Lauren!" I come with a loud shout, my hips bucking roughly against hers as I finally reach my climax, Lauren swallowing my moans as my fingers continue to dance around her clit.

"Yes, that's it," she cries, "yes, right there...yes...oh fuck...Jonny!"

Lauren almost collapses to the floor as I feel her come undone beneath me, but I hold firm, keeping her upright and pinned to the door as I draw out her pleasure for as long as possible. She writhes greedily against my cock, my fingers still working her over, swirling up and around her clit. I feel her core tightening around me all over again and she slams her hands against the door, scoring her nails against the wood as she screams out my name once more.

As Lauren's orgasm finally beings to recede, she falls back against me and I hold on to her tightly. "Jesus, Jonny, where the hell did that come from?" she asks me breathlessly. She flashes me her most satisfied smile. "Not that I'm complaining of course."

I chuckle. "I should fucking hope not." Dropping a tender kiss on to her lips, I say, "And anyway, I could ask you the same question."

She arches an eyebrow up at me. "Erm, you practically pinned me to the backseat of the car when we left the restaurant..."

"Well, can you blame me? Seeing you in that suit today, those heels." I glance down at said heels before lifting my gaze back to hers. "And...well, it's been an emotional roller coaster of a day, hasn't it?"

She gives me one of her mushy looks. The look that simply knocks the stuffing out of me whenever I see it. "Yeah," she whispers, "yeah it has been a roller coaster of a day, but...well, I think we've more than made up for it now."

I grin. "Oh, we've certainly done that alright." I plant

another kiss on her lips before I slowly, and very gently, ease myself out of her. I help Lauren to stand up before tucking myself back into my jeans.

"Holy shit," says Lauren, stumbling slightly. Reaching out for my arm, she says, "I swear my legs have literally turned to jelly."

Pulling her against me, I say, "Mmm, I've turned your legs to jelly, have I?"

"Yeah, you have." She smiles up at me as she laces her hands together around the back of my neck.

"Then my job here is done," I murmur, giving her another quick kiss. Lauren squeals as I suddenly sweep her off the floor and into my arms. "Let's go to bed." I start to walk towards the stairs.

"Erm, what about our clothes? Or should I say, what's left of them? Mine anyway," she chuckles.

Glancing back at the discarded clothing on our hallway floor, I smile, more to myself than to her. "Leave them there. We'll sort them out tomorrow." I head back towards the stairs, Lauren grinning at me like a loon. "What?"

She shakes her head at me. "You're picking up some bad habits, Mathers." She tuts her disapproval. "Ripping my new blouse, leaving clothing on the floor…"

I pause at the foot of the stairs. "I think you'll find the only bad habit I've picked up around here of late is you."

"Oh, I'm a bad habit now, am I?" she says, raising her eyebrows in jest.

"Oh, sweetheart, you are bad," I whisper, "so bad." Brushing my lips softly over hers, I say, "But you taste *so* good" - I kiss her again - "so" - another kiss - "fucking" - and another - "good."

When I pull away for the final time, I watch as Lauren's burning gaze locks firmly on to mine. I feel the air shift between us, the tension palpable. Like a fire sparking back to life, Lauren suddenly grabs at my face, pulling my mouth on to hers with renewed urgency. The next thing I know, I'm pushing her on to the stairs, lifting her legs over my shoulders and we're partaking in round two.

With her high heels resting on my shoulders, I watch as Lauren screams and pants beneath me, her breasts bouncing rapidly as I take her roughly all over again. And after several minutes of what can only be described as the hottest, sweatiest sex I've ever had in my entire life, I decide that this time, we really do need to get up these stairs and into bed.

"Bed," I say to her breathlessly, "and no distracting me this time." She giggles as I haul her into my arms for the second time tonight.

We actually do make it into bed this time, the pair of us crawling under the bed sheets together, still cuddling, still kissing, still making out. My jeans and boxer shorts are long gone and sadly, so are Lauren's high heels, but we are a whole lot of naked under these bed sheets and I am not complaining about that. Not one bit.

We giggle and we roll around like the teenagers we once were, we make out some more, and then eventually, we just lie there together in silence. Completely wrapped up in each other. Finally enjoying the wondrous post lovemaking afterglow that happens when two people are so clearly meant for each other.

"So, how do you feel after today?" Pressing a kiss to her forehead, I cuddle Lauren against my chest even tighter than she was before and she snuggles into me, her head fitting perfectly into the nook of my neck.

"I feel well and truly satiated, Mr Mathers, but I think you already know that," she says with a contented sigh.

I chuckle. "I mean how do you feel after the interview?"

"Oh...sorry." She bites down on a shy smile.

I return that smile with one of my own. "Don't apologise for complimenting me, sweetheart. If you're satiated then I've more than done my job for you tonight."

"Oh, here we go," she says, rolling her eyes at my arrogance. But she doesn't fool me, I can see the smile in her eyes, hear the amusement in her voice.

"Don't pretend that you don't love my arrogance."

"During sex only," she says, raising an eyebrow at me.

"Yeah whatever," I murmur, and she laughs.

"Anyway, you were saying..."

"I was asking, not saying." Placing my index finger beneath her chin, I tilt her face up to meet my gaze. "I was asking how you feel after the interview."

She curls her hand around the nape of my neck, her fingers softly caressing my skin. "I feel a little strange...relieved, a little scared that I've told the world about the most painful parts of my past but, most of all, I feel...proud. Does that sound arrogant?"

I belt out a laugh. Honestly, I could smother her to death with love right now. She is just so fucking adorable at times and so modest. I absolutely adore her. "Oh, Lauren, I fucking love you to death, you know that?"

"What?" She looks confused. "What's so funny?"

"You," I say to her, "you are funny and sweet and adorable but the one thing you are definitely not, is arrogant. I thought we'd already agreed that I was the arrogant one out of the two of us."

She gives me the sweetest, mushiest smile, right before she drops those beautiful lips of hers on to mine. I hum my approval of that, and she giggles.

"Oh, that is the sweetest sound," I murmur, and she giggles again.

Pulling back, Lauren then rests her head against my shoulder, her index finger now trailing its way around the tattoos on my chest. God, I love it when she does that. And so does my cock. Honestly, this horny little fucker never seems to be satisfied where Lauren's concerned. I decide to ignore the twitching going on beneath the sheets...for the moment anyway.

"Seriously though, Jonny, is it okay to be proud of myself?"

I'm about to hit her back with another smart ass remark but when I see she's actually being serious, I frown. I don't like that she's even thinking this about herself, never mind saying it out loud. "Oh, baby, of course you're allowed to be proud of yourself. Why are you even asking that?"

Breaking eye contact, as if suddenly embarrassed, she simply shrugs. "I guess I'm just used to...well...being told otherwise. About myself I mean..."

I know exactly what she means. I also know exactly *who* she means. I swear, the sooner her bastard father is either put away behind bars or better still, suffers a long and painful death after drinking himself into oblivion, the better. Then and only then will I feel as though Lauren will have got recompense for all the years of suffering she endured at his violent hands.

"Hey." Placing the palm of my hand against her cheek, I

gently coax Lauren into looking up at me once more. "You should be proud," I whisper. "Because I am. In fact, I was so proud of you today that at one point, I thought I was going to burst with pride. That's how proud I am of you for doing what you did today, Lauren." Her eyes bounce between mine as the depth of my words begin to sink in. "You are strong and brave for getting out of that life you once lived in with your father. You're even stronger for telling the whole damn world about it. And don't let anybody else ever tell you otherwise."

She smiles at me lovingly. "I love you," she whispers, "the man who made my world a much happier place just by being in it."

"Right back at you with that one." I smile. Tangling my fingers into her curls, I say, "You know, I really don't think I want to wait much longer to marry you, Lauren Whittle."

Resting her hand against my chest, over my heart, she says, "It's funny you should say that, Jonny Mathers, because I've been thinking the very same thing these last few days."

"You have?" I ask, surprised. "Why didn't you say?"

"Well, you know, as usual, things got in the way such as television interviews, meals out with friends, hot sex with my fiancé…"

"Yeah yeah, excuses excuses," I jest, and she smiles. "But seriously. I really think I want to marry you as soon as possible because I really am done with the whole waiting around for you to become my wife."

She beams up at me with happiness. "I'm done with the whole waiting around too."

"So, we're agreed that we're going to get married sooner rather than later," I say, enjoying the look of excitement on Lauren's face, "preferably after we've moved house so we can start off married life as we mean to go on?"

"Absolutely," Lauren agrees, "I'd rather we moved house first too, but, how long will it be until we move do you think?"

"Mmm, you're keen, baby, I like it." I kiss her and she smiles up at me. "But honestly, it won't be long now until we move, as I've been assured by my realtor and my lawyers. It'll be a couple of months at the most I'm sure."

"So…we can maybe look at getting married in a matter of months then," she says to me, her eyes twinkling with excitement.

Honestly, I wish I could bottle her up right now. Seeing her so happy and excited about finally planning our wedding is something I've been wanting for far too long. Or at least, it's felt like a long time anyway. In actual fact, it's only been a couple of months or so since I proposed to Lauren but in that time, so much has happened that it's felt like a whole lot longer. Add to that the years I've spent without her, I just want to get a ring on it and be done with it. With a bit of music and romance thrown in to the mix of course….

"So, we've sort of decided on the when…but now we need to decide on the where," I say to her.

"We could get married in a warehouse and I wouldn't care. Because no matter what, our wedding will be magical. Being married to you will be magical."

"You're the one who's magical," I whisper, feeling suddenly overcome with emotion. "And I'm going to give you the perfect wedding day, Lauren Whittle. The perfect wedding for the perfect bride."

"I can't wait," she whispers excitedly. "I really can't wait."

CHAPTER 13

LAUREN

I wake up the following morning to find Jonny's side of the bed is empty. Well, I am not impressed with that. Not one little bit. Especially after last night. Resting my head back on the pillow, I smile to myself as I replay the dirtiest moments from last night with Jonny over and over in my mind.

I was kind of hoping for a rematch with him this morning. Never mind. I will force myself out of this bed and go on the hunt for my rock star instead. But not before I have my morning shower. It's about time I got back into the good habits I'd started to get into before all of this mess with my dad blew up everything. Good habits such as getting up and ready at a decent hour of the day and cleaning and tidying the house.

I also really need to think long and hard about continuing where I left off with those theatre auditions I'd started going to before all of this shit hit the fan, except now that I've put myself out there in the media, *really* put myself out there, I'm a little hesitant to start auditioning for parts all over again. Especially now that everybody out there knows all about me. Warts and all.

Yes, maybe I need to let the dust settle first before continuing my quest to be a successful actress in a Broadway musical one day. *Yeah right, Lauren, keep on dreaming.* Well, I will keep on dreaming. Because dreams of having a career as wonderful as that one would be are really all I have in terms of the job department right now.

And speaking of dreams…I have an even bigger dream. The biggest dream of them all that is about to be turned into a reality. Our impending nuptials. Shit, I am so excited. And suddenly impatient. Yes, Jonny and I need to get our heads together today and start ringing round the wedding agents or planners or whoever it is you need to ring when it comes to booking something as huge as this. A wedding. *Our* wedding! My entire focus is going to be on that today and nothing else. I can go back to re-visiting my career at a later date, once things have calmed down with the world's media following my television interview.

I think about ringing Stacey to tell her the exciting news about our wedding plans but then decide to wait until we've spoken to the wedding agents first. Once we get more of an idea about the where and when it can happen, we can then focus on the planning part of it all. And there is nobody else I'm more excited about sharing this news with than my best friend.

Stacey will be beside herself with excitement, and I can just see us now, visiting the bridal shops together, drinking prosecco as I try on wedding dress after wedding dress. Stacey doing the same and trying on endless bridesmaid dresses. Oh, this is going to be so much fun and it's about time we had something fun to focus on. I'll just have to make sure that I plan any future shopping trips around Stacey's new job. She's absolutely loving her new role as a backing dancer for one of the local dance troupes in downtown LA, and her shifts vary, depending on the production she's in. I thought about giving it a go myself but then decided on auditioning for actual singing parts instead, up until recent events.

Anyway, at least one of us is now working and even though, like me, she doesn't actually need to work, Stacey wants to. She may be living with a rich and famous bassist these days but Stacey wants to earn her own money and contribute to their life out here together in LA. She also absolutely loves dancing and performing and I don't think that will ever be any different. Same for me, hence why I spent so many years working in a shitty lap dancing club like Carnal Desires. But thankfully, that place is now part of my past and it is staying there. Time to live in the present and move forward with our exciting plans.

I dream my way through my shower, my head filled with wedding dresses and smart suits, heartfelt promises and a beautiful beach laden with rose petals where we'll hopefully be exchanging our vows. I imagine our friends smiling as they stand around us and watch as we make that lifelong commitment to each other. Oh, this is going to be wonderful. So bloody wonderful.

After my shower, I peep through the blinds to check on the weather, laughing to myself when I see the sun shining brightly outside. *You're living in LA now, Lauren, the sun always shines!* Of course it always shines. Well, almost always. It was a little cooler over the winter months, as to be expected, but with it now hurtling towards the end of May, things are really beginning to heat up out there.

I throw on some denim cut-off shorts and a black tank top, scrunch my damp curls with some mousse and that's it, I'm ready for the day ahead. Slipping my feet into my black sliders, I then head out of the bedroom and downstairs to go and find Jonny. Maybe he's in his music studio this morning, weaving his musical magic over some brand new masterpiece. Well Jonny can weave some musical magic over me this morning if he wants to.

As I reach the bottom of the stairs, I notice our clothes from last night that we'd left on the hallway floor have gone. Jonny must have removed them, which is a shame, because I was kind of looking forward to seeing them again this morning. Especially after how he ripped them off me. Well, my blouse anyway. A delightful shiver courses through me as another graphic flashback from last night pops into my mind. *God, the things he did to me against that front door, and on these stairs....*

I bite down on a smile as I descend the last couple of stairs. I so need to get a repeat performance of last night, that's for sure. I head over to Jonny's music studio, expecting him to be in there, but am surprised to find the door is locked. Hmm, he isn't working on his next masterpiece after all then.

It's only when I walk back across the hallway and through the archway into the kitchen that I hear voices coming from outside. Squinting over at the patio doors at the back of the house that lead out on to the terrace, I see they're partially open.

Curious as to who our morning visitor is, I walk outside, across the terrace and towards the stone steps to find that Jonny is sitting down in the garden with...his dad? Shit, now that's taken the wind right out of my sails.

As I start to descend the stone steps towards where they're both sitting around the table beside the swimming pool, I wonder whether or not to turn back. I haven't seen Pete Mathers properly since the day Jonny woke up from his coma in hospital and whenever he's turned up unannounced at our front door since then, Jonny has always protected me by keeping me away from him. Swiftly followed by him closing the door in his dad's face.

Not at the moment though, not since he agreed to help Jonny with this whole bringing down my dad idea. Something that occurred while I wasn't here, which was fair enough, but now that I am here, I'm actually a bit pissed off that they're discussing my dad without including me. In fact, scrap that, I'm really pissed off, my happy mood from moments ago rapidly evaporating.

I continue down the stone steps like I mean business. The shock on their faces as I approach the table is absolutely priceless. I mean, fancy me, Jonny's fiancée, the woman who lives with him, turning up unexpectedly in the back garden! Did they really think I wouldn't come wandering out here when I woke up? Explains why Jonny left me in bed this morning. I thought it was strange he hadn't woke me up for his usual morning sexcapades. Maybe this meeting has been planned all along, and if that's the case, then I've just gone from being really pissed off to being *royally* pissed off.

Despite looking a little uncomfortable at the sudden change in atmosphere my presence has brought to the table, Jonny still tries his usual casual approach with me. The casual approach that has guilt written all over it. "Hey…my dad just stopped by to…"

"Talk about something important that really should have included me?" I snap, cutting him off.

Placing my hand on my hip, I deliberately break eye contact with Jonny, who is now sinking back into his chair I notice, my steely gaze instead coming to rest on the man who, at one time, I feared just as much as I feared my own dad. But not anymore. Whether Jonny wants to press ahead with that whole building bridges thing with his dad after this shit with my dad is done with, is up to him, but for now, in this moment, this floor is mine.

"Do you feel like you've repented for your past sins as yet? Or will that take you a little longer?"

"Lauren…" Jonny starts to intervene but Pete quickly shuts him down before I do.

"No, it's okay, Jonny," says Pete, looking up at me, "let Lauren say her piece. I think it's long overdue." *Long overdue is putting it fucking mildly*, I think to myself.

Wearing a black polo shirt and a pair of beige chinos, Pete is dressed as smartly as ever, but that over confident, cocky air about him I've come to know so well over the years seems to have deflated somewhat. His dark brown eyes that were once cold and empty are looking up at me now in a completely different way to how they used to, a little warmer perhaps than they once were.

One look from Pete used to make me feel like I was a piece of shit on the bottom of his shoe, his pure hatred of me, of where I came from, practically burning its way out of him whenever our paths crossed. He could never hide away his disdain when it came to me and let's face it, he never wanted to. He wanted to make me feel like the scared young girl I already was, deliberately plucking at the vulnerability within me that my dad had ingrained in me from the day I was born.

"But before you do say whatever it is you want to say to me, Lauren, I just want to say that I think what you did yesterday with the television interview was bold and empowering, and if some of the newspaper articles that have been printed this morning are anything to go by, I'd say your interview was a resounding success."

What the actual fuck? Has this man had a personality transplant or something? Jeez, who is this brown nosing suck up sitting before me? At least when he was cold and heartless, I knew where I stood with him. Now I fear he may be playing the being overly nice to me card so he can worm his way back into his son's life only to go and wrench me away from him all over again. Well, not on my watch he isn't.

I start to laugh at him, at his words, and Pete raises his eyebrows in surprise. "You think I'm brown nosing?" Well, at least he's saying it as it is. He must have read my mind.

"Forgive me for being so cynical, Pete, but yes, I think you're brown nosing. For Jonny's sake. I mean, let's face it, you've always hated me and that's not about to change anytime soon just because I grew big enough balls to do a live interview about my painful past in Manchester. *Jonny's* painful past. You remember that past you threatened to send to print yourself?"

"Lauren…"

I glare over at Jonny. With a shake of my head, I say, "Don't say another word."

But Jonny being Jonny simply cannot help himself. He's as stubborn as I am when it comes to things like this. "I will say another word. In fact, I'll say a few. We're not here today to rake over old ground. We're here to discuss…"

"My dad!" I snap. Looking between the pair of them, I say, "And if you're discussing my dad then I want and *should* be involved, but as usual, Jonny, you do it behind my back. What happened to doing things together from now on? What happened to talking through things *together*?"

"And what happened to leaving the shitty parts of our past back in Manchester?" he snarls, "like we promised to do."

Pete sighs. "Look, if you two need a moment…"

"We don't need a moment," I bark at him.

Shit, I'm angry. So fucking angry with Jonny for not waking me this morning and involving me in something as important as this. Pulling out one of the chairs, I sit myself down at that table right along with them, like I mean business. And I really do mean fucking business. I am raging. Just wait until I get Jonny alone after this. He won't know what's bloody hit him.

"So, what shit have you dug up on my dad then, Pete? I assume it's shit that Jonny doesn't want me to know about."

I ignore Jonny's frustrated sigh and instead keep my angry gaze pinned on Pete. If I look at Jonny right now, I fear I may slap him. He can be so bloody infuriating sometimes. His constant need to keep protecting me from things can be so suffocating. Especially when I've just bared my very soul to the entire bloody world. You can't get more out there than that, and yet, he agreed with that decision, he supported me and told me, through his actions as well as his words, how proud he was of me. And now here we are, the following day, and I feel like we're back to square one all over again. Him shielding me from anything to do with my dad. It's pathetic, and I'll tell him as much.

Clearing his throat, Pete sits forward in his chair. Placing his arms on the table, he looks at Jonny first, before finally resting his gaze back on me. "It turns out that your dad is in deep with the wrong people. In fact, how he hasn't got himself killed before now is anybody's guess but, somehow or other, your dad has managed to, shall we say, 'worm his way out of trouble,' up until now."

"Until now? What kind of people is he involved with?"

Sounds like a stupid question but I really am naïve in all of this. All I remember of my dad when he wasn't slamming me around the house with his fists, was that he was either pissing what money he did have up the wall or larging it about the place like he was the man of the town. As I've said before, people seemed to fear my dad and I'd always assumed that was because of how violent he was. Maybe it was for another reason after all. Because of the wrong sort of people he'd been involved with.

"The violent kind of people," says Jonny, "which is why I wanted to…"

"If you say 'keep this from you to protect you' one more

time," I warn, throwing him a glare across the table.

"I'm not going to apologise for wanting to protect the woman I love, Lauren…"

"And I'm not going to apologise for wanting to know the facts about the man who I am sadly related to!" I shout.

Ignoring the look of anger on Jonny's face, I turn back to Pete. "I don't remember very many people turning up at our door when I lived at home with him. I remember him coming home from the pub looking messed up sometimes but I assumed he'd been throwing his fists around at somebody who decided to fight back. Surely I'd know if he'd been in the deep stuff with the wrong people."

Leaning down, I notice Pete reaching into a briefcase that is sitting on the floor next to his chair. He pulls out a chunky file of papers and tosses it into the middle of the table. "It appears that your dad has only got in with these people over the last few months. This file is packed full with the shit he's been up to. He's got himself into a whole load of debt and now that debt is being called in. That probably explains why he sold his story to the newspapers, so he could make some money to pay back some of his debt."

Holy shit, this isn't what I was expecting at all. I should have expected it though. Where my dad's concerned, anything is possible. I open up the file and start to leaf my way through the papers. I have to say, I am impressed with just how much information Pete has managed to get on my dad. Jonny wasn't wrong when he said his dad was the right person for the job. Even so, I'm still royally pissed at him for keeping all of this from me and so I'm holding on to that anger for later on because he is not getting away with keeping all of this from me. Today was supposed to be a happy day, one where we started planning the happiest day of our life together. Instead, he has been keeping secrets from me again and I am not impressed. Not one bit.

As I continue to flick through the information Pete has given to me, I am shocked to learn so many more things about my dad I never ever knew about. That he frequented prostitutes back in the day when I lived at home with him, got violent with a few of them as well by the sounds of things.

"These so called prostitutes he got violent with? How have you got hold of all this information?"

"I know people, Lauren. And I pay a lot of money for private investigators to do a proper job. They've been working meticulously on this since Jonny gave me the go ahead. And they still haven't finished."

Feeling like I've seen enough of my dad's sordid past for the time being, I close the file and sit back in my chair with a sigh. "So, you have all of this information. What now?"

"Now, we..."

"I wasn't talking to you," I say to Jonny, still feeling furious with him. Keeping my eyes on Pete, I say, "What now, Pete? What's your next grand plan now you've dug up all of this shit on my good old dad?"

I really want to know. Because I can't see that digging up any of this helps us with anything. Sometimes, ignorance is bliss, and now I've seen the shit that goes with having a dad like mine, I kind of wish I could now unsee it. Not that I'd tell Jonny that of course. I had a right to see this information because of the fact I'm related to the person involved, whether I *should* have seen it is another matter entirely.

Drumming his fingers over the file of papers, Pete says, "Now, we try and get your dad sent to prison for his past misdemeanours with those prostitutes, amongst other things he could potentially be sent away for. It might not be justice for what he did to you directly, but hopefully it'll be some sort of justice for all the wrongs he did to you back then." Wow. Did Pete Mathers actually just say those words out loud to me? Seriously?

"And what about getting justice for all the wrongs you did to me, Pete? And all the wrongs you did to Jonny? Your own son?"

I can't help it. I really can't. He may be feeling all regretful now but I can't allow him to just sit there and pretend like my dad was the sole destroyer of everything Jonny and I ever had together. My dad certainly played his part, and he played it well, but Pete coming out of all of this smelling of roses is suddenly making me feel sick. And angry. Let's not forget about that burning anger I'm currently holding on to so I can throw it at my future husband later on.

"Lauren…"

I scowl over at Jonny trying to leap to his dad's defence or whatever the hell it is he thinks he's trying to do this morning. I'm beginning to wonder if Jonny himself has also had a personality transplant overnight, because this is not the man who was telling me how proud he was of me last night, right after he slammed me against the front door and fucked my brains out. The same man who made promises to me, and me to him, about staying open and honest with each other, about making a happy future together, planning our wedding.

"It's fine," says Pete, throwing an apologetic smile my way. "I deserve it, and a whole lot more where that came from."

"Damn right you do," I say coldly.

Scraping back my chair, I stand up. "Anyway, I feel like I've seen enough. I'll leave you two to decide what you do with this information, and any more that comes your way, because clearly, I can't be trusted to make that decision with you."

"For fuck's sake, Lauren," Jonny sighs. "Will you just…"

"I'm going to get some breakfast," I say, cutting him off.

I throw Pete a goodbye nod and then storm away from the table, up the stone steps and back into the house, taking my anger right along with me.

****

I sit at the dining table and eat a bowl of cereal for my breakfast as I silently seethe over the morning's events. I also check on my phone to find some of these so called news articles Pete referred to earlier, articles that apparently paint me out to be a resounding success, or words to that effect.

I manage to find one or two that really are very complimentary and empathetic towards my situation and the violence I've faced in the past. They like the fact I'm trying to help others like myself and they think I've done a very brave thing by speaking out. I end the search there, wanting to leave the reading of the articles on a high note rather than a sour one, because there will no doubt be plenty of negative articles about me too. But I really don't want more negativity today. I've had a gut full of negativity already for one day and it looks like I'm about to get a whole lot more, now that Jonny is finally seeing his dad off.

Pete nods his head as he steps into the house and walks past me, Jonny following slowly behind him. Jonny doesn't make eye contact with me I notice. Oh no, he'll be saving that for when he comes back into the kitchen after seeing his dad off, all guns blazing. Well, I'll be more than ready for him, that's for god damn sure.

I stand up from the table and take my pots over to the dishwasher. I have just about loaded said dishwasher when Jonny comes storming into the kitchen like the hurricane I predicted him to be.

"Okay, let's have this out then," he says, standing on the other side of the breakfast island.

Slamming the dishwasher door closed, I swing round to face him. "Oh, you want to 'have this out' do you?" I say, using air quotes at him. I know how much he detests air quotes and because I'm so pissed off at him, I deliberately want to wind him up just that little bit more. Sounds childish and immature but I don't give a shit, not after the stunt he pulled with his dad this morning.

"I know what you're doing," he says, looking mega pissed off, "and it's working, so stop it now and just say what you've clearly been dying to say to me for the last however long it's been since you stormed away from me earlier."

"Oh, I have plenty to say to you, Jonny! Plenty!"

"So say it," he snaps.

Running my hands down my face, I sigh in frustration. "The fact that you're even having to ask me to tell you why I'm pissed off just about sums up why I'm so pissed off!" He screws up his face in confusion, but I continue regardless. "Arranging a meeting with your dad behind my back to discuss my father was wrong. So bloody wrong, and yet somehow or other, you can't see that it's wrong…"

"I arranged nothing," he interjects, "my dad rang me this morning and asked if he could come over to see me, he said he'd found some stuff on your dad that he wanted to discuss. In fact, it was my dad's phone call that woke me up…"

"So why didn't you then wake me up to tell me about it?"

"Because you were asleep and I didn't want to wake you."

"Bullshit. You used the fact that I was still asleep to hide this little meeting from me. A meeting about my dad. *My* dad!"

Jonny frowns. "Look, I was worried about what it would be like for you if you were forced to sit around a table with my dad, after everything he did, and I didn't want to put you in an awkward situation like that."

"Really?" I can't help the derisive laugh that falls from my mouth at hearing him say that. "You were worried about putting me in an awkward situation with your dad when, only yesterday, I put my big girl pants on and deliberately put myself in a really difficult situation by doing a television interview live on air."

Rubbing an impatient hand over his brow, he says, "Look, I was just trying to do what I felt was right. You chose to do that interview yesterday. You wouldn't willingly choose to sit around a table with my dad, given your history with him…"

"Well I didn't get the fucking choice, did I?" I yell at him. "And that's the point!"

"Look, this is all trivial nonsense now because in the end, you didn't need to choose anyway. You came outside and found us in the garden and you said what you wanted to say to him. End of."

"End of?" I screw up my face in anger. "This isn't just about me wiping the floor with your dad, Jonny, this is about my dad too. We made promises to each other back in Manchester. Promises of being open and honest with each other and you've already gone back on those promises."

"I haven't broken any fucking promises. You knew about me looking into your dad because I told you about it on the flight home from Manchester…"

"Yeah, you did, but you didn't expand on exactly what you were digging up on him…"

"Because I didn't fucking know then!" he shouts angrily. "I've only found out that information this morning…"

"Behind my back! Yet again!" I yell. "You should have woken me up and included me in it but you didn't, and don't start with all of this bullshit again about protecting me from your dad or my dad because I've had a gut full of it, Jonny!"

"Says the woman who recently ran off to Manchester all on her own because of her own compulsive need to protect me!" he shouts, thumping a balled up fist into his chest.

"Oh, how lovely of you to start throwing that in my face again when you said we'd put it all behind us!" I spit at him venomously. Jeez, I am seething. How bloody dare he throw that in my face after everything he said to me under our special tree on Heaton Park.

Holding his arms out to the sides, he says, "You throw hurtful shit at me and I throw it right back. It's how arguments work, Lauren."

I shake my head at him. "Well so much for planning our wedding today. You know, I woke up feeling so excited this morning after everything we talked about last night and then, as per usual, you go and pull another stunt that just fucks everything up all over again!"

I get an angry glare for that remark. "This isn't a fucking stunt, Lauren. I'm just trying to get justice for you. For what that evil man did to you for so many years of your life. That's it. Nothing more. Nothing less."

I sigh in exasperation. "And what if I don't want you to pursue this 'getting justice' you seem to need so badly!"

Jonny looks over at me in shock. "Are you for fucking real right now?"

I turn away from him at that point because I feel weary and exhausted. Exhausted from dealing with the very shit we apparently left behind us in Manchester. Resting my face in my hands, I sigh heavily.

"Lauren? Are you okay?" Jonny's voice is gentler now, calmer.

When I don't answer him, he must head straight over to where I'm standing on the other side of the breakfast island because the next thing I know, his tattooed arms are wrapping their way around my waist from behind. I feel his lips in my hair as he pulls me against him, my back to his chest.

"Oh, Lauren, I'm sorry," he whispers. "I'm an idiot. An over protective, hot headed idiot."

I feel my emotions beginning to bubble to the surface as Jonny holds on to me tightly, my anger with him slowly ebbing away. I try to hold on to my tears in a bid to stay strong but it's a pointless venture, as they begin to roll down my cheeks anyway.

Swiping at my eyes, I then turn around in Jonny's arms to find him staring down at me guiltily. "And now I've made you cry," he says with a sigh. "Shit."

He wraps his warm, loving arms around me and allows me to cry quietly against his chest. "I'm sorry," he whispers, his voice barely audible. We stand in silence for a short while before Jonny speaks again. "I guess I see this shit with your dad as my closure, but…that's not fair on you. I know that…I just…"

Pulling away from his chest, I gaze up into the dark brown eyes of the man I love with all my heart and soul. He is my fiancé, my soul mate, my protector, my life. The deep ache I feel in my chest whenever we share a moment like this begins to expand to the point of pain, physical pain. The pain I feel for the man I love so much. Too much. And he loves me back in exactly the same way. Which is why I really need to allow him to do this. Jonny needs his closure with my dad, just as I needed my closure.

"Get your closure, Jonny," I whisper to him. "Whatever you need to do to get your closure with my dad, just do it...and I'll be right there with you, by your side, like you were with me."

I press the palms of my hands gently against his cheeks as I reach up and kiss him. "I love you," I whisper against his lips.

He kisses me right back before resting his forehead against mine. "I love you too, Lauren. Forever and always."

"Forever and always, Jonny." I smile up at him through my tears.

He returns my smile with one of his own. "Now, how about we get started on planning that all-important wedding we were talking about last night?"

A little fizz of excitement goes pop in my belly when he says that to me, my happy mood from this morning beginning to make a re-appearance. "Oh, yes please. I would love that. I really would."

He kisses me softly on the lips and then says, "Come on then, let's go and see if we can get that magical wedding of ours booked into the diary."

CHAPTER 14

JONNY

"So, it's been a while since our last session, Jonny. I'm sure there are good reasons for you cancelling our last few sessions but before we get into those reasons, how are you feeling about coming back here today?"

I look over at Brian, my counsellor, and he smiles warmly at me. Instead of smiling in return, I immediately leap on the defensive. "I feel fine," I say with a frown, "why wouldn't I?"

Placing his notepad and pen down on to the old oak coffee table sitting between us, Brian then sits back in his brown leather chair and studies me for a long moment. I hate being stared at and I tell him as much. "What?" I say to him. "What's the problem? And stop staring. I hate being stared at," I grumble.

I look away from him and fold my arms in annoyance. I've admittedly cancelled the last few therapy sessions with Brian, but only because of recent events, not because I think I'm suddenly better, although right now, I suddenly wish I was.

"I'm sorry," says Brian. I turn back to him and he smiles at me apologetically. "I didn't mean to stare, I was just…"

"Trying to read my mind and figure out what the fuck has been going on with me of late?" I snap.

Shit, poor Brian is really getting it in the neck this morning. I wouldn't mind but I've actually been in a better place mentally this week, especially since Lauren and I have now finally set a date and booked our wedding. In Mauritius, no less. We originally wanted to get married in the Maldives where I proposed but it turns out that unless you're a registered citizen over there, you can't legally get married, meaning we would have had to have a civil ceremony either before or after we got back, which we didn't want to do.

After much deliberation and ringing round, we decided on Mauritius, which I have no doubt will be just as amazing as the Maldives was, only this time, we will be coming home as newlyweds. Yep, come October, I will be well and truly sealing the deal with my girl although right now, October seems like a million years away to me.

Wedding plans aside however, the reason for my short temper this morning is because of the constant war that's been going around in my head all week over what the fuck I should do about Lauren's dad. We had the mother of all rows about it the other day, swiftly followed by me apologising to Lauren for being such an over protective jackass. Lauren however eventually gave her blessing for me to do whatever it is I feel I need to do to get my closure.

Trouble is, I honestly don't know what the fuck it is I want or need to do to get that closure. In fact, I don't even think it's about closure for me anymore. It's all for Lauren. Always has been and always will be. And that's the problem. I will literally do whatever it takes to protect my girl, no matter the cost, but now that the dust is beginning to settle after the difficult events of late, do I really want to fuck up our new found happiness just so I can say at the end of it all that her dad got his just desserts?

Realising I've most likely offended Brian with my angry outburst, I am quick to apologise. "Sorry," I mutter, "I'm just..." I sigh.

"It's okay," replies Brian, "just take your time, Jonny."

Sitting back in my chair, I reluctantly offer up an explanation for my bad mood. "You've most likely seen the tabloids of late, the shit that's been written about me and Lauren, her dad…"

Brian nods. "I'm aware of the news article you're referring to, Jonny, but only because there's been so much press coverage on it. In all honesty, I don't tend to read tabloids or gossip columns. I will admit however that I did watch the live interview you did with your fiancée and I have to say, I thought it was incredibly brave of her, and you."

"It was all Lauren," I say, "she was the brave one that day, not me."

"I beg to differ. I think going on live television after everything you've been through over these last few months was very brave. Just because you remained quiet throughout the interview doesn't mean to say you weren't brave for doing it."

With a deep exhale, I say, "Do you have a point to all of this?"

"Oh, I always have a point, Jonny," he says, a slight smile tugging at his lips.

"Which is?" Yet again, I'm losing patience with Brian and his never ending ability to wind me the hell up.

"That you've made wonderful progress over these last few months and yet somehow, you think you haven't."

I run an anxious hand through my hair, the familiar tremor in my legs beginning to rear its ugly head. Why the fuck am I so wound tight all the time? I never used to be like this. So fucking anxious and irritable. *It's because you want that fix again, Jonny, that's why.* Fuck that, I am not going back to the drugs again, no matter how anxious or irritable I become. I've come this far and I am not going back there again. Ever.

"Can I smoke in here?" I ask Brian, half expecting him to say no.

I've never once asked him if I can smoke in here, usually taking my bad habit outside with me instead. Brian normally allows me a smoke break every so often but as he's only just getting his claws into me this morning, I suspect he won't be allowing me for that smoke break any time soon, but I need a fag and I need one now. Badly.

Brian gives me a wry smile. "I will allow it this once, as long as you open the window to air the room."

I'm off that chair and opening up the damn window quicker than a rat up a drain pipe. Pulling out my fag packet from the pocket of my leather jacket, I then proceed to light one up before sitting back down once more.

"I don't suppose you want one?" I offer one to Brian but he politely declines.

"No thank you."

I put my fag packet back into my jacket pocket and then inhale deeply on my cigarette, hoping against hope that my fix of nicotine will calm me the hell down because, let's face it, something needs to.

"So, do you want to tell me about how you've been? I assume this news article has set you more than on edge."

Blowing out the smoke from between my lips, I say, "I'd say that's putting it fucking mildly." When Brian raises his eyebrows at me in response, as if silently asking me to enlighten him with a more detailed explanation, I begrudgingly give in.

I tell him all about the devastating impact the news article had on both me and Lauren. I give him the full run down of how Lauren and I both ended up in Manchester and the fact she faced her father head on. Basically, I tell Brian absolutely everything as I smoke my way through not one, but four cigarettes, one after the other.

Once I've finally purged myself of everything that's been on my mind of late, I sit back in my chair and wait for the one and only Brian to pass comment. Fuck, if he has the answer to all my problems then happy fucking days. I'll take any shred of anything from him right now.

After scribbling away in his notepad for what feels like an eternity, Brian then sits forward in his leather chair. Steepling his hands together in front of his face, as if deep in thought, Brian remains quiet for a moment. After a beat, he finally speaks.

"Thank you for sharing so much of your troubles with me this morning, Jonny, I know it isn't easy to do." Clearing his throat, he then says, "It sounds to me however like you're holding on to all the hate and anger, which is understandable, after everything Lauren's father did, but holding on to hate isn't the answer, and it certainly isn't healthy..."

"You think I don't fucking know that?" I snap.

"Whether you know it or not, it's something that will continue to eat you up until you decide to let it go..."

"So I just let the mother fucker get away with it then? I let Lauren's father off the hook after everything he ever did to her?" I let out an aggravated sigh. Everything I've just said to Brian was pointless. Completely pointless. "You know, I thought you might have had an answer for me this morning..."

"An answer?" Brian frowns. "Jonny, you just told me that you feel as though you and Lauren are beginning to settle into a happy place together in your life, and that you don't want to mess any of that up by continuing to dig into her father's unsavoury lifestyle..."

"And that's true, I don't want to mess it up..."

"So..."

"So how do I let it go?" I ask impatiently, "how do I just let it all go like you keep telling me to do?"

Brian sits back in his chair and says, "I don't have all the answers for you, Jonny, but I will say this, you need to completely change your perspective on how you view this situation with Lauren's father. It sounds to me like the clock is ticking for him anyway, but even if it wasn't, you instead need to turn all of that anger and hate you have boiling away inside of you into something else. Something good. Focus on all the wonderful things you have in your life, like Lauren, the band, moving house, your upcoming wedding. Remembering all of these positives in your life will soon help to diminish all of the negatives. It sounds so simple and yet it's so much harder to do. Believe me, I understand a lot more than you realise."

Narrowing my eyes on Brian, I say, "Oh, you do?"

He nods. "I do. In fact, my past difficulties are the very thing that pushed me into doing this job."

"Really?" I ask, surprised.

"Really." He smiles.

Well, it just goes to show that appearances really can be deceiving. Just because Brian is a qualified counsellor who appears to have his shit together doesn't mean to say that once upon a time, he didn't have his own problems to deal with. Here I am, offloading my shit on to him, thinking he hasn't got a fucking clue about problems when in actual fact, he's probably had many. After all, he is human. And humans break. I know I broke.

I'm sure that once upon a time, my fans used to look upon me as being somebody who would never ever break. And boy did I love to live up to that reputation. Spectacularly. For so many years, me and my stage mask never seemed to steer me wrong, or at least, I used to think that anyway. Not anymore. Those days are long gone for me and how the fuck I'm ever going to get back up on an actual stage and perform live for my fans again is anybody's guess, but if I want to continue with my music career then I'm going to have to. That however is something I will have to face another day because today is about moving on from the past. Something I've already sworn to Lauren I would do.

Letting go of that hatred I feel towards her father however is a whole lot harder than I thought it would be, but Brian's words this morning have only mirrored my own thoughts from this week. Deep down, I do not want to continue raking up the past. I asked my dad to dig deep on Jimmy Whittle and dig deep he did, but after this morning with Brian, and against all my usual instincts of wanting to forever protect the woman I love, I need to put this shit to rest once and for all and let nature take its course.

In the words of Brian, the clock is ticking on Jimmy Whittle already and it's only a matter of time before somebody out there puts that bastard out of his misery. But that somebody is not going to be me. I want a happy and contented life with my girl and a happy and contented life we are going to have. Starting now.

"Okay," I finally say to Brian.

"Okay?" He looks at me questioningly.

"I'll...let it go," I say, reluctantly.

Brian nods. "It isn't easy to let go, Jonny, but if you remember the positives, and constantly repeat those positives over and over in your mind, they will eventually extinguish all of the negatives. People like Lauren's father don't even deserve to be a thought in your mind. Again, that is something else I'm sorry to say I have experience in. At one time in my own life, I thought I would never be able to break the cycle of negative thoughts over a particular person who had wronged me, but thankfully, through sheer hard work and lots of therapy, I overcame those negatives, and ultimately, I then found my calling by becoming a counsellor myself. I turned my negatives into positives, and my positive was finding a new career whereby I help other people like me. Or at least, I hope I help my clients anyway. I like to think I do, but with you, I'm not so sure."

I give Brian a reassuring smile. "I may seem like an ungrateful asshole sometimes, Brian, but…you've helped me a whole lot more than you even realise." And he has. I owe a lot to Brian really. Considering how against therapy I was in the very beginning, Brian has certainly worked his counselling magic on me, that's for sure.

Brian chuckles. "Well, thank you for that, Jonny. I'll take that as a positive in all of this. As should you."

Right now, I will take all the positives I can get. "I'll take it," I say, "and I promise to create more positive thought processes going forward. It won't be easy but, I'll try. I promise you I will try. For Lauren. I'll do anything for her happiness. Absolutely anything."

CHAPTER 15

LAUREN

"Oh my god, Lauren, you look absolutely stunning. That's it. That's *the* dress!"

Stacey claps her hands excitedly and beams at me through the floor length mirror in the dressing room of the bridal dress shop we are currently in. We've been in a good few wedding dress shops so far today and I've tried on countless bridal gowns of varying designs, Stacey suggesting I just enjoy the day and try on every dress going so I can simply 'enjoy the moment.' And enjoy the moment I have as Stacey has looked on at me proudly, gushing at the dresses she loved on me and pulling her face at the ones she hated.

It's been so much fun, spending the day together, choosing the perfect wedding dress for what I know will be my perfect wedding. *Our* perfect wedding. Mine and Jonny's. Mind you, as it's now the beginning of August and our wedding is in October, I think it's safe to say that I am perhaps cutting it a little fine with choosing my dress, although Jonny has assured me that timescales don't matter. Jonny being Jonny will more than likely pull out his rock star status when it comes to my perfect wedding dress being ready for the big day and so, any worries I had of leaving it to the last minute have thankfully already been quashed.

My grin almost splits my face in two as I smile with happiness at my best friend, twirling around on the spot one more time for her as she does a happy little twirl right along with me. "I think you're right," I say to her, "I think this is the one."

Glancing at myself in the floor length mirror once more, I take a minute to let this happy moment sink in. I can't believe I am the woman in the mirror, standing tall and, dare I say it, looking like the beautiful bride I'd always hoped I would be some day. Before Jonny came back into my life, I never even thought about marriage or weddings. I guess I just always assumed that getting married wasn't on the agenda for me. Until now. Now, I can finally stand here and say I am getting my perfect ending. My perfect ending to what has been an imperfect journey. A journey fraught with pain and heartache, but a journey I honestly wouldn't change for the world.

The heartache and pain that both Jonny and I have endured over the years has led us to this moment. A moment where we are finally allowed to have that long fought for happy ever after together. We're not quite at the wedding ceremony just yet, but we very nearly are, and I am holding on to that. I'm holding on for dear life and I'm never letting go. Wild horses couldn't keep me away from marrying Jonny and I know for a fact it's the same for him. We were always meant to be together, one way or another, and we always will be. No matter what.

"This is the one!" Stacey yells through to one of the female retail assistants who has been more than attentive with me this afternoon, bringing out dress after dress, coupled with plenty of glasses of champagne in the process. Today really has been the ultimate girly day out so far and it doesn't stop here. Hell no. Stacey and I are off for a bottomless brunch after the choosing of the dress is done with. It is something to be celebrated after all, and boy are we going to celebrate. We are going to celebrate our socks off.

The lady comes bustling through into the changing room at

the back of the boutique where I'm currently standing with Stacey, and she smiles at me as I do yet another twirl, for her this time. I honestly don't want to take this dress off. I want to keep it on and wear it forever and ever.

The dress itself is simple yet elegant in its design. Ivory in colour, the lace material clings to my curves in all the right places, the V neck at the front accentuating my ample bosom in a tasteful, classy way, instead of an in your face, spilling out of the dress kind of way. The back of the dress scoops low and the edges of the straps are finished in the same delicate lace as the mermaid style train that flows behind.

It might be a little more restrictive for walking down the aisle in, but this dress is definitely the one for me. It has my personality written all over it, and whilst I have in fact tried on a few more traditional wedding dresses today, such as overly large barbie doll type ones and dresses with much longer trains than this, none of them felt how this one feels. Like stepping into my own skin.

"You look stunning," says the lady, as she hands me and Stacey yet another glass of champagne. "Now, you two have another drink and I'll be right back with my tape measure."

I smile at her gratefully. "Thank you."

Stacey clinks her champagne glass against mine. "Here's to the perfect wedding dress, girl!" she squeals, and I laugh.

"And to the perfect wedding," I say, injecting as much enthusiasm and excitement into my voice as I possibly can.

"Abso-bloody-lutely!"

****

An hour later and Stacey and I are indulging in the bottomless brunch I mentioned earlier, Jonny having made reservations for us at an exclusive restaurant in Beverly Hills as part of our girly day out together. We would have had the bottomless brunch whether or not we found the dress but having now found 'the one,' this brunch has even more of a celebratory feel to it.

The rooftop restaurant which is aptly named, The Hills, is one hell of a posh place for us to be dining at compared to the places where Stacey and I have dined out in the past back in London. We have a table at one of the best seats in the house, on the rooftop terrace itself, giving us a breathtaking view of Beverly Hills beneath us.

Apparently it's one of the largest rooftop restaurants in Beverly Hills, and one of the most popular, giving off a sophisticated garden like ambience with its wooden floors, light green sofas and round marble tables. There's even a large white pergola that wraps around the entire terrace with a snazzy looking bar nestled beneath. A bar that is thankfully well stocked with plenty of alcohol. And speaking of alcohol....

"God, you and I are going to be so pissed when we leave here later on," says Stacey, giggling.

"What do you mean, later on? I'm already well on my way to being pissed, Stacey Kerr. Hey, maybe that's why they ply you with champagne and prosecco in these wedding boutiques, so that you're guaranteed to buy one of their wedding dresses at the end of it all because of how pissed you are." We both laugh.

"You know what? I think you might be on to something there, Lauren Whittle, soon to be Mrs Lauren Mathers."

I glance down at my engagement ring and sigh contentedly. "I love the sound of being Mrs Lauren Mathers."

"Well I know for a fact that Jonny loves the sound of you being Mrs Lauren Mathers," says Stacey, wiggling her eyebrows suggestively. "And speaking of your bad boy rock star...how have you two settled in to your new home? You christened every room yet?"

Biting down on a suggestive smile, I say, "Stace, we only moved in two weeks ago."

Stacey grins and then bumps shoulders with me. "Oh come on, I bet you had every room in that house christened within the first five days of moving in..."

"First four days actually," I tease, before taking a large gulp of my champagne.

"Oh there she is! The dirty girl I know and love that comes out to play when she's had a few drinks..."

"It takes one dirty girl to know one, Stacey Kerr!" I stick my tongue out at her and she throws her head back, laughing loudly.

Shit, we really do need to eat some food and line our stomachs, otherwise we're going to need carrying out of here later on. "And speaking of being dirty, how are things with you and Ben? It feels like it's been ages since you and I had some proper girly time together. These last few months haven't been easy and we've mostly been in the company of the men, so... are you still getting down and dirty with that bassist of yours or what?"

Raising her glass of champagne in the air, Stacey starts to do a little sit down victory dance on the sofa we are sitting on, shimmying her shoulders back and forth to the R&B music which is filtering its way through the speakers from the bar area behind us. She smiles over at me and then says, "I don't think it'll ever be anything other than dirty where Ben is concerned."

I slap my hand to my mouth and burst out laughing. A few people on the table next to us suddenly turn their gazes on both me and Stacey, scowling at the pair of us as we begin to giggle loudly like a pair of teenage girls. Shit, the bubbles of champagne are really starting to run riot through my system and I'd say from the look of Stacey right now, those champagne bubbles are running riot through hers too.

"Shit, I think we need our food now," I say to Stacey, trying to stifle another giggle behind my hand.

"Oh, bollocks to food," says Stacey. Lifting up the bottle of champagne from the bucket of ice next to our table, she screws up her face in disgust when she sees the bottle is empty. "Shit, we've run out of champagne."

Dumping the empty bottle back into the bucket of ice, Stacey then gestures over to one of the waiters passing by our table, asking him to bring another bottle when he gets a spare moment.

"Oh, Stace, we're going to be shit faced."

"And?" She looks at me with a mischievous glint in her eyes. "Who cares? I know for a fact that Ben won't care. In fact, he loves it when I'm drunk."

"Oh, I bet he does."

"Oh, and Jonny doesn't?"

I grin. "Oh, Jonny will take me however he can get me. Drunk or not drunk. However, there is such a thing as being too drunk, Stace, and if we drink any more of that champagne, we are going to be shit faced."

"You've said that twice up to now," says Stacey, flashing me a drunken grin.

"And I'll say it again, we're going to be shit faced!"

She gives me her usual eye roll and then chuckles. "Anyway, back to what we were talking about before..."

"You mean about me and Jonny christening all the rooms in our new house in just four days?"

And we really did christen all of the rooms in our new house in just four days. And the newness still hasn't worn off. In fact, we've been so 'busy' enjoying our new home these last two weeks that we haven't actually given ourselves chance to properly unpack. Not fully anyway.

Shaking her head at me, Stacey laughs. "Oh, Lauren, it's so wonderful to see you finally happy with the man you love. The man you deserve. I honestly cannot wait to be your maid of honour."

I pull her in for a hug when she says that to me. "Speaking of you being my maid of honour…" Withdrawing from her hold, I say, "You do realise that we're going to have to do all of this again very soon so that we can choose your dress too."

Stacey beams at me, her eyes twinkling with excitement. "Another exciting date for what's shaping up to be a *very* busy calendar for the both of us at the moment."

"I'll say, but I am enjoying being so busy with all the wedding planning and everything, and then, when the wedding is over with and I return home from Mauritius as a newly married woman, I am going to set about getting myself a job. I don't know, maybe start auditioning for parts again like I'd originally started to do before all that shit with my dad kicked off."

"I know you don't really want to talk about it today but, how have things been in that department?" Stacey asks me, "Jonny still content to sit back and do nothing? Let nature take its course with your dad?"

I nod. "Yes, and I'm glad, but I didn't force him to come to that decision. Jonny's been working really hard with his counsellor on the whole 'letting things go' stuff and he's made wonderful progress. He's in a much happier place than he was two months ago, and so am I."

"And boy are we all happy to see that," replies Stacey, giving my hand a quick squeeze, and I smile.

"And what about Jonny's dad?" she asks, "how's he been of late?"

I grimace. "Things are never going to be the same between Jonny and his dad after everything he did but, his dad accepted the fact that Jonny didn't want to dig up any more shit on my dad and he's respected that decision."

"And what about the whole band manager stuff and the record label they co-own together? Has Jonny thought any more about that side of things?"

I sigh. "Jonny has surprisingly left the record label side of things hanging at the moment. He said he's got too much on and adding legal shit on top of everything else is just too much to think about. His dad has therefore agreed to stay on as a silent partner for now, which I don't think is a bad idea. Jonny has however reaffirmed to his dad that he definitely doesn't want him to be the band's manager anymore and Jonny has actually said that he doesn't think they even need a manager. They more or less manage themselves."

"I suppose they do," Stacey agrees. "How did Pete take that news?"

"Pretty well. I mean, I think he may have been silently hoping that Jonny would change his mind but he certainly hasn't pushed Jonny on the matter since they had that discussion. In all honesty, I do think Pete has a whole lot of regrets and I do think he wants to change, for Jonny's sake, but whether it's too little too late for Jonny, I'm still not entirely sure."

"Only time will tell I suppose," says Stacey, "although if you ask me, Jonny really needs to keep that man at arm's-length from now on."

"Well, Jonny hasn't invited him to our wedding so if that isn't keeping his dad at arm's-length then I don't know what is."

"It's for the best, Lauren," says Stacey, giving me a reassuring smile.

"I know." I nod. "It just feels a little bit shit that neither of us will have any parents with us on our wedding day, but…we have you and the lads and that's all that matters. Right?"

"Right," Stacey agrees, giving me a quick cuddle.

Our attention is thankfully diverted away from any more serious talk as the waiter finally arrives at our table with a bottle of champagne and a tray of canapes. Stacey and I dive into the canapes straight away, hoping against hope that the food will start to soak up some of the alcohol.

"Mmm, these canapes are delicious," says Stacey. She lets out a little moan of pleasure and the male waiter can't help but smile down at the pair of us.

"You ladies celebrating something special this afternoon?" he enquires, as he pours out the champagne for us.

"Oh yes," says Stacey enthusiastically. Grabbing me by the shoulders, she pulls me hard against her and says, "My best friend has just chosen her wedding dress so we are all about the celebrations today."

I flush pink at suddenly being the centre of attention, the male waiter now smiling away at my best friend as he finishes up pouring our drinks.

"And how about you?" he says to Stacey. "You getting married any time soon or are you already married?"

I can't help but look on in amusement as Stacey's cheeks turn the deepest colour of red I think I've ever seen on her. Okay, maybe not quite as red as when she first met Jonny, or Ben, or the rest of Reclamation for that matter, but right now, Stacey looks shocked that she's actually being hit on for the first time in god knows how long, having now settled down into a happy and contented life out here in LA with Ben.

Hard to believe that Ben wanted to settle down at all but then, my best friend is pretty damn special. In fact, Ben was so smitten with Stacey that once they got back together and sorted out their differences, Ben moved Stacey in with him straight away. And the rest, as they say, is history.

"Erm, I'm not getting married but, I'm taken. In fact, I'm more than taken, I'm…"

"Thanks so much for the champagne and the canapes," I say to the waiter, cutting Stacey off from any further blabbering. "Do you know when we might expect the main course? We're starving."

Placing the bottle of champagne back into the bucket of ice, the waiter gives us a polite smile and then says, "I'll go and check on that for you now. No problem."

He nods and then turns on his heel and walks off, presumably to the kitchen to check on the whereabouts of our food. Turning back to Stacey, I burst out laughing, and she scowls. "Hey, what was that for?"

"I was saving your ass."

"Saving my ass? I was about to tell that flirty waiter just how taken I was…"

"Exactly. And believe me, Stace, he, along with the rest of the customers in this restaurant, do not need to know just how taken you are. God knows what you were about to say to him."

"You really wanna know?" asks Stacey, a slow, suggestive smile creeping its way across her lips.

"Actually, I don't. But what I would really like to know is, how is that man of yours feeling about being Jonny's best man? Has he prepared his speech yet?"

Stacey grimaces. "Erm...not exactly."

My face drops, panic already setting in. "Why are you grimacing? And what do you mean? Not exactly?"

Resting back against the sofa cushions, Stacey sighs. "Look, I don't want to worry you but, now that you've asked, I can't lie..."

"Can't lie about what?"

With a shrug of her shoulders, Stacey says, "Well, Ben isn't exactly great with words, is he?" Okay, blunt and straight to the point, got to love Stacey for never ever mincing her words.

"Okay, but surely..."

"Uh uh." Stacey shakes her head. "Lauren, I'm worried he won't be able to write a speech, or at least, I'm worried he won't be able to write a speech that doesn't have some sort of smut or innuendo in there somewhere along the way..."

"Well it doesn't matter. There's only going to be the six of us at the wedding so whatever Ben says will only be between the six of us anyway."

"Oh I don't know, maybe I'm doing him an injustice by doubting his speech writing skills but I'm only voicing it because I'm worried about him."

"You've got nothing at all to worry about. I'm sure Ben will write a great best man's speech."

Stacey takes a quick sip of champagne before setting her

glass back down on to the table. "I just get the vibe from Ben that he really wants to make something special of this speech. He's honestly so bowled over that Jonny even asked him to be his best man instead of asking Will or Zack, but he's absolutely adamant he doesn't want to have the piss taken out of him at the end of it. Normally, Ben is all about the banter, as you well know, but, I can tell that this best man thing really means a lot to him, and he wants Jonny to take him seriously. Just for this once."

I reach for Stacey's hand and squeeze it gently. "I promise you now that Jonny will take Ben seriously on our wedding day."

"You'll talk to him?" asks Stacey.

Smiling, I say, "You leave Jonny to me and I'll leave Ben and his best man's speech to you. Deal?"

Looking relieved, Stacey is quick to agree to my idea. "Deal."

CHAPTER 16

LAUREN

It's early evening by the time we leave the restaurant and because we are at the happy drunk stage, Stacey and I take it upon ourselves to get Andy, Jonny's bodyguard, to drive us over to the record label to surprise the lads. Andy has been driving us around all day long and I'm actually beginning to feel a bit sorry for him now. Okay, I'm feeling a lot sorry for him, especially as he's now having to listen to the drunken antics of two very loud and very giddy women who are so damn happy that they are literally singing about their happiness from the rooftops. Or in our case, the hills, as in Beverly Hills....

Thankfully, the car journey over to the record label isn't too long although Andy would probably say otherwise, poor man is probably going deaf by now thanks to our endless singing in the back of the Range Rover. And our singing doesn't stop there. Hell no. We continue to belt out one song after another as Andy, bless him, escorts us all the way from the car park, through the bright red double entrance doors, all the way up to Reclamation's recording studio on the top floor, before finally leaving us to it.

Stacey and I have been here before of course, just a few months ago, when Jonny, Ben, Will and Zack gave us a full tour of the place. It was a magical day and one I will never ever forget. This time round however, we are more than a little inebriated to say the least and I'm actually beginning to wonder whether the lads will receive us so well, considering the state we're in. Oh well, only one way to find out.

Stacey and I stumble our way through the door into the recording studio, laughing loudly at the fact that somehow or other, we've ended up here instead of carrying on with our girly time out. We're hardly in any fit state to carry on drinking though, and looking at the now amused faces of Jonny, Ben, Will and Zack, I'd say they agree with us.

"Well this is a turn up for the books," says Ben, grinning widely at the pair of us.

Stacey practically falls into his arms, gushing over how much she loves him, the usual sort of mushy stuff you come out with when you're drunk. "Hey, baby," she says drunkenly, "I've missed you."

That grin of Bens? Just got a whole lot bigger. "Oh, you have?"

Stacey nods enthusiastically before pointing over at me. "Lauren found *the* dress!"

"I found *the* dress!" I shout excitedly, before doing a very drunken dance on the spot.

Jonny, who is sitting over in the corner of the studio with a guitar in his lap, suddenly rises from his seat, places his guitar on the floor and saunters over to me, smiling.

"You found *the* dress?" he asks, reaching for me as I stagger into him.

"I found *the* dress," I whisper, looking up at him hungrily.

I may be a whole lot of drunk this evening but Jonny always, and I mean always, looks so damn hot that I can barely keep my hands off him. Dressed in a figure hugging v-neck black t-shirt, stone washed black denim jeans and biker boots, I take a moment to really appreciate my tattooed rock star standing in front of me.

He looks so much healthier now than he did all those months ago, and so much happier too. I am so proud of how far he has come with his recovery and it just goes to show that being happy in your life, being truly happy, makes all the difference in the world. I should know, because I feel exactly the same as him.

Throwing my arms around his neck, probably a little too enthusiastically, I smile against his lips as I say, "I love you future husband."

Jonny smiles right back at me and then kisses me softly as the others begin to whistle and throw suggestive comments our way. Jonny ignores them and says, "I love you too…future wife."

"Fuck me, could you two get a room?" says Ben, groaning his annoyance. The others all laugh.

Pulling his mouth away from mine, Jonny looks over at Ben and says, "That shit's getting really old, Benny boy, can't you think of something new to throw at us instead of the usual 'get a room' remark?"

"I'll throw a fucking bag of ice cubes over the two of you instead if you want? That should put your fire right out, Jonny." Ben grins and then flashes a wink my way, thinking he's got one up on me and Jonny, and so I hit him right back with a suggestive comment of my own.

"Oh, I highly doubt anything could put Jonny's fire out," I say to Ben.

Will and Zack whoop loudly at my clever ass comeback and I turn back to Jonny who is now chuckling away at my smutty remark. "Nice one, baby."

"She's got one hell of a smart mouth on her, Jonny, I'll give her that," quips Ben.

"Oh, you have no idea," Jonny murmurs, his eyes glittering wickedly.

I can feel the tension crackling already between me and Jonny, that familiar fire sparking to life in my belly, heat pooling between my thighs as I think of when and where to put this so called 'smart mouth' of mine to good use.

"Okaaay," says Stacey, sensing the tension, "I think it's time we left these two 'lovebirds' to it."

I glance over at Will and Zack as they start to pack away their things, and I suddenly feel guilty. "Oh please don't pack up on our account. Shit, we've interrupted your recording time, haven't we?" I pull an overly dramatic face and Will laughs.

"Nah, we were pretty much finished up in here for the day anyway," says Will, "plus, Zack is getting a little antsy for his fix of nicotine round about now. Right Zack?"

Stepping out from behind his drumkit, Zack pulls out his packet of fags from his t-shirt pocket and says, "Too true. In fact, you've done me a favour, Lauren, because slave driver here..." He gives Jonny a gentle smack on the shoulder as he walks past us, "...wanted to start recording yet another song on the new album and the rest of us didn't, because we've been at it since ten o'clock this morning."

Jonny raises his eyebrows at Zack. "Hey, if it was up to you, this album wouldn't be finished for another five years. That's how laid back you are."

I give Jonny a swipe on the arm for throwing an insult at Zack but he laughs. "You think I'm kidding?" His eyes swing back to Zack. "Am I right?"

Pressing a fag between his lips, Zack pretends to think about Jonny's question for a moment. "Yeah," he eventually says with a sigh, "I'm afraid he's right."

"You see?" says Jonny, chuckling away at his friend, "now get out of here before I change my mind."

I suddenly feel Will's head coming to rest on my left shoulder. "Jonny will never change his mind now you're here," he says, smirking up at Jonny.

"You lot are idiots," laughs Jonny. "Now leave me with my girl, would you?"

"What did I tell you?" says Will, finally removing his head away from my shoulder. "I think I've just proven my point." I laugh at Will pretending to look so heartbroken that Jonny has chosen me over his friends. For tonight anyway.

Gritting his teeth at his friend, Jonny says, "Goodnight Will."

Will grins. "Goodnight to you two sickeningly in love but fantastic humans. Oh…and don't do anything I wouldn't do." He flashes us a cheeky wink before heading out of the studio with Zack in tow.

"Goodnight to my bestest best friend in the whole wide world," says Stacey, pulling me in for a hug. "And goodnight to your rock star too." Stacey reaches up to give Jonny a hug and a quick kiss on the cheek.

"Goodnight, Stace," says Jonny, smiling down at my best friend, "I'm glad you two enjoyed your girly day together."

"Oh we most certainly did. And we'll be doing it all over again very soon when I go on the hunt for *my* dress."

"We most certainly will," I say, giving my best friend one last squeeze.

"Well, I hope I'm going to be getting a hug after all of this," Ben says, wanting in on the action.

"Oh, go on then." I pull him in for a hug and he gives me a quick peck on the cheek.

"Goodnight, Lauren, and thanks for keeping this one in check," sniggers Ben, gesturing over at Jonny who is now rolling his eyes heavenwards. Turning to Stacey, he then says, "And thanks for getting this one oh so drunk."

Stacey squeals as Ben gives her bottom a quick squeeze. Pulling her into his arms, he then drags her out of the studio, the pair of them laughing happily together as they close the door behind them. Aww, it's so wonderful to see them so loved up and happy. And speaking of being all loved up and happy...

I turn my attention back to my rock star who is now wrapping those deliciously sexy tattooed arms of his around my waist. "So, this wedding dress of yours...describe it to me..."

"Oh no." I shake my head at him. "You're not allowed to know anything about my wedding dress, Jonny. It's bad luck, and I don't know about you but I think you and I have had our fill of bad luck over these last few months so I'd rather not take that chance. You'll just have to wait until the big day."

Jonny narrows his eyes on me as he scrutinises my face, his hands beginning to smooth their way over my bottom through the fabric of my dress. "Mmm, so you're drunk, but not drunk enough to spill secrets about your wedding dress. Sounds like the perfect amount of drunk to me."

I smile as I feel his fingers skirting their way around the hem of my little pink dress. A gorgeous cerise pink dress that Jonny actually picked out for me to wear this morning. The very same dress that almost got taken off me as quickly as it got put on, thanks to Jonny and his never ending attempts to have his way with me before Stacey arrived at our front door. Unfortunately for Jonny, any attempts at having his wicked way with me this morning were futile…until now. Now, this man of mine can have his wicked way with me as much and for as long as he wants. Right here. Right now. In this recording studio of his.

"I really think I want to christen this recording studio of yours, Jonny Mathers," I whisper, brushing my lips against his, just enough, to really get him going.

He lets out a ragged breath as he backs me up against the main console that sits in front of the large window. The window that looks out on to the room below us. When I first came in here all those months ago, I admit that I fantasised about this moment so many times after I'd visited, wondering if we would ever get the chance to make mad, passionate love to each other in the very heart of Reclamation itself. I can't think of anything that turns me on more than Jonny having me in the very place where his music comes to life.

"Make love to me," I breathe, gazing up at him through lustful eyes.

Jonny's eyes suddenly flicker to life, his burning gaze raking over my face as he drags the tip of his index finger back and forth over my bottom lip. I open my mouth as an invitation and Jonny pushes his finger inside. I suck hard on his finger, moaning softly as Jonny stares at me with an intensity that sets my insides on fire. I want more than just a taste of his finger. I want to taste him. All of him. Right now.

Withdrawing his finger from my mouth, Jonny looks a little surprised when I suddenly push him backwards into one of the nearby chairs. "Lauren, what are you…"

Dropping to my knees right in front of him, I don't even allow Jonny to finish that sentence as I yank down the zipper of his jeans in desperation, quickly freeing his erection from his boxer shorts.

"Jesus," he groans, as I lick the tip of his already glistening cock with my tongue.

"Mmm, you taste so good," I whisper, locking eyes with him as I open my mouth and take him fully in. As far as he will go. Jonny lets out a loud hiss from between his teeth, pulling at my hair as I start to worship him how he deserves to be worshipped. I suck him hard and slow at first, pumping the root of his cock with my fist over and over.

I watch as the colour rises in Jonny's cheeks, his chest rising and falling rapidly, his groans loud and frenzied as I go down on him harder and faster. I love seeing him come apart in front of me because of what I'm doing to him. The power I hold over him right now is immense. So immense I think I might come right along with him, and he isn't even touching me down there.

"Lauren...stop..." Jonny's feeble protests of telling me to stop fall on deaf ears. I want this. I want him to come in my mouth because I want to taste him. "Baby...I want to come inside you..." Oh, I know he does. But I want this. And I intend to get it.

Unable to hold back for a second longer, Jonny comes with a loud groan of release and I swallow down every last drop of him, taking delight in the fact I am sucking him dry. Jonny's head falls against the back of the chair as he tries desperately to catch his breath.

Once I've had my fill of him, I pull my mouth away and stand up, but no sooner have I stood up and Jonny is grabbing me by the hips, pulling me straight into his lap. Fisting his hands into my hair, his darkened eyes sear into mine, and I can see the want, the need, the sheer desperation to have me swirling around in his lust fuelled gaze.

"As incredible as that was...I recall telling you to stop," he says to me breathlessly.

I press a soft, wet kiss to his lips before trailing featherlight kisses along his jawline. He smells intoxicating and he tastes absolutely divine. "But you tasted too damn good to stop," I whisper into his ear.

I begin to wriggle in his lap, the deep ache between my thighs becoming almost unbearable. I am so wet for him, so damn ready that I can't bear the agonising wait for much longer.

Any restraint Jonny had left is suddenly gone. Before I know what's happening, he's grabbing me roughly by the thighs, standing up from the chair, and walking us back over to the main console where we were earlier. He slams me down on to it like he means business. And he really means business.

"You started it your way," Jonny growls against my lips, as he hitches my dress up to my waist, "and now I'm finishing it *my* way."

Jonny yanks my thong down my legs in desperation before dropping to his knees right in front of me. Spreading my legs wide, he looks up at me, his eyes blazing with desire. I sit there, panting in desperation, watching him as he slowly, oh so slowly, starts to kiss the insides of my upper thighs.

I plunge my hands into his hair, my head rolling backwards as I give myself over to Jonny completely. I moan softly as I feel his tongue making its way between my legs, his mouth worshipping me as mine worshipped him just moments before.

I grab the back of his head, urging him on, wanting more of him. So much more. With Jonny, I always want more. "Oh god," I groan, closing my eyes as I feel the familiar deep seated ache building up within me.

Jonny licks and sucks at my clit until I am literally a sopping wet mess of nothing but pleasure. I can feel my orgasm beginning to build already, my body desperate for release, but just as I'm about to come, Jonny then pulls his mouth away.

I look down at him in frustration. "Jonny, what are you…"

Jonny's mouth is on mine so quick, I can barely finish my sentence. He stands up and kisses me deeply, grabbing at my hair as he insinuates himself between my legs. "When I told you I was finishing this my way, I meant it," he growls, before slamming his cock into me. I moan loudly at the sudden invasion.

"Feel how hard I still am for you, baby," he pants, as he thrusts into me hard and fast, "even after you worshipped me with your mouth. Feel what you do to me. All. The. Fucking. Time." *Oh. My. God.*

Jonny's wild and untamed side is definitely out to play tonight and I am lapping him up. Every last drop of him. His dirty words, his roughness, the fact he's still so hard for me, so desperate to always get inside me, it almost blows my head off. I tighten my legs around his waist, the pair of us almost fighting with each other to get to that finish line. Together this time.

And hell do we get there. We scream and shout, our hungry mouths biting and nipping at each other, fingernails digging into flesh, as the sheer ferocity of our orgasm almost rips us apart. It all feels so angry and rushed. So needy. And I get high on that feeling. High on Jonny and what he does to me and my body.

We cling to each other afterwards, both sweaty, breathless and a little dishevelled to say the least. "You should get drunk with Stacey more often," says Jonny with a cheeky smile.

Grasping his face between my hands, I say, "You and I both know that I don't need to be drunk for you to get me into bed, or in this case, your recording studio." Jonny laughs.

"Maybe not, but when you're drunk, you're even dirtier than you are when you're sober, and I like that. I like that a lot."

"Oh, you do?" I say, smiling against his mouth.

"Damn fucking right I do," he murmurs. He plants a deliciously wet kiss to my lips and then says, "Right, home time for us two I think."

CHAPTER 17

JONNY

We are literally days away from jetting off to Mauritius for our wedding and our house is as quiet as can be. Lauren has organised absolutely everything down to the very last detail, and she's loved every minute of the planning that's been involved, particularly over the last couple of months when the planning became really full on.

It's down to her excellent organisation skills as to why our house is so quiet, because everything, so I've been told, is done. There is nothing else left to do apparently. Well, all except one thing of course…the actual getting married to each other part. Which is the best part in all of this. The part I feel I've been waiting for my whole life.

I smile as I watch Lauren swimming length after length in our swimming pool, my girl finally taking the time to relax after all the running around she's been doing of late. I'm led out on one of the sun loungers around our pool, drinking a couple of beers as I smoke my way through a packet of cigarettes. The early October sunshine is especially hot today, and boy do I intend to soak up that rays.

Originally, I was going to head over to the label to continue recording our new album today, but Lauren talked me out of it, telling me I needed to slow down. I reluctantly agreed, and to be fair, I think she's right. These last couple of months have been absolutely manic for the pair of us, Lauren throwing herself into everything wedding related and me working solidly over at the recording studios with the lads.

I really want to get this new album nailed down now and the completion of the album isn't a million miles away, but I can't quite see the finish line as yet either. I'm admittedly not the most patient man when it comes to wanting to get things finished but at the end of the day, the album has to be absolutely perfect, and you don't get perfection from rushing.

I lie back on my sun lounger and peer through my sunglasses at the back of our house, this wonderful new home of ours we have now created. A feeling of contentment settles into my gut, the likes of which I haven't felt since I first moved in with Lauren back in Manchester all those years ago. We've only lived here for a couple of months but it feels like we've been here forever. This house was so made for us. A house that is now most definitely a home. *Our* forever home.

You can see from the exterior design that this property has clearly been inspired by Spanish style architecture, and that Mediterranean/Spanish style theme continues throughout the entire house. From the large white walled foyer with a majestic sweeping staircase leading off, to the grand living room with its original cove ceiling, chandelier, and oversized fireplace, this house is absolutely teeming with character.

With a breakfast island situated in the centre, the kitchen is spacious and a little more low key than the living room, and we also have a separate dining room this time round as well. A dining room with low hanging lights which are suspended above a large rectangular shaped oak dining table with eight chairs, the perfect size for entertaining our friends. Not that we've had much chance to entertain anybody since moving in here. But we have all the time in the world for that. We have forever. Forever and always, as I keep repeating over and over to Lauren whenever I get the opportunity. And she always says it right back to me, smiling as she does.

Finishing up my fag, I stub out the dog end into the ashtray on the little table next to my sun lounger and then reach for my bottle of beer. Taking a quick swig, I look over at Lauren swimming yet another length of the pool. Honestly, I could watch her swimming all day long. And not just because she's wearing a skimpy bikini leaving little to the imagination. Don't get me wrong, I'm all for Lauren wearing skimpy bikinis in our swimming pool but, just seeing her so happy and content is what I love seeing the most. Which is why this really is my favourite part of the house. The outside. The back of the house which is accessed via the second living room or media room as we like to call it.

Light green French doors open up from the media room and lead out through a small archway and into the courtyard area, where the swimming pool is located. Beautiful flowers adorn the archway as well as the two Juliet balconies located on the first floor directly above, which is where our bedroom is.

To the right of the media room, in the far corner of the house, is one of the largest rooms on the ground floor where I decided to house my music studio, my grand piano and the rest of my musical instruments taking up residence in there permanently now. A rectangular shaped window looks out on to a huge rose garden that leads off the courtyard, which is accessed via a large stone archway, that Spanish like feel I mentioned earlier having been woven through the entire inside and outside of this beautiful property.

And that beautiful rose garden is where we intend to scatter Oliver's ashes, when we both feel ready. The wooden box containing his ashes is currently sitting on the window sill in my music studio, overlooking the very same rose garden. We couldn't think of anywhere more fitting than having him spend the rest of his days in a garden filled with nothing but flowers. And colour. So many vibrant colours in a rose garden absolutely buzzing with life. And our Oliver deserves nothing less than that. Even though he is no longer physically with us, his very soul is still a part of us, and always will be.

For as long as Lauren and I draw breath into our bodies, our son will never ever leave us, and having this rose garden will ease some of the grief I think. It will be Oliver's place and nobody else's. *Oliver's Garden*. I love the sound of that. In fact, I'll make a mental note to mention it to Lauren when I feel it appropriate to raise the subject.

Maybe we could get a little sign over the archway or something, if Lauren agrees. We shall see. For now, I will park the idea until another day, because I want Lauren to stay in her happy place in readiness for our wedding, and I intend to stay in that happy place right along with her.

Starting with joining her in the swimming pool and distracting her from this swimathon she seems to be intent on doing today. Not for much longer though. Well, when my girl is wearing a bikini as skimpy as that one is, what's a man to do....

****

It's early evening and Lauren and I are sitting at the breakfast island in the kitchen, eating our meal. Lauren has made a lasagne to die for, proving to me, yet again, that her talents in the kitchen are as outstanding as her talents in the bedroom....

"I still can't quite believe it's only three more days until we fly over to Mauritius with our friends," says Lauren, loading up her fork with more of her delicious lasagne. "I mean, when we initially booked it, even though it wasn't far off, it felt like time was dragging for ages, but then these last few weeks have just flown by. I honestly can't wait to get there now." She beams brightly at me and I smile.

"I know. Me too." Reaching for her hand from across the

breakfast island, I give it a gentle squeeze. Turning my attention back to my food, I then say, "Although, I also can't quite believe I'm going to be in the company of Ben for two full weeks. Now *that's* going to be tough."

Grinning like the childish school boy I can be sometimes, I glance up at Lauren once more and am met with a raising of the eyebrow in return. "Hey, you promised me you weren't going to take the piss out of him…"

"On our wedding day only," I state, chuckling to myself.

"Jonny…"

"Oh come on, baby, you know I'm only kidding."

I'm really not kidding. I can't imagine being able to reel in any sarcasm, banter or quick wit when it comes to Ben, and taking the piss out of him is pretty much what keeps me going some days, when we're in each other's company anyway, but, as Lauren has pressed upon me so many times these last few weeks, I am to leave Ben well and truly alone on our wedding day.

He's taking the part of being my best man very seriously apparently, and both Lauren and Stacey are afraid that if I poke fun at him on our special day, then it'll hurt him. And as much as I love to take the piss out of my best friend, I'd never want to intentionally hurt his feelings. Which is why I promised to behave myself…for the one day at least.

She raises both eyebrows at me this time and I shake my head at her. "Look, sarcasm and banter is how Ben and I roll, but…I promise to take him seriously on our wedding day. I've already promised you I will."

"Hmm, well forgive me for doubting that overly sarcastic tongue of yours, Jonny Mathers."

"Sarcasm isn't the only quality my tongue has been blessed

with, baby. You should know." I flash her a cheeky wink and she raises her eyes heavenwards.

Yep, there it is, my smart mouth running away with me all over again. I can't help it. It's like a reflex or a compulsion, and something I really struggle to suppress. Shit, me being well behaved on our wedding day is perhaps going to be tougher than I first thought....

"I'd hardly call sarcasm a quality, Jonny," replies Lauren, looking none too pleased with how this conversation is going.

"I beg to differ," I reply, shoving another forkful of this scrumptious lasagne into my mouth.

"Of course you do," says Lauren, sighing at me.

I grin over at her. "Okay, okay, I'm taking the piss, I know, but I can't help it."

"Well for once in your life how about you try to help it and behave?"

"Oh, you love it when I misbehave and don't pretend otherwise."

Lauren shakes her head at me but I can see that little hint of a smile playing on her lips that she's desperately trying to hide from me. She doesn't fool me. Not one bit. I decide right there and then to put an end to this conversation, by reaching across the breakfast island and dropping a soft, tender kiss on to those luscious lips of hers. When I pull away, she is smiling. *Of course she's smiling.* She can never stay annoyed at me for too long.

Sitting myself back down on my stool, I continue enjoying my food while Lauren enjoys hers. After a moment or two, Lauren hits me with a question that knocks me back a bit.

"So, have you spoken to your dad this week?"

My fork pauses mid-air and I frown over at her. "Fuck me, that's a conversation changer if ever I've heard one. Where did that question come from?"

She shrugs a shoulder at me. "Nowhere..."

"Well it clearly came from somewhere," I say, feeling suddenly irritated. I almost throw the last forkful of lasagne into my mouth as Lauren looks on. "And why would I hear from him anyway?"

Resting her fork down on to her plate, Lauren looks over at me, a look of uncertainty plastered across her beautiful face. Uncertainty over whether or not to continue this line of questioning no doubt. Well, too late for that now.

Finishing up my meal, I place my cutlery down on to my empty plate and sit back in my stool. Folding my arms across my chest, I say, "Look, you clearly want to say something about my dear old dad so just say it."

With a heavy sigh, Lauren says, "I just thought that as we're getting married soon...maybe he...I don't know...might have wanted to get in touch to wish you well, or..."

"He's not welcome at our wedding, Lauren, and that's the end of it," I snap, feeling pissed off. Pissed off at the fact she's still considering my dad's feelings in all of this. After everything he ever did to her. To us.

"I know," she says, looking a little guilty, "I just..." Her voice trails off and I admit it, my patience with her is evaporating, and fast.

"Just what?" I ask impatiently. "What is it?"

Averting her gaze, she instead looks down in her lap. I have no doubt that she's knotting her fingers together on the other side of the breakfast island right now, something she does a lot of when she's nervous or anxious.

"I can't help but still feel a little upset that neither of us will have any parents at our wedding," she eventually says to me.

"Stacey, Ben, Will and Zack will be there with us. They're our family, Lauren, and they're the only family we'll ever need," I reply, firmly.

I keep my voice firm deliberately, in the hope that Lauren will snap out of any guilt she may be holding on to right now. Guilt over something that neither she, nor I, should be made to feel guilty about. Because none of what happened was our fault. Absolutely none of it. And I especially don't want her to feel guilty over my dad not being invited to our wedding. I want our wedding day to be magical and I will not allow the shadow of my father to taint it.

Glancing up at me once more, Lauren says, "I know they are. It just feels strange, that's all."

I nod. "I know it does, but...do you remember that saying? Something about blood being thicker than water?"

She frowns, clearly unsure of where I'm going with this. "Yeah, I've heard of it, but how is that..."

"Well that saying is complete bullshit," I say, cutting her off, "because blood doesn't run thicker than water. Not for us anyway."

I reach for my bottle of beer from the worktop and take a few gulps, draining the bottle dry. Placing the empty beer bottle back down, Lauren then reaches for my hand. Linking her fingers through mine, she gazes over at me from across the breakfast island and I swear to god, my chest almost explodes with emotion.

How does she do that? Get me all riled up one minute over a subject that is clearly still more than bothering me, and the next, turn my insides to fucking mush with just one look. One look. One touch of the hand. That's all it takes to bring me back down to earth again, and with Lauren, it was always this way. I swear she weaves some magical spell over me that reels me in. Every. Single. Time.

"I'm sorry," she whispers, "for bringing something up that is clearly triggering for you. I just wish things were different."

"And you think I don't? Fuck, Lauren, I'd give my right arm if it meant bringing back your mum and my mum. I'd even give away my other arm if me doing that would take every bad thing away our fathers ever did to us, but I can't, and I'm sorry I can't." And I really mean that. With every fibre of my being, I mean it.

Lauren brushes her thumb back and forth over my knuckles as she gazes over at me longingly. "You don't need to be sorry, Jonny. I'm the one who's sorry for bringing it up."

"How about we both stop saying sorry for the actions of others and instead re-focus on the fact that we are getting married next week."

The excitement soon returns to Lauren's face, her smile almost splitting her beautiful face in two. "But we'll be flying over there in three days," she says excitedly, "just three more days, Jonny!"

"That's my excited girl right there," I reply, reaching over the breakfast island for a quick kiss.

"I love you," she whispers, pressing her hands on either side of my face.

Smiling down at the woman I love more than anything else in this world, I murmur, "I love you more."

CHAPTER 18

JONNY

The following morning, Lauren and I take the time to go through the last few details of our wedding. We check over the booking, we look through our luggage - me being kept well away from the suitcase that contains her wedding dress of course - and basically we work together to tick things off the million and one lists she seems to have made over these last few weeks.

We don't really need to do it but Lauren insists that we do, sort of as a last go over of things to make absolutely sure everything is in place, which of course it is. And with Lauren at the helm, I don't think it could ever be anything else.

I swear my girl could be a wedding planner, she's *that* organised, but, dancing is her passion and I have to admit, I can't imagine Lauren doing anything else. One day, that beautiful fiancée of mine will be showing the world exactly what she is made of, and I'll be sitting on that front row in the theatre somewhere cheering her on. But until that moment arrives, she can continue to dance up close and personal for me and me alone.

Once all the checking through things to do with the wedding is done with, I decide to sit by the swimming pool on one of the sun loungers while Lauren busies herself in the kitchen making us some breakfast. I offered to help but I got told I was nothing but a distraction, so I quickly made myself a coffee and came out here. In the glorious LA sunshine.

I swear I could get used to lounging around the pool every single day, if life would allow. I never used to take the time out to do anything like this but now that Lauren and I have settled into our life out here together, I am hoping to be able to do this more and more. In between being busy with the band of course. Reclamation's diary for next year is going to be packed full and as excited as I am to be getting back out there again, I'm also terrified. Terrified of going back on to the stage and into the limelight and fucking it up all over again. *Keep your mind on positive thoughts, Jonny. Positive thoughts only.*

It's only as I take a sip of my coffee I then realise I forgot to bring out my packet of fags. They're on the breakfast island in the kitchen. I was so busy trying to deliberately distract Lauren from making breakfast that I completely forgot all about bringing them out here with me.

Oh well, looks like I'll have to get my ass back up off this sun lounger and go back inside to get them. I might even try distracting Lauren again, just for the hell of it. She pretends to get annoyed at my ever wandering hands and distracting ways but I know she loves it really. In fact, she pretty much encourages it most of the time. That's my excuse for never being able to keep my wandering hands off her anyway. Not that I need an excuse....

As soon as I step foot back into the kitchen, I know something is off. Lauren is on her mobile phone, pacing back and forth, a look of worry etched across her beautiful features.

Fuck, something's happened with the wedding planning I bet. I can tell. All that meticulous organising and now the shit's hit the fan. This is the last thing we need.

Lauren is biting nervously on her thumbnail, still pacing around the kitchen. She glances over at me as I approach her cautiously, but then she turns away from me. *What the fuck?*

I follow slowly behind her, trying to listen in to what she is saying.

"Look, as I said before, we've been estranged for a very long time. I appreciate you had to let me know but going forward, I don't want to be contacted ever again after this, and I certainly don't want to be involved in anything else to do with him."

Him? Oh fuck. A feeling of unease begins to worm its way into my gut, sweeping all feelings of contentment and relaxation I've been feeling of late to one side. This is to do with her dad again. I know it. I can feel it in my bones, in my very blood. What the fuck has that bastard done now? And who the fuck is on the other end of the phone?

I knew I should have put things to bed with him like I originally intended to. I should have allowed my dad to pursue that mother fucker after all. Someone somewhere would have testified against that bastard for something, both me and my dad were damn sure of that. It would have been a long drawn out process but the ends would have justified the means.

When I try to signal to Lauren to tell me who's on the phone, she turns away from me again. Hell, I'm losing my head here. I can feel the anxiety creeping its way back in, my mind automatically zoning in on the worst case scenario imaginable. I can't handle this. I really can't. I am just about to storm over to where Lauren is standing on the other side of the breakfast island when Lauren finally finishes up with her phone call.

Turning to face me, her sorrowful eyes meet with mine and I swear I nearly crumble. Pain flashes across my chest as I watch the sadness returning to Lauren's eyes, her happiness being washed away and replaced with tears. More tears. More fucking heartbreak. But I don't know why. I have to know why.

"What is it?" My voice is barely a whisper, the fear of the

unknown still strangling its way around me like a venomous snake, suffocating me from the inside out.

Deliberately breaking eye contact with me, Lauren places her mobile phone down on to the breakfast island and sighs heavily. After a beat, her beautiful blue eyes lock with mine once more and she finally speaks. "The bastard is dead," she says to me quietly.

What. The. Fuck. "You mean..."

I struggle to get my words out, this sudden and unexpected turn of events rendering me speechless. In fact, I'm in shock. We both are. So much so that the pair of us say nothing for about a minute or two, both trying to silently process this newfound information. That Jimmy Whittle, Lauren's father, is dead. After all the years of hurt he inflicted upon his daughter, the unspeakable pain he put her through for so very long, and finally, the vile, disgusting human being that was Jimmy Whittle is now dead.

Well, as shocking as this news is, more so for Lauren than me, I couldn't feel more relieved. For her. For Lauren. Even so, whether I feel relieved or not, I am still unsure as to how Lauren is going to take this news. As crazy as that sounds.

"How...who was..."

My words are lost all over again. I have so many questions and yet for some reason, my tongue will not form the words to fucking speak. Lauren sighs.

"That was a police officer from the UK on the phone. They found him a couple of days ago apparently, led out on his kitchen floor. Looks as though he fell and hit his head when he was steaming drunk. Most likely died on impact. His body had been there for a few days by the time they found him, according to the police. No foul play is suspected and they've been trying to trace any living relatives as per the procedures they have to work through…and they eventually found me, his only living relative."

Glancing down at the floor, Lauren then runs her hands up and down her arms, almost like she's feeling cold. And she continues to stand there in silence, in the middle of the kitchen, looking as awkward as can be. Right now, all I want to do is run over to her, scoop her up into my arms and comfort her, but I'm being cautious here, because I really don't know how she is taking this news.

"Baby…I…"

"I told them I don't want to be contacted ever again and that I want nothing to do with anything involving that man, including his funeral. He owned nothing, he has no estate, no will, no money, no anything…the bastard only ever had me. And even when he didn't have me in his life, he still did…up here…" Looking up at me, she taps her index finger against her left temple. "And even now, in death, he still does."

Taking a cautious step around the breakfast island towards her, I say, "Baby, I know this is a shock, but…you're free of him now. Forever. Please hold on to that thought in all of this…"

"Free of him?" She laughs humourlessly, her sadness from moments ago being rapidly replaced by anger. "You think I'll finally be free of him, Jonny?"

"Lauren…" I try to speak but she cuts me off.

"You know, even in death, he couldn't just wait, could he?!" she spits out at me. "He couldn't fucking wait and he had to die now! Three days before we fly over to Mauritius! A week before our wedding! The selfish bastard couldn't have done it long before now or weeks *after* our wedding? He had to do it now! Well, he's had the last laugh after all because look at me now, Jonny!" She thumps a balled up fist into her chest, angry tears now streaming down her cheeks. "That bastard is probably laughing up at me from hell right now!"

I can't stand to see her looking so distraught for a minute longer, so I rush over to her, but she pushes me away. "Don't hug or embrace me, Jonny! I don't want to be comforted because of *him*!" Swiping angrily at her tears, she then says, "These tears aren't for him you know!"

"I know," I say to her quietly. And I do know. I know better than anyone.

She then dissolves into sobs, huge wracking sobs, and that's it, I'm done in. I don't give a shit if she says she doesn't want comforting right now, because I am comforting my girl, whether she wants me to or not.

Lauren comes willingly into my arms this time, her body shaking with the sheer strength of her sobs, years and years of pain spewing out of her like a violent volcano beginning to erupt. The timing is all wrong of course, but I'm silently relieved. Lauren will be too, eventually, once the initial shock has worn off and she's finally wrapped her head around it all.

It's a cruel twist of fate though, her dad dying only a week before our wedding. Lauren wasn't wrong when she said that just now. It's something her evil bastard of a dad would have laughed at for sure, but I can't voice any of that out loud to her. Right now, I just need to be here for her. I only hope that by the time our wedding comes round, Lauren will be back in her happy place once again, because if she isn't, I have no idea what the fuck I'm going to do.

****

After spending the rest of the morning and part of the afternoon calming her down, Lauren finally agreed to allow me to put her to bed so she could get some much needed rest, and thankfully, she's now fallen asleep. Giving me the perfect opportunity to ring Stacey and fill her in on the shocking news.

"Holy shit, I can't believe it," Stacey says to me down the phone. "I mean, this is great news of course but, Lauren no doubt won't be taking it quite that way right now, will she?"

Taking a long pull on my cigarette, I then blow out the smoke from between my lips as I rest my head against the back of the sun lounger. I'm sitting outside by the swimming pool again, well away from the eyes and ears of Lauren. She may be fast asleep at the moment but I'd rather play it safe and talk outside, just in case she wakes up and overhears anything that may upset her even more.

"No, absolutely not. In fact, I think it's triggered her, and that scares the shit out of me. What if she…" I can't even bear to think the words, never mind say them out loud. "Shit, what if she runs away again? Like last time…"

"Oh, Jonny, she didn't run away. Well, she did, but not in the way you think she did. And I know that it still hurts you. Really hurts. But Lauren did it because of her desperate need to protect you at the time. Much like you've protected her so many times in the past. This situation with her dad passing away is nothing like that. Lauren will be feeling all sorts of conflicting emotions right now. Relief, anger, upset. She's most likely reliving everything he ever did to her, as well as feeling heartbroken about the timing of it all. And it's most likely the timing of her dad's passing that has done this to her. Such a cruel twist of the knife but…once the initial shock wears off and the fog lifts, our girl will rise up to the top once more and bring that fighting spirit right along with her, I promise."

Even though she can't see me, I smile down the phone at Stacey. She's such an amazing friend to Lauren, and to me too. We're both very lucky to have her in our life, and I tell her as much. "You know, both Lauren and I are extremely lucky to have you, Stace, and I really need you to know that."

"Oh, I know it," she says, and I can almost hear her smiling away at me, that playful, bubbly personality of hers shining its way through yet another moment of darkness that has descended upon us today. But like Stacey just said, once the initial shock clears and the fog lifts away, Lauren will eventually come to feel that long awaited relief she's been waiting for her entire life. I just have to be careful as to how I navigate her through it over the next couple of days, because I want…fuck, I *need* to get her back to her happy place once more.

"Thanks, Stace, you've already helped me more than you'll ever know."

"I'm here for you and Lauren always. And if you need me to come round to see her before we fly out to Mauritius then please just ring me and I'll be there. I just don't think me calling round right now would help. I think she needs a bit of time to process what's happened and let's face it, she has you by her side to help her with that."

"Always," I say, finishing up my smoke.

"Keep me updated," says Stacey.

"Will do, thanks, Stace."

I end the call and lie back on my sun lounger, pondering over what the fuck to do next. I'll leave her be for now, because that's all I can do really. Hopefully once she wakes up later on, she'll feel a little calmer about the day's events. Here's hoping.

****

It's gone 6.00 pm by the time Lauren wakes from her slumber. She finds me downstairs in the kitchen, contemplating whether or not I should make us something for tea. I admit that I'm absolutely shit when it comes to cooking or anything even remotely food related, but I'm at least willing to try and put something together for the two of us, even if Lauren doesn't feel up to eating.

"Hey, I was just about to make us something to eat. You feeling hungry?"

Even though Lauren still looks a little downhearted and quiet, she still can't pass up an opportunity to comment on something that clearly amuses her. "Seriously? *You're* going to cook?"

Sliding into one of the stools around the breakfast island, Lauren rests her chin in her hand and looks over at me, her lips almost pulling into a smile. *Almost.*

I pretend to look offended. "Hey, I somehow managed to survive without your excellent cooking skills for over ten years of my life, so I think I can just about manage to put something together for us tonight."

That almost smile of Lauren's I just mentioned? It's fading already. "I'm not hungry, Jonny, so save yourself the stress and just sort yourself out."

Walking over to where she is sitting around the breakfast island, I slip what I hope is a comforting arm around her shoulders. Pulling her against me, I kiss the top of her head and say, "You haven't eaten anything at all so far today. You need to eat."

"No, I don't," she replies, glaring up at me. "Now stop fussing over me..."

"Not gonna happen," I state, giving her a glare right back. "Did you sleep? I mean, properly sleep?"

She sighs. "Yes and no...I woke up a couple of times after..."

"After?"

I receive another weary sigh from Lauren, swiftly followed

by the mother of all eye rolls. "Jonny, will you stop badgering me please?"

"Badgering you?" I ask, feeling a little hurt. "Baby, I'm worried about you..."

Shoving my arm away from around her shoulders, Lauren sighs once more and then stands up from her stool. "I just don't want to talk about it. Okay? That man has taken up far too much space in my head to last me a lifetime and I won't allow him to continue to taunt me from beyond the grave."

"Look, I know you don't want to talk about it, but talking helps. You've told me that so many times in our past..."

"Yeah well, maybe I'm eating my own words right now because...I don't want to waste any more time or thoughts on *him*. I want to focus on our wedding and nothing else. Okay?"

I shake my head at her, determined to make her open up and talk to me. I know I probably shouldn't push it with her, but if I don't, and I just allow her to close herself off from me and deal with her own thoughts, then this will eat her alive on the inside. I know it will. Because we've been here before, so many times, and I will not allow this to destroy everything that we've spent the last few months re-building together.

"No. Not okay. Because you are clearly not okay and I want to make you okay. I want to make you better..."

"You can't fix everything, Jonny!" she suddenly yells at me. "You think you can now you've undergone therapy for all of *your* problems but you can't wave some magical therapy like wand over me and make me all better! I am broken! Because of him, I am broken!"

Feeling wounded, I take a step back, almost like she's lashed me in the face with a whip, pain now searing through my heart as her acid like words burn their way through my skin, into my very blood.

"And you don't think I'm fucking broken?" I say to her quietly.

I may be keeping my voice quiet, perhaps for her sake, or maybe even mine, but in all honesty, what I really want to do right now is shout at her. Fuck, I want to yell and scream at her for almost belittling the therapy sessions I've been attending for the last however many months. Therapy sessions Lauren insisted I go to. The very therapy Lauren was apparently so proud of me for doing. The same fucking therapy that managed to pull me out of my darkest ever place!

Lauren of course also helped me a hell of a lot in getting me through that dark time in my life, but, when all said and done, it was the therapy that got me through, and it's still getting me through, even now, all these months later. And yet Lauren is now standing there almost mocking it. And that hurts. It really fucking hurts.

"You know, I've suddenly lost my appetite," I mutter, before storming out of the kitchen and well away from her.

"Jonny, I didn't mean…"

I don't hang around to listen to any pathetic apology Lauren might want to throw my way. Right now, I need to keep my distance from her before I end up saying something I might regret.

****

Lauren and I don't see or speak to each other for the rest of the night after that. I take myself off to my music studio and bury myself in my music, taking any scrap of solace I can get from it. I spend the entire night downstairs, playing my piano endlessly as I try to extinguish that age old anger I feel towards Lauren.

How she can go from making me feel so much love and adoration for her one minute to then making me feel so fucking angry with her the next, I really don't know, but it was pretty much always like that between us. Mostly because we were always so volatile and felt so deeply for one another.

It feels strange, not spending the night in bed with my wife to be, both suddenly at odds with each other just days before we exchange our wedding vows. I so don't want to be in this shitty place with her all over again, which is why I deliberately keep my distance from her all night, in the hope my anger towards her begins to dissipate.

My anger slips away completely when I go upstairs to look for Lauren the following morning. I end up finding her in our en-suite bathroom. Pushing open the bathroom door, my eyes immediately find her, and my chest constricts in pain at the sorry sight I am met with.

She is sitting in the shower cubicle, completely naked, with her legs pulled up to her chest and her arms wrapped around her knees, her head down. The water from the shower is raining down on her and she's shaking uncontrollably from her endless sobbing.

Shit, when I stormed off last night, I thought I was doing the right thing by keeping my distance, allowing my anger to simmer down whilst giving Lauren the space I thought she needed. Looking at her now, I'd say I've gone and royally fucked just about everything up. Days before our wedding and my fiancée is broken.

Well, as I said to her only last night, she isn't the only broken one out of the two of us, but maybe, just maybe, those two broken people can make each other whole again. In fact, we can make each other whole again, and we can heal, I know we can. We just need a fucking break from any more shit from our past being thrown our way, and now that Lauren's dad is out of the picture and gone from our lives for good, that healing process starts now. Right now.

I approach the shower cubicle cautiously, wondering whether or not to strip off my clothes and get in there with her. After a moment or two, I decide to keep my clothes on and get into the shower cubicle with her anyway. The last thing I want is for Lauren to think I'm getting into the shower for any other reason other than to hold and comfort her. I need her to see I am with her in this and that any hurtful words from last night that were thrown my way have long been forgotten. Which they have. Right now, I just want to start mending this broken girl before me. *My* broken girl.

I very slowly slide the shower door open, the noise causing Lauren to look up at me in surprise. Her eyes are bright red and the tears are rolling down her cheeks and I swear it takes every ounce of strength within me to not crumple down into an emotional heap right along with her. But I don't. I need to be strong now. For her. For me. For us.

Stepping into the shower cubicle, which is more than big enough for the two of us, I slide the door closed and then I sit down beside her, fully clothed, and wrap my warm, loving arms around her. She grabs a tight hold of my t-shirt as she buries her face into my chest, her body heaving with the strength of her sobs.

The water falls over the pair of us, my t-shirt and shorts already soaking wet, the material almost gluing itself to my body as Lauren clings on to me in desperation, telling me she's sorry for saying what she said to me last night, sorry for everything. But she doesn't need to be sorry. I am so sick of us both saying sorry that I don't think I want to hear the word fall from our mouths ever again.

"Hush, baby," I whisper into her hair, "I've got you. It's okay.

We're okay. Everything is going to be okay."

As Lauren's sobs slowly begin to fade away, I wonder whether or not I should open up some sort of conversation with her, but I think better of it and instead decide to sing her a song. Lauren's song. A song about her that I wrote for her when we were teenagers. *My Angel.* A personal and private song I never ever released with the band, and a song I never will. This song is for Lauren and Lauren alone.

"Don't you know you'll always be my angel. People said we weren't fit to last, but when I looked into your deep blue eyes, the wind really hit the mast."

Pulling her face away from my sodden t-shirt, Lauren looks up at me in a way like only she can. It's the look she gives me that really works its way inside of me, those deep blue eyes of hers, as referenced in the song, gazing into mine with so much love, so much tenderness, that it stops me in my tracks, making me forget about anything and everything around us. Except for the song. I really need to sing the rest of the song. *Her* song.

"You are my angel, a treasure to behold, you are my angel, my one and only goal. Can you see what you mean to me, my angel, you're all I'll ever need. With all that I have seen, a world so broken and blue, but my angel I exist only for you. Forever yours, forever mine, my angel you are, as though frozen in time. Life after you would never be the same, my one and only angel, forever you remain."

As I finish up the song, Lauren tightens her hold around me, fresh tears now falling from her eyes as the lyrics I wrote for her all those years ago wrap themselves around her, evoking even more emotions from deep inside. I didn't want to add to her sadness, I just wanted to comfort her, in the only way I knew how.

"I always loved that song," she whispers, her voice sounding almost painful, "thank you for singing it to me…and for writing it. It's beautiful. All your songs are beautiful, Jonny. Just like you. You're beautiful. Inside and out."

Trailing the tips of my fingers down her wet cheeks, I press what I hope is a reassuring kiss to her forehead, and she sighs. "You're the beautiful one, baby," I whisper back to her.

"I wasn't so beautiful last night, was I? I'm so sorry…for what I said…I didn't mean…"

"Sssh now, sweetheart, I told you before, it's okay. We're okay."

"I just…don't know how to process it. Any of it. I'm not sad because he's dead. I'm sad because of all the pain he put me through, the son he ripped away from us. And I'm also sad and angry because of the fact he's now gone and had the last laugh by bringing a great big cloud of sorrow over us again, just days before our wedding."

"He's gone, Lauren," I say to her, and she looks up at me. My eyes flick back and forth between hers, the droplets of water from the shower absolutely drenching us, almost like it's purifying us, washing away all the shit from our past once and for all.

"He's gone, and he isn't coming back. Ever. That man will never hurt you again. He might still be in your head right now, tormenting you as you relive all the shit he put you through, but he cannot hurt you again, and he will not ruin your special day. *Our* special day. Because we deserve happiness, Lauren. And I'll be damned if that bastard takes that happiness away, especially from beyond the grave. It's time to move on with our lives. We've said that so many times to each other over these last few months and to a degree, we have moved on, but perhaps we never could, not fully, until now. Now, we really can move on, but I can't do it unless you move on with me. So… are you moving on with me? For real this time?"

Pressing the palm of her hand against my wet cheek, Lauren smiles at me lovingly as she gazes into my eyes. "Oh, of course I'm moving on with you, Jonny…and you're right, I can't allow that man to have a hold over me anymore. And so I won't. I promise you I'll try my utmost to put him out of my mind… forever."

Reaching down, I plant a soft, gentle kiss on her lips. When I pull back, I say, "It won't happen overnight, sweetheart, but eventually it will, and I'll be there with you, every step of the way. One day at a time."

"One day at a time," she repeats back to me.

Raking my fingers through her soaking wet curls, I then say, "So…are you going to marry me next week or what?"

Lauren's happy smile returns to her face when I say that, the truly happy and excitable smile that lights up her eyes, her very soul. "Oh, I'm marrying you alright, rock star. And nothing on this earth, or in the entire universe and beyond for that matter, is going to stop me. You're stuck with me, Mathers, forever and always."

"Forever and always," I whisper, before dropping another kiss on to her lips.

CHAPTER 19

LAUREN

Jonny and I pop the corks on two bottles of champagne as Stacey, Ben, Will and Zack cheer us on, clapping and whooping at the pair of us as we start to get the pre-wedding celebrations well and truly under way. On the plane no less.

Oh yes, we are now on our way to what I know is going to be the most magical two weeks of my life, of *our* life, and I feel so giddy and excited, so bloody happy, that I literally want to scream it from the rooftops. Well, I'll have to settle with screaming it from within the confines of our first class cabin instead.

The cabin crew won't know what's hit them with us six being holed up in here for the next however many hours. And this is just the first flight. We have a change over and a further flight to catch after this one, so god knows what state we'll all be in by the time we do finally get to Mauritius. But, it'll all be worth it in the end. Because, *he* is so worth it. He's worth everything and a whole lot more to me, and I tell him as much.

Turning to my rock star who is sitting in the seat next to me, I smile and then lean over so I can press a quick kiss to his lips. "You're everything to me, Jonny Mathers, you know that?"

Jonny smiles. "Oh, I do know it, baby. Just as you are to me. And don't ever forget it."

"I won't," I murmur, giving him another quick kiss.

"Oh, save it for the wedding night!" Stacey shouts over at me from where she is sitting, directly opposite me. Ben is sitting next to her of course, his hand in hers, grinning over at us suggestively, and Will and Zack are on the other side of the cabin, just a few feet away, laughing away at the never ending banter that always seems to ensue whenever all six of us are together these days.

"Oh, Jonny couldn't possibly wait until our wedding night," I say to Stacey, throwing another suggestive remark into the mix. "Isn't that right, baby?" I turn back to Jonny and he grins.

"Oh, you're right about that, sweetheart. Four more nights before we get married and that would be four nights too many for me."

Our mouths come together once more, Jonny smiling against my lips as our friends begin to wolf whistle and throw yet more suggestive comments our way. All except Ben. Which is a first for him I have to say. Although it soon becomes clear as to why.

"How about you two actually pour out the champagne as opposed to kissing all over it? We're supposed to be starting the celebrations, not watching you two rehearse for your wedding night."

Pulling his lips away from mine, Jonny looks over at Ben and says, "Rehearsal for the wedding night not needed, Benny boy. I've been rehearsing with Lauren from the age of fifteen so I think it's safe to say I've more than locked down my prowess with her in the bedroom. But if you need some extra time to rehearse with your good lady then I'm sure the cabin crew will find somewhere at the back of the plane for you to go and practice. Maybe, I don't know, the cargo hold?"

I can't help it, I burst out laughing when Jonny says that, and Stacey does too. Ben however doesn't look overly impressed at being the 'but' of the jokes all over again. "You always have a smart ass quip to come back with, don't you?" he says, scowling over at Jonny.

Lifting the bottle of bubbles in the air, Jonny says, "Champagne?"

Ben shakes his head at him as Jonny bites down on a smile. Picking up his champagne glass, Ben reluctantly accepts the offer of champagne, allowing Jonny to pour it for him.

"Oh, and just so you know," says Ben, "there ain't no rehearsing needed from me. As Stacey will openly tell you."

Ben shoots Stacey a look and she rolls her eyes at him. "I won't openly tell Jonny anything…"

"But she'll tell *me* everything," I say, flashing her a cheeky wink.

Stacey flushes pink when I say that. Honestly, she pretends to be all sweetness and like around the lads but when she's with me and we're alone, well, needless to say that Stacey likes to share. And she likes to share *everything*. I on the other hand am a bit more picky when it comes to sharing the intimate details of what Jonny and I get up to in the bedroom, or out of it, depending on where we are. But whatever I do share with Stacey, I know for a fact it will never be shared with anybody else. Not even Ben. Thank god. He'd have a field day if he knew some of the things I'd told his girlfriend about the naughty stuff his best friend and I get up to.

"Yeah, okay, enough with all the smutty talk you lot. Hell, Lauren, you haven't even had a drink yet and you're already encouraging them, and believe me, where Ben's concerned, he does not need any encouragement in that department."

"Too true, babe," says Ben, grinning widely, "too true."

"Well, I may not have had a drink as yet, Stace, but I'm giddy and excited and so happy we're all finally on our way to our wedding that my mouth is beginning to run away with me already. Sorry not sorry." I stick my tongue out at her and she smiles, shaking her head at me.

"Well, as you're the radiant bride to be, I'll accept that non-apology, but only if you pour me a drink of those delicious looking bubbles you're holding on to."

"Oh, go on then," I sigh, holding out the bottle of champagne to her. She picks up her champagne glass and I fill it right to the brim.

Jonny then pours out champagne for both Will and Zack as I pour one for myself, and a moment later, we all raise our glasses in the air.

"A toast not only to our impending nuptials," says Jonny, smiling over at me lovingly, "but to friendship…and family."

Turning back to our friends, Jonny looks at each one of them individually as he says, "You four are our family, and without you, all of you, Lauren and I wouldn't be on this flight over to Mauritius with you all today and we certainly wouldn't be getting married. You four are the reason we found each other again, and for that, we love you…all of you." Jonny's eyes swing to Ben. "Even you."

Ben tuts his annoyance but a smile soon follows, because Ben knows, just as I do, as we all do, that Jonny means every single word he just said. Jonny doesn't do over the top soppy public speeches very often, or at all really, always keeping his innermost feelings and emotions locked away for me and me alone, but seeing him say these things today, to our friends, our family, it makes me feel all warm and gooey on the inside for the man I am about to marry. This man who has supported me through thick and thin and got me through the worst of times.

Even just this week, after receiving the shocking news that my dad had finally passed away after all these years, news that admittedly hit me smack bang in the face because it was something that came out of the blue and took me completely by surprise, Jonny was still there for me. Standing tall, unwavering and downright immovable, Jonny never faltered when I needed him the most. Even when I tried to push him away and I hurt him with my nasty words, he still came back to me, comforted me, kissed me, and held me in his arms until the pain I felt inside was no more.

I'm admittedly still struggling with the fact my dad decided to choose now to go and die on me, almost like he was having the last laugh from down below, but, when all said and done, the timing is inconsequential really. As Jonny said to me shortly after it happened, my dad is now gone. Forever. And whilst the memories of the pain he once put me through will no doubt continue to torture me for some time to come, they will eventually begin to fade. In fact, they're already beginning to fade, and I have this lovely bunch of people sitting around me to thank for that. As well as the man himself. My main man. The groom. My husband…almost.

Smiling over at Jonny as though he is the only person in the world to me right now, I can't help but reach over for a very quick kiss before turning back to our friends once more. "I second everything that Jonny just said. We love you all and we really wouldn't be here without you. So, this toast of Jonny's? Is a toast to all of you."

"To all of us," we all chorus together, raising our champagne glasses in the air one more time before clinking them together, Zack and Will standing up and walking over to where we are sitting so they can get in on the action.

The clinking of champagne glasses is swiftly followed by six very thirsty people downing the expensive bubbles far quicker than they should be downed. Champagne is for sipping, but us lot and sipping alcohol don't really fall into the same sentence. We're all fairly hardened drinkers and so, those two champagne bottles of ours won't be lasting long. In fact, I might get Jonny to order us some more. We've got a hell of a long flight ahead of us. And another long flight after this one. I'm suddenly beginning to feel very sorry for the cabin crew who are going to be the ones dealing with us lot later on. Six happy campers raring to go…they're going to need all the luck in the world with that….

****

I don't know what day it is, I don't even know what time it is, but the one thing I do know is that we are finally here. In Mauritius. A place where Jonny and I are going to be getting married in three days. Just three more days! I think. As I said, my body clock is well and truly off and that's all thanks to the long ass flights, the copious amounts of champagne consumed on said flights, and the eleven hour time difference.

It's the middle of the night over here and none of us have even had the chance to properly look round at our surroundings or our accommodation as yet, each of us splitting off into our separate suites and turning in for the night. I can't wait to have a proper look round tomorrow.

I know that there's a swim up pool just off our bedroom. That much I do know. I also know that our bedroom overlooks our very own private beach, much like the private beach we had back in the Maldives, but this private beach is extra special, because it is the very beach where we are going to be exchanging our wedding vows. And I can't wait to see it.

I'll have to wait until the morning to get a proper look at it but I can wait for a little bit longer. Especially as I have an even better view lying before me right now. A stark naked Jonny curled up in the bed sheets next to me, sleeping soundly, both the alcohol and the jet lag having worked their absolute best on him. Needless to say that all promises of having sex before our wedding night have gone well and truly out of the window, for tonight anyway.

I smile over at him in the darkness, my mind unable to relax in order to allow myself to sleep. I'm still buzzing from all the champagne we drank on the flight over here and I'm so bloody excited about the fact we are really here. At long last. After all those years of being apart, all the pain we endured at the end of our relationship the first time round, the pain we've endured this second time round, and we're finally here. I swear I am going to have to pinch myself several times over before I really believe this is happening to me. To us.

At one point in my life, a whole year ago in fact, my life had gone to shit. Literally gone to shit. Jonny's too. I'd walked away from him again and he'd not long lost his mum, and then…he tried to kill himself. Actually kill himself. The word suicide sends chills down my spine whenever I think about the word but hearing the words 'kill himself' strike a chord even more for me.

When I think about what could have been, and the part I played in how Jonny arrived at that low point in his life, I can almost feel my insides ripping apart. But I can't hold on to those painful thoughts anymore, because Jonny pulled through that darkest ever time in his life and he is here with me now, right where he needs to be. And me with him.

****

I get one hell of a wakeup call the following morning, Jonny's magical mouth *arousing* me from my slumber. I fist my hands into the bed sheets as I writhe beneath him, moaning softly as his tongue goes to work on making damn bloody sure I am awake, alert, and more than ready for the day ahead.

And what better way to get me ready for the day ahead than this, by licking me up into a frenzy with his expert tongue, that bedroom prowess of his he talked about on the flight over here only yesterday being put well and truly into action with me this morning.

"Oh god…Jonny," I moan, my hands working their way into his hair, urging him on, desperate for my release.

Once Jonny's fingers join in the party, that's it, I'm gone. I arch my back away from the bed, my desperate cries of pleasure echoing loudly around the bedroom, Jonny relentless in his quest to devour me until he can devour me no more. I am a hot, wet mess once he's finished with me, and boy does he grin up at me like the cat who got the cream afterwards. Panting and breathless, I just about manage to muster up a smile in return before resting my head back against the pillow.

"Good morning, baby," he murmurs, crawling his way up my naked, clammy body. He plants a trail of featherlight kisses along my collarbone, the well of my throat, my neck, all the way up to my mouth, before pressing a final kiss to my lips.

When he pulls his mouth away to gaze down at me, I smile up at him. "And if that's how you intend on greeting me every single morning from this day onwards, then please do."

"Oh, I intend to, baby, believe me," he whispers, his eyes now burning down into mine. Bracing his arms above my head, he then says, "In fact, I'm thinking of incorporating this morning greeting into our wedding vows."

I burst out laughing. "Oh, really?"

He grins like the childish idiot he is. *My* childish idiot. "Yes, really." Leaning down, his lips find my neck once more and I gasp loudly as I feel his tongue sliding its way along my hyper sensitive flesh, goosebumps now popping up all over my body as Jonny and his never ending need to keep worshipping me threatens to send me mad for him all over again.

"But I'm not so sure that the officiant marrying us would approve of such an inappropriate vow, and so, I think it's best we keep this vow between us. Don't you think?" Jonny looms over me once more, flashing me a cheeky smile, and I chuckle.

"Hmm, I think you might be right there, Jonny. Best to keep this vow between us and only us." Biting down on my bottom lip, I allow my eyes to rake over the naked, tattooed wonder bracing himself above me, thinking about how I'd really like him to bring another inappropriate vow into the equation, at least for this morning anyway.

"Fancy adding another inappropriate vow to your list?" I whisper, giving him the look he knows oh so well.

His lips pull into a suggestive smile. "Oh, baby, I thought you'd never ask."

****

Once Jonny and I finish up with our 'busy' morning, we really take the time to look around at our beautiful accommodation which is aptly named, The Wedding Suite. Yep, that's where we are and that's where we will be staying for the duration of our time here. Well, there will be the one night when Jonny and I will be separated of course, the night before our wedding when I will be staying over at Stacey's suite with her and Jonny will be staying here with Ben, but other than that, this beautiful wedding suite is ours for the next two weeks. And it really is stunning.

This oceanfront suite of ours has a full wall of windows overlooking the private beach in front of us, together with the swim up pool I mentioned last night which I can literally step into from our bedroom. Fancy that, being able to step into a pool from my bedroom! Honestly, I'm a total kid at heart and things as grand as this still bowl me over even now. The Maldives certainly worked its luxurious magic on me and this place is going to as well. I can feel it.

A full marble bathroom awaits us, just off the bedroom, with a huge walk-in shower, immense stand-alone handcrafted stone bathtub and two sinks to match. *A sink each for the newlyweds*, I think to myself excitedly, as I continue to walk through our suite with Jonny.

On the other side of the swim up pool is an expansive private terrace, with table and chairs and a large light yellow sofa with yellow and orange cushions to match, sitting along the back wall.

Wooden in design, the terrace looks as though it is floating next to the swim up pool and I love how the bedroom weaves into the terrace area so seamlessly, the open plan layout really hitting the mark with both me and Jonny. Mmm, the fun we can have in here. The fun we've already had in here this morning....

We find another little terrace outside the front of our bedroom, accessed via the wall of windows that slide fully open. I am happy to find two sun loungers, two small tables and a bar stocked to the brim with lots and lots of alcohol out here. Now this is my kind of wedding suite.

Jonny leads us beyond the terrace via the stone steps that take us down on to the beautiful beach. Palm trees and an abundance of greenery and lush flowers greet us along the way, the stunning tropical wildlife and the vivid colours already reeling me in. The crystal clear waters of the Indian ocean glimmer brightly beneath the sun's mid-morning rays, the pure white sand almost blinding us as we saunter slowly over to the water's edge.

We both allow the warm, salty water of the Indian ocean to

wash over our bare feet as we stand together in silence for a moment, hand in hand, taking in the breathtaking view laid out before us.

After a beat, Jonny says, "I know we originally wanted to get married in the Maldives, because of the fact I proposed to you there, but this place, this beach...it certainly matches up to the one back in the Maldives, that's for sure."

"It most certainly does," I agree, smiling over at him.

Jonny turns to me and pulls me in for a hug. Bumping his nose up against mine, he says, "This okay for you then? Are you happy?"

"Oh, Jonny, did you really just ask me that question? I've told you before, I could get married to you in a warehouse and I wouldn't care. This place, this beach, our wedding suite..." I gesture over towards that wonderful wedding suite of ours situated a mere few metres away. "...it's absolutely perfect..."

"You're perfect," he murmurs, before dropping a soft, wet kiss on to my lips. *Oh my.*

Will I ever get enough of this man of mine? Erm, no, I think not. Wrapping my arms around the back of his neck, I deepen the kiss, Jonny suddenly hauling me up from the sand and into his arms. Snaking my legs around his waist, I allow Jonny to walk us back to the very wedding suite we've literally only just stepped out of. Oh well, may as well get our money's worth while we're here....

CHAPTER 20

LAUREN

That afternoon, we reunite with our friends and are given a full tour of the venue which will be hosting our quaint little wedding reception straight after the beach ceremony. Even though there are only six of us, we both still wanted a bit of tradition thrown into the mix, as well as some music. We couldn't get married without Jonny and the lads putting on some music later on. Especially when it comes to our first dance.

I've been told that Ben, Will and Zack will be providing the music for that, while Jonny twirls me around on the sand for the first time as my husband. Yes, I want our little evening do to be on a candlelit beach, much like the night when Jonny surprised me back in the Maldives, when he danced with me under the stars as one of the waiters strummed away on a Spanish guitar in the background. I want to create the magic from that night as much as I possibly can, so I can bottle it all up and remember it forever.

Once the tour of the reception venue is finished with, Jonny and I sit down with the wedding planners and some of the admin team for about an hour or so, just to go through some legalities over the wedding ceremony, final arrangements, finer details of what will happen on the day and such like.

By the end of the meeting, I can tell that Jonny is absolutely itching to get his mouth around a cigarette, as well as a much needed drink. I have to agree with him on that one and we therefore head straight over to meet Stacey and the lads for a late lunch and a few drinks at one of the many restaurants this exclusive wedding resort has to offer.

The restaurant itself is bustling with people and it feels a little strange, going out with our friends in public for the first time ever without any bodyguards in tow. Jonny insisted we leave Tony and Andy behind in LA, wanting our wedding to be a private affair without the need for any entourage or fuss.

When we holidayed in the Maldives, we were pretty much on our own for the entire three weeks, living either in the villa or on the beach, only mixing with the locals who worked there. Mauritius is already proving to be full of life by the looks of things, and whilst we are used to being out of the limelight and away from the public eye more so these days, due to no fault of our own, it's actually nice to be back in the hustle and bustle of things again.

Admittedly, we have been able to live our life out in the open in LA once again since I did my television interview back in May. Maybe not quite as freely as we would like, but, the interview I did certainly helped with that.

As Jonny had hoped and predicted, the fans rallied around both me and him after I went public with the violence I faced as a young girl, and eventually, even the tabloids got back on our side. Well, most of them did. The tabloid that was responsible for printing my dad's skewed version of our past certainly didn't get back on our side, printing a few choice articles about me and Jonny even after my television interview.

Needless to say that Jonny and his team of lawyers are taking them to the cleaners for the despicable things they've been printing about us over these last few months. Lara has assured us that they'll be ruined once Jonny has finished with them, and that they'll most likely be forced to pay up hundreds of thousands if not millions of dollars in compensation to us once the lawsuit against them reaches completion. Any money we do get in compensation will be donated straight to charity of course.

Cancer and mental health charities are high on Jonny's list of donations, as well as the domestic violence and drug addiction charities that are in desperate need of more help. I only wish we could help them all, but if we can at least help some of the charities out there that are crying out for more donations then I can take a bit of comfort in the knowledge that we have tried our best.

And we will continually strive to keep helping and donating where we can. Jonny and I publicly shared the most painful parts of our past for a reason, and that reason wasn't to make money for ourselves or to garner attention. It was to shed light on important subjects in order to help others, and I truly think we have done that.

"Hey, here they are! Almost Mr and Mrs!" shouts Will, laughing at Jonny as he practically slumps his way into one of the chairs as we join our friends around the table at the restaurant.

Looks like we are dining alfresco this afternoon in the gorgeous Mauritian sunshine, the beautiful garden like ambience of our tropical surroundings already winning me over. The same however can't be said for Jonny.

"Somebody get me a drink and fast," complains Jonny, swiping a weary hand over his face before reaching for his packet of cigarettes from the pocket of his shorts. Hmm, my man looks tired, and if I'm not mistaken, a little grumpy.

"Hey Mr Grumpy Pants, what's with the sudden mood change?" I say to him.

Pressing a fag between his lips, he quickly lights it up before turning that grumpy ass face of his on me. "It's called jet lag, baby, made ten times worse by being forced into a room with people I don't know who were so far up our asses, I thought at one point they were competing with each other."

"Jonny," I admonish, frowning over at him. "They were just doing their jobs and going through everything ahead of the big day. I thought you were excited."

Jonny is quick to reassure, instantly reaching for my hand. "Hey, of course I'm excited…I just hate all of that false shit. You know I do. And they were false. All of them were."

I shrug my shoulder at him. "Well, I don't care if they were false. As long as they can organise a wedding without any hitches then that's all I care about."

Pressing a kiss to my hand, Jonny then smiles over at me. "Me too. And I'm sorry for being such a grumpy ass."

Leaning over, he is instantly forgiven when he apologises profusely with that delightful mouth of his. I smile against his lips and the sound of our friends erupting into laughter suddenly reminds us of their presence around the table.

Pulling away from me, albeit reluctantly, Jonny then scowls over at the lot of them. "Yeah, yeah, I may have sent my grumpy ass away for Lauren's sake but believe me when I say, I am one grumpy mother fucker this afternoon, so heed my warning."

Jonny's eyes land on Ben when he says that and Ben immediately responds. "Oh, this is going to be fun," he quips, grinning over at Jonny in a way that silently goads Jonny into biting right back.

"You've been warned," says Jonny, taking a long drag on his cigarette, "believe me, Benny boy, you have been warned."

"I think it's time for some drinks," I say, trying to pull this ever feuding pair apart before they actually get to the feuding part of the proceedings.

Honestly, so much for Jonny not winding Ben up and vice versa. He did only promise to be good on the wedding day itself however so I silently hope and pray that Jonny sticks to his promise, otherwise that smart ass mouth of his is going to get him into a whole load of trouble, and I don't mean with Ben.

Cocking an eyebrow over at my rock star, he rolls his eyes at me, before resting back in his seat. My unspoken warning appears to work, Jonny instead resorting to smoking his cigarette in silence as the others chew over the menu.

"Oooh, they do pitchers of cocktails, Lauren," says Stacey, gushing excitedly over the drink selection.

"Do they do Sex on the Beach?" I ask, wondering if they have my favourite cocktail on offer.

"They don't but I do," replies Jonny, smirking over at me as he continues smoking his cigarette.

"Damn, you beat me to it, Jonny," says Ben, disappointed about the fact Jonny was so much quicker off the mark with a suggestive comment than him.

"Actually, Jonny, they do sell pitchers of Sex on the Beach here so I'm afraid you've just been bumped into second place by a cocktail," says Stacey, chuckling away at her little joke. I chuckle right along with her and I'm met with another eye roll from Jonny.

"Look, are we ordering drinks or what because Jonny isn't the only one around here who's about to get grumpy."

We all turn to Zack who is sitting at the end of the table opposite Will, looking less than pleased with the constant banter we've got going on. I can't say I blame him although I'm surprised at his little outburst. We all are I think. Well, Jonny certainly is anyway.

"Fuck me, Zack Miller has finally found his voice. Welcome to the grumpy ass club, my man," says Jonny, grinning over at him.

Arching an eyebrow up at Jonny, Zack says, "Hey, just because I'm chill most of the time doesn't mean I don't bite."

"Oh, we know you can bite, dude," laughs Will. Turning to me, Will says, "A side of Zack you haven't yet seen and are unlikely to see, unless seriously pushed."

My gaze zones in on the hippy that is Zack, the long haired drummer of the band with his very many piercings and his dark clothing. Even now, Zack still can't tear himself away from wearing his trademark black death metal t-shirt and ripped black jeans. Surely to goodness he has a pair of shorts somewhere. Well, I hope he has something akin to shorts and a little bit smarter, at least just for our wedding day.

I haven't actually imposed any clothing requirements on the lads, instead wanting Jonny to feel relaxed and just be himself on the big day. The only trouble with that is my fear of Zack turning up as he's dressed now, looking all hot and flustered and more appropriately dressed for either a heavy metal concert or a drunken rave in a mosh pit somewhere.

Still, I'd rather he feel relaxed and at ease instead of dressing in something he absolutely detests. I'd hate to put Zack or any of them in suits that make them feel uncomfortable. At the end of the day, our wedding day is about the vows we make, the love we feel, and the people we share it with, and that really is the only thing that matters to me. Well, that and my oh so beautiful wedding dress of course. Stacey's dress too. A shimmering jade green floor length dress that makes Stacey look like the knock out model she is. Boy is Ben in for a treat when he sees her in *that* on our wedding day.

Turning back to Will, I say, "Well, remind me to never push Zack Miller over the edge then." I flash a cheeky wink over at Zack and he breaks out into a huge grin.

"Oh, you're on the safe list, Lauren," says Zack, "as is Stacey. Will too actually. It's more likely to either be Jonny or Ben that push me over the edge."

"Funny that," I joke, smirking over at Jonny, and he shakes his head at me.

"So," says Stacey, waving the cocktail menu around like a mad woman. "Are we going to get this Sex on the Beach ordered or what?"

"Two Sex on the Beaches coming right up," replies Ben with a grin.

****

After spending the rest of the afternoon and the early evening with our friends eating and drinking, we bid each other an early goodnight and turn in for the rest of the evening. We're all still so exhausted from the jet lag and the time change and thought it best we try and catch up on some much needed sleep. With only two more days to go until the wedding, we want to be as refreshed and as spritely as possible, and so Jonny and I crash out as soon as our heads hit the pillows.

Jet lag however has a real knack of messing with your body clock, as I find out however many hours later when I am woken up in the middle of the night to the sound of Jonny strumming away on his guitar. The bedroom is in complete darkness except for a sliver of moonlight peeping its way through the sheer white voile curtain which is pulled across the wall of windows at the front of our suite. Jonny has closed the sliding windows I notice. Most likely because he didn't want to disturb me. The thing is, Jonny forgets that I want to be disturbed by him. *Always.*

Sliding out of bed, I don't bother putting anything on my feet, instead tiptoeing my way across the tiled floor and over to the windows so I can sneak a listen in on what Jonny is playing. I don't recognise the song, but whatever it is, it's beautiful. *Of course it's beautiful,* I think to myself. The melody is slow and soft, Jonny's beautifully rough voice sounding low and emotional.

I want to stand here without him knowing, close my eyes, and just listen to him sing, but the other part of me cannot stop myself from being drawn to him. Being drawn to Jonny and his music. And *that* voice. The way his vocals stir something up inside of me like nothing else I've ever experienced. I can't even begin to explain how hearing him sing makes me feel. Especially when it's like this. Just him and me and nobody else.

Jonny has played in vast arenas and stadiums, he's strutted around the stage at hundreds of concerts around the entire world, and as wonderful as it was to witness that musically talented man of mine work his absolute best up on that stage last year in London, it's moments like these I treasure the most. When Jonny loses himself completely in his music and is at peace with both himself, and the world around him.

A few more seconds tick by and that's it, I can't stand being separated from him for a minute longer. I feel compelled to make my presence known. Pulling back the voile curtain, I then slowly slide open the windows and step out on to the terrace, Jonny looking up at me in surprise. His hands immediately fall away from the guitar and he smiles over at me.

"Hey, beautiful. Sorry if I woke you."

Walking over to where he is sitting on one of the sun

loungers, I reach down to press a soft kiss to his lips. When I pull back, I say, "Number one, don't apologise for waking me up. I want you to wake me up in the middle of the night because I absolutely detest waking up in an empty bed without you lying next to me. And number two, why have you stopped playing?" I raise an accusatory eyebrow at him and he grins.

"I only stopped playing because I was so distracted by your beauty," he says, giving me one of his mushy looks.

"That's a cheesy line for you, Mathers, and an outright lie." He raises his eyebrows at me as I pull up the other sun lounger to sit down next to him.

"I admit to the cheesy line but a lie? Baby, you are the only woman in the entire world who can distract me from my music and believe me when I say, you have done exactly that very many times in our past..."

"But not tonight," I say, fishing for information on the song he was playing just now. He's being secretive, I can tell, I'm just not entirely sure why.

He sighs. "I'm not really sure where you're going with this..."

"What were you playing just now?" I ask him, my curiosity finally getting the better of me.

"Well, that depends," he says, fixing me with a long stare, "how much did you hear *before* you stepped out on to the terrace?" Time for him to raise an accusatory eyebrow up at me this time and I roll my eyes in response.

"Okay, you caught me, I was listening in. Of course I was listening in but...with you, how can I not?"

"That's a cheesy line for you, Lauren Whittle," he quips, throwing my own words right back at me.

"Oh, you're such a comedian, Jonny," I say with a scowl.

"Well, Ben seems to think so…"

"And now you're just trying to distract me…"

"I thought we'd already established that you were the one distracting me," says Jonny, chuckling away to himself.

"My god, you are maddening sometimes, Jonny Mathers," I say through gritted teeth. "Now stop evading the question… what were you playing?" I narrow my eyes on him and he rolls his eyes at my persistence, leading me to continue with my inquisition. "Why are you being so secretive? You've always shared everything with me about your music and your songs." I must be pulling a face because Jonny's jokey like manner soon vanishes when he sees I'm getting a little upset. Am I getting a little upset? Yes, actually, I think I am.

"Hey," says Jonny, reaching for my hands, "don't be upset. It's not that I don't want to share this particular song with you, it's just…" Jonny falls silent as he contemplates his next words carefully.

"It's just?" I say to him, urging him on for an explanation.

Swallowing hard, Jonny pauses for a brief moment before finally responding. "The song I was playing just now is a song I've written for my mum. It's actually the first song I wrote after I had that dream about her, when we were away in the Maldives…"

Jonny's voice trails away as his emotions begin to bubble to the surface, the grief he still feels over his mum still so painful and raw. It's been over a year now since Judy passed away but with our wedding looming, I can't even begin to imagine how he must be feeling right now.

Not having his mum with us on our wedding day is going to be tough. Really tough. But Jonny is clearly finding solace through his music, as he always has done, and he is turning that raw, agonising, grief into something else. Something wonderful. Of that I have no doubt.

"Oh, baby, that's beautiful," I whisper. Touching his face with the tips of my fingers, I turn his sorrowful gaze back on me. "And your mum would think so too." I give him a quick kiss on the lips and he sighs. "So, this song for your mum, is it just a private song you want to keep to yourself for reasons I now understand, or…is there more to it?"

Glancing down at the gap lying between our sun loungers, Jonny says quietly, "This song for my mum is going to be the lead single we release from our new album. In fact, this particular song *is* the name of the album. Well, it will be, once the album's finished."

Now I am shocked. "Wow, you're…you're really going to share something so personal with the world?"

Jonny nods. "I owe it to her, Lauren. My mum appeared to me that night for a reason, and after that, I wrote a song, and not just any song, *this* song. And my mum was my biggest supporter, always the proudest person in the room whenever she watched me play. This song, this album, is for her. It's all for her. But…the reason why I didn't want you to hear the song, or know any details about it, is because I want you to hear it for the first time next year when I open up the comeback concert with it. I want you to experience this song as a fan, Lauren. You are my biggest fan and I want you to have the same experience as all the other fans when I finally reveal this song to the world. That's the only reason why I kept it from you, and I'm sorry if you thought it was for any other reason other than the one I've just told you."

Wow. This man absolutely astounds me sometimes. His words, the love he feels for his mum, the way he still considers my feelings in everything he ever does, it reaches so deep within me that it brings me to tears.

"Oh, Jonny, that's wonderful. You're...you're wonderful," I whisper, my voice sounding all wobbly.

Trapping my face in his hands, he presses his forehead against mine and says, "I love you."

I smile. "I love you more."

Our mouths come together in a soft, tender kiss, and then we wrap our arms around each other in a loving embrace, both enjoying the sound of silence out here on our little terrace at some crazy ass hour of the morning.

We seem to be making a regular habit of this, both waking up in the middle of the night and spending time together, chatting and kissing, playing music. Especially when it comes to staying over in magical far off places with private beaches and stunning sunsets. And now that we're both up and clearly wide awake again, thanks to the good old jet lag I mentioned earlier, I want the very thing I came out on this terrace for.

"So, are you going to play me a song then?" I murmur against his lips, and he smiles.

"Baby, for you? Anything."

"Anything?" I ask, raising my eyebrows at him.

Raking his eyes over my face in that way I love so bloody much, he then whispers, "Anything."

I take a moment to really think about what song I want him to play for me. I think about our upcoming nuptials, about what we've been through these last few months, where we are now in our relationship, back in our truly happy place, and it doesn't take me long to decide on a song I feel is most appropriate for us two right now.

"Would you be offended if I didn't choose one of your songs?" I ask, checking in with him before I throw my request his way.

He frowns. "Of course not. I'm arrogant, but I'm not that arrogant." I cock an eyebrow up at him and he laughs. "Okay. Maybe I am that arrogant...sometimes."

Brushing his hands up and down my arms, he then says, "So, what song would the lady like me to play for her then?"

I bite down on a smile. "How about, I Don't Want to Miss a Thing by Aerosmith?"

Jonny's eyes light up at my song suggestion. "Wow, an unexpected choice but I like it. That is a great song."

"And a song so appropriate for us two right now, Jonny, because, as the song says, I really do not want to miss one more moment with you. Not one."

"Me neither," whispers Jonny, his eyes growing slowly emotional. "Me neither."

I lie back on my sun lounger as Jonny perches himself on the end of it, guitar in hand, eyes well and truly on me. He starts to strum the chords of one of Aerosmith's biggest hits and I can feel myself floating away on a cloud already. We may be sitting outside in paradise but once Jonny's singing voice gets thrown into the equation, I am on that cloud I just mentioned and Jonny is floating away right along with me.

"I could stay awake, just to hear you breathing, watch your smile while you are sleeping, while you're far away and dreaming..."

Our gazes remain locked together as Jonny's voice reaches into my soul once more, his eyes never leaving mine the entire time. By the time he gets to the chorus, I start to sing with him, my mind thinking back to so many other moments like these from our past, when we'd sing together at gone midnight in the tiny confines of our flat back in Manchester.

It was magical then, long before all the heartbreak came

along, and it's still magical now, and with us, I don't think it will ever be anything else.

CHAPTER 21

JONNY

It's the night before our wedding and I'm already feeling wretched about the fact that Lauren will not be sleeping in our bed with me tonight. Just watching her pack her overnight bag to take with her to Stacey's hotel suite is doing me in, but at least I can take comfort in the fact that after tonight, Lauren will be by my side forever, and there will be no more running from either her or me, and certainly no empty beds, that's for god damn sure.

Wrapping my arms around her waist from behind, I nuzzle my nose into Lauren's neck as she throws the last of her toiletries into her bag before zipping it closed. "Are you sure you have to be apart from me tonight?" I murmur, running my nose along the smooth, soft skin of her neck, revelling in her scent. God, she smells absolutely fucking incredible. I swear I could stand here with my arms wrapped around her and inhale her all night long.

Turning around in my arms, Lauren smiles up at me before linking her fingers around the back of my neck. "It's only for one night, Jonny, plus it's bad luck to see each other on the morning of the wedding…"

"So I'll blindfold you from midnight onwards. Problem solved," I joke, although part of me really isn't joking.

"Hmm, nice idea, in theory, although I think we both know how blindfolding me would go…"

She lifts an accusatory eyebrow up at me and I grin. "You make a good point, although…"

"You can stop with all the smutty talk right there, Mathers," she says, prodding me in the chest with her index finger. I feign injury and she just chuckles away at me. "Save it for the wedding night, rock star."

Narrowing my eyes on her, I then press my mouth to hers as I say, "Oh, sweetheart, I will be saving it all up and more, believe me."

She shakes her head at me in mock disgust, but I know she loves our smutty, playful banter as much as I do. It's one of the things I love the most about our relationship. The back and forth between us, the flirting, the mushy stuff and the dirty stuff. It's all part and parcel of what makes our relationship so wonderful, which is why I can't believe I'm going to have to spend the night before our magical wedding without her.

"You do realise that you're inflicting Ben on me tonight for an entire night, don't you?" I say to Lauren, "I mean, have you actually thought about how that might go?"

She grins. "Oh, I'm sure he'll be great company for you, Jonny. Stops you from feeling lonely…"

"I think I'd rather be lonely…"

"Don't start," she warns, giving me 'the look.' "You promised to behave."

Holding out my arms to the sides, I say, "I promised to behave on our wedding day. Tonight is not our wedding day, so…"

"I swear, if you two end up giving each other black eyes then I will not be impressed…"

Yanking her back against me, I chuckle as I try to give her an apology kiss but she shoves my face gently away. "Oh, you know I'm only kidding," I jest, attempting to kiss her again.

"Jonny," she says, giggling like the teenage girl she can be sometimes.

My playful attack against her works, because as per the norm, she ends up melting against me into a great big puddle of mush, and all because she cannot resist me. Of course she can't resist me. Because she loves me. As much as I love her.

After about a minute of me smothering her with playful kisses and whispering sweet nothings into her ear, Lauren eventually says, "Okay, enough with the charm offensive and the wandering hands, Mathers, I actually have something to give you before I leave to go to Stacey's…"

"Mmm, now you're talking," I whisper, nibbling at her neck.

I get another playful shove in the face for that come on, Lauren shaking her head at me again as I am forced to step away from the woman who, in all honesty, I don't want to step away from. I am addicted to her in every way imaginable, mind, body and soul, and my constant need to shower her with love, kisses and a whole lot of dirty will never be any different.

"Okay," I sigh in defeat, "you win…this time." I shoot her a warning look and her lips pull into an amused smile.

"Oh, stop with all the sulking, close your eyes, and hold out your hands."

Wow, my girl ordering me around now, is she? Mmm, I like that, I like that a lot. Not that I'd tell her of course.

"Bossy much?" I joke, raising my eyebrows at her sudden authoritative tone.

She smirks. "Don't pretend you don't love it," she says, instantly reading my mind. "Now close your eyes and hold out your hands."

With a roll of my eyes, I reluctantly do as she says. I stand there in the middle of our bedroom with my eyes closed, hands out in front of me, waiting for whatever it is Lauren is going to place in them. I have to admit that my curiosity over what Lauren is up to is beginning to get the better of me.

Thankfully, I don't have to wait for very long because a moment later, Lauren places what feels like a medium sized box into the palms of my hands. "Can I open my eyes now?"

"And you say I'm impatient when it comes to surprises," she laughs, "but yes, you can open your eyes now."

Opening up my eyes, I glance down to find a black, velvet box sitting in my hands. Frowning up at my girl, I say, "What's all this?"

With a shrug of her shoulder, she gives me one of her shy looks. "It's a wedding gift...but if you don't like it..."

"Why wouldn't I like it?" I ask, wandering back over to where she is still standing by the bed.

Gazing up at me, she says, "Well, I'm just a bit nervous about how you might react to the gift, that's all...because of the sentiment behind it."

Grabbing a tight hold of her hand, I walk us round to the side of the bed and pull her down towards me so that we can sit on the bed together. With the box in one hand, I trail my fingers into her hair with my other hand.

"The fact that you've bought me a gift at all is...well, it's beautiful." She gives me one of her mushy smiles. It makes my chest ache. "But before I open this gift of yours, I've got a bit of something for you too."

"You have?" she asks excitedly.

Biting down on a smile, I say, "Of course I have. It's our

wedding day tomorrow and I couldn't allow that to pass without buying you a gift, sweetheart."

Placing my gift on to the bed for a brief moment, I head over to the wardrobe and rummage around in the bag I'd placed in there on the day we arrived. Hidden away at the bottom of the wardrobe, out of sight and well away from the prying eyes of Lauren, I find what I'm looking for.

I grab the red box containing Lauren's gift, zip the bag up and close the wardrobe door, before heading back over to rejoin Lauren on the bed. Taking one of Lauren's hands in mine, I place the red box into the palm of her hand before reaching for the velvet box containing my gift.

"You first," she says, suddenly looking all nervous. But she really doesn't need to be nervous. Hell, Lauren could buy me a chocolate bar and I'd love it, and all because she's the one giving it to me.

Looking down at the box she gave to me just a moment ago, I slowly open the lid, Lauren's eyes fixated on my face as she tries to gauge my reaction to this unexpected gift of hers.

My fingers slowly pluck out the black leather bracelet from the box, my eyes instantly landing on the silver clasp where an engraving has been etched into the metal. And not just any engraving. Oh no. Lauren doesn't do things by halves and clearly she wanted to get me something really special for our wedding day. Something personal. So personal that I can already feel my eyes beginning to water as they read over the engraving.

Forever in your heart I'll be – Mum xx. A pair of tiny angel wings have also been engraved on to the clasp, just above my mum's name, Lauren knowing full well that angels mean a hell of a lot to me.

I've never really been one for believing in an afterlife, until I had a vision of my mum earlier this year, but I'd always had a thing for angels before that. Not entirely sure what it is about angels that intrigue me so much. Perhaps it's the thought of some invisible being protecting and guiding me along the pathway of life that gives me comfort. Either way, Lauren herself is the very epitome of what I believe angels to be. She is my constant, my love and warmth, my protector and my guide. Without her, I would literally cease to exist, and when I was without her, I did cease to exist, on the inside anyway.

"Lauren, this is..." I gulp down a lump in my throat, my emotions slowly swimming to the surface at the sentiment behind this gift of Lauren's. Shit, she really has hit me in the chest with emotions tonight, that's for sure. And boy do I love her even more for it.

My gaze meets with Lauren's and she gestures towards the bracelet in my hands. "I know how you've always worn leather bracelets over the years and...well, I just wanted you to have your mum with you on our wedding day. I know she won't be there physically but, she'll still be there with you, Jonny. In your heart. And I hope that my gift doesn't upset you..."

I shake my head at her. "This gift is priceless," I manage to whisper to her through my reeling emotions. "Fucking priceless."

I reach for her then, pulling her hard against me as I allow her love and warmth to wrap its way around me. Admittedly, a few tears break free from my eyes, but I don't care. I couldn't stop them, even if I wanted to.

"You are the most thoughtful person I've ever met," I say to her. Pressing the palms of my hands against her cheeks, she too sheds a few tears right along with me, and I kiss them away, one by one, Lauren kissing mine away a moment later.

After a beat, I say, "Now it's time for your gift."

Lauren beams over at me before slowly lifting the lid off her box. She gasps in shock as she lifts the white gold heart shaped locket out of the box. "Oh, Jonny, it's beautiful," she whispers in awe, holding it up between us so she can really take the time to admire it.

"Open it," I urge, hoping I've not gone over the top on the whole emotional gift thing tonight myself. Lauren's gift to me was an emotional one but this, this is a whole other level of emotional, but for an entirely different reason.

Placing the locket down on to the bed, Lauren manages to gently prise the locket open with her fingernails. Picking the locket up once more, she brings it closer to her face so she can study the picture on the inside. Her brow crinkles up in shock. "Is this...how did you?"

Lauren's words are lost as she struggles to contain her emotions, her eyes glistening with fresh tears as she gazes down at the scan picture of our son contained within the tiny locket. It took some doing to get that tiny scan picture in there but somehow or other, I managed to do it. It's the twenty week scan we had done of Oliver, when we found out we were having a boy. The scan that took place just a week before he got ripped away from us. But I didn't put this scan picture in Lauren's locket to upset her. I put it in there so that our son can be with her not only on our wedding day, but for the rest of her life.

"I wanted Oliver to be a part of our special day," I say to her quietly, "but most of all, I wanted you to have a part of him with you, wherever you go...always."

"Forever and always," she whispers to me, an errant tear slipping its way down her cheek.

"Forever and always," I whisper back to her.

"Oh, Jonny."

She throws her arms around my neck and I do the same to her. We cling on to each other as we allow the tears to come and the painful memories to invade. Tomorrow will be a happy day for us, of that I have no doubt, but within that happiness, there will be moments like this. Because this grief journey we are on is part of who we are now, it is threaded within us and will continue to change and grow as we navigate our way through the rest of our life.

We will have good days and bad days. But the most important thing in all of this is that we can finally talk about what we once lost. We can acknowledge it and cry about it, and we can open ourselves up to feeling that pain we once tried so damn hard to push away.

When Lauren finally pulls her face away from my neck, she looks up at me and says, "Thank you for my gift. I love it. And I love you."

I smile down at her. "Right back at you with that one."

She smiles. "I can't wait to marry you tomorrow, Jonny Mathers."

Ceasing the opportunity to lighten the mood a little, I say to her, "What a coincidence, because I can't wait to marry you either."

CHAPTER 22

LAUREN

"Oh, Lauren, you look beautiful. So beautiful that I think I'm going to cry."

I catch another look at myself through the floor length mirror, Stacey standing behind me, admiring me through watery eyes. My hair is done, my makeup is done, my nails are done and the beautiful ivory lace wedding dress I picked out two months ago is on. I have to admit that looking at myself in this mirror right now, I do feel beautiful. In fact, I feel like a princess. I'm sure most brides would tell you that they feel like a princess on their wedding day but honestly, I feel like a million dollars.

Having had a horrendous upbringing, I had to fight tooth and nail to buy myself anything. The trouble was that any money I did earn for myself usually got snatched away from me. And it got snatched away by the one man who should have nurtured me and looked after me.

Standing here now, seeing myself in a dress as exquisite as this one is, it makes me tear up. As a little girl, I used to cower away under my bed and dream about moments like this, in the hope that if I dreamed hard enough, my mind would whisk me away from where I was and take me off to some far away land where my dad could no longer hurt me. Sadly, those dreams of mine at the time were exactly that, just dreams. The dreams of a young girl who, at one time in her life, thought she wouldn't make it out of that god awful house alive.

I shudder inside whenever I think about the monster my father was. But that monster is now long gone and I will not allow the ghost of my father to haunt me anymore. Today is going to be the happiest day of my life and nothing and nobody is going to spoil it.

My eyes drop to the locket I am wearing around my neck, Jonny's wedding gift he presented me with last night shining over at me through the mirror. I run my fingers back and forth over the heart shaped locket containing the precious scan picture of my baby boy, taking a moment to remember him.

I send a silent prayer up to the stars for my son, telling him how much I love him, how much Jonny loves him, how much we'll always love him. Picking up the locket, I place a kiss on the outside of it before gently dropping it back into its rightful place around my neck once more. *I love you, baby boy,* I think to myself. I don't say the words out loud. I want those words to be between me and him and nobody else. Not even Stacey. And speaking of Stacey....

"Lauren? Are you okay?" Stacey asks me, her concerned eyes meeting with mine through the mirror.

Turning around, I give her a reassuring smile. "Of course I'm okay."

"You sure?" she asks, not looking entirely convinced.

With a nod of my head, I say, "I was just…reflecting…but I'm okay now. I promise."

Placing her hands on my shoulders, Stacey looks into my eyes and says, "You look so beautiful, Lauren, and I am so happy and proud that you finally get to have your happy ever after with Jonny today."

Placing one of my hands over hers, I sigh, trying my best efforts to force back the tears. I so don't want to cry today but my best friend is making that really really difficult right now.

"And I have you to thank for that, Stace. You got me back with Jonny. You badgered the hell out of me and pushed me to my limits at one point but *you* did this. You got me here and back with the man I love and for that, I owe you everything."

"You owe me nothing," says Stacey, her voice sounding all wobbly, "now let's stop with all this soppy shit right now otherwise we'll be walking down the aisle with mascara running down our faces. Waterproof or not, I do not want to run the risk on your wedding day."

I burst out laughing when she says that, Stacey pulling me in for a very careful hug. Honestly, she's treating me like I'm a glass vase today, so afraid of wrecking either my hair, my makeup, or of course, my wedding dress. I on the other hand couldn't give a shit about any of that and so I pull her hard against me, to the point where she can barely breathe.

"Can't breathe," she says, pretending to choke.

"Oh, very funny," I say, reluctantly pulling away from her embrace. Sweeping my gaze over my best friend, I let out a whistle of approval. "You know, all this talk about me being the beautiful bride and yet, you're standing there in that shimmering jade green floor length dress looking every bit as beautiful as you say I am."

And she really does look stunning today. Absolutely stunning. Her long auburn hair has been styled to perfection by the very talented on-site hairdressers, her naturally straight locks instead making way for loose curls that flow over her shoulders and down her back. I can't recall ever seeing Stacey with curly hair before, but now I have, I think she should curl her hair a whole lot more, and I'm sure Ben will agree.

"You think Ben will like it?" she asks, her eyes shining with happiness at the sheer mention of her boyfriend.

And that happiness of hers mirrors my own happiness with Jonny, making me feel all warm and squishy on the inside whenever I see it. I am so happy for Stacey having finally met the love of her life, because Ben is so right for her. They are so well matched and so funny together. Of course Ben can be a handful at times but then, so can Jonny, and we wouldn't have them any other way.

"Like it?" I scoff, "Ben won't know what to do with himself when he sees you walking down the aisle with those gorgeous curls in your hair and in *that* dress. Well, he will know what to do with himself, and you, it's whether he can wait long enough for it."

We both dissolve into a fit of giggles, the pair of us knowing full well just how eager Ben is when it comes to Stacey. Mind you, Jonny is exactly the same with me. Barely able to keep his eyes or hands off me whenever we're together. And that's how I hope it will always be between us, but with me and Jonny, I can't ever imagine it being any different.

Jonny is a fiery and passionate man, so wild and untamed, and that wildness within him is what first drew me to him when we were teenagers. He was so carefree and full of life, broke every rule in the manual and pulled me into his wonderful world of music, adventure and passion. So much passion. And now, I get to marry that passionate man of mine, and believe me when I say, it's been a long time coming.

"So, are you ready?" asks Stacey, gushing excitedly.

Taking Stacey's hand firmly in mine, I say, "Oh, Stace, I've been ready for a very long time. Too long. Let's do this."

****

I see him waiting for me by the water's edge. The sun is burning brightly in the sky, the private beach we're about to exchange our vows on is covered in light pink rose petals and my husband to be is standing at the end of a very long red carpet dressed in...a suit? An actual suit? And he isn't the only one in a suit either. Ben, Will and Zack are all kitted out in expensive looking dark grey suits too. Every single one of them.

Well Jonny has certainly pulled that surprise out of the bag, that's for sure. I can already feel my eyes blurring with tears at the sheer thoughtfulness of this wonderful man standing in front of me, and I haven't even walked down the aisle to him as yet. He has his back to me at the moment. A promise he made to me until the moment the music begins to play, because once I step on to that red carpet and start walking towards him, then, and only then, do I want him to turn around and look at me.

I pause briefly at the edge of the red carpet, my teardrop bouquet of tropical flowers in one hand and my other arm linked through Stacey's. Stacey is officially giving me away to Jonny, which may not appear like a traditional move to anybody else outside our bubble, but Stacey is the sister I never had, and I couldn't think of anybody else who I'd rather give me away other than her.

Four white chairs are seated either side of the red carpet, two on the left, and two on the right, in readiness for our friends witnessing the exchanging of our vows this afternoon. The lady officiant stands at the head of the red carpet, in between Jonny and the lads, and other staff from the wedding venue are hovering around the beach where the most incredible moment of my life is about to take place.

As soon as the music begins to filter through the sound system, that's my signal to start walking. But I am frozen to the spot as Jonny finally turns around to watch me start walking towards him. His eyes meet with mine from where he is standing by the water's edge and I swear it feels as though the very ocean he is standing in front of is crashing its way into me.

My heart is fluttering away in my chest, beating so hard as I struggle to compose myself, the expression on Jonny's face working its way inside me. Deep inside. The love and adoration, the sheer emotion on his face right now is like nothing I've ever seen before today. Of course Jonny has always looked at me with love and adoration. *Always.* But for some reason, in this moment, on this our special day, the love within Jonny that's always been there for me is literally pouring its way out of him for everybody around us to see.

Taking a deep, steadying breath in to try and control my reeling emotions, I finally take my first step forward on to the red carpet. It's only as I start my slow walk along the red carpet when I realise the song that's playing, which is The Scientist by Coldplay, isn't actually being sang by Coldplay at all.

Holy shit, Jonny has recorded his own version of the song. I bite down on my bottom lip as I try to quell the tears now threatening to fall from my eyes, but it's all in vain, as they begin to stream their way down my cheeks anyway. Jonny's beautiful heart wrenching singing voice filters its way through the speakers, wrapping its way around me and seeping into my heart. My very soul.

We chose The Scientist as the song for me to walk down the aisle to because of our history. It was a song that we both loved by a band we both loved and Jonny used to play it to me often back in Manchester in our early days.

He's obviously put so much thought and love into doing this for me today. I was expecting the original song to be playing out here and instead, I am being given one of the best gifts I could have ever been given. Jonny and the rest of Reclamation having recorded a song that we definitely consider to be 'our song.'

Jonny and I have very many songs that are special to us, including many written by the man himself, but this one pretty much tops the list for us. And all because of the meaning behind it. The song itself pretty much tells our story, from then to now and how we kept breaking up and parting ways. Well, no more parting ways for us from now on. This is our happy ending right now. Of that I am absolutely certain.

****

JONNY

I have to remember how to breathe as I turn around and set eyes on Lauren for the first ever time in her wedding dress. My god, she is beautiful. So beautiful. And that dress. *Wow... just...wow.* Lauren can barely tear her eyes away from me, just as I can't tear my eyes away from her, not even for a second. Because now that I've turned around to look at her, to watch her walking down the aisle towards me so that she can finally utter those heartfelt vows to me and become my wife, why the hell would I want to look at anybody else?

As Lauren begins her slow walk along the red carpet, I see the raw emotion on her face, the tears glistening in her eyes as she realises the song we chose together for her to walk down the aisle to, isn't the original. Oh no. I wanted to do something extra special for my girl and recording my very own version of Coldplay's The Scientist was something I knew would strike a chord with her. A chord so deep that those tears of hers that were glistening in her eyes just a few seconds ago are now rolling down her cheeks.

Everything all of a sudden becomes white noise to me, our friends and everybody else around us blurring into the background. Because right now, all I see is her. Lauren walking slowly towards me in her beautiful wedding dress. The ivory lace of the dress clings to every contour, every perfect curve on her body, almost as though she has been poured into it. Her hair is pinned up with what look like sparkling diamantes, the tendrils of loose curls here and there framing her gorgeous face, the deep blues of her eyes sparkling over at me and reeling me in. And boy am I being reeled in.

Her full, luscious lips are smiling over at me, the light pink lip gloss matching the very same pink as the rose petals blowing around us right now, the late afternoon breeze beginning to pick up. I swear my heart skips about a thousand beats in the time it takes for Lauren to finally reach me by the water's edge. And when she does reach me, boy when she does, I can't help but reach out for her so I can kiss her. And she welcomes that kiss, smiling against my lips as I return that smile with one of my own.

As I pull away and see the wetness on her cheeks, the tears in her eyes, I can't help but feel that all-consuming yearning, the deep ache within me that wants to wipe those tears of Lauren's away. But I don't wipe them away, not this time, because those tears of Lauren's today aren't because she's sad, they're because she's happy. So blissfully happy to finally be standing here with me. At the end of our journey. A journey fraught with trauma and heartache, a journey so arduous at times that at one point, I feared we would never find our way back to each other again. But here we are, about to make our vows, our promises of forever, as our friends, our family, stand around us and share this happy moment right along with us.

Once Lauren hands her bouquet of flowers over to Stacey, we then join hands and look over at the lady officiant who will be marrying us today. She smiles over at the pair of us, before turning her attention to our friends, introducing herself and explaining a few details about the ceremony that is about to take place.

She talks of love and commitment, the reason as to why two people feel the need to make such a lifelong promise to each other. She talks about us and the few anecdotes we gave to her about our early days so she could share them with our friends here today. But the most special part of the ceremony, the part I feel I've been waiting for my whole life, the part where we exchange our vows and make our promises to each other, is the moment I will remember for the rest of my days.

"I, Jonny Peter Mathers, take thee, Lauren Catherine Whittle, to be my lawful wedded wife. To have and to hold from this day forward, for better for worse, for richer for poorer, in sickness and in health, to love and to cherish, until death do us part."

I say the words with so much conviction, pouring every ounce of love and emotion into those vows. Vows I absolutely one hundred percent stand by. When Lauren came into my life, I fell in love with her instantly, without question, and I always loved her, even when that love was young and naïve and new. But whether we were young or not, I always took good care of her.

Even before I knew about her dad and his violent ways, I just wanted to wrap my arms around her and make her feel safe. Because loving someone so much means that you become their warmth, their safe place, and believe me when I say that I am Lauren's safe place, and she is mine.

****

LAUREN

I look up at Jonny through teary eyes as he makes his vows, his promises of forever, his right hand holding my left hand tightly, his thumb brushing back and forth over my wedding finger in a sign of reassurance. I smile through my joyful tears as I too then step up to say my vows.

"I, Lauren Catherine Whittle, take thee, Jonny Peter Mathers, to be my lawful wedded husband. To have and to hold from this day forward, for better for worse, for richer for poorer, in sickness and in health, to love and to cherish, until death do us part."

I put every ounce of love and commitment into those words, meaning every word and vow with every fibre of my being. I give my entire soul to this man standing before me. And I will love and cherish him until the very last breath leaves my body. Body and soul, I am his, and he is mine.

When it comes to the exchanging of the rings, Ben smiles with pride as his moment in the spotlight finally comes to fruition, Jonny's best man and best friend handing our precious wedding rings over to the officiant at her request. Ben can't help but flash his trademark wink and cheeky smile over at me and Jonny before taking his seat once more next to Stacey.

The officiant hands Jonny my wedding ring, telling him the words he needs to say, although I'm fairly sure that by now, Jonny knows exactly the words to say to me in this moment.

"Lauren, take this ring as a sign of my love and fidelity. I pledge to you all that I am and all that I will ever be as yours. Forever and always."

Jonny smiles down at me as he slips the wedding ring on to my finger, his little addition of our three special words at the end of his vows there making my chest expand even more for him.

As the officiant hands Jonny's wedding ring over to me, I take a moment to draw breath, before looking up once more into the eyes of the man I love with all my heart and soul. Without breaking eye contact, I say the vows I've been longing to say to him for what feels like an eternity.

"Jonny, take this ring as a sign of my love and fidelity. I pledge to you all that I am and all that I will ever be as yours…forever and always."

I can't help it. I had to include those three special words into my vows too, Jonny smiling down at me with happiness. Sheer happiness. Once Jonny's wedding ring is firmly in place, the officiant looks over at us with a huge smile on her face.

"Jonny and Lauren have made their commitment to each other today, in front of their friends, their family. Their love and devotion to one another is clear to see, and so without further ado, it gives me great pleasure to say the following words. Jonny and Lauren, I now pronounce you husband and wife."

No sooner has the officiant said those words to us and Jonny is scooping me up into his arms, spinning me around on the spot as he kisses the very life out of me. Our friends behind us jump up from their chairs, clapping and whistling, whooping loudly. The officiant herself is clapping right along with them, and after kissing Jonny's lips for the first time as his wife, I then throw my head backwards and let out an overly loud squeal of happiness. Jonny is laughing right along with me, still spinning me around on the spot as our friends look on.

The next thing we know, we are being covered in rose petals by everybody around us, including the officiant and the staff from the hotel. The sun beats down on us all as Stacey, Ben, Will and Zack crowd around us both in a huge group hug. We've finally done it. We have finally become husband and wife at long last, and what a wonderful feeling it is.

CHAPTER 23

LAUREN

Straight after the wedding ceremony, we are whisked off to our little reception gathering over at the venue. A small but quaint little garden area which is located around the back of a beautiful Italian inspired bistro is where the six of us are seated right now. Situated amongst palm trees and well away from the prying eyes of everybody else in the main restaurant, this beautiful little haven is exactly the place I had in mind for our intimate wedding reception.

Twinkling fairy lights and a trail of ivy weaving its way between dozens upon dozens of tropical flowers adorn the expansive wooden pergola above us. A large circular table has been set up for the six of us beneath the pergola, the white tablecloth and fancy looking napkins and tableware looking as perfect as can be.

A large spray of pink and white lilies sit in a tall glass vase in the centre of the table with tealights scattered around. The lilies themselves smell sublime and they look absolutely stunning, really finishing off the whole newly married, romantic vibe I had envisioned for our cosy little gathering this afternoon.

A small bar area is situated at the very back of the garden, together with a music system, several speakers of which are dotted around the place I notice. I am more than ready for some music. Jonny's music preferably but we shall see how we go.

Once the food has been brought out and demolished, the lot of us absolutely starving, the champagne then gets poured out and it's time for the all-important speeches.

Not looking at all nervous, Jonny stands up beside me, his suit jacket long gone, along with his waistcoat and tie. How he and the lads actually wore those suits out there on that red hot beach this afternoon, I will never know, but I love him all the more for it, for the sentiment behind it.

Looking up at Jonny right now, as he's about to make his speech, which I have no doubt will be heartfelt and sincere, I can't help but still feel so taken aback by how gorgeous he actually is. Especially in a suit. I never thought I would ever see the day when my rock star wore a suit but as per the norm with Jonny, he wore a suit today and he wore it well.

His crisp white shirt is now open at the collar and he's rolled up his sleeves to just below his elbows, giving me one hell of a view of those tattooed arms of his I adore so much. The tattoos on his chest are just about peeping out at me from the open collar of his shirt too, now that he's loosened up a little bit after the ceremony. Mmm, I have my sexy tattooed bad boy standing before me once again. And that sexy tattooed bad boy of mine is now my husband. *My* husband. My stomach flips whenever I think of Jonny as my husband. But he is. And believe me when I say that my new husband is going to find out just how much his new wife wants to love and adore him later on.

Looking down at me, Jonny smiles his happiest smile, before turning his attention back to our friends around the table. "I could tell you all a thousand stories about Lauren and me, about when and how we met, about how crazily stupid we were as young teenagers and about how in love we actually were. Back then. Right now. And not forgetting all those lost years without each other in between."

Our eyes meet for a brief moment when he says that, my emotions from earlier during the ceremony beginning to bubble to the surface all over again. Turning back to our friends, Jonny continues.

"But I'm not going to stand here and tell you about any of those stories, because if I did, then you'd all be old and grey by the time I finished telling you all about them." We all chuckle, Jonny trying to lighten the mood a little, which I'm more than grateful for. The last thing I want right now is to burst into tears in my champagne glass.

"But the one thing I will say about Lauren is this. Lauren is my soul mate, my one and only. She is the love of my life and the very epitome of what a person should be. Beautiful inside and out. Kind, thoughtful, loving and generous. She wants for nothing and yet I want to give her everything. Absolutely everything."

Turning to me, Jonny's gaze locks with mine once more as he raises his champagne glass in the air. "Mrs Lauren Mathers, my beautiful wife, the love of my life. I love and adore you more than life itself. This toast is for you, my radiant bride, my angel, my light in the darkness and the rainbow in my many storms. Happy wedding day, beautiful."

Jonny flashes me one of his trademark winks but even that cannot stop the tears of emotion now rolling their way down my cheeks. So much for not crying into my champagne glass!

I stand up from my chair and practically throw my arms around him, almost knocking the champagne glass right out of his hand and on to the floor below. But I don't care. I just want to shower him with love and kisses. So many kisses. Our friends whistle and clap as Jonny places his champagne glass down on to the table before hauling me up into his arms, Ben yet again shouting at us to get a room. Well, we don't have a room. We instead have an entire suite to take advantage of later on....

"Dude, you gonna find the time to put her down so that I can take centre stage for a few minutes?" says Ben, finally forcing us to pull apart so we can allow him into the limelight for his big moment. I really want Ben to shine during his best man's speech and so, albeit reluctantly, I allow Jonny to place me back down on to the floor before taking my seat around the table once more, Jonny following suit.

"Okay, Benny boy," says Jonny, "let's hear it."

I elbow Jonny in the ribs, silently warning him yet again to not take the piss. He gives me his usual eye roll in response before turning his attention back to Ben who is now standing up from his chair with a piece of paper in his hands. Smoothing down his shirt, Ben looks over at Jonny to begin with.

"Well, what can I say?" Ben smirks over at Jonny in his usual cocky like manner, almost like he's goading his best friend already. Jonny narrows his eyes on him but Ben just shakes his head in response. "Only kidding."

Clearing his throat, as if suddenly nervous, Ben then glances down at the piece of paper in his hands before finally mustering up the courage to speak.

"I first met Jonny when we formed the band, so I've known Jonny now for over ten years of my life. In that time, we've made music together, drank together, toured the world together, and, dare I say it, we've also fought together. But, throughout all those years of knowing Jonny, being his band mate as well as one of his best friends, I feel like I've only gotten to know the real Jonny since Lauren came back into his life in July last year. Believe me when I say, the Jonny I know now, the one beneath all the big bravado, the man behind the stage mask, is so much more than the Jonny I knew long before Lauren came along."

My hand sneaks its way into Jonny's, our fingers knotting tightly together as Jonny looks over at me through yearning eyes, the pair of us remembering our reunion fondly, at how we both found each other again, and how finding each other made us whole once more.

Turning our attention back to Ben, he continues with his beautiful, heartfelt speech. A speech that at one point, Stacey was really worried he may not be able to write.

"Like Jonny just said in his own speech about Lauren a few minutes ago, I could stand here right now and tell you a thousand stories about the time me and Jonny have spent together over the years, some of the hilarious moments and memories from our time in the band, but instead, I'll settle for this. I've known you, Jonny, with and without Lauren. I've seen you at the top of your game when you were strutting about that stage with us in the band, and I've seen you fall and hit rock bottom, but what I've seen the most throughout all of that, is how much love you have for that beautiful woman sitting beside you, and how much love she has for you in return."

Ben smiles over at the pair of us, pausing briefly. "And as much as I profess to hate all the soppy romantic stuff that seems to have descended upon our tightknit group since you two reunited back in London, I've actually grown to quite like it. So much so, that I went on to meet Stacey, the girl who turned my head more than just the once, and the one who kept me going back for more, and for that, I thank you, Jonny. For not only bringing Lauren into our lives, as lovely as she is, but for bringing Stacey into our lives too. Into my life."

Gazing down at Stacey who is looking about as emotional as I feel right now, Ben then says, "I love you, Stace." He flashes her a cheeky wink and then looks between the rest of us as he says, "I love you all. But that is the one and only time you will ever hear me say that...except for you, babe."

Turning back to Stacey, Ben grins like the loved up loon he is before he plants one hell of a smacker on the lips of my best friend, Stacey trapping his face in her hands as the rest of us stand up from our seats and applaud Ben loudly for his wonderful speech.

That really was the most wonderful speech Ben could have ever delivered, and any doubts over whether or not he would be able to do it or whether he would make a joke out of it all have now been well and truly put to bed.

I watch as Jonny pulls Ben to one side a moment later, the pair of them seemingly having a serious conversation before doing the whole back slapping, man hug stuff they sometimes do. I can tell that Ben has hit a bit of an emotional nerve with Jonny this afternoon, and I am so happy that all my worries about them taking the piss or winding each other up have gone out of the window for today. This wedding day of ours has been perfect from start to finish, but the day isn't over just yet. In fact, it's only just getting started....

****

Our wedding celebrations carry on well into the night, the six of us heading back to our private beach where Jonny and I exchanged vows earlier on. Tealights are scattered upon the sand, the champagne is still flowing, and Jonny and I are dancing away to the sound of acoustic guitars and bongos as Ben, Will and Zack put on a bit of a performance for us newlyweds. Even Jonny can't resist playing his guitar later on, serenading me with Bruno Mars' Marry You. It's all wildly romantic and so much fun.

The stories we've all shared together today, the laughter

we've had, the high emotions and the happy tears have made this wedding day of ours as magical as Jonny and I envisioned it to be.

And it's about to get a whole lot more magical as Jonny finally manages to steal me away from everybody else, the pair of us finally bidding our friends a goodnight as we head back to our wedding suite, desperate for some alone time.

I've been dreaming about this moment all day long, the moment where Jonny slowly, oh so slowly, peels me out of my wedding dress, leaving me standing in nothing but my bridal lingerie. The bridal lingerie I picked out especially for tonight. All so I can get my rock star husband all hot under the collar and worked up to the point where he can no longer handle it.

Needless to say, my ivory sheer lace bra with matching thong, stockings, and suspender belt goes down very well with Jonny. He stands behind me next to the bed, his chest to my back, as he drags the tips of his fingers back and forth over my shoulders, my collarbone, my neck.

"You look exquisite tonight," he whispers, his breath dancing across the overly sensitive skin just behind my ear. It gives me goosebumps. "And you looked beautiful today. So beautiful. My angel. My wife."

My stomach clenches at hearing him call me his wife. There is something so erotic about the way he utters those two words to me. It does wondrous things to my insides. Snaking one of his arms around my waist from behind, Jonny then places his mouth against the nape of my neck, where the locket he bought for me containing Oliver's scan picture still hangs.

"He was beautiful too," Jonny whispers, his voice almost breaking with emotion, "and I'm so glad that a part of him got to be with us today."

Jonny falls silent for a moment, and I rest my head back

against his right shoulder, melting into his embrace, his words, his love for me and for the son we lost. "Me too," I whisper back to him.

"Just as a part of my mum got to be with us today too," says Jonny, glancing down at the leather bracelet I bought for him. With my left hand, I reach out to touch the leather bracelet adorning his wrist, sweeping my thumb back and forth across the engraving on the silver clasp as I remember the wonderful woman that was Jonny's mum.

"I'll never take this bracelet off," says Jonny, pulling his emotional gaze back to mine. "And as much as I don't want to remove that locket from around your neck, knowing what it means to you, knowing what's inside, I really think that I'm going to have to take it off, at least for tonight."

Jonny presses a soft, gentle kiss to my lips and I turn around in his arms, placing the palms of my hands against his cheeks as I kiss him right back, telling him I understand exactly why he needs to remove my locket, even if it is just for tonight. This locket means the world to me and yet, I want to treasure it and look after it, and so, whenever this locket isn't around my neck, it will be safely locked away in my jewellery box until the next time I come to wear it.

Removing the locket ever so gently from around my neck, Jonny locks it safely away in my jewellery box before returning to where I am standing by the bed. He then takes the time to carefully remove every single clip and pin that had been holding my hair together today, allowing my mass of long blonde curls to tumble over my shoulders and down my back.

After that little job is taken care of, he stands in front of me for a long moment, the need and the want in his eyes so clear for me to see. He appraises my every inch, his fingers softly caressing the skin of my stomach before skimming their way around the lacy hem of my thong.

"I want you badly," he whispers, his eyes now bouncing back and forth between mine, "so very badly."

"Then have me, husband," I whisper back to him, Jonny's eyes flaring at the endearment. "Take me for the first time as your wife, and don't hold back. I never want you to hold back when it comes to having me."

Cupping my face in his hands, Jonny closes what little distance there was between us. "I want to savour you tonight," he murmurs, pressing a featherlight kiss to the corner of my mouth. "But the animal within me is really struggling to contain himself right now."

Gazing up at him through hungry, lustful eyes, I say, "Then savour me, make love to me, fuck me."

Jonny's eyes darken at hearing those words fall from my mouth, the flames of passion igniting between us like a lightning bolt from the blue. "Say that again," he mutters, his voice sounding all gruff, "please god say that to me again."

Raking my teeth back and forth over my bottom lip, I thread my hands together around the back of his neck as I repeat the words back to him. "I said, savour me, make love to me, and then fuck me."

I know Jonny is dying to do exactly that, shove me back on to the bed and fuck the living daylights out of me, but the gentle, softer side of him seems to win the war currently raging inside of him. Instead, he gently lies me down on to the soft silk duvet beneath me before taking a step backwards.

I gaze up at him standing at the foot of the bed. Showing a restraint I never thought possible, he begins to unbutton his shirt. Almost like a stripper doing the ultimate tease before the main event, Jonny slowly begins to reveal the tattoos on his chest and arms to me, peeling off his shirt in what feels like super slow motion capture. It is without doubt one of the hottest moments of my life, watching my new husband doing a full on strip show for me, with his eyes on me the entire time.

The belt goes next, shortly followed by him pulling the zipper down on his trousers. He allows both his trousers and his boxer shorts to drop to the floor before standing proud in front of me, his long, thick length already glistening at the tip and just begging for me to be on the receiving end of it.

Eyes still well and truly on me, Jonny then slowly crawls his way on to the bed, bracing himself above me as he takes a moment to drink me in. Reaching up, I brush my fingertips across the skin of his cheek, and he closes his eyes on a sigh, turning his mouth into my palm as he presses a kiss there. "I love you," he whispers, "I love you so fucking much."

Opening his eyes once more, Jonny's dark browns blaze down into my blue ones as he begins to kiss the tips of my fingers, one by one, at an agonisingly slow pace that has every nerve ending in my body standing to attention. I watch him intently as he licks and kisses my fingers, the intimacy and the raw openness of the moment literally turning me into a puddled wet mess beneath him.

God, how does he do that? Turn something as innocent as kissing my fingers into something so scorching hot that I feel I might explode if he carries on like he is doing. I'm barely holding on to my own restraint here, never mind Jonny and his.

"Make love to me, Jonny," I plead, wanting him to put me out of the agonising wait for him to be inside me. I want him desperately, and I don't want to have to wait a second longer. "Please," I beg.

Hearing me beg and plead has the desired effect on Jonny I'd hoped it would. Ripping my fingers away from his mouth, his lips suddenly crash into mine as his fingers go to work on ridding me of my lingerie as quickly as possible.

"As much as I love seeing you in stockings and suspenders, I still prefer you naked, wet and completely open for me, baby." *Oh my god.*

No sooner has my bridal lingerie been torn away from my body and Jonny is thrusting into me, causing me to cry out as he buries himself deep inside, touching that special place within me only he can reach. We are husband and wife now, coming together as one for the first time as a married couple, and what a feeling it is.

Jonny pauses momentarily as he gazes down at me lovingly, and with so much passion, so much want and need, that it marks me, it burns its way into my skin, into my very blood. When Jonny reaches down to kiss me once more, I wrap my hands around the back of his head and claim that mouth of his as mine. This man is all mine and more, and I am going to show him just how much I love and adore him.

Opening my legs that little bit wider, I then smooth my hands down his back, from the nape of his neck and his shoulders, all the way down to his beautifully taut bottom, urging him to move inside me. I want to feel him thrusting into me, over and over, so madly, so deeply, to the point where we drive each other insane with the feeling.

As Jonny begins to slowly move inside me, I dig my fingernails into the bare flesh of his bottom, silently telling him I want more. I want him harder, deeper, and I want all the rough, untamed wildness that goes hand in hand with the man I love.

With one hand braced above my head, Jonny drags his other hand down my face, allowing his fingers to trail over my eyes, my mouth. I close my eyes, allowing my head to fall backwards as I revel in the feel of Jonny's fingers coming to rest against my mouth, his cock now driving into me at a much faster pace than it was just a moment ago.

I kiss the tips of his fingers in desperation, my tongue darting out every now and again as I feel Jonny's cock swell inside of me, the inner animal within him about to be unleashed.

"Fuck...Lauren..." Jonny lets out an agonised groan as I squeeze his bottom that little bit more, and he surges into me faster, harder.

"Oh god...Jonny...please," I beg.

"Open your eyes," he pants, "I need to see those deep blues when you come, baby."

At hearing his command, my eyes flash open and Jonny roars like a wild animal, his gaze searing into mine as he finally loses all sense of control. Ripping one of my hands away from his bottom, Jonny then presses it into the mattress above my head, his fingers linking with mine at the exact moment his orgasm hits.

"Fuuuuuck..." he growls, his forehead pressing hard against mine as I feel the warmth of his juices flooding into me.

Seeing him come apart in front of my very eyes, watching the pleasure take over, the pure desperation on his face because of what I do to him, it breaks me apart, and I come with a loud cry.

Jonny watches me as I thrash wildly beneath him, wave after wave of pure nirvana washing over me. Neither of us look away in that moment, and it is so primal, so raw, that I come again. I can't help it. Jonny rips my emotions to pieces, shattering me, every single time. And I cannot get enough. I will never be able to get enough of this man and what he does to me. Ever.

Jonny collapses on top of me in a heap afterwards, panting,

breathless and well and truly sated. I curl my hand around the nape of his neck and press a soft kiss to his left temple. Jonny then nuzzles his nose against my cheek and pulls me in close, his hot sweaty body clinging to mine, reminding me yet again of why I always, and I mean always, want to get to work on him all over again.

Looking over at me, Jonny flashes me one of his cheeky smiles. "So much for savouring each other."

Biting down on a smile, I say, "There's plenty of time for savouring each other, Jonny. In fact, we have the rest of our married lives to savour each other."

"Oh, we most certainly do," he murmurs, before reaching across to drop a deliciously soft kiss on to my lips. Resting his head into the crook of my neck this time, he then says, "We also have the rest of tonight to savour each other, and just so you know, I intend to make you come every single hour for the duration of our wedding night." Mmm, I love the sound of that, and I tell him as much.

"Is that a promise?" I whisper.

Meeting my gaze once more, he whispers, "Damn fucking right it's a promise."

"I'll hold you to that promise, Mr Mathers."

"Oh, I have no doubt that you will, *Mrs* Mathers."

Brushing my knuckles back and forth across his cheek, I gaze down lovingly at my new husband as a whole flurry of butterflies begin to take flight and do a happy dance in that tummy of mine.

"You know, I love hearing the sound of my married name on your lips, as well as you referring to me as your wife. It does things to me like you wouldn't believe."

Brushing a stray lock of hair away from my right cheek, Jonny then runs his fingers into my mass of curls, a mischievous smile tugging at the corner of his mouth.

"That's good to know," he says, "and believe me when I say, it's exactly the same for me too."

Resting my hand against the side of his head, I let out a satisfied sigh. "Thank you for today," I whisper to him. "Thank you for making our wedding day so special. Your wedding speech was absolutely beautiful, the things you said about me. About us. And Ben's speech was pretty amazing too."

"I meant every single word of that speech," he says to me, his eyes suddenly misting over with emotion. "And I have to say, Ben's speech really did hit an emotional nerve with me today. He did me proud. He did us all proud."

"He really did," I agree, feeling so very grateful for the wonderful friends we have around us, because, let's face it, without them, Jonny and I wouldn't even be here right now. "We're very lucky to have friends like them in our life," I say, voicing my innermost thoughts.

"We most certainly are." He smiles.

"And speaking of our friends, I couldn't quite believe it when I first saw you and the lads standing there in suits. I was so shocked."

"Well I wanted to make the effort and surprise you. Admittedly they weren't overly keen at first but they knew, just as I did, how much it would mean to you."

"Well it meant the world to me, Jonny, as did the Coldplay song you re-recorded for me, especially for our big day. I will never forget that for as long as I live and breathe."

I reach across so I can place a tender, loving kiss on to those yummy lips of his. The yummy lips of my husband I will never ever tire of. When I pull back, Jonny says, "And that song is a special, private version by Reclamation that will only ever be for the ears of you and you alone. Because if it ever got leaked out into the world, I would have one hell of a copyright lawsuit on my ass."

I chuckle. "Yeah, we wouldn't want that, and so I promise to keep that special version of yours for my ears only."

"That's my girl," he murmurs, before pressing another delicious kiss to my lips. "You know, I don't think I'll ever be able to get enough of kissing these soft, sumptuous lips of yours, Mrs Mathers." *Oh my, here we go again.*

"And I'll never be able to get enough of you kissing said lips and saying my married name over and over," I tell him.

With a naughty glint in his eye, Jonny then shifts himself so he is on top of me once more. Placing his hands on either side of my head, he gazes down at me in that oh so familiar way that tells me he is more than ready for round two.

"Oh, Mrs Mathers, I am about to make good on that promise of mine from earlier."

"Is that so?" I tease, my teeth sinking into my bottom lip as Jonny's lips find the well of my throat, his tongue darting out to lick at the skin there.

"Abso-fucking-lutely," he whispers.

I gasp as I feel Jonny's mouth travelling south of my neck, leaving a trail of open-mouthed kisses in his wake, over my breasts, between my breasts, across my stomach, my hips, all the way down until that godly like mouth of his is buried between my legs. Holy shit, he really does have the mouth of a rock god. And I am now married to that rock god. Lucky me.

CHAPTER 24

LAUREN

We return home from our wedding/honeymoon as newlyweds two weeks later, feeling happy and content with the new home we have started to build together, as well as the fresh new chapter in our lives that we more than deserve. Jonny and I have been through so much heartbreak over the years, both together and apart, but that heartbreak is now well and truly behind us as we embark on married life together.

We have so many exciting things to look forward to over the next twelve months, such as Jonny and the rest of Reclamation exploding back on to the stage next year with one hell of a comeback concert, as well as the release of their new album, me hopefully finding that longed for career in the theatre somewhere, and of course having lots and lots of fun with our friends in between.

Making happy memories together is a promise both Jonny and I have made to each other, but not before putting the very last painful memory of our past to rest once and for all. The sprinkling of our son's ashes in our beautiful rose garden, which we have now officially named 'Oliver's Garden.' An idea that came about from none other than my loving husband.

When Jonny first suggested his idea to me one evening while we were away in Mauritius, I felt so overcome with emotion at the thoughtfulness of the man I had just married, I honestly didn't quite know what to say to him at first. I was so taken aback by the beautiful idea that I admittedly cried a few tears. In fact, we both cried a few tears that night. But we need to cry those tears for the boy we lost, because locking up that grief inside of ourselves after it initially happened just wasn't healthy. Sadly, whether it was healthy or not, grief isn't something you can control. Once it takes a hold of you, that knife cuts deep, so very deep it can send you spiralling into a world of nothing but darkness and pain.

Thinking back to how I buried my grief back then, at how I pushed it all down in the hope I could pretend I hadn't lost my baby boy, it makes me feel ashamed. Ashamed because of how it must have looked to everybody else around me. As though I was trying to forget about my little boy when in reality, I was just pretending inside my head that he did still exist and that he hadn't been cruelly ripped away from me.

Glancing at the stone archway entrance as we walk into the garden, Jonny and I smile up at the sign we had specially made in readiness for today. Oliver's name sparkles down at us in the early afternoon sun, each letter of his name having been done in a different colour, like a rainbow.

Rainbows have become a bit of a thing for me and Jonny, him telling me many times over recent months of how I became his rainbow in his many storms. And we now like to think of Oliver as our rainbow. *Our* rainbow in *our* many storms that Jonny and I may still face together. I really hope and pray that most of the storms we ever faced are behind us, but sometimes, with life, you just never know what's around the corner.

Either way, whatever life throws at us from now on, Jonny and I are back together, and this time it's for keeps. We are married and happy, so deliriously happy that I have to pinch myself sometimes to make sure what's happened to us is real, that this wonderful thing called fate has finally turned a corner and given us our long fought for happy ending after all. A happy ending that's been a long time coming for us.

"Are you ready?" asks Jonny, giving my hand a gentle squeeze.

Standing next to my new husband, hand in hand, with the locket he bought for me hanging around my neck containing the scan picture of our son, I squeeze his hand right back and nod my head.

"I'm ready," I whisper. And for the first time in my life, since the day I lost him, I really do feel ready to sprinkle the ashes of our son, and Jonny feels ready too.

"I love you," he says to me, his eyes full of nothing but love and adoration for me, "and I love our little boy. More than I've ever loved anything or anyone in my life."

I smile over at the man I love more than anything else in the entire world. My rock star. My husband. My life. "I love you too, Jonny. And I love our little boy. So much."

Reaching across, Jonny presses a soft, tender kiss to my lips. When he pulls away, he whispers, "So let's go and set him free."

Walking deeper into our rose garden, Jonny and I set our little boy free that day. We cry so many tears as we sprinkle his ashes in a garden that will be the perfect place for him to run free, amongst so many flowers and colours, a garden absolutely teeming with life. I think a part of us is also freed that day in the garden, like an unburdening of so many emotions after so many years of closing ourselves off to all the pain.

When we walk out of Oliver's Garden over an hour later, feeling content that his soul has been put to rest at long last, it feels as though we are stepping into our next chapter together, a brand new exciting chapter in our lives that is about to begin, and what a chapter it is going to be....

****

JONNY

10 Months Later – Rose Bowl Stadium, Pasadena, California – August 2017

"Where is she?" I ask, my anxiety beginning to worm its way into my gut as the thought of stepping back on to the stage in front of sixty thousand Reclamation fans, as well as the ones tuning in from all over the world, begins to get the better of me.

"She'll be here," says Stacey, trying her best to reassure me. "She wouldn't miss this for the world, Jonny, you know that. Her audition must have run over or something. Let me try ringing her again."

Five minutes. That's the only time I have left before I have to get up on to that stage out there, and I can't do it without my wife standing by my side. I just can't. And I won't.

I pace back and forth in my dressing room, Stacey trying her best efforts to get hold of Lauren, but for some reason, Lauren's phone isn't even ringing when we've tried calling her, and that only adds to my already anxious state. What if something bad has happened to her? What if she's had a car accident? *Stop it, Jonny. You're doing that whole leap frogging shit you used to do, and you really don't need to start with that shit again, not after how far you've come.*

"It still isn't ringing," says Stacey, frowning down at her phone.

"So try Andy again," I reply, sounding a little more abrupt than I intended to sound. I am quick to apologise. "Sorry, Stace, I'm just worried, especially as Andy's phone isn't ringing either."

"Hey, I know you're worried, but I promise you she'll be fine..."

"So why aren't either of their phones ringing then?" I snap, forgetting myself once again. "Shit, I'm sorry, I just..." Letting out an aggravated sigh, I run my hands back and forth through my hair as I start to spiral.

Twenty one months I've been clean and free of the drugs. I feel like I've come so far with kicking that horrendous drug habit of mine, and yet, it's moments like these that really punch me in the gut, reminding me yet again of my need for a fix, and all because I cannot get a handle on my anxiety. Especially when it comes to Lauren.

The fear of losing her is something that won't ever fully leave me, not after everything that happened to us in our past, and sadly, that fear of mine sometimes tips me over the edge, leading me to panic. Really panic. Brian, my counsellor, is still working with me on this crippling anxiety of mine, and he's got me to a much stronger place than where I originally was nearly two years ago, but I'm admittedly still struggling. I thought I was ready to go back up on to that stage tonight but as it turns out, I'm not, so what the fuck do I do now?

I can hear the deafening roar of so many Reclamation fans filtering its way through to me in my dressing room. I can hear the stamping of their feet, the shouting and the chanting as they wait with baited breath to see the long awaited return of a band they've come to love and adore. Shit, I can't handle this. I really can't.

Ben comes strolling into my dressing room a moment later, all geared up and ready to go for the comeback concert we've spent months and months planning. A comeback concert that was supposed to signal the return of our band, but if Lauren isn't here within the next five minutes, then that comeback concert of ours won't be happening.

"Dude, they've given us the five minute call, we need to get our asses up there pronto." Looking between me and Stacey, he then says, "You okay?"

I shake my head at him. "No, I'm not okay. Lauren isn't here."

"She isn't?" he asks, looking surprised.

Stacey rolls her eyes at him. "Well, do you see her anywhere in this dressing room with us right now, Ben?"

He narrows his eyes on her. "Yeah, okay, no need for sarcasm. I've been busy running around out there like a headless fucking chicken. Lauren could have arrived and gone to the toilet and I wouldn't have known. Where is she?"

"Well if I knew that, I wouldn't be fucking panicking right now, would I?" I snap at him.

Ben is about to respond when suddenly, the door to my dressing room opens once again and Lauren comes dashing in looking panic stricken. "Oh, Jonny, I'm so sorry I'm late," she says, rushing into my arms.

And boy do I haul her up into my arms, relief flooding through me like you wouldn't believe. "Shit, I thought something bad had happened to you," I whisper, feeling suddenly teary. I run my hands through her hair as I hold her tightly against me, my heart still thudding against my ribcage in panic. So much panic.

"We got stuck in traffic," she says, placing her hands against my cheeks. "And then for some reason, the phone signal on both Andy's phone and mine just dropped out, so we couldn't call you. We're on the same network you see, and…"

"Sssh, it's okay, baby, you're here now and that's all that matters." And it really is all that matters to me right now.

Walking over to where we are embracing by the dressing room mirror, Stacey gives Lauren's arm a quick squeeze. "So glad you're here." Glancing up at me, she then says, "You gave this one a fright."

"Oh, I'm sorry," says Lauren, looking terribly guilty.

"No need to apologise," I say to her, "it was something beyond your control and thankfully, no harm done." I give her a quick kiss on the lips, and she smiles. "So, how did the audition go?"

"Oh, you know," she shrugs her shoulder at me, "I kind of got offered the part on the spot…"

"You what?" I ask excitedly, my panic and anxiety about going on stage in a few minutes time going by the wayside for the moment. "You got the part?"

She beams up at me. "I got the part!"

"Oh, baby, I am so fucking proud of you!" I exclaim, before picking her up from the floor and spinning her around on the spot, both Stacey and Ben joining in on the mini celebration we've got going on in the corner of my dressing room.

"Oh, Lauren that is amazing!" screeches Stacey, doing a happy little dance for Lauren as Ben looks on, chuckling away at the happy scene unfolding in front of us.

"Congrats, Lauren," says Ben, giving Lauren's shoulder a quick squeeze as I place her back on the floor. "If anybody deserves their big break, it's you." He flashes her a cheeky wink and she returns his wink with one of her own.

The door to my dressing room then opens for the third time in as many minutes. This time it's one of the production crew shouting for me and Ben to get our asses on to that stage, and fast. Fuck, this is it. Time to step back into the spotlight.

Nodding my head over at the male crew member, I say, "I'm

coming. I just need a minute alone with my girl first." And I really do need a minute alone with Lauren. In fact, I need a whole lot more than just a minute but if a minute is all I've got then I'll take it.

"See you up there," says Ben, bumping fists with me before he leaves the room.

"Good luck, Jonny," says Stacey, squeezing my arm. "Not that you'll need it. You'll be back to your best out there tonight, I have no doubt about that." Turning to Lauren, Stacey then says, "See you out there in five, girl."

"Thanks, Stace," I shout over to her as she walks out of the room.

As soon as the door closes and we are alone, I am kissing Lauren like I've been starved of her. And of course she responds, as she always does, wrapping her hands around the back of my head as we share one final kiss before I take to the stage for the first time in almost two years. Two years. How the fuck am I going to do this?

"I can't do this," I suddenly blurt out as I wrench my lips away from hers, "I honestly cannot go out there tonight and perform…"

"Yes you can," she says, firmly. Holding my gaze, she brushes her thumbs ever so softly against the skin of my cheeks, and I sigh into her touch, my eyes closing briefly. "And you can do it because you are Jonny Mathers, rock god of the stage, and rock god of the bedroom too, as my memory likes to recall so often."

She bites down on a cheeky smile and for the first time since I stepped foot into this dressing room tonight, I feel the anxiety over performing beginning to dissipate.

I smile down at this wonderful woman standing in front of me, thinking how fucking lucky I am to have found her.

"Damn right I am rock god of the bedroom, and don't ever forget it," I murmur, before planting another kiss on to those soft, sweet lips of hers.

When I pull away, I press my forehead against hers as I try to work through my spiralling anxiety. "What if I fuck up again though?" I ask, "like I did in Chicago."

Running a reassuring hand through my hair, Lauren says, "Jonny, you were high on drugs, and you were unwell at the time. Really unwell. That time in your life is now long gone and you and the rest of the band have worked your asses off these last ten months to get this comeback concert together, and don't forget about why you are doing this concert. Not just for your fans but…for your mum too."

Placing her hand on my chest, over my heart, Lauren then says, "Your mum would be so proud of you for getting yourself back to this point, for getting yourself strong enough again so you could plan this comeback concert, for writing and recording your new album that's shortly going to be released into the world. And I promise you that from wherever she is, she will be right here with you tonight, cheering you on from the side of that stage, just as I will be. Me and Stacey. And… selfishly, I really want to hear you perform the song you wrote in memory of your mum. A song I am sure will be as beautiful as the man who wrote it. A song that deserves to be heard. You are more than ready to get back out there and do what you love doing. And I know you're ready. You just have to believe that you are."

Wow, Lauren has done it again. Rendered me completely speechless with her beautiful words, the emotion in her eyes as well as her voice as she talked about my mum just now. I swear she literally reaches deep into my soul sometimes, settling me and calming me from the inside out. Which is exactly why I wanted her here with me tonight. Hell, I need her here. And I will always need her. For better for worse, she is stuck with me now. For the rest of eternity. And I tell her as much.

"You do realise that you're stuck with this broken down wreck of a rock star for the rest of your days, don't you?" I jest, trying to make light of my anxiety and my spiralling emotions.

Dragging her teeth over her bottom lip, Lauren rakes her eyes over my face as she says, "Oh, there's nothing whatsoever broken about you, Jonny Mathers. And even if there was, I'd just pick all your broken pieces up and glue you back together again."

I grin, thinking how utterly cute and sweet she is for coming out with a line like that. "You kind of did glue me back together, because I did break." And I really did, but then, so did she. We broke together and now here we are, two years down the line, and we've glued each other back together again.

"Well, I broke too," she says, as if reading my mind, "and you glued me back together again. So we're stuck together now. No matter what."

"Mmm, I kind of like the thought of being glued to you for the rest of my life, baby," I murmur, giving her ass a quick squeeze through the material of this hot looking outfit she's wearing. An all black jump suit with thigh high slits and a plunging neckline, complete with five inch sparkling silver killer heels on her feet.

Lauren really does look like the knock out she is tonight, with her smoky eyeshadow, full pink lips and long blonde curls tumbling over her shoulders. I can see I'm going to have real trouble prising myself away from her to go up on to that stage, although I won't be away from her for very long.

"Me too," she smiles, gazing up at me in that way I love so damn much. After a beat, she says, "So, I think it's time for you to get this deliciously taut leather clad ass of yours back up on to that stage, Jonny Mathers."

I belt out a laugh as she gives my so called deliciously taut leather clad ass a squeeze with her hands. "You missed the leather pants I take it?" I jest.

"Hell yeah I've missed them," she says, her eyes twinkling mischievously. "I've missed this leather jacket of yours too."

"I always wear a leather jacket," I say to her.

"Yeah, but this one is special, it has your name on the back in silvery letters and everything."

She then turns the collar of what she now refers to as my 'special' leather jacket upwards, much like she did two years ago in London, right before I went on stage to perform the last concert of our five night run at the O2 arena. Back then however, I was bare chested beneath this leather jacket. Tonight, I'm not. My chest is staying well and truly under wraps for this comeback concert.

Whilst I'll still be banging out the rocky numbers later on, the opening of this concert is in memory of my mum, and it's going to be a highly emotional moment for me when I first take to that stage. Putting myself out there in front of all those fans, as well as the fans tuning in from around the world, is not going to be an easy feat after a two year absence, and with the loss of my mum still very raw, it's going to be even harder.

I just hope that our fans out there are ready for the real Jonny tonight, because the real Jonny is the one they are going to be watching. I am at least more than assured that my biggest fan, my favourite fan of them all, is more than ready to see the real Jonny perform up on that stage tonight.

"Are you going all fanlike on me, Mrs Mathers?"

Her lips pull into a suggestive grin. "Too damn right I am," she whispers, before pulling me in for yet another kiss. I only wish I could do so much more than kiss her right now, but sadly, the man from the production crew who came in here earlier, is now gracing us with his presence once more.

"Time's up Jonny," he says, looking less than pleased with me being so last minute. "You needed to be on stage three minutes ago."

"Our fans have been waiting for this moment for the last two years, so I'm sure a few more minutes won't make much of a difference," I say to him as I walk past, Lauren's hand firmly in mine as I pull her along with me.

She chuckles. "There's my arrogant rock star, I knew he was in there somewhere."

I drop a kiss on to her hand, swiftly followed by a cheeky wink as we continue to walk down the long corridor towards the stage together. "And you damn well love it," I mutter, grinning like the conceited idiot I can be sometimes. Yes, I can do this after all. I know I can. *Okay, Jonny, let's do this.*

****

LAUREN

It's been over two years since I last saw Jonny and the rest of Reclamation perform at the O2 arena down in London. Two entire years. And now here I am, two years on, with Stacey standing beside me, at the Rose Bowl Stadium in Pasadena, California, where Jonny and the lads are about to perform for sixty thousand screaming Reclamation fans, as well as the hundreds of thousands of fans tuning in from all around the globe.

It's taken a hell of a long time to get here, Jonny working his absolute ass off to get himself both physically and mentally better after suffering so badly with his mental health following his suicide attempt, but being the strong man he is, he's finally done it. And I honestly cannot wait to watch him take to this stage tonight, not just because I adore watching him perform live, but because of how this wonderful husband of mine is about to honour the memory of his mum.

Paragon is the name of the song Jonny wrote for his mum, way back when we were in the Maldives after he had that vision like dream of her one night. And whilst Jonny hasn't actually performed the song to me, him wanting to keep it under wraps so I can experience it for the very first time tonight at the same time as all their other fans, he eventually gave me the name of the song. He wanted that to be a gift to me. Just me, and only me.

Curious as ever, I had never even heard of the word paragon, and so I grilled Jonny about it straight away, desperately wanting to know the meaning behind the word and the reasoning behind him choosing it.

It turns out that paragon means a person or thing that is regarded as a perfect example of a particular quality, or a person or thing viewed as a model of excellence. Needless to say that in Jonny's eyes, his mum was exactly that, a paragon of virtue, patience and love. So much love. *This song is going to be immense,* I think to myself. But where Jonny's concerned, I don't think it could ever be anything else.

As soon as the stadium lights fade into darkness, the crowd go absolutely berserk, the screaming and chanting ratcheting up to an ear splitting level. Stacey and I are of course stood to the side of the stage, once again being given the best view in the house, and boy are we excited. Really excited. But as excited as I am, I somehow can't manage to muster up enough excitement to jump up and down on the spot and chant along with the rest of the fans as yet, because I am also nervous. So nervous for Jonny and about how he must be feeling right now.

Even though he has worked hard to overcome a lot of his

anxiety and the withdrawal related symptoms that went hand in hand with his past drug addiction, certain events and situations can still trigger him, and you can't get much more triggering than doing something like this. Stepping back on to a stage you once performed on after a two year hiatus. But, as I told him only a few minutes ago in his dressing room, he is ready for this. I know he is. He just has to believe that he is. *You can do this, baby, I am with you every step of the way.*

Stacey grins over at me and then takes a hold of my hand, squeezing it tightly in a show of reassurance. She knows how nervous Jonny is tonight. Hell, she knows how nervous I am for Jonny, and as always, she is standing by our side, supporting us, her strength and friendship having never faltered. She is my best friend, my sister from another mother, and I absolutely love her to death.

Squeezing her hand right back, I give her a nervous smile and then turn my attention back to the stage, where a bright spotlight is slowly beginning to glow. The spotlight grows ever brighter, the crowd busy stamping their feet and chanting Jonny's name, absolutely desperate to set eyes on their idol after not seeing him perform live for far too long.

All of a sudden, Jonny, Ben, Will and Zack walk on to the stage from wherever they were hidden. As they approach the front of the stage, slowly walking towards their fans, the spotlight grows brighter still, gradually basking them all in its warm glow. And no sooner have the fans clapped eyes on all four of them finally gracing them with their presence, and they go absolutely nuts. And I mean nuts.

I thought the O2 arena back in London was wild but this is something else. The amount of fans in this stadium is triple the amount of fans they performed to back in London, not to mention all the fans watching from around the world, cameras upon cameras set up on and around the stage to film the wonderful spectacle that is about to take place here tonight.

When the four of them finally reach the front of the stage, they take a huge bow, the fans still cheering and screaming for them, posters and signs being waved around the stadium, camera flash after camera flash going off, chanting and singing. You name it, this place seriously has it going on tonight, that's for sure. What a welcome Reclamation are receiving right now. A welcome I am so bloody happy to see. In fact, I'm feeling teary and emotional already and he hasn't even started singing as yet.

"Hello everybody!" Jonny finally shouts into the microphone, already sending his crowd of fans into an absolute frenzy. I'm fairly sure Stacey and I will be deaf when we walk out of this stadium tonight, that's how loud their fans are right now.

"I said hello everybody!" I look up at the large screens just above the stage, Jonny putting his hand to his ear as if he can't hear them, smiling over at his audience, much like he did when I saw him perform in London. "I can't hear you! I said hello everybody!"

Stacey and I laugh as we watch Ben, Will and Zack running along the front of the stage, flailing their arms around at their fans, encouraging them to shout even louder. Oh, this is priceless. Seeing this tonight is absolutely priceless. Jonny is already doing what he does best and I bet he doesn't even realise it.

Whether he's still feeling nervous or not, it certainly doesn't show. He absolutely adores performing live and this is why I refused to allow him to quit his music career. As stubborn as he was at the time, I bet he's so glad he powered on through and got himself to this point, because what a showman he is. All of them are. We are in for one hell of a comeback concert tonight, that's for sure.

"Boy are we glad to see you all here tonight!" Jonny shouts into the microphone. "All of you here in this stadium, waiting so patiently for us to begin the concert, and all those fans who are also watching us from around the world. Wherever you are, all four of us are so grateful to all of you for the unwavering love and support you've shown the band over these last two years, and believe me when I say that it feels damn fucking good to be back!"

More screaming and more foot stomping from the crowd as Jonny begins to win over his audience in a way like only Jonny can. His smile, his demeanour, his heartfelt thanks to the fans which is so genuine, they absolutely adore him. I adore him too but then, we already know that.

Looking over at Ben, Will and Zack, Jonny then turns back to his audience and says, "As you all know, this comeback concert came about as a way of making right all the wrongs that happened two years ago when I lost my way after my mum sadly passed away after a long battle with cancer." The crowd fall silent for a moment, all acutely aware of Jonny's public health battle and his former drug addiction.

"But this concert also came about because of my mum. I wanted to honour my mum in the only way I knew how. Through my music. The first song we as a band are going to perform to you tonight is the name of our new album, an album that is about to be launched in the coming weeks and admittedly, an album that's been a long time in the making. But not only that, this song we are about to perform is a song I wrote in memory of my beloved mum, and I ask you all to take this song into your hearts, as I took it into mine when I first wrote it. So, this song is for you, Mum, and it's called Paragon."

The fans descend into more screaming and clapping as Jonny waves over at them all in a show of gratitude and appreciation, true appreciation, the emotion on his face now clear for everyone to see. He then blows them all a bunch of kisses, Ben, Will and Zack joining in and waving over at the crowd once more before they all turn away and head towards their musical instruments in the middle of the stage.

The stadium fades into darkness once more and the deafening roar of sixty thousand Reclamation fans returns with a vengeance. Shit, this is it. This is the moment for Jonny to shine like the wonderful performer he is. Stacey wraps her arms around my shoulders and pulls me tightly against her, clearly sensing my spiralling emotions, because believe me when I say that I am terrified for Jonny. Excited too of course, but terrified. Terrified for him and how he's most likely feeling right now.

A couple of minutes roll on by, my own nerves being shredded to pieces the longer we stand and wait, the fans as loud and as wild as ever, but thankfully, the waiting game is now over with as the bright lights from above suddenly flash to life, the large screens above the stage all now displaying a beautiful photograph of Judy Mathers with the words 'In Loving Memory of Judy Mathers, 1961 – 2015' underneath.

I try to quell my already reeling emotions, and I think I'm just about managing to do it, until I look over at Jonny sitting by the piano in the middle of the stage, with his head bowed, as if sending a silent prayer up to his mum.

I notice that Ben, Will and Zack are all standing by their musical instruments and bowing their heads as well, all remembering Jonny's mum for the beautiful person she was. Stacey and I follow suit, bowing our heads as we take a moment to reflect, the crowd now a little quieter than they were a moment ago.

I can feel the tears threatening to fall down my cheeks, the well of emotions brimming just beneath the surface. And those emotions of mine come spilling out from within the moment Jonny starts to play the piano, his fingers flitting across the keys as I, and the rest of the fans both here and around the world, finally get to hear the song he wrote for his mum. A song that finally gave him back his song writing prowess. And what a beautiful heart wrenching song it is. I bite down on my wobbly bottom lip as I allow Jonny's lyrics to work their way inside of me, as they always do, whenever I hear him sing.

"Archangel falling, archangel falling, give me a reason, a reason left to stand. Send me a message, a way to hold your hand. Tell me a story, the story of your life, we all need comfort in a world full of strife."

"Archangel falling, archangel falling, tell me your heartache, the pain we all bear. Give me a ray of hope, a momentary prayer. Send me a shooting star, down to earth below, I feel so close to you, so never let me go."

Jonny and the rest of Reclamation then descend into a beautifully haunting instrumental, Will playing a powerful electric guitar melody alongside Jonny's piano playing. The bass guitar and the drums kick in about thirty seconds later, taking the song into another place entirely, a soul destroying crescendo that builds and builds until it suddenly drops off, Jonny then playing solo on the piano once more, the emotion on his face so clear for everyone to see as the final lyrics of the song fall softly from his lips and into the microphone.

"Archangel falling, archangel falling, falling on and on, you're my paragon."

The moment Jonny finishes playing the song, the crowd erupt into an explosion, clapping and screaming, more feet stomping, and flashes upon flashes of cameras from every direction. I look up at the screens to see some of the faces of the crowd now being displayed on them as the film crew pan out to catch glimpses of the fans and the looks on their faces.

Most of them are smiling and waving like mad at the cameras but I notice some of them are crying, most likely extremely moved by that performance of Jonny's just now. And they aren't the only ones moved, because Jonny's song has knocked me sideways. To the point where I end up turning and sobbing on to Stacey's shoulder, Stacey being her best self and comforting me when I really need her the most.

I so wish I could run over to Jonny right now and hug him tightly. God, what a song. His mum would be so proud of him tonight, for the loving son he is and for the musically talented musician he has become. What started off as a real passion for Jonny from a very young age soon turned into one hell of a talent, and Jonny has honed that talent over the years, going from strength to strength in spite of all the challenges and difficulties he has faced in his life, particularly over the last couple of years.

When I finally manage to prise myself away from Stacey's shoulder, I look over at Jonny who is literally just standing up from the piano after finishing up his song. As if sensing my gaze, his eyes suddenly lock with mine from across the stage and the next thing I know, he's running over to me. And I run to him.

I don't care about the fact that we're being watched by thousands upon thousands of fans both in this stadium and around the world. All I care about right now is him. My husband. My rock star who admittedly broke in front of the entire world but a rock star who pulled himself out of the darkness and got back out there again tonight. Back at his best, doing what he loves. Along with the woman he loves.

We practically crash into each other up on that stage, Jonny hauling me up into his arms and clinging on to me tightly, kissing me in desperation as the emotions of the night do their work.

"That was amazing and beautiful," I say to him between kisses, "I am so proud of you. And your mum would be proud of you too." He spins me around on the spot, beaming with happiness as the world looks on.

"You're amazing and beautiful," he murmurs against my lips, "and I want to take on the world with you, Mrs Mathers."

Pressing my forehead against his, I say to him, "Just you and me against the world again?"

Jonny smiles, the recognition in his eyes so clear for me to see at hearing the words we used to say to each other so often in our early days, the very same words that have come along on this journey with us since our reunion back in London.

"Damn right it's just you and me against the world again, baby," he says. "Just you and me. *Always*."

Epilogue

JONNY

Three Months Later – Hollywood Pantages Theatre, Los Angeles – November 2017

From the minute I met Lauren at the tender age of fifteen, I feel like I've been waiting for this moment. The moment where that beautiful, kind and incredibly talented wife of mine finally gets her chance to shine. She's honestly waited so long for this big break to come along, and thankfully, that wait of hers is now over with.

As the lights of the theatre begin to fade into darkness, I turn to look over at Stacey who is sitting next to me on the front row, Ben, Will and Zack sitting either side of us, and she gives my arm a quick squeeze, smiling over at me in excitement. I'm as excited as Stacey is of course, but I'm not going to lie when I say that I'm also nervous. Nervous for Lauren making her big theatrical debut in here tonight. In the Hollywood Pantages Theatre in Los Angeles no less.

My girl certainly bagged herself the part of a lifetime and boy does she deserve it. Every bit of it. She's worked her absolute ass off for it too, spending the last three months rehearsing non-stop while I, along with the rest of the lads, have been busy promoting our new album. A new album that went down a storm after our comeback concert kicked us back into the limelight once more.

Both our album and our lead single, Paragon, the song I wrote in memory of my mum, went straight to number one in both the US and the UK charts, as well as a whole host of other countries I've admittedly lost count of.

The welcome back we received from our fans back in August and in the months that have followed has been absolutely wonderful, not to mention a whole lot of crazy. So much so that Lauren and I have been a bit like ships in the night of late, both heavily involved in our work and not having anywhere near as much time together as we used to, but we wouldn't have it any other way. And anyway, the time we do get to spend with each other when we are together is priceless. Absolutely priceless.

Turning my attention back to the stage, I wait in anticipation for the curtain to go up. I am so desperate to see Lauren strutting her stuff up there, and not only because I just want her to shine for the beautiful performer she is, but also because I have absolutely no idea what part she is playing. Lauren has kept her part a secret from me for the last three months, insisting she wants me to be surprised when I first see her walking on to that stage.

I do know the musical she's bagged a huge role in has something to do with circus performers and features a lot of acrobatics and stunt work, as well as pyrotechnics and the like. The show itself is apparently a huge hit, having been performed in many other theatres around the world over the last year or two, but I'm admittedly not well up when it comes to theatre productions and musicals.

I've spent so many years having my head buried in my own music that I haven't had much chance to look up and take note of anything else outside of Reclamation's bubble. Until now. Now I am getting the chance to not only take in something fresh and new, but to also see my stunning wife play a starring role in a huge Hollywood theatre production. And for me, life really doesn't get any more perfect than that.

As soon as the curtain begins to go up, a very excited Stacey is suddenly grabbing a tight hold of my hand, and I welcome her holding on to my hand right now because believe me when I say that on seeing the curtain go up, I'm even more nervous now than I was just a moment ago. In fact, I'd go as far to say that I feel more nervous tonight than I did when I took to the stage at our comeback concert back in August.

I was absolutely terrified that night, not wanting to go on stage after spending almost two years out of the limelight, my anxiety almost crippling me to the point where I couldn't see myself even getting beyond the dressing room door. But then Lauren swept her way into that dressing room and took every last shred of anxiety away from me that night, her calming demeanour, her smile, her playful banter and her beautiful words reaching inside of me and settling my very soul.

Thinking of her now, of how she's built on her own confidence over these last however many months, of how she didn't even want or need me to calm her down in her dressing room before stepping out on to this stage tonight, it makes me feel proud. Proud of how far my girl has come.

I admit to feeling a little dejected when she first told me she didn't want me to visit her in her dressing room before the show, but of course, I understood. The not seeing her before the show is all part and parcel of the build up to the surprise of her performance tonight. I therefore stood by her decision, as sulky as I was about it at first.

Me being the grumpy ass I can be sometimes didn't let her off the hook all that easily, but eventually, I relented. And I'm so glad I did. Because Lauren needs the space to grow and thrive, she needs that time on her own sometimes to gain the confidence she's always lacked over the years thanks to her shitty father. She also needs to believe in herself a whole lot more and I really do think this production is going to be the making of her. In fact, I know it is. I can feel it.

Once the musical starts, I am gripped, my eyes fixated on the stage wondering when Lauren is going to make her appearance. Will it be straight away? Will it be halfway through? I don't know! And that's all part of the excitement and the build-up I suppose, although for me, I just want to clap eyes on her and applaud her already for the knock out performer I know she is.

The musical production itself is an absolute wonder to watch, the stunts, the music and the performers themselves simply spellbinding as they acrobat their way across the stage, taking to the high ropes above, dancing in the air as they whisk us audience off into another world entirely. It really is a sight to behold.

But there is no other sight in the world more captivating to me than the one now making her way on to the stage in a pure white satin ballgown billowing out around her.

I can feel Stacey's eyes on me, but I can't look away from the beautiful vision now walking towards the front of the stage. I am enraptured by her beauty, as I always am, but there is something about her wearing a ballgown, something so pure about the moment, that I simply have to remind myself to breathe. Shit, she looks…fuck, I can't think straight at all right now. That dress, and her hair, her long blonde curls pinned up in a way that reminds me so much of how she wore it on our wedding day. *My god, she's beautiful…so fucking beautiful.*

The audience have fallen silent around us, waiting with baited breath as to what comes next. And what comes next threatens to absolutely destroy me. On the inside. Because when Lauren starts to sing, her voice is like nothing I've ever heard before. Not from Lauren anyway.

She sounds like an opera singer, singing a song that is so heart wrenching and so beautiful, I can feel the tears beginning to prick at the back of my eyes already and she's only just started singing.

Fuck. Me. I understand now why Lauren didn't want to tell me anything about the part she's playing, and all because she's been having opera lessons. For three entire months. Without me knowing a thing about them. Fuck, I can't believe what I'm witnessing here tonight. Lauren is singing much like a star on Broadway. In fact, fuck that, she is the brightest star on LA's equivalent of Broadway right now, belting out opera like that. I don't tear my gaze away from her for even a second, the entire audience around me as entranced by her performance as I am.

I am one proud husband tonight. The proudest husband in the whole wide world. When I look at how far she's come, from the young fifteen year old girl who got beaten badly by her own father, to this, to stepping up on to a stage in Hollywood all these years later, sounding like the angel I always professed her to be, it makes me want to throw myself at the stage and worship her. Truly worship her. Because she is the angel I always professed her to be. *Oh, she is.*

I'm vaguely aware of Stacey's fingernails digging into me, her grip around my hand growing ever tighter, Lauren's best friend most likely as shocked and as proud as I am right now, but I still don't turn to look at her. I can't look away from Lauren. I want to be in this moment with her for as long as she's up there. So many doors are going to open for her after tonight. As I always told her they would. *You've done it, baby. You've really done it.*

The song doesn't go on for anywhere near long enough, me wanting it to last a lifetime, but when the moment does finally arrive, Lauren finishing up her song on the highest of highs, every single person in the theatre stands up from their seats, giving my wife the standing ovation she well and truly deserves.

I'm admittedly the last one to stand up from my seat, my emotions finally getting the better of me, tears of pride and joy and so much love now swimming around in my eyes as I look over at Lauren standing on that stage, smiling over at her audience and curtsying.

I clap along with the rest of the audience, Stacey, Ben, Will and Zack all turning to look over at me, the shock and surprise on their faces an absolute picture. Lauren really has knocked the stuffing out of all of us tonight, along with the rest of Hollywood by the looks of things.

As Lauren turns to leave the stage, she somehow manages to catch my eye from where I'm standing in the front row, and she waves over at me excitedly, smiling her most wondrous smile. I mouth the words 'I love you' to her, placing my hand over my heart as I do, and she gives me her mushy look before blowing me a kiss. I blow her a kiss right back and then I have to deal with the fact she now has to walk off that stage and away from me. Whether she returns to the stage again after a knock out performance like that one was, I'm not entirely sure, not knowing how big her role actually is.

Lauren returning to the stage isn't really registering on my radar right now however, because after seeing her performance, I just want to go and throw my arms around her and tell her how proud I am of her. But the impatient man within me will have to wait a little bit longer for that moment because somehow or other, I'm going to have to get through the rest of the show before I get to see my girl, but the wait will be more than worth it. *Patience is a virtue, Jonny, patience is a virtue.*

****

After the show, I am taken to Lauren's dressing room by one of the production crew whilst Stacey and the lads get whisked off by Andy to a nearby bar. I told them I wanted to see Lauren on her own after the show. At least initially. We'll be joining them for a celebratory drink in a short while, Tony doing his usual job of ferrying us around in the Range Rover.

As things went a bit nuts after our comeback concert and the release of our new album, fans and paparazzi alike have taken to following us around a lot again. Something I don't think I'll ever feel entirely comfortable with, but something I've had to adapt to all over again. I feel more at peace these days with being followed around, more so than I ever did, and that's because I'm finally happy and settled. My life is no longer the soap opera it once was and I have my beautiful wife to thank for that. And speaking of my beautiful wife....

No sooner am I through the dressing room door and I am all over Lauren like a rash. She's barely stood up from her seat by the mirror and I'm dragging her into my arms, holding her against me as tightly as I can, my face in her neck, my emotions from earlier beginning to resurface.

"God, I am so proud of you," I say to her, my voice thick with emotion, "so fucking proud."

Lauren's soft hands work their way through my hair as she allows me to find my inner calm, the love and pride I have for this woman threatening to rip their way out of me. I really don't know how to get a handle on my feelings for her sometimes, my love for Lauren completely overwhelming me, as it so often has done over the years.

"Are you okay?" she asks me, her soft, gentle voice helping to settle the storm of emotions whirling within me right now.

"Oh, baby, I am more than okay," I whisper.

Finally pulling my face away from her neck, I press the palms of my hands against her cheeks and gaze down into her ocean blue eyes, and she smiles up at me. "You were...fuck me...you were fucking astounding out there tonight."

I struggle to find the words to speak, to express how I really feel about what Lauren did out there on that stage earlier. "Do you have any idea how utterly talented you actually are?" I ask her. "I mean, you were...you were singing opera out there tonight...fucking opera...how did you...just...how..."

Lauren can see I'm unravelling here, really unravelling, and she manages to roll my frayed ends right back up when she presses her lips to mine, silencing me, calming me, loving me. Oh, the love she has for me. The love I have for her.

"I love you," I murmur against her lips. "So fucking much."

"I love you too," she whispers, "and I'm so happy you finally got to see me up there on that stage tonight. It's been agony, keeping it a secret from you."

"Oh, that was the best secret you could have ever kept from me," I say to her, brushing my hands through her hair as I gaze down at her with pride. So much pride. "I mean, I always knew you had the voice of an angel but...learning to sing opera? In just three months? That's a hell of an achievement, and you should be proud of yourself for doing that. I really hope you can see now what I see. What everybody out there in that theatre saw tonight."

She beams up at me. "I think that I'm maybe beginning to see what you see. Not in a Jonny Mathers arrogant kind of way perhaps..." I narrow my eyes on her in jest when she says that. "...but more in a modest, yeah I think I absolutely kicked ass out there tonight kind of way, and I'll hopefully kick yet more ass when I do it again tomorrow night, and the night after that."

"Oh, you have more than kicked ass tonight, baby. In fact, you've just kicked the backside right out of Hollywood, and believe me when I say, you are going to be one busy lady after tonight, because the offers are going to come flooding in after that performance. You'll have so many offers to choose from after you've finished your stint in this show, you honestly won't know which one of them to choose first."

Suddenly growing all coy on me, Lauren shrugs her shoulders before taking a step back out of my embrace. I frown. "What is it? You think you won't get any offers after that performance?"

"No, it's not that. It's just…" Lauren blows out a shaky breath, her voice trailing off, as if she's suddenly nervous. I'm sensing something is a bit off here, and yet everything appeared fine with her a moment ago.

"Baby, are you okay?" I ask, feeling concerned about her sudden mood change. "Or are you doubting yourself again?"

She shakes her head at me. "No, of course not. It's just…I'm not so sure how much time I'm actually going to have to devote to a career in the theatre…"

"What are you talking about?" I ask, not entirely sure where her concerns are suddenly coming from.

"Well, you're starting your US tour in the New Year and then you're talking about doing a world tour after that…"

"The world tour won't be until the back end of next year, most likely September or October, that's nearly a full year away. And anyway, what I'm doing with the band shouldn't have an impact on you and your dream career. A career that's only just begun…"

"Jonny, I'm pregnant."

I draw back from her in shock, Lauren's sudden announcement hitting me slap bang in the face. In fact, I'm fairly sure I didn't just hear her correctly. Surely to god my wife didn't just tell me that she's pregnant…did she?

"You're…you're…" I glance down at her tummy that's currently hiding away behind her tank top and the waistband of her jeans, before pulling my gaze back to hers once more. "Did you really just tell me that you're pregnant?"

Biting down nervously on her bottom lip, Lauren then gives me a reluctant nod before breaking eye contact. "Yes, I really did."

"Wow," I say to her, "I...I'm..." Taking a step backwards, I swipe a nervous hand through my hair as I try to process this unexpected news. "When...how..." Yep, that's me, going to absolute shit in front of her because I seriously don't know what to say to her.

Lauren looks up at me then, her eyebrows shooting up at me in surprise. "You're seriously asking me when and how? The amount of sex you and I have and you're asking me how it happened?"

"No, I didn't mean..." I sigh, taking a few seconds to compose myself in the hope that when I next speak, I don't put my foot in it all over again. "I just meant that...you're on the pill... aren't you?"

She rolls her eyes at me in annoyance. "Yes I'm on the pill but...well, we've been so busy these last few months, what with your comeback concert and the album launch, me rehearsing endlessly for this show. So busy that I've admittedly lost track of my periods, and clearly I've also lost track of taking my pill too, so...here we are..." Lauren looks away from me once more, almost like she's ashamed of herself for falling pregnant. "I'm sorry," she whispers, and that's it, I'm done in.

Striding my way back over to where she is standing by her dressing room mirror, I gently place my hands on either side of her face, coaxing her to look up at me. Her uncertain eyes meet with mine and it almost crushes me to death on the inside to see her looking so nervous and upset about something I think is wonderful. So fucking wonderful that I suddenly feel overcome with emotion all over again. But my emotions need to be put to one side for the moment, because Lauren is clearly beginning to panic here and it's up to me to douse that panic right out.

"Don't you dare apologise to me for giving me the best news I could have ever been given," I say to her, hoping against hope she will see I'm genuine. Genuinely happy that I, Jonny Mathers, am going to become a father.

"You're...not mad?" she asks, looking shocked.

"Mad?" I almost laugh. "Lauren, it takes two to make a baby and...you've just given me the most wonderful gift in the entire world. You've just told me that I'm going to be a father, and as shocked as I am at hearing the news, I'm absolutely fucking ecstatic!"

"You are?" Lauren still doesn't look convinced.

"Oh, I am. Please believe me, baby, when I say I am thrilled."

"But having a baby right now wasn't part of our plan..."

"Sweetheart, our plan was that we never had a plan. We didn't have one back then, and we don't have one now. Our plans were dreams, remember? Your dreams of performing in the theatre one day and my dreams of having some sort of music career. Needless to say that you and I have managed to smash those dreams of ours right out of the park. But the real dream. The biggest dream of them all, is happening right now...in here."

Reaching between us, I slowly, and very gently, slip my hand beneath the hem of her top, placing my palm flat against her tummy, much like I did all those years ago when I first found out she was pregnant with Oliver. I can't help the pang of grief that suddenly hits me in the chest whenever I think about our little boy, at what could have been. But I don't allow that pain to show, instead focusing on the here and now and the happy news Lauren has just shared with me.

Looking up at me with so much love, so much emotion that it makes my chest ache, Lauren then places her hand on her tummy along with mine, our fingers linking together in silent acceptance of our future. Our future that is happily growing away in there, safely cocooned inside Lauren's womb for the next however many months, which leads me to my next question.

"How far on are you?" I ask, becoming ever more curious about the when, more so than the how this time.

Lauren pulls a face. "When I said I'd lost track of everything, I really meant it, but…hazarding a guess, I would say between two and three months, although a scan would have to confirm that…"

"Really? That far along?"

"It's not that far along, Jonny. Not really. Not far along enough to be out of the danger zone anyway," she says quietly, averting her gaze once more.

"Hey," I say, placing my hand firmly under her chin so she can turn those worried eyes of hers right back on me. "I know you're going to naturally worry about the early weeks of your pregnancy, as I'm sure all mothers do, but please don't let it consume you, Lauren. I want you to be happy and excited…"

I hesitate for a moment, trying to gauge if Lauren is in fact excited right along with me. I know she placed her hand against her tummy just now, and she certainly seems more relaxed after knowing how excited I am about the baby, but I want to be sure that Lauren is okay. I *need* to know she's okay.

"Are you happy and excited?" I ask her, fearing she may be

spiralling. Spiralling into the trauma of our past once again.

Lauren sighs. "When I first saw the positive line flash up on the pregnancy test this morning, I admit that I panicked, but… after the initial panic wore off, I started to feel excited. Nervous too of course, about telling you and how you might react to the news, about how our lives will change when the baby arrives, but then…"

"Then?" I press, urging her to get whatever worries she has right off her chest and out into the open.

Blowing out another weary sigh, Lauren says, "Then I felt guilty."

"Guilty?" I ask, not quite understanding what she means.

She nods. "Yeah. Guilty for feeling excited over a new baby when Oliver didn't get to live."

"Oh, baby," I whisper, my heart breaking apart on the inside for her. "What happened to Oliver wasn't your fault. Or mine…"

"I know it wasn't, but…that doesn't make me feel any less guilty for feeling excited about having another baby."

Brushing the pads of my thumbs across her cheeks, I gaze down at her lovingly, hoping against hope that she really takes in the next words I am about to say to her.

"I understand why you feel guilty, and I can even sort of relate to it myself, but…Oliver wouldn't want us to be unhappy, Lauren. He would want us to bring his baby brother or sister into this world and shower them with nothing but love. So much love. The very same love we gave to Oliver. He may not have had the chance to live his life, but that didn't stop us from loving him endlessly, unconditionally. And we'll never stop loving him. Ever. And he knows that. I promise you he knows it."

Stroking her knuckles back and forth over my jawline, Lauren finally smiles up at me, and for the first time since she delivered the news, I think she looks excited. "You know, it's in moments like these when I'm reminded of exactly why I married you, Jonny Mathers. Not that I need reminding. It's just…a wonderful rush all over again when you do remind me, unwittingly, of the wonderfully kind and loving man you are. And you really are."

"Right back at you with that one, sweetheart," I whisper, grinning down at her like the loved up loon I am.

Wrapping her hands around the back of my neck, Lauren then kisses me gently on the lips, her mouth moving over mine so slowly, so softly. When she eventually pulls away, she smiles up at me once more and says, "You ready for the next part of our plan then, Mr Mathers?"

I smile. "Like I said to you before, this isn't our plan, Lauren. This is our dream. A hard fought for dream we have waited so long for."

"We really are living the dream at long last, aren't we?" she says to me, her eyes twinkling with excitement.

"Oh, too damn right we are, Mrs Mathers. And the best part of our dream is yet to come."

*****

LAUREN

Six Months Later – Cedar-Sinai Medical Center, Los Angeles – 5th May 2018

"Oh, just look at him," says Jonny, gazing down in awe at the miracle in my arms, our newborn son wrapped up in blankets, looking up at us through the most beautiful dark brown eyes I have ever seen. Well, the second most beautiful dark brown eyes I have ever seen. Because these eyes of his are an exact copy of Jonny's, much like the mop of jet black hair atop of his head.

This precious gift we have been given, our brand new baby boy, who was delivered by caesarean section earlier this afternoon, really is a carbon copy of his daddy, and I cannot begin to tell you how in love we both are with our new addition.

The last six months have certainly gone by in a whirlwind, this unexpected but delightful surprise really cementing the dream for us. And this little surprise of ours may have forced me to take a break from the theatre for a good while, but looking down at him now, at my son, my healthy, bright eyed bouncing baby boy, I couldn't care less about any of that. I now have everything I want right here in this hospital room with me, and I will never want for anything else. Ever. Well, all except for one thing maybe.

"Have you spoken to your dad and told him the news?" I ask Jonny, finally broaching the elephant in the room.

Jonny is sitting on the hospital bed next to me, one hand smoothing its way through my dishevelled hair, the thumb of his other hand stroking the tiny fist of our son, Jonny barely able to tear his eyes away from our brand new bundle of joy.

He instantly sighs at my question. "I texted him earlier to tell him the news, and I think a text is more than enough."

After everything that happened, things haven't been and most likely won't ever be quite the same again between Jonny and his dad, which was to be expected, but somehow or other, in spite of all of that, Jonny has never quite been able to find it within himself to completely cut his dad out of his life. He even ended up keeping his dad on as a silent partner permanently at the record label, not wanting to add stress to either his life, or his dad's. And staying true to his word for once in his life, his dad has stayed exactly that. Silent. At least for the most part.

Even though we didn't invite him to our wedding and Jonny has kept his dad at a distance, we of course still shared the happy news with him about my pregnancy. And we did that face to face, Jonny inviting him into our new home for the first ever time only a few months ago, Pete accepting our invite wholeheartedly. And he was happy for us when we told him the news. Genuinely happy. Hard to believe that genuine and Pete Mathers go together in the same sentence but he was genuine that day and I can't take that away from him.

I only wish things were different, that Jonny could perhaps reach out to his dad a little bit more in the hope they could somehow move forward. I may have wiped the floor with Pete when I finally got my chance, and I may have hated him for over ten years of my life, but seeing how torn up Jonny still is about the strained relationship he now has with his father, it kills me inside.

And he's never talked about it at great length with either me or his counsellor. Brian may have cracked the nut wide open with Jonny in many areas during their very many counselling sessions, but one area he could never crack open was the dreaded 'dad' subject. Maybe Brian will one day be able to get Jonny to open up to him about his dad, but until that moment does or doesn't arrive, I have to accept things as they are.

Trying to steer Jonny's mind away from all things dad related, I decide to talk about something else. A much happier topic of discussion for the both of us. "So, are we agreed on his name then?" I ask, thinking back to our conversation from a few moments ago.

Even though we'd already decided on both a girl's name, and a boy's name, Jonny and I not knowing the sex of our baby until he finally graced us with his presence earlier this afternoon, we were still unsure about a middle name. Up until ten minutes ago, when a middle name hit me right in the face. When I suggested it to Jonny, he simply smiled down at me and told me yet again how much he loved me. And he's doing the whole smiling down thing at me again right now, his nose just touching mine, his hand still in my hair, his other hand still gently stroking the fist of our little miracle.

"We are definitely agreed on the name," he says to me.

We both look down at our newborn son at exactly the same time, his dark chocolate brown eyes still gazing up at us in wonder, his little tongue darting out of his mouth every now and again as he wriggles away in my arms.

"Welcome to the world, Noah Oliver Mathers," whispers Jonny.

Biting down on my wobbly bottom lip, I whisper, "And one day, when you're old enough, you're going to know all about that wonderful big brother of yours, and the reason for us giving you that middle name."

Shit, I really am turning into an emotional wreck today, my post pregnancy hormones playing absolute havoc with me right now. Seeing that I'm beginning to get upset, Jonny wraps a comforting arm around my shoulders, pulling me in close.

We both cry a few tears together in that moment. Tears of both joy and grief. The grief we still feel for the boy we lost. Grief that will always be there, lingering just beneath the surface. But Noah is the rainbow in our life now that will help to heal our inner pain. And we will never forget about our other precious boy who came before him. The boy who will be forever running free in his rose garden. *Oliver's Garden.*

"When are Stacey and the lads coming for a visit?" I ask, trying to lighten the mood a little, "I know when I spoke to her earlier, Stacey was so excited to meet little Noah. And I can't say I blame her. He's a right charmer is this one. Much like his daddy."

I'm met with a huge grin on the face of my husband, swiftly followed by him reaching in for a quick kiss, thanking me for the compliment in a way like only he can.

When he pulls back, he says, "What can I say? Like father like son." He flashes me a cheeky wink and I smile. "And as for Stacey and the lads, they'll be along later. After you spoke to Stacey, I then rang Ben and told him I wanted a bit more alone time with you two. Just for a little while."

"Well, that's absolutely fine with me," I say, giving him another quick kiss. "But be prepared for Stacey when she does eventually arrive, Jonny, because believe me when I say, that girl was born to be an auntie, and a fun auntie at that."

Jonny chuckles. "Oh, believe me, sweetheart, I am more than used to Stacey by now. And I can't wait for her to meet Noah. In fact, I can't wait for them all to meet him. Especially Ben. Now *that* is going to be fun to witness."

"Oh, here we go," I sigh, giving Jonny my usual eye roll.

"Oh come on, Lauren, you know for a fact that Ben will be like a fish out of water when it comes to meeting Noah. I can't imagine Ben ever wanting to hold a baby in his arms, never mind actually have one."

"Well, that's what you said about him getting married, and yet again, he proved you wrong, getting down on one knee on Christmas Eve all those months ago and proposing to Stacey, taking her completely by surprise."

And he really did take her by surprise. In fact, he took us all by surprise, but most especially Jonny, who still seems to think they won't quite make it down the aisle. I however think otherwise. I think Ben is so head over heels in love with my best friend that he'll do anything for that girl. Absolutely anything.

"Look, I have no doubt that he loves Stacey to the moon and back, and I have no doubt in my mind that they will last the test of time…but they won't get married. Getting engaged is one thing, but getting married is something else entirely. Take it from someone who knows Ben well."

"We'll see," I say to him, a slight smile playing over my lips.

"Are you disagreeing with me, Mrs Mathers?" asks Jonny, grinning over at me like the childish idiot he can be sometimes.

I pretend to think about his question for a moment. "Hmm, let me think…erm, yes, I'm disagreeing with you, Mr Mathers."

Narrowing his eyes on me, he says, "God, you're naughty. Even now, a few hours after giving birth to our son and you're still disagreeing with me."

"And I'll always disagree with you if I think differently to you, Jonny. It's called a difference of opinion."

"And boy do I love it when you do disagree with me," he murmurs. Suddenly turning playful, Jonny then decides to start kissing me all over my face, making me giggle.

"Stop it," I protest, "your son is watching."

Jonny smiles against my cheek. "He'll understand when he's older."

I gently shove his face away, still secretly loving the fact that my playful husband finds me attractive enough to be kissing me so much, especially not long after giving birth. I must look a fright in my unflattering maternity nightie and dressing gown.

"And anyway, you're the naughty one out of the two of us, Mathers," I say to him, "and don't ever pretend otherwise."

"Wouldn't dream of it," he says, his eyes sparkling with mirth, "because I remember with great fondness just how much you love and adore my naughty side, and don't *you* pretend otherwise."

I shake my head at him, and am just about to send another smart ass comeback his way when the door to our hospital room suddenly opens.

Jonny and I turn to look over at the friendly looking midwife slowly walking into our room, thinking she's most likely come in here to help me start feeding Noah, but as it turns out, she hasn't come in here to help me start feeding Noah at all.

"Mr and Mrs Mathers." She smiles down at us both, her eyes coming to rest on our precious bundle of joy. "I'm sorry to intrude on you during what I know is a private time but you have a visitor."

"A visitor?" I ask, thinking it's most likely Stacey and the lads. "Well they're a bit early but they can come in. Right, Jonny?"

"They?" The midwife looks a little confused. "This is just one visitor." Turning her gaze on Jonny, she then says, "And he said he's your father."

I watch the colour drain from Jonny's face as he draws back in shock, his dad turning up at the hospital, unexpected, uninvited, throwing him completely off kilter. I then watch as Jonny stands up from the bed, looking less than pleased with this sudden turn of events.

Shaking his head at the midwife, he says, "No."

"Jonny..."

Turning to me, Jonny shakes his head again. "He shouldn't

be here, Lauren. I texted him earlier on to tell him the news and that was that. This is a private moment. *Our* private moment..."

"Jonny, we've had a good couple of hours of privacy with Noah up to now, and we have all the time in the world with him. So much time. But your dad...he's come here to visit us. To meet Noah. He clearly wants to make an effort..."

"He should have made the fucking effort way back when," snaps Jonny, swiping an angry hand over his face as he turns away from both me and the midwife.

"I'm sorry," says the midwife, suddenly looking uncomfortable, "I'll send him away and leave you both to enjoy the precious time with your newborn son." I give her an apologetic smile before she turns and walks away.

She has just about opened up the door to walk back out into the corridor when Jonny suddenly calls her back. "Wait."

The midwife stops in her tracks, chancing a quick glance over at me, before resting her gaze back on Jonny.

With a heavy sigh, Jonny turns around to look over at the midwife. "Tell him he can come in, but do it quickly, before I change my mind."

The midwife nods her head and then dashes out into the corridor, closing the door behind her. Looking up at Jonny, I can see the tension working its way through him already and he hasn't even set eyes on his dad as yet.

"Look, I know I was trying to convince you to allow him in to meet Noah just now, but you don't have to do this if you don't want to," I say to him. "I'll support you whatever you decide. You know that."

Running a shaky hand through his hair, Jonny sighs once more, before dropping back on to the hospital bed to sit beside me. "I know I don't have to see him but for some reason..." He blows out a breath, as if trying to compose himself, the war inside of him still raging on. "...now that he's here. I think I want to see him. I think I want him to meet our son." Jonny's sorrowful eyes meet with mine, and with my free arm, my other arm still wrapped ever so tightly around our son, I pull him into my embrace.

"I'm with you in this," I whisper, "and no matter what happens with your dad today, or after today, just know that whatever you decide to do, I am with you every step of the way. It's you, me and Noah against the world now, Jonny, and believe me when I say that we're going to be one hell of a force to be reckoned with."

Jonny gives me a grateful smile. "Oh, I have no doubt about that." He drops a soft, sweet kiss on to my lips. "I love you, Mrs Mathers," he whispers.

"I love you too, Mr Mathers," I whisper back to him.

Jonny's dad knocks on the door and walks into our hospital room a few moments later, a look of trepidation written all over his face. He closes the door behind him, approaching us cautiously. "Thank you for agreeing to see me," he says, looking grateful.

Jonny gives his dad a reluctant nod but I stay silent. Because I really don't think I should say anything right now. I think for once in my life, it's time for me to say nothing, sit back, and allow these two to do the talking. Fingers crossed.

Gesturing over at Noah, Pete says, "Congratulations to you both. He looks absolutely perfect."

Glancing down at our son, who has now fallen asleep in my arms, Jonny then brushes his hand ever so gently over the top of his head. "That's because he is perfect," says Jonny, now smiling down with pride at the gorgeous bundle of joy we made together.

I still can't quite believe he's ours. It all feels so surreal to me at the moment, almost like I'm in a dream. Well, I'm most definitely living the dream right now, that's for sure. And Jonny is living that dream right along with me. But whether or not he wants his dad to be on the periphery of that dream of ours is all down to Jonny.

Taking another step towards the bed, Pete asks, "Have you named him as yet?"

Jonny nods. "Yeah, we have. We've named him Noah Oliver Mathers."

Suddenly looking overcome with emotion, Pete smiles. "That's a beautiful name and a lovely tribute to…to Oliver."

Jonny nods once more. "Yeah…yeah it is."

"Your mum would be so proud of you, Jonny," says Pete. "I only wish she were here now. She would have doted on Noah."

I can see the emotion whirling around in Jonny's eyes, the muscle ticking in his jaw as he tries his best to put any type of feelings or emotions over his mum to one side, not wanting to show any form of weakness in front of his father. Not that showing any type of emotion is a weakness, but with Jonny being so wary of his dad these days, I can't say I blame him for being so on his guard around him.

Clearing his throat, more so as a distraction I think than anything else, Jonny then says, "Yeah, she would have adored him."

"I'm proud of you too, son, and I'm sorry it's taken me so long to say it to you, but I am, and I need you to know that."

When Jonny doesn't respond to Pete's sudden declaration of pride, instead deciding to stay silent whilst turning his gaze back on Noah, Pete then takes another step closer towards us.

"Look, I know I've got a hell of a lot to make up for with you two, and I'll more than likely never be able to fully make up for what I did, but know this, know that I will never ask either of you to forgive or forget, because I don't deserve your forgiveness, and I never will. All I ask of you two right now is hope. Hope that maybe, just maybe, we can move forward, and that one day, in the future, you might allow me to be a part of your life once more. A part of your son's life. My grandson's life."

Swallowing hard, Pete continues. "Is there hope?" he asks, his uncertain eyes now landing on Jonny.

Finally tearing his eyes away from our son, Jonny briefly looks up at me before resting his gaze on his father. After a long moment of silence, Jonny finally speaks. "There's hope."

A glimmer of hope flickers to life in that moment, Jonny opening himself up to the possibility of re-building some sort of relationship with his father, and it's all thanks to this beautiful newborn baby boy of ours.

Noah really is the rainbow Jonny and I have been looking for. A rainbow so bright and colourful, a rainbow of hope in our lives that shines brightly in the darkness, much like his brother who came before him. *Oliver and Noah*, I think to myself, the rainbows in our many storms.

THE END...FOR NOW...

ACKNOWLEDGEMENT

Thank you for purchasing and reading this book. I am so grateful that you took the journey with both Jonny and Lauren as they battled their way through to that hard fought for happy ever after.

I truly hope I did the characters justice, giving them the happy ending they truly deserved after all the heartbreak and trauma that came before. It has been an honour to write this series of novels and I will truly miss these characters who have worked their way into my heart over the last ten years, although this may not be the end for the world of Reclamation.

There may be a story or two to follow in the future, perhaps in the form of a novella or a spin-off, but for now, I reluctantly have to bid a fond farewell to Jonny, Lauren, Stacey, Ben, Will and Zack, six wonderful characters who will forever be in my heart.

To keep up to date with any further releases, you can follow me on Amazon, Instagram, Threads and Tik Tok, by following JFrances81author.

Thank you for reading and love to all. J x

Printed in Dunstable, United Kingdom